Trial of Katy Wilkins

Other novels by H. F. Beaumon:

The Wiloby Estates
Stockdale Avenue
Descending the Spiral Staircase

Trial of Katy Wilkins

H. F. Beaumont

Library of Congress Control Number:		2020918707
ISBN:	Hardcover	978-1-6641-3325-9
	Softcover	978-1-6641-3324-2
	eBook	978-1-6641-3341-9

Print information available on the last page.

Rev. date: 09/25/2020

To order additional copies of this book, contact:
Xlibris
844-714-8691
www.Xlibris.com
Orders@Xlibris.com
815980

ACKNOWLEDGMENTS

I would like to personally thank all of those listed below for the encouraging words which prompted me to write, The Trial of Katy Wilkins.

My God, who still encourages me to continue writing. I thank him in prayer every night, to fulfill my calling in life, please lord you allowed me to live after a brain bleed, five weeks in a coma and ninety days in therapy, to restore my body to a working order.

The therapists who worked with me from losing all my motor skills to walking with a cane, thank you from the bottom of my heart.

Eric Ludy, lead pastor, president, Ellerslie's Bible College, dear friend and customer and his entire family, gave me hope and strength. Working side by side for many weeks to restore his landscape from prior mishaps, was very fulfilling for me. Sharing his novels and sermons was extremely inspirational.

Barbara Beaumont, my second wife, County of Orange Purchasing Operations Manager, Metropolitan Water District, Senior Contract Anaylst, my first reader of my manuscript and short stories, such an inspiration with many encouraging words to allow me to write The Spiral Staircase.

Melisa Ruelas, Master of Science, Licensed Marriage and Family Thereapist, my stepdaughter, who told me years ago to write. I wrote for her a manual on how to do landscape take-offs, what to look for in the specifications and plan notes and details. She started the whole process of burning into my brain, you need to write.

Teri Iverson, CPA, Iverson & Associates, LLC, my second reader of my manuscript, without her telling me, the book is well written, gave me an 'A' plus, plus, plus and even circled words which needed corrected. Teri, is also one of my landscape customers.

Kari Aston, Controller for McGee Contracting, Inc., my stepdaughter, she received birthday and holiday letters from me for the past few years, always said, these are better than, any Hallmark card, thank you.

Nichole Ward, my daughter, Administrator for Rez Church, who has read some of my short stories, birthday and holiday letters, always stating how much she appreciates the stories. Loves to read about my early childhood.

Justin Beaumont, my son, Bachelor of Science Degree in Electronic Engineering, Production Technician and Small Group Leader, Rez Church, he and I have spent hours playing video games, he always won of course, he also enjoyed reading his birthday and holiday letters. When just a young fellow, we would sing 'Oh, my Darling Clementine', while driving around town. We only got to the second verse and started all over again. He would also help me with the garden, I taught him how to plant the vegetable seeds, he would giggle as the seeds fell into the groove, I dug with a hand pick.

Mom and dad, telling me to go outside and play, while you're out there pull the weeds, in the flower beds, make sure, you get the roots. Then my brother and I got to mow the lawn, with a hand push mower. in Bermuda grass. That started my landscape career.

CONTENTS

1

The Trial of Katy Wilkins

Early this morning, we were packing up the vehicles, going for our last meal at the restaurant, and saying our goodbyes to the aquarium. The girls were saddened as they dressed. My bride had on her wool hat, scarf, sweater and designer-lined gloves. Marie was dressed the same, and Sophia and Agnes wore their wool hats, scarves, sweaters, and designer-lined gloves. We guys were roughing it with shirts, jackets, and baseball caps. I had my floppy hat on, just to show the guys that they, too, could be stylish.

As we arrived, we met Susanne, who was also wearing a wool hat, scarf, sweater, and designer-lined gloves. She said, "Twins," as the ladies stepped out of the vehicles. They all had a group hug with the girls.

The film crew followed everyone inside the restaurant, where they filmed the gift shop for the audience. The girls were talking to their fish friends and, of course, Mister Frog.

The manager gave the girls some worms to feed the fish. Susanne made sure the cameras were in position before the girls fed them the worms. She asked them, "How do the worms feel?"

Leslie said, "Soft and wiggly. We drop them in the tank as quickly as we can." The cameras caught some great shots of the fish feeding. Even Mister Frog got a piece of worm dropped by one of the trout.

Now it was time to fill our bellies with the Albright scramble, hash browns, two link sausages, two pieces of toast, and hot chocolate with a squirt of whipped cream. We adults all ordered the Albright Scramble with coffee, hash browns, link sausage, and toast, and I had a goose juice to celebrate my new hat. Our waitress and another waitress both came over and put real lip prints on the hat for good luck.

The chef first brought out a plate of dollar-sized pancakes, with homemade maple syrup, for the girls and everyone else. This made for a nice snack before the real meal. He also later brought out a dessert dish with red raspberries, cooked apples, peaches and apricots, shredded chocolate, whipped cream, coconut, and pineapple for toppings.

It was going to be really hard to leave this place today. They had treated us like royalty. Every night a piece of chocolate was placed on each pillows, the beds were neatly turned down, and smooth jazz was playing on the television set. A note from the maids expressed the hope that our stay with the resort was memorable and asked us to fill out the feedback form on the dresser before we left. They also thanked us for being guests and said, "Come back soon."

After our breakfast and desserts, we headed home. Leslie and Sarah rode with us so they could talk to my parents. Kim and Rebecca rode with Susanne; Marie and John had Mama and Papa as well as Jessica and Mickey. All told, we formed a six- vehicle caravan back to our home. The film, sound, and makeup crews, with hair stylists and wardrobe, were in two vehicles, and an equipment van brought up the rear.

We made fairly good time, with little or no traffic on the highway. Of course we stopped at the halfway point for potty call and snacks.

My parents were really having a good time with Leslie and Sarah. They asked numerous questions of the girls and got answers that I know they did not expect. One question my mom asked was "Do you have friends besides the four of you?"

Leslie responded, "We have the Wiloby family and over three million followers, and our staff responds to the letters, postcards, and emails we receive every week."

"Do you play with other children?" asked Mom.

Sarah said, "We have guest children on our show, if not daily at least three days per week. We spend the whole day with them and teach them how we do what we do to please our parents, adults, and other children."

Then my mom asked, "You don't have a regular friend who visits all the time?"

Leslie said, "We could have what you're asking about, but we work, we get tutored every day at least six or eight hours, and we get home maybe two hours after we leave the studio. Then at home, while our dads and moms prepare dinner, we help set the table and make salads and dessert with Grandma, we don't have a lot of time to socialize."

Sarah said, "Our bedtime is at nine o'clock. We say our prayers with Mom and Dad, and we get a good-night kiss and lots of 'Love you' and hugs. We love our life; we have no complaints. We don't get yelled at or scolded, like some of our classmates talk about at school, and we don't get restricted. We have all learned to be respectful, and in return we get respected."

Leslie said, "If we do bad things, we get treated badly. We love being loved. We're not looked down on or belittled, and when we speak, our parents listen because we do the same for them. We're not bratty or snooty and we don't pout;

if we don't get what we want, no is no. Why push your parents, to make them mad at you?"

Mom asked, "When was the last time you got a spanking?"

Leslie asked, "Have we done anything wrong the whole time you have been visiting that you would have spanked us for doing?"

Mom said, "Well—no, not really. You're polite, kind, and willing to help without being asked. You pick up after yourselves, and you help clear the table and do the dishes, without complaining."

I intervened. "Mom, is there anything that you would punish them for doing?"

She answered, "Well ... they don't act spoiled. Nope, I can't think of one thing that would justify even raising my voice." Then she turned to the girls. "Who taught you all of this?"

Leslie said, "We have daily a meeting in our home, where we work out every scenario that we encountered during our day. If there's an issue that we caused, then we learn how not to do that again. We talk about everyone we have come in contact with and determine whether they are on the invite list, whether we need more time, or whether we should never invite or allow them into our space."

Mom asked, "How did Susanne become the one who watches over you?"

Leslie said, "When we had our housewarming party, she came with the magazine staff. We met the governor and his wife as they entered our home. The governor and Diane got down on their knees and hugged us. They didn't push us away; they were polite, kind, and courteous to us. We all returned to our house and a quick meeting and decided to have the governor and Diane join us for dinner. Susanne was the nearest staff member, and we asked her to deliver a note to them. She was a hesitant but then decided this would be a great opportunity for her to meet the governor.

"Susanne had to pass through his security personnel, but after that she handed him the note. The governor and Diane read it and said they would be delighted to join us for dinner at our house.

"In about a half hour, Susanne with a microphone announced our dinner guests. Then she handed me the microphone, and I told everyone, 'Our space is small and our budget is small, but we would love to have all of you join us. We hope that soon you can be invited; our parents have plenty of space and an unlimited budget. Please enjoy your dinner, and welcome to our home.'

"We had dinner with the governor and Diane. Susanne helped us carry the food and beverages to serve our special guests, and then she fixed her plate and ate on the seat wall below our house. Once she was finished, she came back upstairs and waited by our door for the governor and Diane to exit.

"I asked her if she still had the microphone. She handed it to me, and I announced our guests for viewing the light show. We asked Mama and Papa to join us with the governor and Diane. When Mama and Papa arrived, I asked

Susanne to join us as well. She started to weep, and we all hugged her and asked what was wrong.

"Susanne said, 'This is the happiest day of my life. I love you girls. Thank you so much for asking me to join you.' Mama and Papa and the governor and Diane all gave her a warm and loving hug.

"The light show was amazing; from our balcony the whole courtyard comes alive. We all went downstairs so others could see the courtyard from our house. We saw the rest of the yard, and the stream and waterfall had everyone saying how pretty and what a wonderful space. Diane and the governor and Mama and Papa all sat on the benches. Then, with the cameraman filming, Susanne held the microphone and asked everyone questions. Mom and Dad joined us on the bridge, watching leaves float in the stream. The lights were shining on the leaves; it was very pretty."

Delores texted Marie: *Big sister, I hate to ask, but you're such a wonderful sister, I'd give my life for you. You're so dear to me and my daughters. You know you're the best thing that has happened to me and my family. We have a little problem, which you could make go away with a simple okay.*

Our little problem is Leslie has been talking to Agnes about your party. They have not seen your home. Would you be so kind as to allow them the golden opportunity to see just what their son does for a living, giving you and all such joy and happiness?

Marie texted back, *Let me think, were you nice to me today? You could have been nicer, but okay, nice enough counts. Did you make me feel special? Well, you teased me a couple of times; you bumped me into a display rack in the gift shop and you smacked me on my behind—with love, I'm certain. You didn't treat your older sister very well by doing that; are you sorry?*

Delores replied, *I was only trying to get your attention; you were ignoring me. I'm sorry. I'll try to be more respectful next time.*

Will this be the full tour, or are you trying to get out of cooking dinner?

I'll be a good girl and make the side dishes, harass my husband, and make beverages for your guests, stated Delores.

Marie texted, *And help with the dishes?*

Okay, but you will owe me at the next event, texted Delores.

Give me an hour to get the house ready for the tour. Marie went on, *The girls all want to stay at our house, they had it planned early today.*

We will drop off Leslie and Sarah. Can you contact Susanne? asked Delores.

I already have contacted Susanne. She will stay the night with us, and her crew will continue on to the studio, replied Marie.

Delores told everyone the plans for today. "This will bring everything Leslie and Sarah have told you into reality."

Agnes said, "You mean we get a tour of their home?"

"Yes. Marie is a gracious hostess. And she has photo albums taken daily, so you will see your son's vision become a reality."

Agnes said, "This will become one of our greatest days. Thank you all for sharing."

We were about ten minutes away from Marie and John's house, and the girls were getting excited about seeing it again. Being gone for two days is very trying on them.

When we arrived at Marie and John's, the girls hopped out of the vehicle and gave everyone hugs and cheek kisses. "See you in about an hour; love all of you," and they were hugging their little sisters and Susanne. Grandma, Grandpa, Marie, John, Jessica, and Mickey all got hugs from the girls.

We headed home, freshened up, and offloaded the luggage and fishing gear. Then we hopped back into the vehicle and stopped at the market for hunger pain medication as well as and snack foods and two bottles of champagne for the grand entrance set to occur during the tour.

I was tempted to get a three-dollar bottle just for giggles. But as I grabbed the bottle, I recalled that it could be used as a weapon. The ladies had been that upset with the first sip; "rotgut garbage" was the consensus. I decided to get three of the high-priced bottles instead—the kind with a real cork, not a screw cap.

Then it was back into the vehicle and off to John and Marie's, with Mom and Dad in tow.

Marie met us at the door to welcome my parents to the Albright tour. She would be their guide, and Susanne, with a microphone, became the master of ceremonies.

They started in the foyer and showed Mom and Dad the staircase, which had started the whole project. Marie had her photo album for this particular part of the project and explained that the carpet had to be replaced. The company they hired to replace the carpeting in the bedrooms wanted too much money to remove the old carpeting from the staircase.

Marie said, "They claimed disposal fees had nearly doubled from last year. Your son found a recycle center that would give him a low disposal fee if he would cut the carpeting into five- or six-foot lengths; the width was perfect." As Marie was showing mom and dad the photo album and explained each photo, they got more interested in what happened next; they spent nearly an hour just on the staircase.

They entered the backyard with a margarita glass in hand, tradition for all tour members until they get to the staircase. Marie had put on the sound system before entering the rear yard. It took a few minutes just to cross the first bridge; they were mesmerized by the view from the bridge to the waterfall as well as a couple of leaves floating down the stream.

Everyone arrived at the benches, where they sat down and chatted all the way to a refill of the margaritas. I brought out the pitcher; Mom said, "He was always such a good boy, right, honey?" Dad was dozing off; too much soft music, and the warmth of the margarita was taking its toll.

They all decided to look at the rest of the landscape and crossed the second bridge. Mom asked, "Where does the stream go?" So they stood there for a few minutes watching a leaf make it to the vault.

Marie told them to follow her to the courtyard. They arrived at the staircase, and Mom was utterly amazed at what she was viewing.

Marie and Delores showed them their grand entrance. They had Mom try, and after two margaritas and a glass of champagne, Mom and Sophia did make a grand entrance. The girls were on their balcony cheering on their grandmas, telling them, "You can do it, Grandma!"

After Mom saw the girls' house, we broke up the tour for lunch. John grilled hot dogs for the girls, hamburgers for the rest of us, and pork chops for grandmas and grandpas.

The girls invited the grandparents to their house for lunch. We of course got the losers' table; nothing new.

Delores and Marie got the candle with the holder to complete the ambience. Leslie and Sarah came down to visit John, with their hunger pains almost gone. "But if you have just a few more cooked meats, we'll share them with our guests; they also have hunger pains." John lifted up the grill cover and found six more pieces staying heated for the girls.

Marie said, "Someday the cupboard will be bare; then what will you gentlemen say to our lovely daughters? You'd both better have a speech ready. It'll have to be good, or those girls will tear you apart, verbally."

Delores said, "They'll tell them they can be replaced with our buff gardeners."

Marie said, "That gives me a wonderful idea. Does your buff gardener speak English?"

Delores said, "He only knows pleasure; no other language is required."

It was time for dessert. Marie and Delores both said, "We already had ours, 'Dream Lover,' with whipped cream and of course our red cherry."

While heading toward the tunnel, Marie said, "With chocolate shavings."

John said, "Simple things amuse simple people." He was brushing the grill for tonight's grilling.

Jessica and Mickey, returned from their home, told us they had a letter on their table about what they can and cannot do until the forensic team is completely finished with the investigation. "Please do not go down into the lower area," Jessica said. "We are waiting for some results of tests taken. Tomorrow we're packing up boxes and furniture for the movers. We talked to Stuart; he will have the movers at our home on Friday. He wants Mickey to start work on Monday for his firm.

"Mickey said he hasn't given his company notice. Stuart said, 'Tell them you're leaving on Friday to move to Oregon; your wife got promoted.'

"Stuart has a friend who owns an eldercare facility and is looking for a registered nurse. He would be happy to send Mickey a letter if required by his firm; just let him know."

The tour continued after dessert. Mom and Dad were impressed by all the details that Marie had captured in her photo albums. They had a greater appreciation of their son, claiming that they never knew my capabilities.

Dinner was superb, and the light show was amazing, with Mom and Dad seeing the project lit up. We finished the day sitting on the benches at the waterfall, listening to the sound of the water and soft music in the background. Mama and Papa joined my mom and dad, with coffee for all.

We returned to the courtyard, making for another grand entrance by the ladies. The girls were on their balcony with their hot chocolate, raising their mugs in appreciation of what their moms were doing. John and I hugged our wives once they were on the patio decking.

After Mom and Dad said prayers with the girls and us, kissed their foreheads, and gave them hugs, we took Mom and Dad home. Delores and I tucked in the girls, gave them our love, and proceeded to our room for another great night's sleep.

2

The next morning the girls pounced on our bed. "Good morning, Mom and Daddy!" They got under the covers and shivered. We cradled them in our arms to warm them up and stop their shivering.

Delores whispered in my ear: "Good thing we didn't stay naked.'

We kept huddled under the covers until Sarah said, "Daddy, can we start making breakfast? My hunger pains are acting up."

I looked at Delores. "Darling, our little ones are starving. Would you be so kind as to start making the coffee and hot chocolate? My little chefs and I will conjure up a meal fit for our queen."

Delores made the coffee and hot chocolate. After joining her, the girls and I mixed up the batter for pancakes and heated the pan for our sausages and another pan for hash browns. Rebecca started making toast and, of course, the Albright scramble. My largest pan was for frying the bacon, chopped onions, and chopped green peppers, with a pinch of spice per the chef at the Whispering Pines Resort.

Mom and Dad smelled the breakfast cooking and joined us for breakfast, Mom helping the girls. Our doorbell rang. Delores answered the door and invited the Albrights to pitch in on making breakfast.

Delores poured me a cup of coffee and added a smidgen of milk. The girls were busy making pancakes; Rebecca took a plate full of toast to the table; Sarah was in charge of the sausages. Leslie and Kim were flipping pancakes like nobody's business; Leslie was turning the pancakes like a pro at the perfect moment.

Marie was pouring orange, apple, or tomato juice, taking requests. My Albright scramble was nearly finished, and Delores brought me a bowl.

Marie poured salsa into a bowl for the eggs. A bottle of ketchup was on the table for the hash browns and sausages, with three different jellies, syrup, and butter.

Mom and Dad set the tables, one in the kitchen for the girls and the dining room table for us much older guests.

The breakfast was astounding, lip-smacking good. Soon all bellies were full, ready to take on the day. Mom and Dad are going to spend the day with their son, while Delores and Marie headed to teach their next class, all excited to meet new faces and raw talent.

The girls were preparing for their show. They would also be hosting four children, wearing their fishing gear for Whispering Pines Resort. Susanne asked for a representative from their organization to surprise the girls and promote their remodeling, starting in a couple of weeks.

"John, Marie, mama, papa and I, headed off to the showers; time's a-wasting." The girls had taken their baths last night before going to bed. They all went into their bedroom while the girls got ready for today.

Marie sat down in the living room and clicked on the morning news. They were showing protesters in front of the courthouse. "Free Katy" was their slogan, and they were waiting for the prosecutors to give the people an update.

Delores sat down with Marie and watched the protesters. The media had to have someone off camera encouraging the crowd to get louder and more threatening. Soon the prosecutor strode to the podium and stated that jury selection would be starting this afternoon. Then he said, "Katy will not be freed, nor will any of those arrested. Wait until you see the evidence against these people before you pass judgment."

The defense attorney put in his nickel's worth, stirring up the protesters, assuring them, "The state has no case; it's all circumstantial evidence. Katy will be freed."

Delores and Marie talked about what they'd just witnessed. It reminded Marie of all the press attacking her front door. "They will do anything for ratings. I'd love to watch them get into a frenzy as they lead Katy into the courtroom with all the protesters screaming, 'Free Katy!' Then the trial starts and they'll see just what they have been screaming for, and it smacks them in the face with truth."

Delores asked Marie, "How long will the trial last?"

"Once there are no more protesters to promote ratings, a couple of weeks. All of her supporters have been arrested. If they call on those arrested to testify on her behalf, that testimony will be used against them. If their lawyers are in it for press exposure, their clients could be found guilty without a trial."

Our telephone rang. It was the FBI agent handling the case, telling Delores to make sure everyone was wearing their devices. They are calling all the ladies to make sure they were wearing their devices. "Be on full alert every day," the agent said. "We still don't know if we have everyone involved."

Papa called Marie. After the call, she turned to me, saying, "Fred, they have more eyes on everyone until this is over and those involved are behind bars forever. He's sending a driver over to pick up your parents. They will be safer with him than at your office; he knows they'll understand. He says you should keep your travels minimal today and all this week as this starts to unfold into the public eye. Oh, one other thing: he said don't visit new customers; that could be a setup, to get kidnapped."

I went upstairs to get ready for work, and Delores came up moments later. I told her, "Not that, not now, silly girl."

She said, "You wish that was why I'm watching you get dressed; no sir. Don't forget to wear your device."

I lowered my underwear to show her my device.

Delores said, "Great place, it will keep hummingbird company. Thanks for sharing—like I needed to know."

The limousine was here to pick up the girls. They had two escort cars with security personnel.

Papa put his people on drone watch, along with the eyes on the ground. He called around to see if any contracts had been issued. He also set a team of men to the cabin to keep an eye out for any activity— food delivery trucks or smoke coming from the chimney.

I left for work after kissing everyone goodbye. Mom and Dad were worried about our safety. We assured them that we had been through this more times than we cared to remember. As I was leaving my home, I saw a couple of cars following. I just put on my radio and listened to good music.

I was thinking about what else my drawings needed before I handed them over to Denise and Melanie. I almost drove through McDonald's for a coffee but remembered that Papa had warned not to make unnecessary stops, so I continued to the office. I arrived, unlocked the building, and started to make coffee for my office wives. I thought I could sneak a snack, but Charise had locked it up; no belly filler with my coffee. *This is going to be a long day; chained to my desk is never much fun.*

The office door opened, and in walked my first office wife, dressed to the nines in business attire. "Charise, I love the look."

Charise said, "Let me rephrase that into reality—you love to look; you forgot. Great, you did your chores: fresh coffee."

"Are you wearing your warning device?" I asked.

Charise said, "You know, I grew up hearing the phrase, 'Hey, baby, what's your sign?' Now you've come up with a new one: 'You wearing your device?' What's next? 'Are you on the pill?' Men, always trying to trip us up."

"The answer to your personal question is yes, and no, you can't see it."

We headed to my office. First she took a detour, and then she joined me with two, two-packs. She said, "Yes, it was one of those nights."

"Wow, a two-packer night. Must have been exhilarating."

"You'll be way ahead if you just enjoy your gift," said Charise, taking a bite of one of the cupcakes.

"Did you see the news this morning?" I asked Charise.

"Parts of the special alert," she answered. "Such lies are being told by the defense attorney. Does he really believe his client will be freed? Either he's a complete fool, or he's trying some reverse psychology on the public. If he believes he can defend her from execution or life in prison without parole, he needs to go back to law school and this time attend some of the classes."

"I would be surprised if any of those arrested ever see the light of day outside prison walls. I hope they all get put into a maximum-security prison, in the general population, not isolated or put on death row. Let the inmates have a field day with that pompous, rich and famous crowd."

Charise said, "You think since they all have a social status that the juries and judges may give them a lighter sentence?"

"From talking to Papa, who is a highly skilled attorney, there is enough evidence collected that we know of that no defense attorney, no matter how famous or skilled, could soften the outcome.

"Let's take one of those arrested. They present a delivery order for concrete, a copy of the original delivery ticket, with their signature. The defense attorney states that someone forged the signature. Then they lay a bank signature card in front of the accused: 'Is this your signature?' They can show signatures for years on tax records, mortgages, loan papers, country club receipts, a nice grocery list of signatures, impossible for a forger to be everywhere you have traveled to sign your name exactly the same every time. On the exact date that you were there, that would be the equivalent of winning the lottery back to back to back."

Charise asked, "How long do we have to wear these warning devices?"

"Until the FBI knows we are safe from kidnapping or hits put on us. Papa is in constant watch. Most of his competitors, who may get contacted for a hit or kidnapping, are alerting him. He alerts his affiliates, and they track down the perpetrator. They follow the money, even before the FBI has a clue."

We were joined by Janice and Melanie. Both looked refreshed after the arduous weekend.

Charise asked if they were wearing warning devices. Janice said she was; the FBI had contacted her early this morning. Melanie said she was not; since she rides and lives with Janice, they thought they would swap off each day.

Charise said, "Girls, you both must wear the device."

Janice said, "But if we're together all the time why would we both have to wear the device?"

I said, "During the day, how many times are you left alone? Restroom trips, out shopping, one looking at one rack of clothes and the other looking at another rack, one goes into the dressing room while the other is still looking, or all the rooms are occupied, and you're waiting for a room to vacate."

Charise said, "You both must wear your devices every day, even while you're sleeping. Criminals rarely sleep at night."

I said, "The last I heard, there is no set time when abductions take place. Be very careful. Keep a watchful eye open."

I told them, "If it weren't for Papa, Marie and Delores would be in pieces. There's evidence that both had parts of their bodies already spoken for. A couple more days and they would no longer be with us.

"I have about an hour left on the construction drawings; then you both can proceed to input the data and order me three sets of plans. Forward the data to Angel; she can get copies for Murray and his foremen. Oh, three plan sets to Phillip as well."

Our receptionist joined us just before we adjourned, and then the girls all went back to their offices. Phillip's office staff were filtering in; I gathered it had been a long, hard weekend for a few of them.

I refreshed my coffee, returned to my desk, and finished up the construction drawings for our home and Marie's home. I gave the drawings to Janice and returned to my desk to draw Mama and Papa's house.

I called Delores to make sure everything was okay and that she and the girls had all arrived at the studio safely.

She told me that the class was packed with women; it might take the entire morning to get them all registered. They had four staff members in the studio to help with the registering.

They had the magazine's office manager explain the forms the ladies had to sign for insurance purposes. Our three branch offices were starting their first classes this morning as well. The magazine was filming the registration process, and all three offices were watching the live filming right now.

Marie got on the phone, thanking me for all that I had done for her and the magazine. "Can you believe there are four classes going on in each location?"

I told her, "You and your grand entrance have inspired many ladies to follow you."

Marie said, "Your vision got me out of my shell. Then the crew applauding me—all of that made me want to do more. Then came your lovely wife with her moves, and it's now a way of life for both of us."

"Don't forget, John and I reap all the benefits."

"Well, they're calling us, so talk to you tonight. Have a wonderful day," said Marie.

I started drawing Mama and Papa's landscape construction plan. I put a half circle patio with the patio cover for shade, three ceiling fans, barbecue island—only a barbecue and side burner and one storage compartment—and a firepit. I included a craft room for Mama on top of the patio cover, fifteen feet by fifteen feet. I made a note to talk with Murray about adding an elevator to allow her to get to the craft room without making a staircase. She could enter the elevator from the patio and go up one floor.

The girls could learn to sew from Mama, and I held out the hope that my mom and dad would move to Oregon to be with their grandchildren. That would work out wonderfully for all the families. It occurred to me to also add a wooden dance floor under the craft room.

The plan was nearly finished when Charise brought me another cup of coffee and one more cupcake. It seemed that being such a good office husband, keeping our office daughters busy, had earned me one more cupcake.

I told Charise, "Whatever happened to you this past weekend? Can it happen again tonight? Three cupcakes in two hours—I'm all for a repeat performance."

Charise said, "My office husband, a repeat of the performance that inspired me to give you two cupcakes this morning won't happen. I want you to understand one thing: it was not pleasure that got you the cupcakes. I didn't eat breakfast, so those were my breakfast, and they don't last very long and I knew you would be pleased to get another one, since you did not have your Happy Meal this morning.

"Do you and your missus have cupcakes after an evening of pleasure?"

"Nope, she wants a full-on breakfast: Albright scramble, pancakes, toast, sausage, hash browns, Bloody Mary or margarita, orange juice, and coffee, just to get her ready for pasture. You know, grazing in the grass type of thing."

"You're not saying your wife is bovine?"

"Oh no, she is a thoroughbred, Arabian, from the finest stables in the world. She even has a buff bronzed body handler, who only speaks pleasure; no other language is necessary."

Charise said, "Does she have a backup that she could share?"

"She's a thoroughbred, from the finest stock in the world, so she more than likely has a backup in every track she runs."

Charise said, "At least she's not an old nag—still able to leave the rest of the stable in the dust."

After Charise and I had our cupcake treat, I returned to drawing Mama and Papa's landscape construction plan.

I decided to attach the patio cover to the house, centering the posts between the house and the outer beam. *That will keep the elements off the homeowners and give them more shade. I want to add paver walkways from the front of the house and side garage door to the patio; there will be a perimeter fence surrounding the property to slow down wildlife.* I also added raised planter seat walls to the perimeter planters and added a circular planter which would have a large multi trunked tree for shade; this would invite guests to the center of the landscape. *I don't think Papa will mind not mowing a lawn.*

Mama likes roses, so part of the raised planters will be roses. I'll have to teach her how to maintain the roses. They're ready to hand it off to the girls.

Maybe I can get my next cupcake as a treat for being such a good boss. No, buddy, don't push your luck; finish up your messages to make the chief office wife happy.

I booted up old Jezebel, opened the file for my messages and found a bucket load of spam messages; the delete button got my stack down to just a few. I flagged the people looking for an estimate and the account calls. I replied to the do lunch requests, politely stating that I didn't have the time. Then there were my office managers, all wanting some attention from their office husband. I responded to them: "Not today, sugar, hubby's on a texting diet. Call me if it's earthshakingly important."

I called the five customers wanting an estimate and told them I was waiting for the all-clear from the FBI before I could make an appointment. "I will contact you once I'm able to set up an appointment."

Our receptionist called me on the intercom: "Gloria is holding on line one."

"Thank you, I'll talk to her.

"Good morning, Gloria, how may I be of help to you this fine morning?"

"First, get off your texting diet. 'Texting diet'—for the life of me, you do come up with some doozies. I have your room reserved at a local, five-bat-rated hotel, Rest in Peace, separate coffins, with free burial service if you happen to pass away in the night."

"Very nice, I'm sure we will enjoy our stay. I'll have Delores dress up like Morticia, and the girls will follow Mom's wardrobe."

"Well, office husband, you know you have been slacking in your chores, answering messages with your texting is on a diet if far below reasonable. We are starting three new projects today. We are of course shorthanded. Should I take the crew working on my house to start one project to appease the customer or contact the customer and delay the start time once my home is finished?"

"Well, in my experience, that calls for a face-to-face meeting. Either you or Nadine needs to visit the customer and explain you are running a couple days behind, and you're sorry for any inconvenience. If they have a patio cover, then see if Phillip can start a crew on digging the footings for the posts."

"Okay, I'll send Manuel to see them this morning," said Gloria.

"I said either you or Nadine. Make sure you both have your devices on and call the local FBI office and alert them to the address you'll be going to. They can tell you a time to arrive at your address. Be very careful; we don't need another kidnapping caused by those incarcerated."

Just as we were finishing up our conversation, Charise came in and told me to tell Gloria to turn on the computer and watch what the protesters were doing now.

"The driveways and parking structure are being blocked so those called to jury duty can't park their vehicles. The police are in riot gear and armed, and they have hooked up fire hoses to the nearest hydrant ready to disperse the protesters.

"The governor said he will call out the national guard if necessary. 'This ruckus will end now, either by force or in a peaceful manner,' he said. 'If you all choose by force, you will be charged with aiding and abetting this case, and you will be prosecuted to the furthest extent of the law; there will be no plea bargaining.' The police chief told the protesters they had five minutes to disperse, or else they'd go to jail.

"Some of the protesters started a countdown, and that got the chief to say, 'Three minutes, so you all can count to one hundred and eighty.' The national guard was arriving to surround the protesters and keep them from escaping.

"The courthouse had routed the people called for jury duty to another parking lot. They shuttled those called to jury duty past the protesters, since they were surrounded and could not stop prospective jurors from entering the courthouse.

"The police chief said, 'You have one minute to decide your fate.' The protesters waited until the countdown was in the teens before they said they would disperse. Those called for jury duty were safely in the courthouse; they could not stop them, and they were surrounded, with no escape.

"The governor told the protesters and the public, 'Let the courts decide the fate of those who were arrested, not the media. And the less disruptions, the quicker; after all, these people are in custody.'

"The protesters were escorted out of the area still surrounded by the national guard and the local police department. The cameras were rolling from a distance, not allowed to mingle with the protesters."

It later developed that out of all the people called for jury duty, over two hundred, they selected three who were agreed to by the prosecutor and defense teams. Another pool would be called for the next day, and this process would continue until they had the fourteen needed jurors. The three selected jurors were sequestered in a nearby hotel. They were allowed to contact their families to arrange for the sheriff's department to retrieve clothes and toiletries.

The news coverage was more than any of us wanted to hear. We knew they were just trying to keep the audience in an uproar.

We all sat in my office discussing what we'd just seen and decided that Chinese food would be a perfect lunch for all of us. Charise ordered from a local restaurant, and soon they delivered it to our office. We also ordered beverages and egg rolls. This was our third order from the restaurant, the food was that good. We also ordered all three rice dishes.

Janice asked about the construction drawings, whether I would provide details of the tunnels connecting the two playhouses. They wanted to see how the tunnel system would work; it was a lot of wood flooring for the girls to clog.

"You'll need to buy them hard-soled shoes once a month," said Janice. "If those girls don't get tired going from one house to the other, I'd be shocked at their endurance."

I told her, "They clog back and forth bringing items to the patio table, laughing and giggling the entire time. They wear out their moms and grandmas. I'm putting a seating area about halfway for us adults to catch our breath."

Charise asked, "Will there be a blender, cabinets, and refrigerator for that rest?"

"You know, that's not a bad idea. The ladies will love it, and the girls can have sodas and water stored in the refrigerator."

3

When our food arrived, the office wives set up the conference room table with a fancy plastic tablecloth, paper napkins, plasticware, and plastic cups. They constructed a five–pickup truck-rated eatery.

After our Chinese lunch—no leftovers, which surprised all of us, as the last grain of rice was consumed after the girls flipped the coin to see which one would tease out the last grain—cleanup took about three minutes. We took the trash bag out to the dumpster so it would not stink up the office for the entire day.

I returned to my desk with a two pack from Charise. I had rid my account of messages, so this was a bonus for being such a great employee. Leading by example, doing your homework without being scolded, was a real plus. *Thank you, girls, for teaching Daddy a valuable lesson.*

I got a clean sheet of velum paper and began the design of the playhouses with tunnels to show Phillip. The girls could later computerize them using AutoCAD to complete the submittal package to the city. The connection to the house could be tricky; I might just use verbiage and let the general contractor come up with the connection. *Merrily I draft along, draft along, draft along, merrily I draft along all throughout the day.*

Janice and Melanie came into my office. "You know, you were singing, out loud," said Janice. "You may want to consider taking singing lessons, or tell us what key you were singing in; that would be nice."

Melanie said, "Whatever key it was in, it was flat."

I told them that I don't charge for my concerts.

Janice said, "That's s good thing. I know I wouldn't pay to hear that voice."

Melanie said, "Maybe Phillip can build you a shower so you could practice."

Charise said, "Girls, you know we don't want to encourage any more of his singing, shower or no shower."

She saw my two-pack wrapper in my trash can; clearly she'd been thinking about taking back my bonus for punishment.

Delores and Marie walked into the office, and our receptionist informed me my ladies had arrived. Too late for the three in my office to look busy, I handed Charise a yellow pad to act like we were having a meeting. Not quite quickly enough; they arrived way too fast.

Marie said, "So you're wasting more payroll?"

"No dear, I was giving them singing lessons."

Delores laughed. "You were teaching them how to sing? You poor girls, you need to order a box of earplugs, his singing is not for humans to endure. He sings in an unknown musical key and in a flat monotone key."

I said, "Now that all of you have taken my ego out and squished it into my carpet, how else my I amuse you?"

Charise said, "We use you to sharpen our claws, meow."

I now had all five women sitting in my office. I turned to my drafting table and returned to my detail drawing. I cleared my throat and mock-prepared to start singing another tune, "Do, re, mi, fa, so, la, ti, do." My office emptied quickly.

Charise said, "I just ate. Please don't make me lose my lunch. See you later, my office husband."

Alone at last. The wrapper that Charise saw in my trash can was from early this morning; my afternoon bonus was in my desk drawer. All was quiet, the ladies back at their work stations. I thought this was the perfect time to unwrap my bonus.

Nope, thought wrong. In came housewife and saw the two-pack in my hand, grabbed it, and took it to her office, where she and Marie paid homage to the contents.

Marie said, "Thank you, my adopted husband, for thinking about our needs."

Charise came on the intercom. "You tricked me. That's the one and only time that will happen. I'm just letting you know."

I had the playhouse, patio cover, barbecue, smokehouse, staircases, and tunnel for our home all detailed along with the planter seat walls. I was starting on John and Marie's when the whistle blew for quitting time. My housewives came into my office and sat down. Marie asked, "Just when is your quitting time?"

I turned around in my chair and asked them if they wouldn't mind to stand up and turn around slowly.

Delores asked Marie, "Why does he want us to stand up and turn around slowly?"

Marie said, "He's trying to see if we'll respond."

Delores asked, "Why would he want us to respond to that?"

Marie said, "Hummingbird wants to leave his nest."

Delores said, "Mrs. Hummingbird says, Sorry, Charlie, no free show."

Marie said, "Put a Franklin on your desk, per quarter of a turn, for each of us. Then we'll proceed."

I told her that would be a very expensive pay per view, quite a bit out of my Happy Meal range of payment.

Marie stood up and told Delores, "He's comparing us to a McDonald's child meal."

Delores put a five-dollar bill on my desk. "Here, sport, see if Happy Meal will turn around in your stomach slowly."

They both left my office and the building. As I was locking up behind us, Delores said, "On your way home we need hunger pain medication for all of us."

I stopped at my favorite grocery store. The clerks immediately went to the back room and brought me a case of cupcakes, three bottles of champagne, and three different types of fancy chocolates.

They had all of that waiting in a shopping cart. Being one who has a bag of tricks, I told them, "Oh, I came in for a pack of gum."

One clerk said, "Sir, your wife called a few minutes ago and stated exactly what you are supposed to bring home. We know you always want to please the ladies of your home, and we would hate to see you without your skin. She did say they would skin you alive if you came in without these items.

"She also added, 'Only these items; no screw-on caps for the champagne or penny candies would be acceptable.' You see, sir, she said they would scalp *me* if I didn't follow their wishes."

I asked the clerk, "How much is my bill?"

He handed me a receipt, I handed him my debit card, and the other clerk loaded everything in the backseat of my pickup truck.

As I walked out of the door, I told the young clerks, "Stay single for as long as you can."

The clerks laughed, and one responded, "Too late, we're both married."

I told them, "I feel for you. I'm too late again. Have a great day, gentlemen; see you soon."

When I arrived at Marie and John's, everyone was home. John was preparing the burnt offerings for tonight's meal. The girls got two two-packs; only one cupcake each this close to dinner.

Delores and Marie were comparing the goodies to the list they'd called in to the grocery store. They agreed that the store did good, and at no time would I be allowed to depart from their list; done deal.

Marie told me to go outside and play with John. "Make sure he does a good job on grilling, or else we'll need to write another list to the grocery store."

Soon the men were outside, and the ladies were inside. John already had the goose juice to enhance the flavor of the grilled meat. We were all talking about the episode on the television earlier today.

Papa said, "This is going to be an ugly trial. The media will keep criticizing the proceedings to rile up the viewers. They can't give her a life sentence, or this will never end."

He went on, "We're looking into the law firm defending Katy. We are checking everything: what is the connection between Katy and her puppets to this law firm? Financial and business doings are being looked at very carefully.

"Someone is funding these protests. Did you notice, not one of the protesters were questioned as to why they are protesting. The shots of the protesters were from a distance; the ones who were in the camera frame are people who Katy would never associate with. These aren't upper elite type of people; they are lower middle to lower class people looking for a paycheck."

Papa said he talked to Mr. Barns about planting a cable network news crew during the next protester rally and interview some of the protesters, telling them they are live. "Mr. Barns told me he would have to talk to the networks to see what they need to do to film the protesters. He called me back and told me they needed to reach the organization sponsoring the protesters to get approval. They are checking now as to who is organizing these protests. We checked with the city to see if permits were pulled, but nothing was filed."

I asked Papa, "How will you find out who is organizing the protests?"

"We have a few of our elite staff hanging out near the law firm making sure they are noticed if you know what I mean—bait. Even lawyers are only human and can endure only so much temptation. One will get hooked, and they'll reel 'em in.

"Remember, gentlemen, we want this to end. There is no nice way to play with these people. The FBI called me this morning; they've arrested three more people that were found from the files."

The girls were bringing out the salads, sides, and dinnerware, everything for the patio table along with the loser's candle and candleholder and a book of matches.

Leslie asked if the grilling was about done; their hunger pain was getting pretty strong.

John told her, "In about three minutes we will cure those hunger pains. Love you, my dearest child."

The girls returned to the tunnel and clogged back to the kitchen, where the ladies wee polishing off their first margarita, and the blender was creating another masterpiece. The girls announced that the grandparents would be joining them for dinner. "Maybe tomorrow, Mom, you and Dad can join us."

With drinks in hand and another batch prepared, the ladies and the girls all clogged through the tunnel. It sounded like a stampede was approaching the courtyard.

Once dinner, dessert, and the light show were completed, with everyone all tucked in, prayers said, kisses on foreheads, hugs with Mom and Dad, we headed home, off to fast-approaching marital bliss. Heart rate was increasing, thinking about all of the possibilities. Soon we were alone in our room.

Delores said, "Can you wait until tomorrow night?"

What? Are you kidding me? After all the anticipation, racing heart, into turn four, finish line in sight, she breaks the fuel line, and everything comes to a halt? No finish line for this race, no doing donuts for the fans, no checkered flag. Only disappointment, discouragement, a hug and a kiss and "Night-night, dear."

Well, at least I could get a good night's sleep, once I regained my composure.

4

The next morning before the rooster crowed, the girls hopped on our bed and clambered under the covers to get warmed by us parents. They squirmed up next to us and absorbed all our body heat; their little hands were cold every time.

It was the usual drill: make coffee for the missus and get that breakfast onto the stove; these girls have severe hunger pains. Marie, Leslie, and Kim were due any minute. Our girls were now all warmed up and ready to take on the kitchen.

The race was on to see who could complete their portion of the breakfast first and rub it in on those less fortunate.

As the coffeepot was nearing completion, our doorbell rang, and in came more kitchen help and supervision. Each girl had her job title down pat: flipper, turner, toaster, table setter, beverage maker, hash browner, and cheese shredder, all working to make another fabulous breakfast.

As I completed the Albright scramble and bowled and served it, the feeding frenzy began. It seemed that each day the food disappeared faster.

The girls were starting to mimic their moms, lean back in their chairs, saying, "Ahh, so good. That was perfect; no more hunger pains here."

We all headed upstairs and got ready for work, school, and shows.

The girls' special guests were two girls and their moms. The guests had written letters to the girls explaining how they cherished their program and would be honored to spend time with them. Both were special needs little girls; it should be exciting to share their experiences with other children.

Marie and Delores were starting their second day with a full slate of ladies taking their class.

I had the honor to get chained to my desk for another day. *I'm going to stop and pick up a box of Twinkies for my office and lock my desk drawer. I'll tease them when they sit at my desk being so pristine and proper.*

I stopped at my market and bought a box of Twinkies, a box of cupcakes, and a bagel with strawberry whipped cream cheese to taunt the girls.

I got to the office and made the coffee. I was almost done when in walked Charise.

"Good morning, office husband," she said in a very welcoming voice.

I told her, "Good morning; I hope you had a two-cupcake-in-the-morning evening."

Charise said, "No, actually I had a wonderful evening, and breakfast this morning was superb. Is the coffee ready?"

"Allow me to pour you a cup to complete your joyous morning."

Charise said, "What's up with you this morning? Not prodding me for treats?"

"No, I'm turning over a new leaf: I only get a treat if I do good and please my office wives."

We both went into my office, she sat down on the opposite side of my desk, in came Janice, Melanie, and Marsha. All sat down with their coffee and started talking about last night's adventures.

I turned toward my drafting board, glancing at what was needed to complete my morning task.

Charise asked if they could watch more of the trial.

I told them, "You can unless it is utterly boring and spokespeople dominate the news coverage. I really don't want to hear a celebrity talk about something they've never experienced in real life."

Papa called. When Charise answered, he told her to turn on the computers. She told us, "It's starting to look like a riot could erupt at any moment."

Once again, the police and national guard surrounded the protesters. This time, they gave the protesters no time to consider a peaceful departure. Reinforcements entered the circle and started putting a hurt on the protesters. The arrested them and loaded them into waiting vans to haul them into headquarters for processing.

It was starting to look like the civil rights riots of the 1960s when the protesters, being outnumbered, just sat down. This forced the officers to pick them up and drag them off to the police station.

Again, like yesterday they rerouted the arriving pool of jurors to another lot and shuttled them to the courthouse. Once all were safely inside, the protesters grew quiet, headed to their vehicles, and dispersed.

Before we turned on the computers, Papa called and said, "They now know who is financing the protesters. The funds are being funneled from all of those arrested to the organization putting on the protest."

The organization was of course headed by the law firm. Papa said, "Let them run Miss Katy out of money; she won't need much where she is going anyway."

By the end of the day they added six more jurors. Tomorrow the same scenario would take place: more of the same, with a crowd trying to disrupt the process. The more delays, the more likely the public's interest will dissipate.

By the next day, once the protesters were leaving the courthouse grounds, they now had enough jurors to start the trial. The jurors were to be sequestered throughout the trial. The prosecution and probably the defense attorneys would give their opening statements the next day, more than likely taking until court would adjourn for the weekend.

This would be the first weekend the jurors get to watch television for seventy-two hours.

The defense attorneys used up every minute they could muster, sticking to their line: "All the evidence is hearsay. Nothing has been found to convict poor Mrs. Watkins or any of the others who've been jailed."

On Monday, with their first witness the prosecutors will begin to unravel the hearsay defense with evidence and facts. By Tuesday or Wednesday the courtroom should get heated up with prosecution witnesses.

We returned to normal procedures, I gave the girls Mama and Papa's construction plan and explained how the patio cover would attach to the house. I had one phone call to make to clarify whether the spa could remain and ask if adding the elevator in lieu of a staircase would be allowed.

I called Murray to get the specification for an elevator and explained the situation to him. He said, "No problem; I'll have the elevator subcontractor design a one-floor elevator. That is a great idea; would you mind if I used it idea on another project?"

"Let me see—do I need to apply for a patent?"

Murray said, "I don't believe your idea would necessitate a patent unless you come up with an idea that revolutionizes the industry."

I called Mama and asked about the spa. She asked Papa, came back on the phone, and said, "I love you. My dream will finally come true."

I returned to Janice. "Both ideas are a go, so an elevator and spa for Mama and Papa."

I returned to my desk, grabbed a two-pack of Twinkies, and realized I'd forgotten my coffee. I took my cup and filled it. When I got back, sitting in my office was Charise, she had a Twinkie in her hand and asked for my cup of coffee; busted. Like a whipped puppy I got another cup of coffee and returned to my doghouse.

Charise had polished off both Twinkies and found my entire box of Twinkies and cupcakes, which now sat on my desk in front of her.

As I sat down at my desk, she was waving her index finger at me. "You sneak. No wonder you told me you changed your attitude, not begging for treats any longer. You bought your own. What kind of example are you setting? Lead by example—don't you remember your speech when you hired us?"

She said, "No treats until Monday for you. You're on restriction, do you understand me, mister? I have texted your wife and Marie, so they also know you're on restriction. Gloria is next on my list. You were bad, very bad. I'm so disappointed in your actions."

Charise called in Janice, Melanie, and Marsha, had each of them take a two-pack of their choice, and told them that I was on restriction, no treats until Monday.

Janice took one of each, and so did Melanie and Marsha. As they were leaving my office, each one gave me a hug, saying, "It's only four days; they will just fly by, you'll see."

"We love you and thank you for the goodies; you know how girls like their goodies, not things."

"Things are bad for our figures," said Janice.

Charise took the rest of the goodies, walked over, and kissed my cheek. "This hurt me more than it did you. I still love you. Try to be a good boy the rest of the day."

I took a drink of my coffee and looked at all the ladies on my walls. Then I asked the Lord, *Why?*

I received an email from the elevator subcontractor wanting to know the exact location of the elevator. I went to Janice, had her email them the site map showing the location of the elevator. As I gave her his information, lying on her desk was the two-pack of Twinkies. Her back was turned, and the devil was working hard on me to "Just take them; she won't care."

Just as I was ready to pocket the Twinkies, Charise grabbed my ear and led me out the door and back to my office. "Bad boy. You know better than trying to sneak a treat. Sit in your chair for one hour facing the corner. I don't want to see your face. I'm so ashamed of your actions."

She went out and told the office staff, "Don't go into his office for one hour. He's being punished. No visitors either."

Charise went and said to Marsha, "Tell all those who call for our boss that he is on another call or out of the office, due to return before lunch."

While I was sitting in my chair, I broke her rule and sat at my drafting table to complete the details for the tunnels and playhouses. I added two staircases and a porch to the tunnel at the property line heading back toward each home. All that would be required if one or the other sold their property would be a wall panel; the interior of the tunnel would be framed with a surround to accept the panels. The roof would also be designed to be separated, and a portion of the tunnel would be removed per city building codes.

This is becoming an intriguing project. I hope all parties concerned will be impressed.

It seemed only minutes had passed when my office wife came in. Charise said, "Did you learn your lesson?"

I told her, "You know, I totally forgot about why I was being punished, since I was the one who spent the money on the treats but never ate any. I know it was being sneaky, but I didn't want to take goodies from the girls. I felt guilty with each bite, that they would miss out."

Charise said, "That was an awfully good excuse. That does not make it right. It doesn't matter who purchases the goodies; we all chip in and buy the goodies, and we are willing to share."

She fixed me with a look and asked, "Will you do that again?"

I told her, "Of course; it's my nature to please the opposite sex. I'm a well-trained puppy, house and office broken, obedient, loving, your perfect lapdog. I even give kisses. Do you want to see?"

Charise said, "Maybe after lunch or before I head home; not right now."

Then she asked, "You don't drink out of the toilet, do you?"

I asked, "Bowl or tank?"

Charise said, "Forget the kisses. I can do without those, for right now."

5

When we ended our day, the plans were completed, and the girls were enjoying their final snack, all my office wives devouring my Twinkies. As they all exited, I followed and locked up the office and wished them all a good night, no hard feelings.

I texted Delores to ask just where we were dining tonight. She texted back: *You have been a bad boy today. We will meet at Marie and John's since your mom and dad are with Marie's parents. We will talk when you arrive.*

So, knowing she more than likely notified the store not to sell me any goodies, I stopped at McDonald's and ordered two small burgers with a small Diet Coke. I know they would never stop anyone from getting McDonalded.

Received my burgers and small Diet Coke and headed to Marie and John's for my talking-to by my housewives.

I took an alternate route so that I had enough time to eat my two burgers before the housewives grabbed them from my hand. I checked my rearview mirror making sure no ketchup leavings were still present.

I walked into the courtyard via the arched gateway. John was at the grill, doing his best to stay out of harm's way. I startled him when he saw me.

John asked, "Are you trying to avoid seeing the women?"

"I have had enough of women today to last me a lifetime."

"I heard Charise sat you in a corner after you tried to sneak a Twinkie from Janice."

I explained to John that I got a cup of coffee from the break room and returned to my desk to find Charise eating my Twinkie which I set on my desk while getting my cup of coffee.

"I forgot to put it in my desk drawer." John shook his head. "Let me explain, she has rules to earn a treat. The day before, you must get through all your messages on the computer. Our receptionist puts messages into your box for you to respond to.

"Charise and Marjorie dreamed up this idea, to eliminate time spent writing the messages on a message pad. So if you don't respond to messages, then you get no treat.

"So, being smarter than an average person, I stopped this morning and bought a box of Twinkies and cupcakes for my own desk. I told Charise earlier that I'd learned my lesson yesterday about bugging her for a snack, so I did my messages, drew three plans, and answered phone calls as they came from our receptionist. I would just wait until she had time to bring me one.

"She was very impressed by my response. I thought I was home free. I could even tell her later in the day to save it for tomorrow, really putting a thick layer of icing on my earlier remark.

"She saw my Twinkie on my desk. She does not have Twinkies to hand out, only cupcakes. She knew I was up to no good. She put me on restriction until Monday; no goodies for me. No matter how good I'm being, no treats will I receive.

"She saw that I was going to take Janice's Twinkies from her desktop while her back was turned to her computer. That's how I got put into a corner and scolded."

John said, "You own the company. How does she make the rules for you to follow?"

Just then Delores said, "Yeah, dear, just how did she make the rules?"

"Okay, here it goes. See, I try to be fair and balanced—no favoritism, no special treatment. Even though I'm technically the owner, I'm also an employee. It wouldn't be fair for a lesser employee not to receive a cupcake for doing a good job while the owner is doing less work and gets rewarded."

Delores said, "So you were told you are on restriction, no goodies, and then while your employee was distracted, you were going to take her reward?"

"You made that sound really bad."

Delores said, "Honey, did you hear what you said before about being fair?"

"Well, yes, and I fully intend to follow that procedure, but the devil told me to take it: 'You bought it. Don't be a fraidy-cat; take it back—it's yours.'"

Delores said to John, "Burn his meat offering. Better yet, cremate his meat offering." She walked away, saying, "God help me. Please, God, help me."

John was laughing hysterically now. "Boy, you can step into it with both feet; amazing."

During dinner, Marie said, "No dessert for you tonight. You were bad, and rewarding your bad behavior would not make for a good learning experience for our daughters or your housewives. Your office wives do have some authority; they are in charge of you while you're at work.

"We are going to take your parents to Cheyenne tomorrow afternoon to get them Western outfits for Gloria's party. We would invite you to join us, but you're on restriction; such a pity."

About an hour after the lighting ceremony we all headed home for our night's sleep.

Then Sarah asked me why Charise was angry with me today.

Delores had her arms folded and said, "Tell her, dear," with a snide tone.

I said to Sarah, "You know when someone tells you that you did something bad, and you find a way around what they told you not to do?"

"Yes, Daddy. That can get you a spanking. We talk about that all the time; would you like to attend one of our meetings?"

Delores leaned back in her seat and looked over at me. "Would you like to join them in one of their meetings, dear?"

I told Sarah, "Not right away. I've learned a valuable lesson today from Charise."

Sarah said, "Daddy, was it over cupcakes? Did you have a hunger pain?"

"Yes and no—not really a hunger pain, but the devil prodded me into being bad."

Sarah said, "Daddy, you have to learn to tell the devil to go away. Jesus will guide you in the right direction. You can ask Jesus to forgive your actions tonight, at prayer time."

We arrived home, and Delores called Marie and told her what Sarah and I were discussing on our drive home.

Marie said, "Video that prayer session, and we can use it in our class tomorrow morning before heading to Cheyenne. That will be priceless. Make sure Susanne gets her people to put it on a DVD for future reference."

Delores did as Marie suggested and videoed the entire prayer session, to be aired during the class tomorrow. Just to make matters worse, they also aired it during the girls' program, all over the world.

Sarah told their audience that their daddy had received a one-hour time-out in the corner of his office with no dessert, and had to talk to Jesus during prayer time. Being bad, not listening or following the rules, is always bad behavior and needs punishment. She said, "My daddy is also on restriction for three more days."

Leslie said, "We don't do bad things, and this is the best reason why: you let down the people who love you the most, and disappointment is very hurtful to those who respect and look up to you."

Of course, Delores and Marie texted Charise, Marjorie, Gloria, and Silvia to watch the girl's program today; priceless.

I was bombarded with "Shame, shame, shame on you" from all of my office managers. "We are so proud of Sarah for teaching you how to lead by example. The prayer was very nice, from the heart and everything."

Gloria texted, *You better hope God overlooks that error you made; a pack of Twinkies. Good thing Charise stopped you from committing such a sin.*

Remember, "Thou shalt not steal" is a very bad sin, texted Silvia.

The all sent their texts and emails to Charise, Marie, Delores, and each other. Marjorie said, *We will get even with him at the party. Wear some spurs on your cowgirl boots.*

Charise came into my office. "See what you caused?"

"My dearest love, *you* caused this to spread like a wildfire. I know I did wrong; I more than likely would have picked them up and put them back. I didn't need the Twinkies; it was more a rebellion than a need."

Charise got a cup of coffee for each of us and stopped at her desk for a two-pack of cupcakes. The Twinkies were all gone. Something new besides cupcakes was the general consensus. Charise said, "I was going to leave one on my desk to let it get stale and give it to you this morning, but one of the girls saw it and said, 'He's on restriction; it wouldn't be nice to tease him.' Janice ate your Twinkie; in fact, she ate three two-packs yesterday."

I opened up my mail box and started to respond while Charise was sitting at my desk.

I read a very strange email: Would I be in the office in the afternoon? They wanted to stop in to say hello. Didn't say who they were or what company or vendor they represented. I contacted the FBI and forwarded the email to the agent, who sent it to their team to analyze where it originated.

The agent replied to my email: "Tell them that you will be out of the office until 2:15 p.m. Leave in about ten minutes; we will have an escort vehicle follow you, and be sure you're back in the office before 2:15 p.m. We will have the place secured with armed agents. Tell your staff to close the blinds on any window facing the street or parking lot. If you have venetian blinds, turn them to see out but not in. We will have three agents at your office in ten minutes dressed like foremen attending a meeting."

The agents pulled into our parking lot with a construction pickup with a pipe rack in the bed, tools, and a tool box. The men sported worn blue jeans, work boots, hard hats, and safety vests; one of them was carrying a handheld radio. You would never know they weren't part of a construction crew.

They were escorted into our conference room where Charise briefed them on the email. She had a computer set up for them to use.

The lead agent at our office got a text from his commander that the email had come from a personal computer; they were checking the exact location.

They called in about ten minutes. The lead agent turned to the room: "It came from a laptop computer, which could be anywhere by now. They are checking the GPS, to see if they can trace the exact location. Their office is contacting all the women, the magazine, and the studios to be on full alert."

They traced the laptop location to the country club frequented by all those who'd been arrested. The FBI dispatched three vehicles with agents dressed up like golfers to locate anyone with a laptop and check all offices, personnel working

The laptop was still at the location; the agents found it sitting in a corner of the country club, against the wall out of sight from anyone passing by. They talked to the waitress and bartender on duty, asking who was sitting at those tables and whether they had videos from early this morning to the present.

The manager took the agents into his office, where they viewed the security tapes. It was a woman, who sat closest to the area. They ran the tapes back to the beginning, and she had a large purse, big enough to hold the laptop. The agents confiscated the laptop and the security tape since the country club had a backup video. They left two agents at the country club just in case the woman returned. They also alerted the other agents in the area to be watching out for her.

The laptop had two fingerprints, which led them to her name and address. Agents were dispatched to her home.

The FBI set to work at their office trying to open the computer, since it had a locking device in the program. The agents at my office were told, "Have the office staff load into our vehicles en route. We'll take them to a safe zone; there are female agents on their way to fill their positions."

They contacted Delores and Marie to forgo their trip to Cheyenne. "Stay at the studio; we will have it surrounded in about ten minutes."

They found out the lady in the country club was Katy's sister, Catharine. She was apprehended as she pulled into her driveway by the agents watching her home. She surrendered without a struggle. The lead agent told me later, "She was a plant, poised to be apprehended. Just who are they after?"

They called Papa and Mama, who said everyone was safe at the house. "All window shades have been drawn all day; no one has been outside."

"We don't know who they are after," the agent told them. "Everyone is being watched or is secure except Fred. We have two cars following him and have just reached him to pull into the nearest parking lot and get into one of our vehicles. Lock up the truck, act like it's a luncheon meeting."

Papa told the agent, "Have your men watch overhead for a drone. Over all locations, they have been using drones to watch suspected people." While Papa was talking to the agent, three armed agents arrived at the home. Over the phone, they verified the badge numbers as actual agents.

Catharine was being questioned, but they did not gain much information from her. She had been instructed to drop off the laptop at the country club, hide it in a specific location, and leave. The FBI office was on full alert; all entry doors were locked, and all parking structures were blocked with steel gates and being scanned for anyone not supposed to be there. The robot was filming all license plates.

They posted ten armed guards at the hotel where the jurors were being sequestered. The judge and attorneys were all being watched and guarded.

Papa made his calls to find if any contracts were looming. There was nothing on the radar screen that anyone could follow. Papa called the FBI agent to inform him that there was nothing specific in the system. As the two were discussing the situation, Papa remembered years ago that a competitor organization wanted to see how the police force operated. They set up a dry run and took notice of the time line, who was first to respond, and where they were approached. All of that was documented. They wanted to know how much time was used up.

Papa asked, "Is Catharine still being interrogated?" The agent said yes. "Hold her until I arrive; I need to question her as well."

Papa hung up and called for his escorts to pick him up and stay with the vehicle while he took care of business. He told my parents, "Do not answer the door for anybody, and stay away from any window." He also instructed them that the armed guards would stay with them while he was away. "Listen to what they tell you, and follow their instructions."

Within a few minutes, my parents were well protected, and Papa was on his way to interrogate Catharine.

Papa was taken to the interrogation room and sat down across from her. His first question was "Do you know why your sister was arrested?"

Catharine said, "Yes, I heard she was charged with murdering people."

Papa asked, "Did you know you can be charged with the murders as well?"

Papa was watching her expressions; never did she show any concern at the pressure being applied.

Papa asked, "Aren't you concerned about being charged with twenty-eight counts of murder and facing the death penalty? Do you also know you could be charged with kidnapping and bank robbery, extortion, tax fraud, forgery, and receiving stolen property besides the murder charges?"

Catharine said, "Sir, if you have evidence of any of these charges, book me."

Papa said, "You must know you were used as a pawn. Who gave you the laptop?"

Catharine said, "Sir, I don't know who gave me the laptop. I already told the agent I got a phone call, stating they had a gift for my sister and asking if I could deliver it to her. I was told to meet them at the country club for the package."

Papa said, "I had the agent bring in a computer and install the disc that they received from the country club."

Catharine said, "What disc, are you talking about?"

"We will show you some evidence. You said they would meet you at the country club with the package, correct?"

"Yes, that's what I said."

The agent ran the video disc for her to watch. "Here you are, ma'am, carrying a large purse. You sat down and set the laptop on the tabletop. The waitress brought you a beverage, so we gather you frequent the country club often if the waitress already knows your choice of beverage.

"Now, where are the people who gave you the laptop computer?" The woman gave no answer.

"Let me back up one more time. We have another video showing the parking lot and entrance to the country club. You were never approached by anyone. Here you are getting out of your vehicle, with your purse on your shoulder. You entered the country club; no one approached you, and you still have the purse on your shoulder."

Another agent approached the man and handed him a piece of paper.

The lead agent said, "Catharine, we have a receipt from a major retailer showing the laptop in question was purchased by you with your credit card. This is your signature, correct?"

Catharine said, "That proves nothing; that could be planted evidence."

"Okay, ma'am, we understand you may have a point, but let me insert this disc. The sale was videotaped by the retailer. Here you are, ma'am, and lo and behold, you were signing for it, and we have a copy of the exact piece of paper, sitting in front of you."

Catharine said, "I want my attorney present before I say another word."

Papa and the lead agent left the room to discuss what had just occurred.

Papa said, "Book her, put her in solitary confinement away from the others, and charge her with all counts. Check all the fingerprints taken by the forensic team to see if she matches." Once their quick meeting ended, entering the office was a lawyer, dressed in a very expensive suit and carrying a briefcase .

"Where is my client?" he asked.

His attitude seemed to rub the agents the wrong way. "Who are you representing?" asked the lead agent.

"You know damn well who I'm representing. I want to see her now!"

The agent said, "You appear to be a well-groomed gentleman lawyer, but we don't care who you think you are. Tell us whom you are representing, or, guards, get him out of my face."

Papa said, "Let's book him, too. The roaches must have seen the light come on in the room."

The lawyer said, "Catharine Thompson is my client."

The lead agent said, "You know, if you had told us from the beginning, we could have shut out that pesky light."

They took him to the room where Catharine was seated, where they did the client and lawyer hug and dance before the agent and Papa entered the room. They had watched the exchange from the two-way mirror.

The lawyer said, "I want her released into my custody, right now."

The agent instructed his assistant, "Could you see if we have another room available at the FBI Bed and Breakfast for our newest guest?"

The lawyer said, "Under what evidence would you charge me?"

The agent said, "You have the right to remain silent," and finished his Miranda rights.

Then the agent told the attorney the charges against his client: twenty-eight counts of murder, aiding and abetting a known murderer, tax evasion, and so on for the entire list of charges. "As for you, sir, we are running your involvement in all of the charges at this moment."

The agent was handed another piece of paper from his assistant. The agent read the paper and told the attorney, "Your client's fingerprint is a match found in the slaughterhouse on several documents. Shall we continue< or would you like to confer with your client?"

The agent said, "Maybe we can make this a sister act and save the taxpayers lots of money. What evidence do you have beyond a couple of fingerprints?" They showed the lawyer the videos. "She has no defense for any of this. Everything she has told us, we have proof that she is lying."

The agent instructed his assistants to escort Mrs. Thompson to her suite at the FBI Bed and Breakfast. Then he asked the attorney, "Would you also like a suite? Oh, don't leave town, and here is an ankle bracelet for you just for being such a welcomed guest at our establishment. Your vehicle was impounded for our forensic team to detail for you. One of the perks in our brochure, to make sure your stay at our B&B is enjoyable."

The lawyer got boisterous, using terminology not becoming for a highly paid attorney. He offered no apologizes, no "very nice meeting you," nothing polite, but he was exercising his First Amendment right to freedom of speech.

The agent made a quick phone call and decided an overnight stay at the B&B just might settle this attorney down. His assistant did say they had a couple of rooms available If necessary.

Catharine Thompson and her attorney were escorted to the suites at the Bed and Breakfast sponsored and owned by the FBI. "Did we mention it comes with three meals, buffet style, daily?" the lead agent asked with a chuckle.

Papa said, "So this is how you win friends: offer them free room and board." Then he headed home, which allowed the gentlemen guarding my parents to return to their normal positions.

Charise was being awfully nice today, feeling her punishment might have far exceeded the penalty incurred.

The clock on the wall chimed three times, so it seemed my guest would not be showing up this fine day. We still had the curtains drawn and doors locked, with men stationed out in our parking lot in addition to three men stationed inside.

The agents in our office escorted the girls to their vehicles, and an escort followed them home. They also escorted me to my pickup truck, and a vehicle followed me home as well.

Everyone was safely at home, and I called all of the branch offices to verify all was well. I got an earful from every office manager: "When is this all going to end?" "Will we ever get to return to normalcy?" "How many other residences are you going to find relating to the murders?"

All the questions had no real answers. I could only say, "We are doing everything to rectify the situation. They arrested another person today, Katy's sister, whose fingerprints were on some of the papers in the files. The roaches are finally coming out from their hiding places.

"They have now separated all those arrested into different facilities. When their trial dates approach, they will rotate prisoners to accommodate the courts. The prosecutors are writing down the arguments that the defense will throw up during the trial, preparing to answer each of their so-called hearsay defense the very first day during the shuffling of the witnesses to be called.

"They want to erase any doubt the very first day that this lady was the prime reason that the murders occurred."

Gloria said, "How confident are you that they have the right person?"

I asked her, "Your re-landscape project, how many invoices or delivery tickets have you personally signed?"

Gloria said, "Too many to count, why?"

"Your signature states that you received the product, correct?"

"Yes, that's why I signed; the product was delivered."

"You didn't have someone sign the receipt for you, did you?"

"No, I wanted to make sure the items on the list were accounted for and in good condition," said Gloria.

"If you were the only person on the jobsite at the time of the delivery, you couldn't say you had the foreman or supervisor sign your name. Katy's signature is on at least ten delivery tickets for concrete received when no concrete crews were present. There's no way the defense could possibly argue with the facts—logbook, time of day, her signature, no human bones in the concrete mix, the driver was watching the chute full of concrete as he poured the mix."

Gloria said, "What if the defense unnerves the driver, questions his testimony, trying to cause doubt in the jurors' minds? The driver has moved up in the company, to dispatcher and sales. He is very credible and solid. I'm thinking they'll try to get him off the stand; 'No further questions' will be the normal response by the defense.

"I can't wait for Monday when the evidence is presented with the witnesses."

I told her, "I can't wait for the Western party at your home. Will you have your bathing suit under your outfit?"

"Maybe," Gloria said. "You'll just have to wait. You know I'm up to surprising you. Make sure the girls all pack suits; we all can splash around in the spa on Sunday if convenient."

The dinner bell was ringing, so we said our goodbyes, and it was off to the burnt offerings, sides, and salads, this time with homemade dinner rolls that Mom and Mama had made from scratch. The girls also helped knead the dough and put them in the bread tins. They even made three loaves of bread for tomorrow's breakfast feast.

Dinner was fantastic. At dessert, as the ladies forgot I was on restriction, I received some peach cobbler, homemade as well. They even put a scoop of vanilla ice-cream on it, with chocolate shavings, whipped cream, and a cherry on top.

Marie and Delores were in a marvelous mood. They shared with their class the video of me getting lectured by Sarah on our drive home. They even showed it on the girls' show, and the magazine and cable networks received calls all day long once it was aired.

6

After the light show we all headed to our homes for another wonderful night's sleep. The girls were getting all excited about going to Utah for the Chuck Wagon Extravaganza at Gloria's. I told them to pack a bathing suit. "Gloria has a spa and wants you to join her before we leave on Monday morning."

We all said our prayers, thanking God for returning us all home safely. "Please bring all of this to an end. Annie wants to be free of all of this as well." The girls were tucked in, foreheads kissed, and "I love you"s said all around. Mom and Dad were going back downstairs to watch some television before retiring, Delores and I moseyed off to our bedroom for some needed rest.

I asked her on the way whether this would be a good night or a "not tonight" night.

She reminded me that I had gotten dessert. "The girls felt bad that you could not eat some of the dessert they made, so you have had goodies. Once you're off restriction and have learned a valuable lesson, you will get rewarded." Delores shook her head. "This hurts me as much as it does you. I'm very disappointed in your actions. You're a much better person than what you showed your office staff."

The next morning before the rooster crowed, in came our lovely daughters, who climbed into our bed and shook until they got our warm embrace. They were chilly, with hands were like icicles. It took longer than normal to warm them up, but their hunger pain got the best of them, so I was off to the kitchen to get breakfast started.

Soon coffee was brewing, and hot chocolate was almost ready. I got out the can of whipped cream to garnish the hot chocolate while the pans were heating up. The pancake batter was ready, the bacon was starting to fry, and the sausages were ready to hit the heat.

My fair ladies all arrived, in their robes and slippers, hair in ponytails, ready to transform from little girls to little chefs. Delores poured us cups of coffee and sat down at the kitchen table to watch the masters prepare a breakfast fit for our queen.

Our doorbell rang, and I reminded Delores to make sure it was Marie and the kids as she headed to the door. It was safe, and Marie and the girls brought a loaf of fresh bread to be toasted.

Leslie, our head flipper, was all poised to perform her magic; Sarah was stationed at the sausage pan; and Kim and Rebecca were setting the table while Marie was slicing the loaf for the girls to toast. I was making the Albright scramble.

Leslie was giving me instructions, keeping an eye on my preparation. "Our reputation depends on that scramble. If you do it perfectly, we'll have you on our show to share with our audience. We will also have three other chefs preparing the same dish and have our staff judge whose is number one. Keep practicing, Daddy, we want you to win the contest." She gave me a hug.

I asked her, "What if it's a tie or all four dishes are the same?"

Leslie said, "Me and the girls are the final judges," with a twinkle in her eye. "No ties."

Then pancakes were done, sausages were cooked, the Albright scramble perfected, and toast finished and on the table. Everyone was digging in.

Leslie said, "Daddy, your scramble is perfect. Great job."

I got thumbs-up from all diners, their mouths too full to express a verbal comment. Marie and Delores raised their cups, letting me know they needed a refill. I also got the girls more hot chocolate; they were dunking the homemade bread into the hot chocolate. They got the idea from watching their moms do it with their coffee.

I asked if all of the hunger pains had gone away. The girls were following their moms' lead, rubbing their tummies and saying, "Just enough good food always rids us of hunger pains. Good job, Daddy."

Marie and Delores added, "So what's for dinner?"

"Albright scramble on homemade rolls, covered with marinara sauce and parmesan cheese and dinner salad on the side, with a glass of Chianti. Oh, by the way, find a red and white checkered tablecloth, linen, with matching napkins, for our patio table and the girls' table. And we need two candles in red glass jars. You'll want to put on your favorite Italian CD and dress in Italian clothes."

Marie said, "You will be a busy boy today making sure all of your dream comes true. We have a class to teach, eight hours of strenuous maneuvers, completed in four or five hours so we can come home and pack for our flight to Utah early tomorrow morning."

The girls, defending Daddy, said, "Mom, we can help Daddy, and Grandmas would love to make this happen. Mama has recipes that we can help her with, and you have the music already. We love Daddy's idea. This will be our treat if that is okay, with Daddy."

I stood up and gave each girl a real daddy hug. "Maybe Grandmas can put something other than Albright scramble in the homemade rolls. Thank you, girls, this will be a great dinner. Something different than off-the-grill meats."

We all headed to our showers or bedrooms to get ready for the day. I gave everyone hugs and kisses before I left for the office. I gave Marie an extra special hug and kiss and told her, "I look forward to seeing you every day. You make my day complete."

Marie said, "Whatever you're up to, it won't work. Christmas is too far away for a special gift, and your birthday has passed. I'm leery of your intentions."

With my arms still around her, looking deeply into her eyes, I told her, "You are my vision. I created you; that will always be my reward."

Marie said, "If only I could believe that. There is something else you are hiding; I can feel it inside."

Off to work I went; *leaving her in suspense is the greatest gift I can give myself. Now I'm ready to face the office wives.*

Again I beat the staff into the office. I was making coffee when my first office wife, Charise, arrived. She said, "For their birthdays I have to get each of the girls a watch that shocks them about a half hour before starting work."

She got a coffee cup and poured herself a cup of boss made coffee. She asked, "Just what do you put in your coffee that makes it taste so good?"

"I can't tell you. It's a family secret from the old country, handed down from my foremothers."

"Foremothers, isn't that forefathers?"

"I'm trying to be politically correct. Would that be *forepersons*? I get so confused with all the new garbage being presented."

Charise said, "It's designed to be that way so you don't know if you're stepping in a fresh pile or yesterday's pile."

"You're correct about one thing: they are piles."

We took our coffees into my office and settled down for a nice prework conversation. Charise was all excited about seeing Gloria and her landscape remodel.

I told her, "If you think that Marie and John's is beyond belief, get ready for another moment of awe. Phillip's men are getting highly skilled, and the cabinet maker is fine tuning the playhouses to act as actual living quarters for our parents if necessary. I have designs established now where the entire patio cover is the playhouse, with a sun deck or another room."

Charise asked, "Will you eventually make a second residence above the barbecue and spas?"

"Phillip and I have discussed such a thing for certain clients who need more space, but their current home is as big as the city will allow.

"I actually want a space created for the children to call their own. It gives them responsibility, not trying to give moms something else to add to their already crazy lives."

Charise said, "When I saw your playhouse and the one outside, the girls and I have all had lunch in the playhouse. It's quite nice to have the cabinets with necessities in case we're missing plasticware or a cup or napkin. They're right there and handy.

"Our cleaning staff cleans the playhouse while cleaning our offices. They also use the playhouse to eat their lunches. They appreciate having a place to sit down and relax without feeling that they are imposing on the staff."

"Well, I'm glad the playhouse is getting some use. It's made to be used."

By now the rest of the staff had arrived, all with cups of coffee. They are all seated in my office poised to hear today's agenda. I told them, "Hold on to something. This is big, really big. I mean, there is nothing bigger than this. Are you ready?"

Charise said, "If this is not really big, nothing bigger, you will be wasting our time."

"Well, since tomorrow is Gloria's Chuck Wagon Extravaganza, you can all go home and pack at lunch. I will give you an extra fifteen minutes."

Charise said, "Hold me back, girls. That was way more than I expected— fifteen minutes to pack for three days away from my closet, my makeup, my shoes. Fifteen minutes, so generous. This might be the big one, I feel it coming.

"Take away a man's cupcakes, he get beside himself with generosity," she said, fanning her face.

"Okay, they get the message, Charise. You're overjoyed. You can't explain your total excitement. I know fifteen minutes is more than what you would need, but it is Friday, and you all have worked so hard since Monday, I felt a little additional time would be a blessing in disguise."

Charise said, "Your blessing is not disguised; it's out there for us all to grasp. Could you squeeze that dollar bill a little tighter to at least a half hour so we don't pad the police force's wallet with a speeding ticket? In fact, give us an hour longer, and we'll stop and get you a Happy Meal!"

"Okay, you win. Take the rest of the day off after lunch. You drive a hard bargain, but don't tell Delores or Marie I caved in, or it will be a long weekend for me on top of my restriction."

They all went to their desks to complete all of their work before lunch.

I started working on the details of the tunnels and playhouses. *Phillip will need to see just how all of this will work; he also may suggest another way to make it all happen— enhance the appearance and functionality of the structures.* I trusted Phillip's suggestions, since when we created the layout on the Wiloby estate, everything just fit better to the lot. I thought of one thing that we might need to provide due to a fire. There were only two exits to the tunnels; I'd have to install another way out of the playhouses, or the girls could get trapped in the tunnel between them, unable to reach the staircase by the property fence line.

The tunnel would have windows in every panel—*but it stands eight feet off the ground with pavers below—not a safe scenario for the girls. We'll add a sprinkler system to the tunnels and the playhouses as a precaution.*

If the properties were not so wooded with pine trees, this would not be much of a concern. A forest fire could become disastrous.

I made a notation on my yellow pad for Silvia to find a local arborist to inspect the pines surrounding the three properties for dead trees, diseases, and insect infestation. I didn't want to put my family or the Albrights, Mama and Papa, in harm's way.

Okay, genius, you got sidetracked again. When will you learn to stay on track? That train you're engineering might never return to the tracks; then what will you do?

Okay, brain, you're starting to sound like Delores and my office wives. Stay focused until one task is finished.

I know the drill. Man, this is tough, fending off my own scolding's.

Just then a little voice was piercing my eardrum. "Hello in there—hello, it's me," said Charice. "I've been talking to you for at least five minutes, but no response. Hello, are you in there? Once you are in a zone, it's impossible to get your attention. How does your wife cope with that?"

"What? I didn't hear you. What is it?"

Charise said, "It's quitting time. We're all getting ready to head home. I didn't want us to just up and leave you alone."

I merely shook my head and returned to my desk. Charise sat down in the chair facing me. "Talk to me. I've never experienced that from you before, you scared me."

I told her, "I do this once in a while. I get so focused on the task that I drown out everything around me. While I was designing the Albrights' place, I got stuck on a problem. Delores asked if I would like to take a break and go grocery shopping with her. I was out of my zone and agreed to go.

"Then while pushing the shopping cart, I fell back into a zone. I was driving in the Indy 500, leading the race by a couple of car lengths with two laps to go. As I was navigating the track, Delores kept interrupting the race: 'Hello, in there— oh, for crying out loud, hello … There you are. We need some bread; remember the aisle? Go get some bread,' she said.

"I had no clue what aisle it was on and backtracked the store. After I found the bread, now how to join up with Delores without getting another earful of 'What took you so long?' She said, 'The bread was just the last aisle we walked up. Men—you're impossible.'

"I was back into the race, white flag, last lap. The other car had gained position, now only a half-length back and he's pushing me to go faster. Holding the car in my lane took much more strength. I'm focused on going into turn three when I get a poke in the ribs. 'What is wrong with you? I've been near screaming at you for two aisles now,' said Delores. 'Why, oh, why did I put myself through this? I hate it when you're zoning; what is wrong with you?'

"'I'm driving the Indy 500 turn three heading to turn four. What is it you want from me?'

"'You're pushing a shopping cart, not driving the Indy 500, for crying out loud. I'm trying to get the shopping finished so I can pick up the girls from school, and you're not even on the planet.'"

Charise said, "Did you win the race?"

I told her, "After we picked out the snacks, heading to the checkout line, I was back in the driver's seat on turn three; entered and exited the turn smooth, heading to turn four. My pit boss was telling me not to back down, push it to the finish line.

"Entering turn four we are wheel to wheel, no chance for error. I'm on the inside, and he's hugging me on the outside. Engines are screaming, nearing the redline on my tach. Then out of turn four, and there is the finish line, the bricks, the bottle of milk—only a few seconds more, then the sputter, sputter, sputter and nothing. I see his rear spoiler, then another rear spoiler, then another; I'm out of gas. Then another poke: 'Hello, the groceries don't jump out of the cart onto the belt.'

"The cashier asked if I was all right. Delores said, 'That depends on your definition of all right.'

"I loaded the groceries onto the belt and then put the sacked groceries back into the shopping cart. When we left the store, she was not happy."

Charise said, "How often do you space out like that?"

"If I'm troubled about a situation is really the only time. I'm not aware of what is going on around me."

"Have you ever done that while driving?" asked Charise.

"No, never while driving or I would give up my driver's license."

"Well, boss, we're leaving. Are you all right to drive home?" she asked.

"Yes, I'm fine. But a cupcake would make it all better."

"Sorry, Charlie, you're on restriction, remember? This is reality. Maybe when you're home you can envision eating a cupcake while driving the Indy 500."

All the girls said, "See you tomorrow at the airport."

"Off to Utah we go," said Janice.

7

Chuck Wagon Extravaganza

At home we met for a great Italian dinner, everything we talked about at breakfast was prepared, even the checkered tablecloths, linen of course, candles in red glass jars, Dean Martin playing in the background. The girls and grandmas outdid themselves, complete with spumoni for dessert. At home we did our prayers, kisses, "I love you"s, and "Not tonight, dear; remember, you're on restriction."

The girls awakened us with a pounce on the bed, squirming under the covers and shaking with chills, borrowing our body heat to warm up.

I asked Sarah, "Who wakes up first?"

Sarah said, "Some days me and some days Rebecca. We just give each other a little loving nudge, not to scare one another. We always hug each other before getting out of bed to visit you and Mom."

Delores asked Sarah, "You like waking us up?"

Sarah replied, "We get chilled coming from our room to your room and need to get warm again, and we know you really don't mind, do you, Mom?"

"Nope, we look forward to you two snuggling up against us. Having your hugs and cheek kisses starts our day out on a positive note."

I asked Delores, "Should we make a small breakfast to fill up the hunger pain?"

"Marie and John should be here to meet the limousines in about an hour," she replied. "We have time, and they would enjoy some belly filler.

"Remember, girls, Gloria has breakfast planned for all of us at her and your dad's favorite eatery, so take it easy with breakfast."

I got up and made coffee and hot chocolate to get the breakfast brigade started. Fired up the stove and put two pans on the burners, mixed up some pancake batter and pulled out three packages of sausages from the meat drawer which we put in frozen last night before going to bed. We got up just in time: the Albrights, Mama and Papa, were ringing our doorbell.

The girls all went into Grandma and Grandpa's room to wake them up. Boy, were they surprised. I know their heart rate jumped from being startled. Being hugged and kissed by their granddaughters was well worth the higher heart rate.

Everyone was sitting at the kitchen and dining room tables, and the girls were our waitresses. We were all ready for the limousines with ten minutes to spare.

We arrived at Denver Airport, we again had to tell security that we were wearing wires and explained why. We had to get the supervisor involved when one TSA agent tried to make us go through the metal detector. That would cause the units to malfunction. When we refused, he got threatening. Our bodyguards politely and firmly took him aside to explain that if he persisted in drawing attention, then he would be spending the rest of his life serving prisoners in the cafeteria.

Another FBI agent got the supervisor. We explained the situation, and they allowed us to pass all the gadgets that could harm the devices.

The TSA agent blew the cover of the FBI agents, so they arranged to have three other agents meet at the airport. Too many passengers on the flight knew they were with the FBI from the loudmouth at the scanner.

If the agents had not done their jobs, my parents' warning devices would have been destroyed. Papa would have been thrown onto the ground, he was that angry with the agent. Mama would have kicked the TSA guy into next week more than once for being such an idiot. We all would have been put into the interrogation room and missed our flight.

At the terminal, the airline was very gracious, asking if we needed anything to settle us down. Papa told the boarding agent that no further disturbance would be greatly appreciated. They upgraded our seats so we could board the plane ahead of most of the passengers.

Two of the TSA managers approached us and gave us cards for future flights. We could show them to the agents and be escorted around the scanners, patted down, and allowed to proceed to our terminals. They apologized for their agent's behavior; he was concerned about the other passengers' safety.

The agents unmasked during the TSA debacle approached us and told us they were to ride on the plane to Utah; no other agents were close enough. The FBI didn't want us unprotected even for less than an hour flight.

We arrived in Utah and were escorted to the baggage claim area. Our agents disappeared during the journey to the baggage claim, and we didn't know who our new bodyguards were. They just got handed the baton, and we all were the batons.

Then Gloria appeared, and oh, what a vision she was. She and Nadine hugged Delores, Marie, Mama, my mom, and all the girls; then they proceeded to hug us gentlemen, who were anxiously waiting for the embrace of a lifetime.

Gloria looked prettier every time I saw her. Nadine was no slouch, but Gloria was my creation, just like Marie.

Gloria had three limousines waiting for all of us to take us to our favorite breakfast eatery. Susanne and her staff had arrived on Friday and were joining us for breakfast.

The restaurant was virtually ours. Only a couple of tables had customers; the staff was waiting for our ladies to arrive. The owner restaurant owner had told them he was having celebrities arrive on Saturday morning.

Silvia, Angel, Juanita, Marjorie, Janet, Jerome, Jonathan, and Matthew had arrived on Friday as well from Texas. Jennifer and the twenty ladies arrived about an hour before we arrived; they also were waiting at the restaurant. Sally and Maggie came with Silvia.

The owner of the restaurant was in seventh heaven when he saw all of the ladies enter his establishment with the film crew, sound men, makeup, hair stylists, and wardrobe poised to make every lady look her absolute best for the filming. We pulled in with the three limousines and found no place to park; it looked like a limousine car lot.

We hopped out and approached the door, where we were greeted by Susanne and three of her staff members. This was very similar to the red-carpet treatment you see on television. As we entered the restaurant, everyone was on their feet and applauding Marie, Delores, Sophia, and Agnes. Mom had no clue she was now famous.

Susanne had the owner play the CD she had given him earlier. Gloria led the ladies' grand entrance; she was a showstopper all on her own. She got loud whistles from the gentlemen and played right into the ovation. Susanne was introducing all the ladies one by one with the little darlings between Sophia and Delores.

Our little ladies' applause was loud as well. They have become little showgirls, with their own style of entrance. Delores followed the girls, and Marie was the anchor—and what an anchor she was, so poised and graceful. She floated across the floor to her favorite song, "Return to Me."

Marie told me one afternoon, after doing her grand entrance, that when she hears "Return to Me," she is returning to him. She gets so emotional inside, her whole body is warm and loving. Everybody wants to be wanted and loved that much. She actually started to tear up as she was talking. "My hope for my girls is to love that much," said Marie.

After breakfast, our limousines dropped us off at the hotel to freshen up before proceeding to Gloria's home. Gloria's family members also attended the breakfast, so I finally met her sons and daughters. All were married but had no little ones as yet. I made sure that our daughters shared their joy with her family members before the afternoon's festivities.

Gloria told me she had the waitress who told everyone to purchase an eight-second clock. She will be out on the driveway teasing the boys to give it a try. She will be dressed up like Daisy Duke in front of the curtain, and if the boys want to give it a try, she'll take them behind the curtain, and an electronic bull will be waiting for them. Jason will be operating the bull, and he who stays on the longest will compete for a gold opportunity to try their luck.

Jason, who is the current Professional Bull Riding champion five years in a row, was bucked off before the eight-second bell rang.

Denise said, "He gave it a shot, and boy, was he horrible." He told me riding a bull is much easier than eight seconds with her. It is in comparison to staying on a tornado for eight seconds.

They have a video of Jason being put on the floor three separate times, with several seconds remaining on the clock.

Denise said if she could teach some of her moves to the bulls, there would be no champion bull rider.

We headed over to Gloria's after freshening up. The wardrobe trailer, was set up for all the ladies, girls, and boys. Jerome was taking lessons from Jason; he wanted to become a professional bull rider. He already had two bull riding events under his belt. First time was a learning experience; the second time he was much better, not so scared.

Marjorie told me she can't watch him ride, it scares her too much. She keeps her eyes closed until Janet says, "He did good."

The ladies and girls were going to get ready in about two hours. Gloria took the girls, Janet, and her brothers up to her playhouse. It was decorated like a bunkhouse with lassos hanging on the walls, horseshoes and longhorn steer horns above the entry door and French doors. She had cattle hides draped over all the benches and a lantern in the middle of the table. Poker chips and three decks of cards with shot glasses set up as if there were cowboys ready to play cards for keeps.

She had a full bar set up next to her spa, with Silvia as the bartender. There would be a mixture of guests, so the bar would definitely be useful. Silvia was a highly skilled professional, gifted in making even nondrinkers feel at ease. She planned to make nonalcoholic drinks for anyone who wants them.

Gloria fired up the spa, and the caterer fired up the grill. They already had prepared barbecue meats for the guests. Now they were making lunch for all the performers, bands, waitresses, sound and lighting personnel, Susanne and her staff, wardrobe and makeup people, stylists, the decorating crew—all were getting fed.

It always amazed me how the magazine arranged the festivities. You'd give them a theme, and they'd make it happen, lining up donors and businesses to make the theme and dream come true, not just for the host and hostess but for the invited guests around the world. When they aired the program live, or taped for later viewing, you were at the event. Production made it happen in your time zone, along with viewing in the time zone in which it took place.

Susanne told all the diners that in a half hour all of the ladies should head to the trailers to get ready. "Gloria, we need you and your female family members to get ready first. We'll need all of you to welcome your guests as they arrive." The magazine got permission to use a church parking lot for a charitable donation. They also got mentioned in the issues used to advertise Gloria's house. Gloria is a member of the church, so getting permission was fairly easy.

I don't know how the makeup people and stylists can improve on perfection, but she did come out of the trailer as a polished gem. She has such a sparkle about her; infectious.

Gloria's two daughters closely resemble her, but mom received some genes that the girls didn't get all of. The younger daughter was very bubbly and liked lots of attention. That she got from Gloria; as she ages, she will be Gloria in personality.

All of the ladies were lined up to get beautified—going in one door as plain Jane and out the other door with all sorts of wow added. Angel received her black bow tie to accent her cowgirl outfit. That will be her trademark forever; she has been notified that organizations are requesting her for their events.

Susanne had been busy with her schedules. She had even denied a couple who wanted Angel to drive the owner of the corporation to a gala event. Susanne said, "She is not a chauffeur. If you want a chauffeur, we can provide you one and a car. She's a construction worker dressed up like a chauffeur for that one event." The secretary said he would pay whatever price; he wanted her to drive him to the gala.

"She is not an escort or a chauffeur. She won't do that for any amount of money offered."

The secretary said, "I'll have him call her direct; we don't need to talk to a go-between."

Susanne said, "Good luck with that approach. I'm the final word; they're under contract with us, not independent. Have a great day."

The secretary called our office in Oregon. "I need to speak to Angel."

"Okay, leave a phone number and name, and she will call you when she returns to the office."

The secretary asked, "What time is she due to arrive?"

"Once per week, for an hour, construction meeting."

"What day?" asked the secretary?

"Whenever the vice president of the company schedules the meeting, he notifies them. We don't have a specific day set aside for meetings."

"Let me talk to your manager."

"I'm the manager, ma'am. Why do you want to talk to Angel?"

"We want her to drive the owner of our company to a gala."

"Ma'am, she is not a driver; she has no license for such a thing. Call a local escort service. Thank you for calling; goodbye."

The phone rang again. This time Silvia answered, "Hello, who is this?"

The secretary told Silvia her name. "Are you one of our clients?"

"No, I'm the personal secretary for Applewood Industries' CEO. I need to talk to Angel," said the secretary.

"She's working in a sewer right now." Silvia gave her an address and said, "Yell down the manhole. If she hears you, talk away. We will bill your firm five thousand dollars for disrupting our employee. Have a great day."

Silvia, Angel, and Susanne were having a blast telling the other girls how they handled a high-ranking company. Silvia said they'd received a letter stating that we were rude to their employee; they said they would talk to our owner, who would have heads rolling.

Silvia asked me, "Will our heads roll?"

"Did they give you the pervert's name? On Monday, contact that secretary, and ask for her boss. Your boss wants to discuss the matter with him personally. I'll have Marie read this entrepreneur the riot act. She will refer the matter to the authorities for solicitation.

"Inform the secretary that she's also going to be questioned since she was acting as a pimp."

8

The guests were arriving. Gloria and her daughters and daughters-in-law were in position. The guests came in wearing their Western outfits, with the cameramen filming them. Our waitress was urging the gentlemen to beat the eight-second clock.

One of the lady guests stated, "Honey, that would be three or four love sessions for him. Eight seconds just might leave me craving for more. Go ahead, honey, give her your best second." She was about five feet from the gate. "Let's see if you can beat me to the gate."

Gloria and her daughter were out of control with laughter. The guest was one of Gloria's best friends. They hugged, and out he came from behind the curtain.

He said, "That bull threw me off on the first buck."

His wife said, "You paid her a buck?"

"The bull bucked me off," said her husband.

The wife told Gloria, "Don't ever get married; this is as good as it will ever get."

Gloria's daughter said, "He'll be known in these parts as One-Buck Chuck."

That whole scenario became the talk of the town. Some lasted for two bucks; one fell off the bull while climbing on.

Jason was laughing so hard he nearly peed himself. He told the waitress the winner may be less than a second in time. She answered, "Welcome to my world."

Before the evening was over, Gloria had over fifty orders for the eight-second clock. "Great idea," one lady said. "I'll start the clock during foreplay to give my husband a fighting chance."

One of Gloria's guests asked if they make a clock that marks hundredths of a second; he might hit eight with that type of clock.

Once all the guests had arrived, and the ladies had belittled their spouses beyond salvaging any egos, the bands were playing country-and-western songs, and couples were dancing. The girls were having a great time dancing with anyone who asked. Now and again the call went out for line dancing, and there was little room to dance so the band split the crowd into two groups. The kids watched the adults dancing and laughed, discreetly of course.

One of the gentlemen was showing off and landed in the spa. That was caught on video, which brought down the house with laughter. Gloria sent a waitress to get the gentleman a towel from the kitchen, but his wife said, "No need, I'll go get one for him."

She brought out a washcloth, said, "Here, dear," and walked away, shaking her head. "Fell off a bull in less than a second, falls into a spa—what's next, lassoing himself? Cowboy, an outfit does not make you a cowboy," she said.

The band started playing songs John Travolta danced to in *Urban Cowboy*. They had a member of the band, who taught some of the men the steps; he was really good. The cameramen were filming like crazy. "This will become priceless," said Susanne. This also got the kids excited; I'd never seen all of them laugh so hard.

They all watched through a couple of songs and then headed down the staircase. They had the band play one of the songs again and did really well at following the instructor, getting everyone to applaud. Even most of the ladies joined them; that was a great moment in video history.

The caterer told Gloria that his crew was ready to serve her guests. The staff was busy putting up tables, and the band was now playing dinner music. The girls had two of Gloria's best friends dine with them. They were still laughing about the man falling into the spa. They had only heard the splash until Susanne showed them the video from the handheld computer.

Leslie produced a piece of paper and wrote a number eight on it. She had Susanne show the video again, and she flashed up the eight to show the diners.

That got everyone laughing: "She gave him an eight!"

Each of the kids had a different number as they judged the splash. Susanne ran the video on the big screen so all the diners could watch, and the kids all graded the dive into the spa.

One of the female diners said, "Let's have them grade our husbands on that bull; that will be worth the price of admission."

I asked Gloria, "How did you find so many Deloreses in such a short time?"

Gloria said, "We all have a Delores in us. You men just keep bringing it to the surface. That's what keeps us from going stir-crazy."

Gloria asked for a vote to have the kids judge the dads' and moms' performances on the mechanical bull. Those in favor outnumbered those opposed. Jason would control the mechanical bull. The kids were the first to ride, and of course Jason made the mechanical bull friendly. With warm embraces from Silvia, who helped the girls onto the massive bull, they all got an eight-second ride..

Jason asked the crowd if the waitress who started all of this should show her abilities. He helped her onto the bull and set the speed for lady beginners. She also got an eight-second ride, and the kids gave her very high marks. When Jason helped her off the bull, she gave him a hug and said, "Thank you for being so kind"; she knew he could have tossed her to the ground.

Now the men, Jason asked if they have ever ridden a mechanical bull prior, if so he upped it a notch. The first rider was set, and the ladies were putting money on how long each rider would last. One rider had under a second; his wife pointed out that his abilities of doing anything were marginal at best.

The rider's wife yelled "Fire away!" to Jason, and her husband did as his wife expected. He was a male beginner and was off after the second buck. He was renamed Two-Bucks Jefferson.

Kim gave him one point, and Susanne asked her why. Kim said, "He didn't get hurt."

The gentleman who fell off the bull before Jason even bucked it did it again, and the kids gave him high marks. When Susanne asked why, they said, "He was funny; he landed on the mats like no one else has before."

Leslie said, "He must have had a protective childhood."

One lady started naming their husbands. The best was "good old In and Out"; others were "One and Done," "Good Old Wrong Hole," "Hole in One," and "Satisfaction." One man lasted only three bucks, but his wife was so proud that she said, "Three bucks, almost a second, dear." The kids all gave him one point, they liked his name: "Where Is It?" That made the crowd of ladies burst into applause for his wife. "Oh, my God" received some high fives from the ladies. He made two bucks from one lady, when he got to his feet—the only rider who received real money.

Next to ride was "One Buck Short"; he did exactly as his name suggested: he was thrown off after two bucks. His wife said, "Ladies, sorry he's mine. Oh, dear God, my wake-up alarm just rang."

Jason told Denise this was the most fun he'd ever had. The names the wives gave their husbands were hysterical. Remember, this was being filmed and aired live on all seven networks. Two of the cameramen were laughing so hard the cameras were shaking.

"Do You Believe in Magic" mounted the mechanical bull. He had ridden in the past and even dared Jason, "I never get bucked off." Now he was talking to the five-time world champion, looking down on his accomplishments, so Jason flipped the control to "not preprogrammed" and adjusted the speed to fit his comments. He asked, "Are you ready, rider?" The rider took the first few bucks and a couple of turns with grace and poise. Then Jason sent the mechanical bull to the right followed by a quick left, and off the rider went.

"Do You Believe in Magic" got to his feet and said, "I want to ride again," sounding assured that Jason could not throw him off again. So he remounted the bull, and at the very first move Jason made—fast forward and down, then the buck and a quick double spin to the right and then left, and off he flew.

The fallen rider's wife rushed to his side. "Are you okay, dear?"

The rider glared at Jason. "I'll bet you could not stay on with those moves." Now the men were whipping out their wallets and slapping their money on the judges' table. Jason handed the controls to the waitress who started all of this, showed her how the joystick operated, and set the speed to "professional rider."

He told "Do You Believe in Magic," "It's set up, and she is at the controls. I'll ride first, and whoever gets the most seconds on the eight-second clock wins, agreed?"

"Magic" said, "Let's ride, talk is cheap."

Jason stayed on for the eight seconds, and the waitress made his ride very impressive. Jason dismounted and said to her, "Do you remember the moves you put on me? Return the favor to my competitor."

Jason stood next to Denise and told the crowd, "Let's give him a hand for challenging a five-time bull riding champion to a match."

The rider got set and looked toward the waitress. "Let's rock." Three seconds into the ride he was on the mat.

Jason went over and helped him up. "She is a really good operator, almost as good as a champion bull in the circuit. You did well to stay on for three seconds." He handed him a business card. "If you want to pursue a riding career, contact me."

Jason had everyone applaud his ride. The kids gave him high scores on all his rides.

"Dust in the Wind" was hilarious. He even mounted the bull backwards. Jason said, "You have to turn around, sir."

The man's wife said, "The other way—you remember how I showed you, the first time we were together, on our honeymoon?"

"Okay, dear, I remember now." He fell off the bull trying to get turned around. As he mounted the mechanical bull, he did what one other had done and fell off before the bull started to buck.

The man's wife came over to him. "It's okay, dear. It only took you three years to get it right in our marriage."

"Slow Learner"—his wife named him perfectly; that said it all. Even Leslie tried to teach him how to mount the mechanical bull, but he tried a sidesaddle approach and fell off the bull backward.

Up next was "One, Two, Three, and Done"; yep, three bucks and done.

Susanne was on the microphone and said she had just received a phone call. "The phones are ringing off the hook at all of our locations. People are saying this is the most enjoyable, the funniest program ever aired. Thank you all for making this a moment to remember. You all will get a free video and magazine, as our thank-you for being such good sports. We have prizes for all the riders today; you will get them in the mail in a week or so. This was so much fun—I have never laughed so hard in my life."

She gave Jason a huge hug and kissed his cheek. "You are beyond remarkable. They want to hire you to go on tour; they will fill stadiums with this show.

"Ladies, the magazine wants you all to keep thinking up names for Jason's tour. The riders will have the names on the backs of their shirts.

"'One Buck Short' received the most likes," said Susanne. "Priceless names, all of them.

"One lady said her husband's name was 'The Buck Stops Here'; he's pretty tight with his wallet. The magazine wants viewers to make up names for the next 'Buck Off'; watch your local listings for the next event."

The event turned to the backyard for some boot stomping. The girls were all excited to make noise with their cowgirl boots on the wooden floor by the spa. The band was happy to play two-step, waltz, and boot-scooting tunes.

Silvia was very busy with drinks, both alcoholic and nonalcoholic. She had three waitresses serving the guests nonstop. I asked her if she needed some help.

She said, "I'd love some help."

I told her, "I'll find someone to help you." She threw an ice cube at me, apparently finding no humor in my remark. I did find an ex-bartender who rolled up his sleeves and helped until she got caught up and could take a breather. I returned and was the official beer top opener—the extent of my bartending experience in a nutshell.

Oh, except I could also pour a glass of wine, straight, nothing fancy, pop the cork and pour.

It was getting near dusk and everyone was positioning to see the outdoor lighting event. Gloria had a professional company light up the playhouse and patio for additional effects. The kids invited the grandparents up to the playhouse to view the event from their viewpoint.

Gloria did a fantastic job decorating the playhouse. She uses it to get away from everyday hassles. It's her me-alone place; her view from the playhouse is the best we have ever done. She has a great mountain view to the east and a great city view to the west. At night the lights of the city are astounding.

A few of the lady guests wanted to take a dip in the spa, so off with the Western outfits and into swimwear and into the heated spa.

Gloria had said on the invitations that if you so desired the spa would be available, so about a half dozen ladies took her up on the invite.

Gloria's invitation did warn to keep the swimming attire modest; there would be youngsters about, and the neighbors didn't need free entertainment.

Gloria had arranged for towels and robes for the ladies to move from the spa to the restrooms inside the house.

A couple of the girls actually danced some songs in their swimsuits.

The light show was unbelievable. Gloria and her family were allowing photos to be taken, and all the ladies were asked to pose for photos. Then they all decided to do the grand entrance from the playhouse staircase. Susanne had the stylists and makeup personnel fix up the ladies to perform. The crowd was positioned to give them some space to perform.

The band had a list of tunes the girls wanted to perform to, descending the staircase. There were six cases of champagne chilled with glassware suitable for the queens.

Susanne had the drummer perform a drumroll, and she introduced the ladies one by one, forty-nine of them in all. The parade of beauties was about to begin.

At last Jennifer and the twenty newest ladies started the descent. The band had a list of tunes that they instructed the sound people to put on a CD that would provide the music the ladies requested, the band would just butcher the tunes. They'd asked for ballads from George Strait, Kenny Rogers, Eddie Arnold, Alabama, and Brooks & Dunn. They moved with grace and glamour to each song played. Jennifer and two others had formed classes for the ladies to perfect their moves. Marjorie and Denise both aided her once they arrived in Texas.

Eileen performed in total awe of the crowd. Clearly, she had perfected the grand entrance beyond the rest of the ladies; her confidence level was off the charts. As if feeding off her vibe, as the ladies descended, each lady was outdoing the last time they performed.

Marie was telling Delores, "These are our girls; we have done well." Marie and Delores were in an embrace when it dawned on them that it was almost their turn.

Following Eileen came Gloria, then Nadine, Denise, Juanita, Angel (with her chauffeur outfit), Sophia, Delores, and finally Marie. She loves being the anchor for the grand entrance; She has mastered every step with poise, grace, glamour, sophistication, elegance—and of course "Return to Me." There can't be one man watching her who wouldn't want her to return to them.

There were a couple of cowboys who got sore ribs from their spouse during her descent. The girls all met her at the bottom of the stairs and group-hugged her. That alone showed the viewers what a special lady she truly is, someone to look up to and emulate to the best of your ability.

The evening was winding down, and guests began heading for the church parking lot in the limousines. A few stragglers were sitting at the patio table reminiscing about old times. The crews were restoring the backyard to its original condition. Finally, we all headed back to the hotel for a long-needed sleep.

We of course stopped in the lobby and gathered some rolls, coffee, hot chocolate, and vendor snacks, just in case that pesky hunger pain should return.

Marjorie and her family had the suite on the other side of Marie and John. All three suites had common doors so the kids could visit on another without going into the hallway. We are all still under the watchful eye of the FBI and local authorities.

9

The girls were all ready for bed, jammies on, teeth brushed, stuffed toys in their arms, all four girls in their king-size bed. All the parents were present, along with grandparents. so let the prayers begin. Each girl said her own prayer, thanking God for this day. "Please watch over the farm animals; we will be there in a few weeks. We hope they remember us," said Leslie.

They thanked God for all of us adults chosen to protect them and love them. They lifted up the hope that all the children of the world might have food, fresh water to drink, and shelter. "Thank you for your Son, giving his life so we are free of sin," then they all said amen.

After kisses on foreheads and cheeks, lights were turned out and Delores plugged in the night-light they'd received at the Whispering Pines Resort. Marie plugged in one on the other side of the room, and the girls were very happy.

Kim said, "We forgot our fishes in the aquarium and Mr. Frog." So the girls said another quick prayer for the aquarium fish and Mr. Frog.

We grown-ups all went into the living room of the suite and drank our coffee and had a sweet roll.

Delores said, "Silvia told me that Murray is flying in tomorrow, and they will show photos of Scooter and Lulu as well as their lambs and calves waiting for them to return. They have the ranch hands' young children come to the corrals to make sure that Scooter and Lulu are truly kid friendly. The dogs love being around the kids."

I told her, "You know that is going to charge up our girls beyond belief. It's going to be hard for them and us; are you all sure you want them to know now?"

Delores said, "They will film the animals and dogs every day so the girls can see their friends."

Marie said that we could all fly over to Oregon so the girls can see and play with the dogs, lambs, and calves.

I told them, "That is a torment. Our girls will be so sad on the flight home. Can you both tolerate seeing the girls weep, come home, and cry on their pillows for hours? You all know how sensitive they really are. We have always been so supportive and pumping them up with positivity. We don't hurt or sadden our girls; I don't think this is a great idea."

Delores said, "You don't know how tough your daughters really are."

"Maybe you're right. You two will have to deal with what you cause. I can't bear to watch them saddened. I saw the looks on their faces when their fish friends were put into the aquarium. With a stroke of luck, the owner told the girls that he would take good care of their friends; he promised them."

Papa and Mama said, "You girls did not see your daughters when you were kidnapped. I agree with Fred; sleep on this idea tonight, and alert Silvia and Murray not to proceed with their plans. It's only a few weeks; the girls will be so overjoyed once they see their lambs, calves, and dogs. I know it must be killing Silvia inside, but it will do more damage than good."

Papa said, "Those dogs will sleep with the girls. I had a border collie as a boy; he was beside me all day and night long. They are very loving and caring animals. Their job is to protect the flock, shepherds, and cattle at all costs. You both will have to fill in while the girls are at school." Papa said I might have to take them to work with me once in a while.

"As those young animals mature," he continued, "they will have to return to the herds, waiting for the next young to be born. The dogs will be bored; they are herders. Murray and I will talk about just how he will make adjustments. Remember, everyone, this is a business operation. They raise cattle for food and sheep for wool and food. They are not raising animals for pets.

"I remember as a young boy, I went to the barn to say hi to my friends, the pony and the two steers. I would give them hay that my grandfather handed me. One Saturday I went to the barn when our family arrived at Grandma and Grandpa's to see my friends. The pony was in his stall and I gave him some hay and a cup of oats that my grandfather gave me, holding me up to feed the pony.

"When I finished, I wanted to feed the steers, but they were gone. My heart was in my throat, and I started to cry. 'Where are my friends?' I asked Grandpa. He said, 'Come with me, son,' and we went into the garage part of the barn, and he told me that they went to heaven to be with Jesus.

"He told me that the next week I would have two new friends to feed. 'They are much smaller and will need some milk, so you can feed them a bottle of milk when you come.' That next week seemed like a year.

"When Saturday came around, my dad had to work. We only had one car, and he told me we might go the next week. He tore my heart out and stomped on it—no hugs, no kind words of encouragement; just 'Deal with it, you're almost in school; you will have many times you can't have your way.'

"It was a way to toughen up your children, prepare them for letdowns; society is great at taking away dreams.

"We lived in an apartment. When my brother had a cast on his leg—a girl had pushed him off the slide at school—I just played by myself on the living room floor. Mom was pregnant with our new sister, getting up and down was not easy for her.

"Don't put my granddaughters through this," said Papa. He got up from the sofa, excused himself, and went to his hotel room. Mama followed him.

Marie said, "I never saw my father like that before."

I told her, "You and Delores being kidnapped, we dealt through quite an ordeal. Your father took the bull by the horns and freed you without any harm. No FBI, no local authorities were involved. Annie and her friends allowed you to be freed without a scratch. It took a toll on your father and mother, the girls, and John and me. You don't want to have the girls in tears for days. It is gut-wrenching, the hurt they felt; ask Diane, ask Susanne. They will confirm what your dad has said."

Delores said, "You're telling us that our daughters were distraught?"

"Distraught, devastated, saddened beyond your wildest imagination. We had no way, no matter how hard we tried to settle them down, nothing, absolutely nothing returned them to the girls we know and love."

John told Marie, "I could not even go to work the whole time you were kidnapped. I couldn't leave the girls. Susanne finally got them to go to the studio to plead with your captors to let you return to their home.

"After the first airing, the next morning the staff rolled in three large bins of mail from all over the world. They went through an entire case of copy paper with emails from all over the world. I could not even tell you how many offers the girls received to come live with families. Prayers were nonstop."

We all decided to sleep on the decision that they would make before Silvia and Murray met us for breakfast in the morning.

The next morning all four girls pounced on our bed all snuggled up to us under the covers to get our warmth. I told them I would go to the lobby and gather up some breakfast rolls and thermoses of hot chocolate and coffee and would return in a few minutes.

Off I went and the girls all stayed in bed with Delores, keeping nice and warm. Delores turned on the television so the girls could watch whatever program they chose. The girls rarely watched television—or any electronic device for that matter.

Leslie said, "The programs are boring and not very educational." She even said they look down on the viewers intelligence—"not worth wasting my time."

I returned with two bags of rolls, two thermoses of hot chocolate and one full of coffee. The hotel desk clerk said if I needed more, I could just call her and her assistant would bring us more. As I entered the room, our table was full of guests; not enough goodies, I'm afraid. So I called the desk clerk, and soon the assistant arrived with a cart full of goodies for everyone.

By the time we finished our rolls and beverages, we all got ready for the day, just in time for the limousines to escort us to the restaurant. There the girls ordered Albright scramble. Gloria told the chef about the meal, and he was more than happy to give it a shot for the girls. He asked Leslie about the ingredients; she has the recipe down pat.

All the girls, myself, John, and Papa all ordered the Albright scramble with pancakes, the ladies ordered different meals. Silvia and Murray met us at the restaurant. Marie talked with them privately; later she told me they both understood. There were no hard feelings; they didn't want to upset the girls. They are just excited that the dogs love children and watch over the animals with eagle eyes.

Marie told them, "We love what you are both doing for our girls. They talk about the lambs and calves with everyone they meet. They are really excited about joining the 4-H club. They have printed everything on the internet for the Oregon 4-H Club. We're just concerned that they will get too emotional once they see the dogs."

Marie said, "We even looked into getting airline tickets for tomorrow morning to let them see and play with the dogs, but my dad told me, please wait. He saw something in the girls when we were kidnapped that was very unsettling for him and my mom."

Marie gave them both a huge hug and told them, "Go see our little buggers, and give them your love."

As soon as the girls saw Silvia and Murray walk into the restaurant, they ran to them and gave them their signature hugs. They invited them to sit by them and tell them about their pets.

Murray showed them photos of their ten lambs and eight calves. He showed them his ranch hand feeding and watering them and giving them love—"So they won't be afraid of you when you arrive." He showed them photos of the houses. "As soon as they get some carpet and painting is finished, you're ready for move-in. Give me two more weeks, and get your stuff packed for my moving company to load up and bring you to my ranch."

I asked Murray, "You'll be ready in two weeks?"

"Yes, that will give me a couple extra days for the final cleanup and detailing the inside. Mama and Papa could move tomorrow if they like. All the utilities are turned on; telephone, internet, and cable are already. Your homes have everything ready; just need us to give them the start date. The gas company checked everything out yesterday, and we have the green light for the heater and water heater, oven and stove; they're all working perfectly.

"Electrical was ready on Wednesday, and our crews have been using the power for their tools and lighting."

We all returned to our seats and enjoyed a delicious breakfast. The chef brought the girls a special cake he'd made early this morning. He even put their names on the top of the cake and gave them all a hug. This was being filmed by the magazine, and Susanne was busy talking to customers with the cameras rolling. They were live on location giving the restaurant lots of free publicity, which was dearly needed.

As we were leaving, lines were forming to enter the restaurant. The ladies got applause from the crowd, and they gave a little show tor the waiting customers. The busboys and waitresses were busy seating new customers. Our waitress ran up to us and gave everyone a huge hug, thanking us for all we had done for them.

Susanne texted her staff to forward a wall of fame to the restaurant for next-day delivery. She told the manager, "All the photos are signed by the ladies, and the kids' photos are coming as well."

She also put in for a free subscription and a rack to display the magazines for their clients. The restaurant will be shown in the upcoming issue; she even secured the front cover with the ladies all posing.

The restaurant ran the Albright scramble as their special of the day. The chef called Susanne the next morning to say they had run out of eggs—the first time in his career he ever ran out of eggs.

We all headed back to Gloria's for some hanging out time. The ladies and the girls all got into bathing suits and lounged in the spa. Sylvia poured champagne and sparkling cider and then climbed into the spa, bringing two bottles of champagne in ice buckets and a bottle of sparkling cider for the girls.

When she got out of the spa, she shook all over like a puppy would to dry off its fur. The girls were all giggling and asking their moms, "Did you see her do that?" They each got out of the spa and did the same thing, laughing while they shook. Then they all went upstairs to the playhouse; they sure loved having their own space. They took the bottle of sparkling cider with them just in case they got thirsty. Since there were eight of them, Silvia gave them two more bottles just in case.

We guys just sat at the patio table and enjoyed the view of the ladies getting in and out of the spa. The more champagne they drank, the friskier they became.

Gloria's family all joined us after about an hour, and Gloria asked if we would do the honors of burnt offerings for lunch. John said, "Madame, we are highly skilled grillers, but you will have to provide us with our secret sauce, to burn the meat to perfection."

Gloria asked, "What is your secret sauce?"

"Goose juice. Silvia knows how to perfect the sauce."

Silvia asked Gloria, "Do you have red lipstick and a pad of Post-its?"

Gloria said, "I'm sure I do; why?"

Silvia said, "Come with me. I'll show you why."

As Gloria was gathering up the lipstick and Post-its, still puzzled as to why these items were important, Silvia told her, "This is tradition thanks to Delores."

When Gloria found the items, Silvia put red lipstick on Gloria and had her kiss a lip print on the Post-it. "Not bad," she said; "a little more pucker and it will be perfect. Try not to smear the print."

Gloria referred it to fingerprinting, only with your lips.

Silvia had her sign it, and she stuck it on a glass. "Now you only have to do twenty or so. I'll go make the goose juice—by the pitcher; the girls like it as well."

Gloria asked Silvia to have all the ladies come to her aid; twenty lip prints could take a while.

Gloria asked, "Delores, how did this get started?"

Delores said, "You know my husband has the gift of stepping into it, often. He is well-meaning, sometimes speaking before his mind catches up to his mouth. I started feeding him crow for lunch and dinner, and he got clever with me and said, 'Next time, honey, could you remove the feathers first before serving?'

"So one afternoon while making him a sandwich, I told him I'd run out of crow, so I used the goose he ran over a couple days ago—"too far gone to make a real dinner, but enough to make a sandwich. Hope you enjoy your lunch.' I took a can of 7 Up, put a lip print on it with red lipstick, and called it Goose Juice, to go along with his sandwich."

Gloria and her daughters and daughters-in-law were laughing hysterically. "You feed your husband road kill for lunch?"

Delores said, "You know, scraping it off the grille of his truck can become an arduous task."

"Do you have recipes of your road kill dishes?" asked Gloria's daughter.

"If you catch it right after he hits one, no need to reheat the bird," said Delores. "If it's on there for a while, then you can microwave it for a few seconds."

Marie said, "You know, he always remarks about how good a cook Delores has become. Her first meal she made him was a bit hard to swallow. Too many feathers, and got stuck in his throat.

By the time they had enough stickers made, Silvia returned with a pitcher of goose juice for the ladies to sample. The general consensus was "This is really good. What did you add to the 7 Up?"

Silvia said, "A touch of lime juice. I also added grenadine at one party to make his drink look more exotic, and he gave me a quarter tip. A whole quarter, just for me; I was so honored. I didn't need to share that with the busboys, no sir; pocketed that shiny quarter. I earned it.

"I had a tip pitcher filled with paper bills; not one person put in change, except my boss. He ordered the same next time and gave me a shiny nickel. That got the rest of my customers saying who is the cheap Charlie? That increased my tips the entire party."

Marie said, "But, Silvia, you were showing a lot of skin at that party. A couple of guys would chug their drinks just watching you make another one."

Silvia said, "I watched those guys, and would show just a little more with different angles. They went from one dollar, to five dollars, to ten dollars. The more I showed and the longer I held a pose, the more money they put into the pitcher."

Delores asked, "How much did you get in tips at that party?"

"Enough to pay all my bills for the month," said Silvia.

Gloria's daughter asked, "Didn't you feel cheapened by doing that?"

Silvia said, "I could have been a schoolmarm and not wear a revealing outfit at a luau, with all the other ladies sporting skin, and got maybe a hundred dollars at best for six or eight hours of hard work. Or I could sport some skin and pay all my bills. What would you do?"

Gloria said, "Show it. The drunker they get, the less they'll remember you or your name by the end of the evening. If I remember correctly, there were no preachers at that luau."

Silvia said, "Ladies, my God gave me a talent. Not denying I may have stretched that talent to the extreme, and I'm sure I will get questioned regarding my intentions on the day of judgment, but I needed the money to pay my bills. If they were willing to up the tip by seeing what God gave me, I was only sharing my assets."

Gloria explained that Silvia was a bar tender by trade. "She has seen things none of us have ever seen. I could not do what she does for a living. I would have been fired after my first encounter with an idiot."

Delores hugged Silvia, saying, "She is my alter-ego. I'm so proud of her and what she brings to all parties."

Denise and Jason, just arriving, entered the backyard. Gloria said, "Girls, watch what happens to your mates with her just strolling into view."

Gloria's daughter said, "I'll kill him, tonight."

Gloria said, "No, my love, get me a grandchild. Capitalize on what just occurred."

Delores told them, "It's a game she plays. You should see her at an airport. Guys walk into walls or trash cans, step on moving walkways and nearly fall over. She even had two men run into each other head on."

Marie said, "Girls, look at your mom. She has stopped traffic. She is gorgeous but not flashy. She knows she is eye candy for all men, but she doesn't flaunt it; she doesn't need to flaunt it. She has what other women around her want, attention.

Marie asked, "How many men have had their ribs bruised by you?"

Gloria said, "At one grand entrance, a lady elbowed her husband so hard she knocked his fork out of his hand. I think she knocked the wind out of him as well."

The girls practiced in the kitchen to enhance their grand entrance for their husbands.

"Ready, girls?" asked Gloria. "Let's treat them to some eye candy." Gloria turned on the stereo with her favorite CD—Brooks & Dunn, *Greatest Hits*. Her favorite song was "You're Gonna Miss Me When I'm Gone." She got her kiss from all the men upon her arrival at the "burn 'em again grill" and Chef John. He did a great job on the hotdogs the girls crave. Only John blackened them to perfection.

I grilled the pork chops, hamburgers, and steaks while John was busy blackening the hotdogs. We of course goose juiced the meat to give it that added zing.

While we were all sitting at the firepit, Gloria said, "Can't you all just move to Utah? I miss everyone. I get so lonely; you all bring me such joy. We can find some condos nearby, like a vacation home."

Jason told her, "They are opening up a bull riding school in Utah. There is a demand for bull riders, and we will fill that demand."

Gloria said, "I can check around and find you multiple choices if you would like."

Denise asked, "Could you take photos and give us your honest opinion of the complex?"

Gloria said, "I'll do my best for you two. No matter where you choose, the complex will never be the same. You're both celebrities, and home rates will triple in value when you move in."

Gloria's daughters and daughters-in-law all agreed. "You got our husbands' attention in seconds."

Jason said, "Yeah, I know what you mean. I picked her up at the airport and three men walked into trash cans and walls. I was amazed. I know she's beautiful or I would not have approached her as she was getting out of the limousine when I first put my eyes on her. Oh, by the way, wait a minute, will it be okay to tell them, my darling?"

Denise said, "Only them until we let my parents know."

"We're getting married right after Silvia and Murray," said Jason. "We don't want to cut in line."

Every one of the ladies stood up and hugged the bride-to-be. Joyful tears were flowing. We guy were giving Jason manly hugs, congratulating him. "Great choice; she's a wonderful girl."

10

We all returned to our hotel and packed for tomorrow's flight back home; only a couple of weeks later we would be off to Oregon. Mama and Papa talked to Murray about moving in by Friday to their home if he thought the movers would be able to move them on short notice. Murray assured them that a Friday move would be easy for the moving company to make happen.

The girls were all excited that Mama and Papa would be there to help with their friends. They had already named the new lambs and calves and made sure Papa would call them by name and give them daily hugs.

Marie said she would help them prepare for their move and get Charise to arrange for the flight. This of course brought lots of tears just before bedtime. They mean so much for all of us.

Mama said, "Whoever gets chosen to dine with my babies, bring them their flowers or candy. Don't disappoint them; they will call me daily, right, girls?"

There was so much hugging going on John and I went to the lobby and stocked up on coffee, hot chocolate, and rolls to restore some of the fluids lost during the exchange.

Silvia is on cloud nine, so excited to have Mama and Papa in Oregon. She told them, "Every morning before work I will stop by to bring breakfast rolls and coffee. I'm so excited, I can't express how I feel right now." She started tearing up, but Susanne had her signature box of tissues handy, with a shoulder and a hug.

Delores said, "Now I have to butter up my girls so we get on the list of guests for dinner."

I told Papa, "I'm giving Phillip the plans for the playhouses and your plan tomorrow afternoon so he can start right away with all the structures. We can't have meals with no diner available. We may have to rough it for a month with charcoal grilling. I'll have to train John all over again. I'll send Murray the plans on Tuesday."

Murray said you know we have a backlog of two months?"

I told him, "I'm certain we can muster up a few more crew members to facilitate our family's needs."

Murray said, "Great, two bosses."

Delores said, "Honey, you don't have enough fingers to count how many bosses you just inherited."

Silvia said, "I forgot to tell him, his life will change forever once everyone has moved into their homes."

After some well-deserved rolls and coffee and hot chocolate, we tucked the girls in the king-sized bed; they sure liked sharing a large bed together. The night lights were all plugged in and shining brightly, as designed. All the adults were poised and ready for some much-needed prayers.

The girls all started by thanking God for a wonderful day. "Please be with us as we return home tomorrow. Watch over everyone in Ladies' Club; return them home as well. Watch over our friends in the aquarium, and our lambs and calves; protect them until we can love them every day."

As the prayers were being said by each girl, the tears started rolling down our cheeks. They had a way of making us humble and thankful for being alive and able to contribute to their well-being. When they said amen, we were all sniffling, and Susanne's box of tissues was depleted, Delores found another box in the bathroom closet just in time to catch more tears flowing.

We all retired to our rooms; the girls were already warm and cozy and starting to fall asleep.

Delores told me, "You know, it just dawned on me that we will be moving from Colorado to Oregon in just two weeks. We have a lot of work to complete in two weeks' time. I'll miss our home; it's where both the girls were brought home to their first days of life. It will be so sad leaving our home."

I told her, "You know we still own our home; it will just be rented to good people. We will eventually own the Oregon home if we choose to continue to live in Oregon, and we can return at any time we choose."

Delores said, "You know our girls. They will fall in love with Oregon, with all they can do at the house and being right next door to their sisters. We won't return anytime soon."

I told her, "You will have Marie right next door, with her parents next door to her. My parents are planning on moving to Oregon. What about your parents? Would they like to move to Oregon?"

"I talked to Mom and Dad last week," said Delores. "They are thinking about it but still have too much going on where they live. My mom is involved in her church group, and Dad plays golf nearly every day."

"I don't want to seem uncaring, but there are churches in Oregon, and golf is year-round there, except when it gets rained out, but give the clubs a day off once in a while, or play after it stops raining. They will get far more from our daughters than what they cherish today."

"Mom said they would come and visit us once we are settled in. She wants to see the new house first before they decide one way or another."

"Would you mind them living in our neighborhood?"

"My mom and I were very close until I got into high school and found new girlfriends, and I spent most of my free time with them. I think I left my mom out of my life for a few years, and that may have hurt her feelings. We have gotten closer in the past few years, but there is still an uneasiness between us."

"I know the solution: sit her out on our new deck with the lounge chairs, and watch the girls going from house to playhouse to barnyard, playing with the dogs, visit the waterfalls, have dinner with the girls, starlit nights with our outdoor lighting event, music playing in the background, with my parents, Marie's parents. Your past is your past. This will be a memorable experience for everyone."

Delores said, "If only half of what you just said becomes reality, Mom and Dad will agree to join us in Oregon. Can we pray about that tonight? We may need God's help in making that happen."

I told her I had more in my vision.

She gave me that look of disbelief; then she said: "I know I should never ask such a silly question, but here goes: what more did you see?"

I put my arms around her and snuggled up close to her. She said, "That was not part of your vision. You're ad-libbing," said Delores.

"Do you know how my vision ends?"

"A broken rib and a trip to the emergency room?" said Delores.

I told her, "That might be your vision, but mine? I tell the buff gardener, 'Not tonight, she's all mine.'"

"I told you and Marie, he only speaks pleasure, no other language. Does he understand?"

"I'm starting to learn pleasure; I took an online crash course and received very high marks."

"There's only one thing against you," said Delores.

"What might that be?"

"You speak another language," said Delores. "Actions speak for themselves."

The next morning, reclothed of course, the girls all came in and squirmed under the covers and snuggled up against us to restore their warmth. After a few minutes Sarah asked, "Daddy, you know how sensitive our tummies are, how the slightest change, can make them rumble, and that agitates our hunger pains."

"I'm aware of the symptoms, my dearest darling. Would you all like Daddy to get some hunger pain medication before they expand?"

"Oh, Daddy, we would be so appreciative if you would be so kind to help alleviate the temptation before it goes out of control."

Up I got, and away I went on a mission to cure the hunger pains of my daughters and wives.

I got to the lobby just as the hotel desk clerk was preparing our thermoses. She said, "You are at least a minute late. Do you have a legitimate reason or the one I normally hear, 'I overslept'?"

I turned my backside toward her and said, "Whip me, whip me as hard as you can bear. I've been bad, disrespectful of your time. I don't deserve even one crumb of a roll or a sip of coffee. I could blame the elevator for being slow, I could say your alarm clocks are not in sync with your wall clock or your watch, I could say the sun did not rise at the exact minute that the news channel stated, but those are just blame-it-on-someone-else excuses. I deserve your most severe punishment. One minute is one minute; you never can get that minute back no matter how hard you try."

The clerk said, "You make me sound so guilty over a lousy old minute."

I gave her a hug. "You know I love you; I would do anything for you. I only ask for your forgiveness. I promise to do much better the next time I stay at your fine establishment."

She handed me two bags of rolls, two thermoses of coffee, and one thermos of hot chocolate. She said, "As soon as you reach your room, my assistant will bring the same order to your room. He told me you were having a slumber party yesterday."

"No, you see we have our parents and a cameraman with sound, makeup, and hairstylist crews on our floor. We're celebrities, you know."

She looked at me and said, "Do I know you?"

"Honey, we have spent two wonderful mornings together; we're practically married. The third morning together would be, aside from the piece of paper, you're mine for life."

She told me she'd been dating a guy for four years, and they aren't married yet.

I said, "Tell him you were nearly married, just missed it by twenty-four hours."

She said, "If I told him that, he might say goodbye, and I'd have to start looking all over again."

I told her, "If you are serious about this young fellow, tell him four years is an eternity to wait. He needs to ask the question today, and be prepared for a short engagement. You're ready, and each day he waits makes it that much harder for you to resist other men who are serious."

She said, "That sounds like an ultimatum."

"You were four years younger when you first started dating; what age is your limit? Add eighteen years to your age, and that's when your first child will be getting out of high school. How much hair color and makeup do you want to wear? Will you be your child's grandparent in age?"

She stepped to the desk phone, dialed a number, and said, "Either we get married this year, or I'll become my child's grandparent at their graduation," and she hung up.

She held up her right hand and counted down from five, "Four, three, two, one," when the phone rang, and her boyfriend said, "Will you marry me?"

She said, "I will. Please call me back in a few minutes; I have a customer who needs my help."

She gave me a hug and a kiss on the cheek. "You're remarkable. Thank you."

I told her, "Name your child Monday Morning."

She laughed and said, "Probably not, but nice idea anyway."

Off I went and returned to our room with the slumber party in full swing. The bag of rolls was snatched out of my hand, and the thermoses were snatched out of the other hand. I went to the door, and in came the bellhop with two trays of goodies and beverages. He said, "The hotel desk clerk told me to say you're welcome." Before I could get my wallet out to tip him, Delores pushed me out of the way and pushed the roll cart to the table.

I told the young man, "She's hungry; there's no stopping them when they're hungry. Tell your boss thank you, and I'll return the carts as soon as it's safe."

Marie pushed the beverage cart to the table; this was really serious. I'd hate to be near them if we ever had a famine.

When both carts were empty, I told them I had to return them to the front desk for others to use. "I shall return. Is there anything else I might retrieve for you while I'm your servant?"

Delores said, "My nonspeaking buff gardener. I want to compare your schooling to his profession."

"I'll be back as soon as allowable."

I returned the carts, and the hotel desk clerk's boyfriend was at the counter. She said, "Sir, just leave those there; we'll take care of them for you. Thank you for everything."

I told her, "No, thank you. If those carts had not shown up, they would have turned on me and eaten me alive. You know how long plastic ware takes to cut through skin and bones. It would have been agony."

They both laughed and told me to have a great day. "Come back anytime," said the clerk.

When I got back to the room, my suitcase was the only thing left; the suites were empty. I grabbed my bag, made sure the night lights were packed, and scurried to the elevator and then to the front door just in time to hop into a slow-rolling limousine.

Delores addressed the driver. "I said punch it. Men—I swear, simple directions, can't follow simple directions, none of them."

She turned to me. "You know you were about to be left in Utah. So slow. You're lucky, we had to fit all the luggage into the trunk. One less bag, and you would be standing on the sidewalk thumbing your way to the airport."

Marie asked, "Did you give the desk clerk a tip?"

I told her, "A big one. She's been dating her boyfriend for four years, so I told her, 'That's long enough. Figure out how old you will be when your child is eighteen and graduating high school; will you be their parent or grandparent in age?' She called him and said, 'Today either ask me to marry you, or I'm gone.'

"She counted down from five on her fingers, and at one the phone rang and he proposed marriage to her."

Delores said, "You know, you could have destroyed that relationship."

I told her, "I did destroy the dating relationship, and now they both have a permanent relationship to work on."

On the way to the airport, Marie said, "You need to start a wall of your handiwork: changing me to what I am today, Gloria's hair color and style, Marjorie's and Denise's marriages, Silvia's dead-end user of a boyfriend—I still can't believe that he offered her to his friends for money. Today's encounter with a hotel desk clerk and her four-year dead-end relationship. What's next, start healing people?"

Delores said, "How about parting a sea? Maybe we can take him to Sea World and have one of those whales swallow him."

Marie said, "No, that won't work. The poor whale would get him lodged in its throat. Too many crow feathers."

Delores said, "It might tickle its throat and make it sneeze."

John said, "At least it would be a quick, painless death after the first bite."

I told John, "Only if he swallowed me head first. If feet first, I don't know; f he had to stop and chew my bottom half—horrible, simply horrible way to go."

Soon we were through the strip search and at the gate awaiting our flight. At the gate next to us were the girls from Texas, and across from them was the flight to Oregon. The cheering for each gate was getting loud.

Texas has fewer letters; they were able to spell their state twice while we Coloradoans barely got out the first three letters. Some of our passengers had to teach us to spell.

Gloria texted me to say she had over a hundred calls wanting an estimate to remodel their homes. *I'll be busy for a few days, incoming.*

She still sends her measurements and photos to Janice and Melanie to put into the computer to create the plans.

We landed in Denver to find waiting limousines. The camera crew from the office was there filming us heading to the baggage claim area. Susanne was being interviewed while walking with the girls, telling the audience to please watch the upcoming special to see the Western themed party. "The mechanical bull riding by the guests is absolutely priceless; the girls were grading the riders.

"Some of the names the wives called their husbands are so funny. Please, everyone, order a copy now; don't wait. This was not rehearsed or scripted; it's pure side-splitting humor.

"Also watch for our next 'Buck Off,' scheduled in two weeks. Send in your favorite name for the husbands."

We had our luggage all loaded, and Susanne rode with the girls. We had Mama and Papa, John and Marie; the ladies were making their margaritas. I had a ginger ale with a cherry, living high off the hog this trip.

We all voted, and it was unanimous: we had a great time, it was a perfect weekend. The girls had a great time as well.

Marie said, "Delores and I will send flowers to Gloria at the office and a gift certificate to her favorite eatery or hair salon or wherever she would like to go."

We arrived at Marie and John's house and offloaded the luggage and our precious cargos. The girls and Susanne went to the playhouse. We went into the kitchen area and made some refreshments.

"It's nice to be at home," said Marie. " I hope our new home makes me feel this way. You know, you have to make all of this happen again; no letdowns. I could not bear being let down, you know me."

I said, "With the plans I have, you'll have all this and a touch more. The playhouses are bigger, the tunnel is longer, and you can go to either playhouse without getting in the elements unless you choose. You can go house to house anytime you wish, night or day, rain, snow, sleet, or gloom of night; the girls must have freedom to choose."

Marie asked, "So you joined the two playhouses together?"

"They are joined by one continuous tunnel. If for any reason you decide to separate the tunnels, each property has a staircase with a side door, and there's a sliding panel to separate the tunnels. Phillip and I are designing to separate the roofs at the property line. There are two separate waterfalls with a connecting stream feature which we can separate if need be."

Marie said, "Are you hinting that maybe you might move back to Colorado or elsewhere?"

"Delores and I decided we're not doing anything unless we confer with you and John and the girls, no matter what. We hope you both will do the same. You are both too dear to us; we're closer than family, we're soul mates."

Marie said, "You want us to be soul mates?"

"Only if you feel the same."

Marie put her arms around Delores. "We are now soul sisters!"

John and I hugged, and I said, "Soul brother—nice ring to that title, is it not?"

The girls were having a hunger pain; three days without one chocolate cupcake is devastating.

We told the girls that they all have a new title: soul sisters.

They were a little confused with the term and wanted to know what it meant.

Marie explained, "You were just friends earlier, very close friends I might add. Your mom and dad want us to be together for eternity, so you are now soul sisters; your souls and spirits are together."

The girls were all hugging at their new titles, with hugs for us parents and both grandparents, hoping to have all four grandparents from both sides of the family join us in the new titles.

The girls got the cupcakes and ran to tell Susanne and Annie their new titles.

Marie said, "You both know those four girls made this happen. They are miracle workers, so warm and loving. I thank God every night for having those four girls in my life."

Delores said, "I do the same and add you, John, and Mama and Papa as well."

It was getting near lunchtime. "Do we fire up the grill and have hotdogs or go to the girls favorite hangout?"

"Well," John said, "I cooked yesterday. My grilling hand is sore."

Marie said, "Honey, you cooked two packs of hot dogs. Fred did the pork chops, hamburgers, brats and steaks; won't his hands be sore as well?"

Delores called to the girls and Susanne to make the final decision.

The girls came in and rubbed their chins, giving it lots of thought. Susanne said, "I go wherever you all decide. I'm good with both ideas."

The girls looked at John and me. "You make a better dinner than lunch, most of the time," said Leslie. "Moms, you need a break from dishes. Let's go get some crow, like Daddy gets."

We all loaded into the vehicles and off we went to the girls' favorite eatery.

We were received with open arms. "Where have you been? We have been heartbroken for days." We were hugged by our waitress and the manager, even the owner and his wife hugged us.

The service was extraordinary. The girls ordered crow just like mine. Our waitress said, "You know, the chef will give you extra chocolate feathers. If you don't want the crow, you can have anything on the menu."

They thought about what the waitress told them and decided on the crow. They are starting to like how it tastes, and with French fries and coleslaw, it makes a nice combination. The chef suggested that he give them some macaroni and cheese in a side dish just in case; he makes it special.

Delores already knew she had fries sitting a couple feet from the center of her plate. She ordered the rib eye steak, medium, with baked potato, steamed vegetables, and a salad. Marie, Mama, Papa, John, and Susanne ordered the same. We all ordered goose juice—"with lots of lips," said the girls.

In a few minutes the waitress brought out the first pitcher of goose juice with at least ten stickers on the pitcher and one per glass for the girls. She and the other waitresses needed a break to get their kissers back in shape; too many days of goofing off. Their lips were out of practice.

The girls nearly killed the pitcher by themselves. They chugged the first glass and slammed their glasses on the table and wiped their lips and said, "Ahh, that's good."

Just like Mom with a margarita.

I told Delores and Marie, "See what you taught our daughters?"

"Excuse me," said Delores, "remember at the patio table the girls were working for you, and you drank some lemonade and did exactly what they just did and they followed your actions? Sir, *you* taught them. Marie and I, even our dearest friend Susanne, we saw her at the bar after Silvia made her a drink to settle her nerves.

I told Delores, "I'm a good teacher."

Marie said, "I don't know, the jury is still out on that issue."

Our meals started to arrive. The chef came out with his special macaroni and cheese and had the girls sample a bite; the glow on their faces was priceless. Then he had the staff bring out the birds for the girls—twice as many feathers as I normally receive—and an extra plate of french fries for them to share. Their smiles were wide, their eyes glowing with joy. The rest of the meals followed, and the aroma of the steaks was fabulous.

Delores didn't let me down. She snatched the chocolate feathers from my crow and reached in for a handful of fries. "You were eating those, were you?" she asked.

Marie asked, "Are those fries like the last time?" Delores handed her a couple of hers. Marie said, "Even better than last time."

Delores grabbed another handful and said, "You don't mind sharing, do you, dear?"

Our waitress came by and said to me, "You must have been starving. The others have barely touched their meals, and you're nearly finished." I just pointed over to Delores, the food snatcher. I had a piece of chicken on my fork, and she took it and plopped it in her mouth.

"This is very good. Delores, have you tasted his crow?"

"Not yet, I'm putting ketchup on the fries, just a second." The waitress took my knife and cut off a piece with the cheese and cream filling and used my fork to feed a bite to Delores and one to Marie.

Delores said, "You know, Marie, I think he orders crow just to tease us; don't you agree?"

Marie said, "He knows we love what he eats, so different than our steaks. Even though they're mouthwatering, the difference drives us crazy. Can we have another bite?"

The waitress just stuck a fork into the rest of the bird and plopped it on their plate. "No sense asking, just take it; you're married, so it belongs to you. Remember the fifty–fifty rule established by the courts: you get it, he pays for it; pretty simple." The entire restaurant was in hysterics over this encounter.

Susanne said, "You know, the next time I'm bringing the film crew. This is better than any *Lucy* show that was ever created."

The chef and his one assistant brought me another crow. "Here, sir. The ladies told us last time what they planned to do to your meal. Bon appétit. "The owner and his wife got some still shots with their cell phones and forwarded them to Susanne. They too were laughing at the encounter.

My little darlings came and gave me a hug and snatched my chocolate feathers, just the way Mom did. There were two feathers, so they broke them in half and ate them while returning to their seats. "His are much better than ours," said Leslie.

Lunch was an adventure as normal. The girls got their chocolate cupcakes with chocolate icing and their names in white icing with three red hearts around their names. Everyone had their cell phones out taking photos of the cupcakes. Customers around us stood up and took photos of the cupcakes. They were warned earlier not to take photos of the ladies or the girls; "They are under contract, and your photos could land you in jail or a healthy fine. Give us your name and address, and photos will be sent to you."

11

Prosecution Begins

The prosecution called their first witness, Ronald Carter, the concrete delivery driver for Round About Concrete. Ronald was sworn in by the bailiff and seated in the stand. The prosecution attorney, Natalie Morgan, asked Ronald if he know the defendant seated at the table.

Ronald stated he did know her. Ms. Morgan asked, "Just how did you meet Katy Wilkins?"

Ronald stated that he delivered concrete to her home, gave the address, time of day, and the amount and type of concrete delivered.

Ms. Morgan asked, "Was there anything odd about your delivery that morning?"

The defense attorney objected to the question, and the judge overruled the objection. "Please answer the question," Ronald was told.

Ronald said, "There was no concrete crew there to start processing the pour. I just ran the concrete down the chute into the forms, it took a little more time; the crew would have moved the concrete into position, making the delivery quicker."

Ms. Morgan asked, "Did you notice anything in the concrete mix beyond the normal rock, sand, cement, and water?"

Ronald said, "No ma'am, normal concrete mix I deliver all day long."

Ms. Morgan asked, "How do you know the exact date and time of your deliveries?"

"For years I have kept a diary of the mixes delivered, the time and date of delivery, and names of those signing the delivery tickets."

Ms. Morgan showed Ronald a document. "Is this the copy of your diary on the date you delivered the concrete mix?"

Ronald said, "Yes ma'am, that is the copy I submitted to you a couple of weeks ago."

She showed Ronald a delivery ticket. "Is this the delivery ticket for the concrete delivered?"

Ronald looked at the delivery ticket and said, "Yes ma'am, that is the signed ticket of the delivery of nine cubic yards."

"Whose name is on the ticket?"

Ronald replied, "Katy Wilkins."

Ms. Morgan asked, "Do most of your delivery tickets get signed by the homeowners or property owners?"

The defense attorney objected to the question: "Leading the witness."

The judge overruled the objection and warned the defense attorney that if he kept objecting, it would take longer for this witness to finish. "Please use your objections sparingly."

"You may answer the question," the judge said to the witness and warned Ms. Morgan about leading the witness.

Ronald said, "Not very often. It does occur; usually the concrete contractors sign the delivery tickets, since their accounts are being charged for the concrete."

Ms. Morgan asked, "Did you ever see a concrete crew on any of Katy Wilkins's concrete deliveries that you personally delivered?"

"I never saw a concrete crew during my deliveries."

Ms. Morgan asked, "Were you ever involved in collecting payment for the concrete being poured?"

Ronald said, "No ma'am, I just deliver the concrete. The office handles the money. Our sign states the drivers carry no cash; it's much safer that way."

Ms. Morgan asked, "How many times did you deliver concrete to Katy Wilkins's address?"

Ronald said, "Five loads on five different days. You have the delivery tickets, with the dates and times and the amount and type of concrete mix."

Ms. Morgan asked, "You saw no concrete crews?"

Ronald said, "No ma'am."

Ms. Morgan turned to the defense attorney. "Your witness."

Jonas Smith, who happened to be a very high-profile attorney, approached the stand. He asked Ronald, "How long had you been a driver at the time of your first delivery to the Wilkins residence?"

"I was just starting my third year," said Ronald.

"During your three years of delivery service, did you ever offload concrete at a construction site without a concrete crew?"

Ronald replied, "No sir, she was my first to have me offload without the concrete crew."

Mr. Smith asked, "Why did you offload without the crew present?"

Ronald replied, "She said they were on their way. 'Just pour; they'll have to deal with the outcome.'"

Mr. Smith asked, "Did you check with your office to see if that would be allowed?"

Ronald replied, "Yes sir, they instructed me to follow the customer's order. 'If a form lets loose, then stop the delivery, and the customer will be charged for the concrete poured at the time.'"

Mr. Smith asked, "You keep accurate records. Whom at the company did you talk with during the first pour?"

Ronald replied, "Our dispatcher, Ralph Jones. The time was 7:30 a.m. on the delivery date."

Mr. Smith asked, "Is Ralph Jones still employed with your firm?"

Ronald replied, "No sir, he passed away three years ago."

Mr. Smith asked, "So there is no one who could verify that conversation?"

Ronald replied, "Yes sir, all calls are recorded and put on permanent records. I brought the call with me." He reached into his suit coat and handed the disc to the bailiff.

Mr. Smith immediately objected.

The judge asked Ronald, "How long have you had that disc?"

"I got a copy yesterday," replied Ronald.

The judge asked Ms. Morgan if she was aware of this disc. She replied, "No, Your Honor, I was not aware of the disc."

The judge addressed Ronald. "You know, sir, this is very much against court procedures. Counsels, approach the bench."

They had a short meeting and allowed the disc to confirm that Ronald did indeed call into his office to get authorization to pour the concrete into the forms.

Mr. Smith asked Ronald, "Do you have any other surprises in your pockets?"

Ms. Morgan stood up and objected. The judge sustained the objection and warned Mr. Smith about badgering the witness. "If you do that again, you will be held in contempt of court." The judge instructed the court reporter to strike that question.

Mr. Smith stated, "No further questions at this time, but reserve the right to call the witness back." Ms. Morgan stated the same.

The judge told Ronald he could step down and thanked him for his testimony.

Ms. Morgan called her next witness, the concrete superintendent who was in charge of the concrete finishing.

The superintendent, Charles Wilson, took the stand and was sworn in by the bailiff, who said, "Please be seated."

Ms. Morgan began: "Mr. Wilson, why were your crews always late at Mrs. Wilkins's concrete pours?"

Charles replied, "We were told to start at nine o'clock, because she likes to sleep in."

Ms. Morgan asked, "Is it customary for you to arrive after the concrete has already been poured into the forms?"

Charles said, "No ma'am. I was shocked when I arrived to find the concrete had already been setting up, making finishing nearly impossible. I had her sign a waiver that we were not responsible if the concrete failed."

Ms. Morgan showed Charles the paper he had Katy Wilkins sign. "Is this the paper?"

Charles looked at the paper and said, "Yes, that is the paper, dated and time-stamped."

Ms. Morgan asked, "Were you given any other instructions by Katy Wilkins?"

Charles said, "Not Katy Wilkins. We were instructed by the general contractor, or else the developer, Stephen Delany, instructed us to just put on a rough finish; this was just the subfloor."

Ms. Morgan asked, "Is this a customary practice?"

Charles stated, "No, not even remotely reasonable."

Of course, the defense objected to that comment. The judge sustained it and said, "Please strike that from the records. Mr. Wilson, just answer the question asked."

Ms. Morgan asked for a meeting at the bench. There she asked the judge if Stephen Delany, who was serving a life sentence for the murder of Annie, could be called to confirm what Mr. Wilson stated.

The defense stated, "No, he's been convicted of murder. My client is on trial for murder. It would give the jury reason to believe they were working together; there's mistrial written all over that."

The judge told Ms. Morgan, "This could backfire and you could lose the case completely. I agree with Mr. Smith; not allowed."

Ms. Morgan apologized to the court for the interruption.

"Mr. Wilson, how many times were you called to finish already delivered concrete for Mrs. Wilkins?"

Mr. Smith objected to the question, but the judge overruled the objection

Charles answered, "Five times."

Ms. Morgan showed Mr. Wilson four separate papers with different dates and asked, "Do you recognize these papers?"

Charles said, "Yes ma'am, we gave these to you as evidence. They are waivers stating our firm is not responsible for the concrete finish."

Ms. Morgan asked, "Why did you have to have the customer sign the waiver?"

"Just like our first pour, the concrete had already been poured in the forms," replied Charles.

Ms. Morgan asked, "Could you read the signature on the waiver?"

Charles stated, "Stephen Delany, contractor."

Ms. Morgan asked, "Why did Stephen Delany sign the waiver?"

This got the defense to call for another bench meeting. Mr. Smith asked the judge, "How often are we going to go down this road? We talked earlier about how this could lead to a mistrial. One more time and I'll request a mistrial and demand my client be absolved of all charges."

The judge called for a brief recess. "All attorneys meet in my chambers."

They met in the judge's chambers for half an hour, discussing this case in detail. Then they reentered the courtroom, and the judge announced that they would recall Ronald back to the stand. The judge asked Charles to please step down and sit at the prosecutor's desk.

Then Ms. Morgan called Ronald back to the stand. "You are still under oath. Please be seated."

Then she asked, "Ronald, during your concrete pours did you ever see anyone else but Katy Wilkins?

Ronald replied, "No ma'am, just Mrs. Wilkins."

Ms. Morgan asked, "Did you see any other vehicles parked at the home during your concrete pours?"

Ronald replied, "No ma'am, I was focused on pouring the concrete and watching the concrete forms in case of blowout."

Ms. Morgan asked, "Could you see the front of the house from where you were pouring?"

Ronald replied, "No ma'am the house blocked the view of the street."

Ms. Morgan asked, "Did you ever go to the front of the house after or before the pouring of the concrete?"

Ronald replied, "No ma'am, I stayed on the alley which led me back to my batch plant. No need to go another direction out of my way. I had more deliveries to do, and time is very important."

Ms. Morgan asked, "When your truck was offloaded, how did the concrete pour appear?"

Ronald replied, "I'm proud of my workmanship. I tried to keep the pour as even as possible, not knowing when the crew was to arrive; I tried to make it easy on them to finish."

Ms. Morgan stated, "No further questions at this time, but I do reserve the right to recall this witness."

Mr. Smith stood and asked, "How long did it take you to offload the concrete?"

Ronald asked to see his delivery tickets; "It varies."

The bailiff handed Ronald his delivery tickets. Ronald looked at them and responded, "The first pour, foundations, was twenty minutes. The second pour, the concrete floor, thirty minutes," and he continued to give the time of each pour.

Mr. Smith asked, "So between twenty and thirty minutes, or thereabouts. So you were usually gone from the construction site within forty-five minutes on average?"

Ronald stated, "According to the delivery tickets, that would be correct."

Mr. Smith said, "No further questions at this time, but I do reserve the right to recall this witness."

Ms. Morgan stated, "Would Charles Wilson return to the stand."

Charles sat down and was reminded by Ms. Morgan that he was under oath.

She asked, "Mr. Wilson, you just heard from the prior witness that he took pride in his pouring of concrete, tried to leave the site so your company would have an easier time finishing, correct?"

Charles replied, "Yes, I heard his comment."

Ms. Morgan asked, "Did the site reflect those conditions when you arrived?"

Charles stated, "No ma'am, it was very bumpy. It looked more like no concern at all on how the concrete was poured."

Ms. Morgan asked, "Just how did you finish the concrete in such a condition?"

Charles stated, "That is why I had them sign a waiver. We could not guarantee a clean finish under those conditions."

Ms. Morgan asked, "Did you ever see Katy Wilkins while you were finishing the concrete pour?"

Charles stated, "No ma'am, never saw Mrs. Wilkins. Only Stephen was present during the finishing."

Ms. Morgan asked, "Do you know if Katy Wilkins was home?"

Charles stated, "She waved goodbye a couple of times to Stephen."

Of course, this caused the defense to object to the questioning, asking the witness to assume. The judge sustained the objection and asked the court reporter to strike the question and answer of the witness and instructed the jury to disregard the question and answer.

Ms. Morgan looked puzzled but went on, "Ronald claims he did his best at filling the forms so the pour would accept an easy finish. You said the pour was less than professional. You arrived at nine o'clock, and he left at a little after eight or just before eight o'clock. Would the concrete change that much in that short a time?

The defense objected, stating the witness would have to make an assumption. The judge called for a meeting at the bench. "I'm going to have to ask both of you to stop this line of questioning. It is extremely difficult to put witnesses into this position. Ms. Morgan, Mr. Smith, work with the court on this matter."

Ms. Morgan said, "I have no further questions for this witness but do reserve the right to call him at a later time." Mr. Smith echoed her words.

The judge recessed the court for a lunch break.

Upon returning to the courtroom the press was all over the attorneys, all wanting a scoop, but they got nothing from either side.

The bailiff announced, "Please rise for the Honorable Judge Adamson presiding."

Ms. Morgan called Vanessa Danielson to the stand. She was sworn in by the bailiff and told to please be seated.

Ms. Morgan welcomed Vanessa to the courtroom and asked her to state her title.

Vanessa replied, "I'm the lead forensic investigator for the FBI, in this local area."

Ms. Morgan asked, "Are you familiar with this location?" and she gave Katy Wilkins's address.

Vanessa stated, "Yes, we were called to investigate after receiving a phone call from Stockdale Landscape Construction."

Ms. Morgan asked, "Why would the FBI follow up on a private business phone call?"

Vanessa stated, "They were the ones who contacted local authorities regarding human bones found in a concrete pour."

Defense objected to the line of questioning as having no bearing on the Wilkins case.

The judge asked Ms. Morgan, "Where is this line of questioning going?"

Ms. Morgan stated, "Your Honor, we are trying to establish why a federal agency would honor a private company's call. These types of call are routed away from any concern by the federal government."

The judge said, "Do not refer anymore to another solved case."

Ms. Morgan asked, "Was the decision yours alone to investigate the Wilkins residence?"

Vanessa said, "No ma'am, we had a fifteen-person panel discussing whether we would investigate or pass on the idea."

Ms. Morgan asked, "What was the deciding factor that triggered the investigation?"

Vanessa said, "Who made the call and the sincerity of the call."

Ms Morgan, "What was found at the site?"

Vanessa said, "We started in the bomb shelter, but the structure was not how we would expect to find a bomb structure. Our scanning devices did not find the structure bombproof in any way."

Ms. Morgan asked, "What determined your findings?"

Vanessa replied, "The walls were too thin, and the structure flimsy and not airtight. There was no system installed to filter the outside air. It had no source of running water or heat or ventilation."

Ms. Morgan asked, "What else did you find?"

Vanessa said, "There were two areas where the wall was not more than four inches thick with no reinforcement."

Ms. Morgan asked, "What was the reason for the thinner walls in the bomb shelter?"

Vanessa said, "We removed the thinner walls and found two separate entries."

Ms. Morgan asked, "Where did those entries lead?"

Vanessa said, "The entry to the west led to a stairway from the existing house. The entry to the south led to the basement under the new addition to the existing home."

Ms. Morgan asked, "Did those entries lead anywhere else?"

Vanessa said, "I'm sorry, if you turned to your right on the west entry, you went back into the house, but if you went left, you proceeded down a hallway which had three rooms—two on the right and one on the left. If you continued, you ended up in the basement under the new addition."

Ms. Morgan asked, "What were those rooms you found?"

Vanessa said, "The basement area was the embalming room, with three refrigerators to chill the bodies. I'm sorry, I thought this would be easy for me. May I have a few minutes to regain my composure?"

The judge called for a recess of a half hour and instructed the bailiff, "Please empty the courtroom." He had Vanessa brought to his chambers with Ms. Morgan and Mr. Smith.

Vanessa said with deep emotion, "I've done forensic work for fifteen years. I've seen some brutal killing sites, but this place gave me nightmares. All those poor innocent people dismembered, body parts sold, and for what purpose? They inherited property from their parents or grandparents. This was horrible; you don't understand. This place reeked of death and dismemberment." She continued to sob. "We were sickened every day at what we found over three weeks, and now I have to relive this again. We haven't got into any of the evidence. You won't believe anyone could do such a thing. Not just once, but routinely for years. These people are not sane."

Mr. Smith asked, "Is there anyone else on your team who could account for what was found who might be less emotional?"

Vanessa stood up and opened one of the photo albums. "Here, look at each photo. You stand up there and describe each photo for the jury in detail."

She sat down on her chair as the attorneys flipped though the photo albums with the judge. The photos were all dated and time-stamped. The judge said, "This is absolutely sick. This will cause the jury nightmares."

Ms. Morgan said, "You know this has to be done. We could not allow this woman or any of those arrested to ever walk on the streets free again. Would you like to take the rest of the day off and resume tomorrow?"

Vanessa said, "No, let's continue. The longer she is on this planet, the worse for civilization. I just have to tell myself one more photo or one more question ends her time."

Mr. Smith said, "So you believe my client did all of this?"

Ms. Morgan stood between the two and turned to Mr. Smith. "If you cause her to go berserk in front of the jury, you will be disbarred and arrested as a coconspirator.

The judge nodded. "Badgering a witness will see you removed from the courtroom, counselor, and put into custody. I will not tolerate any grandstanding during this proceeding.

"Let's return to the courtroom and proceed with the questioning, hoping to wrap up your testimony by tomorrow."

Soon the courtroom was filled, counselors were seated, and Vanessa was seated with Ms. Morgan. the judge reentered the courtroom, with the bailiff announcing to the courtroom, "Please rise for the Honorable Judge Adamson, presiding."

They asked Vanessa to return to the stand; she was reminded that she was under oath. "Let's begin," said Judge Adamson.

Ms. Morgan asked, "When you saw the basement, what did you instruct your forensic team to do?"

Vanessa said, "We first returned to our vehicles and put on protective gear. We used our equipment to spray Luminol everywhere, being very careful not to disturb anything. We photographed the entire embalming lab and used the black light to see if there was any blood splatter. We all left the scene immediately; we were all getting ill."

Mr. Smith objected, stating, "She is speaking for everyone."

Judge Adamson overruled. "She is describing what actually occurred as a highly skilled observer. If the staff was ill, that would contaminate the evidence before it was collected. She did what she is trained to do, protect the crime scene."

Ms. Morgan asked, "Did you return the next day?"

Vanessa said, "We returned with my staff and another team of experts who specialize in blood splatter crime scenes."

Ms. Morgan asked, "What did you and your staff do that day?"

"We investigated the other hallway and stairwell and found more blood evidence on the staircase and hallway."

Ms. Morgan asked, "How else did you investigate the scene?"

Vanessa said, "After lunch they brought a machine to scan the walls and floor of the bomb shelter."

Ms. Morgan asked, "Did they find anything?"

Vanessa said, "The walls and flooring had shown imperfections not customarily found in a concrete pour. The floor was to be removed first and taken to the lab to continue the investigation in a sterile environment. We didn't want any contamination to occur."

Ms. Morgan asked, "Is this a customary practice, scanning walls and floors?"

Vanessa said, "Based on the evidence we had discovered, yes, we would scan the floors and walls for additional evidence."

Ms. Morgan asked, "Did you investigate any more that day?"

Vanessa said, "Yes, we went down the hallway to the south to the three other rooms."

Ms. Morgan asked, "What did you find in those rooms?"

Vanessa said, "The first room on the right-hand side of the hallway was an office full of file cabinets, a telephone, and a desk. The room across the hall was a storage room full of plastic totes sealed with tape. The other room was full of freezers and refrigeration units."

Ms. Morgan asked, "Did you examine the contents?"

Vanessa said, "No, we all stayed in the hallway, which was secured as evidence, and I took photos of the rooms to bring to my superiors. We ended our evidence gathering for the day and yellow-taped off the area so the homeowners would not go into the crime scene to contaminate the evidence."

Ms. Morgan said, "I have no further questions at this time," and looked at the clock.

The judge stated, "Let's adjourn for today and resume tomorrow at eight o'clock." He reminded the jurors not to talk about this case with each other or with anyone. "Our staff will take you to your hotel. Enjoy your stay, and get a good night's sleep."

12

The next morning before court was in session, the media and protestors were having a field day calling for the release of all those arrested on "trumped-up charges"; "Release them now!" was the chant. The signs showed the prosecuting attorneys as those who should be charged. Of course, media reps were interviewing the sign carriers—as if they knew anything about the trial going on inside the courthouse.

This morning the judge banned all press from the courtroom stating that this was not going to be a media circus. Those allowed to sit in the courtroom were family members of those slain; no one else was allowed. They also were told to say nothing to anyone or they as well would be held in contempt of court and prosecuted.

As the eight o'clock bell rang, the courtroom was full. Counselors were seated at the proper tables, Vanessa was seated next to Ms. Morgan, and Wilson and Carter were seated behind the prosecuting attorney's desk along the railing.

The bailiff told the court to rise as he introduced Judge Adamson. They called Vanessa to the stand, reminded her she was still under oath, and directed the prosecutor to proceed with the witness.

Ms. Morgan asked, "The next day when you returned to the crime scene, were all the others assigned to your case still working there?"

Vanessa said, "The team scanning the floors and walls were not present. They were at the FBI lab waiting for the concrete floor to arrive."

Ms. Morgan asked, "What about those assigned to the embalming room?"

Vanessa stated, "They returned to gather evidence and secure the site for my team to proceed with our investigation."

Ms. Morgan asked, "What did your team work on?"

Vanessa said, "We started on the file room, logging in the files and sealing them in evidence bags for our forensic lab to inspect them under sterile conditions. You can see the process taken in the video to be shown in a couple of minutes."

The bailiff had the clerks setting up monitors for the attorneys, jurors, judge, and court attendees to view. Once all was operating as designed and everyone was in position, they ran the video.

Ms. Morgan asked, "Can you describe for us the procedures taken to secure evidence?"

Vanessa said, "Gladly. You see the agent has protective gear covering his entire body. One file is taken from the file cabinet, and another agent is holding open a sterilized plastic bag designed especially for files. The first agent places the file in the bag, and the other agent seals it, making it airtight."

Ms. Morgan asked, "How many files were processed in this manner?"

Vanessa said, "Three hundred and seventy-five files. It took a week to process the files."

Ms. Morgan asked, "What happened to the file cabinets?"

Vanessa said, "In another video you will see we encased the file cabinets in sealed sterile plastic bags designed for file cabinets. They were taken to our lab to be examined under sterile conditions and that process also recorded on video."

Ms. Morgan asked, "Just how long did removing everything from the office take?"

Vanessa said, "Two weeks and three days to gather evidence which ended up under the cabinets and desk."

Ms. Morgan asked, "The other two rooms—when were they started?"

Vanessa said, "The storage room was started the same day as the file room. That took over a week to secure, and we sealed off the room once cleared so no further contamination would occur in case we needed to return at a later date."

Ms. Morgan asked, "And when did you start on the third room?"

Vanessa said, "Once the storage room was emptied and secured, that team gathered evidence in that room following the same procedures shown in the video."

Ms. Morgan asked, "How long did that room take?"

Vanessa said, "One full week."

Ms. Morgan asked, "When did your team reenter the embalming room to gather evidence?"

Vanessa said, "Two weeks from when the other team collected blood evidence and removed the drain line from the lab to the sewer connection."

Ms. Morgan asked, "What was found in the floor and walls of the bomb shelter?"

At that question Mr. Smith rose to say, "That would be hearsay since Vanessa was not present at the lab."

The judge sustained the objection, instructed the court reporter to strike the question, and told the jurors to disregard it. He also instructed Ms. Morgan to restrict her questions to what Vanessa had clearly witnessed.

Ms. Morgan asked, "Was there anything else your team discovered during their time investigating the crime scene?"

Vanessa said, "We did get evidence from the light fixtures, wall receptacles, and restroom drains."

Ms. Morgan said, "I have no further questions for this witness but do reserve the right to call her back at another time. Your witness, Mr. Smith."

Mr. Smith stood and said, "Good morning, Vanessa. I have a few questions for you this morning. First of all, how long have you been collecting evidence from crime scenes?"

Vanessa said, "I started with the agency twenty years ago. They promoted me to the forensic department fifteen years ago, and I became the head forensic agent nine years ago."

Mr. Smith asked, "From your video the evidence at the scene was collected with care. What about in the lab—how is that evidence handled?"

Ms. Morgan stood and objected, reversing field on the defense's earlier objection. "Hearsay: she was not present at that point of the investigation."

Judge Adamson sustained the objection and instructed Mr. Smith to ask questions pertaining to her part of the investigation. "She cannot be expected to answer questions about which she has no direct knowledge."

Mr. Smith asked, "How is the gathered evidence transported to your lab?"

Vanessa said, "In a sterile van. Those loading the van stay in the van and do not exit the van until it is emptied and all evidence is securely in the lab."

Mr. Smith asked, "Those loading the van ... how sterile are they?"

Vanessa said, "Our team in the crime scene stays in the crime scene. The evidence is handed off to the transporters to the van, at no time is the evidence ever in contact with the ground or mishandled. If by chance something goes wrong in the handling, that evidence is taken in a separate van to the lab."

Mr. Smith asked, "From what you collected, what percent of the evidence could have been contaminated?"

Ms. Morgan stood up and objected. "Calls for hearsay. There is no way anyone could answer that question."

Judge Adamson sustained the objection, saying, "Rephrase or delete that question."

Mr. Smith said, "I have no further questions for this witness at this time but do reserve the right to question her at a later time."

Ms. Morgan called Justine Waterman, the FBI forensic examiner supervisor, to the stand.

Justine was sworn in by the bailiff and directed to be seated.

Ms. Morgan stated, "Good morning, Ms. Waterman. Could you tell the court your position with the FBI?"

Justine stated, "I'm the forensic supervisor for our local division."

Ms. Morgan asked, "Just what is your responsibility as a forensic supervisor?"

Justine stated, "As forensic evidence is gathered in the field and delivered to our labs, I oversee the procedures taken to ensure all evidence is handled with the utmost care, so no cross-contamination occurs."

Ms. Morgan asked, "Are you familiar with the Wilkins evidence?"

Justine stated, "Yes, I oversaw all of the evidence examined by my staff."

Ms. Morgan asked, "How long did it take to go through and document the evidence collected from the crime scene?"

Justine stated, "Nearly four weeks with a staff of twelve highly skilled examiners."

Ms. Morgan asked, "Did you find the evidence received secured to prevent any outside contamination?"

Justine stated, "Every bag was properly sealed per FBI standards and logged in so we could proceed with our portion of the examination. There was just so much gathered it took a considerable time."

Ms. Morgan asked, "Was everything fingerprinted?"

Justine stated, "Yes, fingerprints were taken, and evidence was photographed, all per FBI procedures."

Ms. Morgan asked, "Was there anything unusual about the evidence gathered?"

Justine stated, "Everything was unusual, we don't see this type of crime committed, but the earlier files were not as well organized as the rest."

Ms. Morgan asked, "What do you mean?"

Justine said, "Some of the papers were out of order, datewise—not in chronological order. Other than that, the files were exquisite."

Ms. Morgan asked, "So papers were just out of order in the earlier files?"

Justine said, "The first files had numerous different fingerprints on the papers. The later files only had two or maybe three."

Ms. Morgan asked, "Were the prints of Katy Wilkins found on the papers?"

Mr. Smith stood and stated, "You're asking the witness to draw a conclusion. She is an examiner?"

The judge asked Justine, "Does your job require you to distinguish whose fingerprints are found on evidence?"

Justine said, "Yes, Your Honor, we have to distinguish the fingerprints making sure one of our agents' prints are not contaminating the evidence."

Judge Adamson said, "Overruled, answer the question."

Justine said, "We found numerous fingerprints of Mrs. Wilkins on the file jackets and pages."

Ms. Morgan asked, "From the earliest to the latest files dated?"

Mr. Smith stood again. "She is leading the witness, Your Honor."

"Sustained. Rephrase or move on, Ms. Morgan."

Ms. Morgan asked, "Did the majority of the files have Mrs. Wilkins's fingerprints?

Justine said, "The majority did have her prints."

Ms. Morgan asked, "Did you examine the skulls found?"

Justine said, "No ma'am, another department handles that type of examination."

Ms. Morgan asked, "Did you examine the blood evidence taken?"

Justine said, "No ma'am, that too is another department. We primarily handle documents."

Ms. Morgan stated, "I have no further questions for this witness; you may cross-examine, Mr. Smith."

Mr. Smith said, "I have no questions for this witness."

The judge thanked Justine and reminded her that she was still under oath and could be called back. "So please don't leave the courtroom until dismissed by the court.

"Next witness, Ms. Morgan," said the judge.

Ms. Morgan said, "The next witness will require some time. Could we recess for lunch?"

Judge Adamson said, "Court is in recess for one hour. Jurors, do not talk to anyone or among yourselves about this case. Enjoy your lunch."

*

Once everyone returned from lunch, the bailiff called the court to order: "Please rise for the Honorable Judge Adamson."

"Please be seated, said the judge. "Ms. Morgan, call your next witness."

"My associate, Mr. David Greenspar, will question the next witness."

Mr. Greenspar called James Wildom to the stand. The witness was sworn in by the bailiff and seated.

Mr. Greenspar asked, "Mr. Wildom, please tell the court your occupation."

Mr. Wildom stated, "I'm the director of the forensic division for the FBI in Denver, specializing in skeletons and bones."

Mr. Greenspar asked, "Are you familiar with the Wilkins case?"

Mr. Wildom answered, "Yes, I have been examining the evidence for three weeks."

Mr. Greenspar asked, "Have you been able to identify any or all of the victims?"

Mr. Wildom answered, "We have identified all but one of the victims."

Mr. Greenspar asked, "How did you identify the victims?"

Mr. Wildom answered, "Mostly from the skulls in the containers. Dental records identified most of them, but three were identified through DNA samples."

Mr. Greenspar asked, "How many skulls?"

Mr. Wildom answered, "There are twenty-five skulls in those storage containers."

Mr. Greenspar asked, "Were you given any information from any other department prior to your investigation?"

Mr. Wildom answered, "No, we were given the skulls and some bones removed from the concrete. There are eight different victims from the bones extracted from the concrete; they match eight of the skulls."

Mr. Greenspar said, "You mentioned you have twenty-five skulls. Where are the rest of the skeletons that match the skulls?"

Mr. Wildom answered, "We were only given bones extracted from the concrete taken from the crime scene."

Mr. Greenspar asked, "Can you determine the time and date that the death occurred from each victim?"

Mr. Wildom answered, "Not the time; just an approximate date."

Mr. Greenspar asked, "Do any findings match certain victims to missing persons reports?"

Mr. Wildom answered, "All we do is determine the identity of the victim and approximate time and date when the death occurred. We don't match such data. We turn in our findings to management and move on to the next investigation."

Mr. Greenspar stated, "I have no further questions for this witness but do reserve the right to recall him later. Mr. Smith, your witness."

Mr. Smith with yellow notepad in hand approached the stand. "Mr. Wildom, the evidence you received, bones and skulls—what were you told when you received the evidence?"

Mr. Wildom stated, "Just normal protocol: the case number and the inventory of the evidence submitted. They asked for the identity of each victim."

Mr. Smith asked, "There was nothing else, just 'Here, do your job'?"

Mr. Wildom replied, "Our department is nonstop with numerous cases. We need to identify victims; we don't have time to chitchat and get particulars of any case. Identifying persons with no fingerprints or blood samples is not a walk in the park."

Mr. Smith asked, "Where are the other seventeen skeletons?"

Mr. Greenspar stood and objected. "How would he know where the other seventeen skeletons are located?"

The judge sustained the objection and told the court reporter to strike the question from the record and the jurors to disregard it.

Mr. Smith said, "I have no further questions for this witness but do reserve the right to requestion him later."

"Witness, you're excused," stated the bailiff; "please step down."

Ms. Morgan called Abigail Stephson to the stand.

The bailiff swore in Abigail Stephson and asked her to please be seated.

Ms. Morgan asked, "Ms. Stephson, what is your job title?"

Abigail stated, "I work for the FBI as the blood and tissue supervisor."

Ms. Morgan asked, "What does a blood and tissue supervisor do for the FBI?"

Ms. Stephson stated, "We receive blood evidence or tissue samples from evidence gathered from a specific crime scene to determine whose blood and tissue this is."

Ms. Morgan asked, "How do you receive the blood and tissue samples?"

Ms. Stephson replied, "Our field collectors gather the evidence in sterile containers and submit it to our lab to determine identity."

Ms. Morgan asked, "How long can blood and tissue remain on a crime scene and still be used to identify a victim."

Ms. Stephson stated, "No longer than ten years, or we cannot get actual trial data."

Ms. Morgan asked, "How many victims were you able to identify?"

Ms. Stephson stated, "There are seven victims identified and four nonvictim blood samples, which we have identified."

Ms. Morgan asked, "Are the four nonvictims identified?"

Ms. Stephson stated, "Yes, all blood and tissue samples submitted have been identified and turned over to management."

Ms. Morgan asked, "Did you find anything out of the ordinary?"

Ms. Stephson stated, "The collection samples were immaculate; nothing out of the ordinary was discovered."

Ms. Morgan stated she had no further questions for this witness but reserved the right to call her back at a later date. "Your witness, Counselor."

Mr. Smith stated he had no questions for this witness but did reserve the right to call her back at a later date.

Judge Adamson said, "This ends our second day. Please return tomorrow at eight o'clock." He reminded the jury not to talk to anyone regarding the case, not even among themselves. "Court is adjourned."

13

Ms. Morgan and Mr. Greenspar went to the local restaurant to talk over tomorrow's witness list. The office staff had assured them that each one was available and poised to testify.

They were also summarizing today's results. They had witnessed a couple of the jury members fighting sleep. Nodding off in the jury box can lead to indecision. Ms. Morgan decided to write a recap of testimonies given to refresh the jury's memory. Maybe five minutes tops so the defense can't object.

She tried to determine a break point, for the morning, lunch, after lunch, and ending the day. It was determined by the two that the defense was playing very cautiously, allowing some testimonies without rebuttal; why?

Mr. Greenspar said, "I'm sure Mr. Smith was seeing what we were seeing. A couple of the jurors were nodding off, bored, or not interested in what was being said. No reason to question something if the jury is not paying attention."

They discussed a hand signal to call for a short recess, to allow the jury to wake up. Some of the information given now would be crucial during the next few days of testimony.

Ms. Morgan asked, "Do you think Mr. Smith is waiting for a statement that could cause doubt among the jurors that collecting practices or lab testing was mishandled?"

As they were refilling their coffee and sweet rolls, Ms. Morgan got a phone call from the court to please return for a short meeting with Judge Adamson.

She and Mr. Greenspar returned to the courthouse for the meeting with Judge Adamson and Mr. Smith.

Judge Adamson thanked both attorneys for attending his meeting. The judge stated that his office had been in contact with the governor's office and determined to keep the protesters from gaining popularity. The way they would try to accomplish this was to show the proceedings on a closed-circuit program airing in a separate room for the press corps. They would not be allowed inside the actual courtroom and would be given the last two days of testimony. There would be only one person per news broadcaster allowed, with the governor's office supplying names of those allowed in his press briefings.

The judge asked, "Are there any objections?"

Mr. Smith asked if they could pick the reporters.

The judge said, "You will be given a list of those who have passed the governor's strict rules and standards; no others will be allowed. They all will be warned against any outbursts or inappropriate conduct. If they misbehave, they will be asked to leave, and their agency may not be able to replace them."

Mr. Smith pointed out, "We just don't want a one-sided presentation of this trial."

Judge Adamson replied, "This will be fair and balanced. No documentation will be distributed that can be altered in any way. So are there any objections?"

There were none.

Judge Adamson thanked everyone and told them, "As of tomorrow there will be four cameras recording the proceedings."

Ms. Morgan and Mr. Greenspar returned to the restaurant to finish their conversation, checking in with their office to see if any new developments had occurred.

Their assistant told Ms. Morgan they had two concrete construction foremen from Smooth as Silk Concrete Finishing ready to testify. "Do you have time tomorrow to interview them?"

"No. Our trial resumes at eight tomorrow. But Mr. Greenspar can be there."

"Okay," said the assistant, "he can meet with them around eleven o'clock. I'll contact them immediately."

They discussed what to do about the seventeen victims with a skull but no skeletal remains. They decided that they had to find answers to the whereabouts of the sixteen other skeletal remains; they knew where Annie's bones had been disposed of.

On the drive home, Ms. Morgan remembered that the case against Stephen Delany might reveal a few more skeletal remains if the bones matched the skulls found in the plastic containers.

When she arrived at her home, she wrote down what she remembered: *Check to see if the bones uncovered during the Stephen Delany case match our skulls.*

She also noted, *Verify with David that the workers from Smooth as Silk can lead us to the missing bones.*

She prepared some dinner for her and her family. Then after dinner she sat down and scanned tomorrow's witness files before retiring to bed.

The next morning heading to the courthouse the media had it normal display of players trying to get anyone involved in the case to say something they could call their exclusive. Police security escorted the attorneys through the gauntlet of microphones jammed into their faces, cameras only inches away. Ms. Morgan, a seasoned veteran, used a straight arm technique to help clear a pathway to safety, the officers doing their best to give aid to the attorneys.

Once inside the courthouse she headed to her office for some quiet time, again going through her notes and questions for each witness called. She had a little over a half hour, and her assistant brought a fresh cup of coffee and a breakfast roll. She was grateful, since the press were lingering outside her door.

Soon courthouse security personnel were herding media into the closed circuit room, checking the names on the list. All electronic devices were either put into a secure box or handed to an associate for them to retrieve after the day's events came to a close. Many chose the secured lockbox, put their devices in the box, and handed one key back to the officer. It required the box holder's key and the officer's key to open the box—an extra layer of security for the electronic devices.

They also had to surrender any briefcase, backpack or hand-carried notebooks; all paper and writing implements were provided for the reporters. Five security personnel watched the reporters during the proceedings.

The county employee in charge of the room gave the rules to the reporters. Any breach of the rules, and they would be removed from the room and not allowed to return. "You will follow the court's protocol," she said, "rising when the judge enters the courtroom and so on."

She asked if there were questions.

One reporter asked about restroom breaks.

"Raise your hand, and one of our security members will contact another security worker, who will escort you to the restroom and back here. All paper and pens will remain on your desk."

Before entering the courtroom, Ms. Morgan received a call from her office. "There's now evidence that the doctor sold the blood to an organization that sold it to hospitals. They ran across this operation thanks to the files." Ms. Morgan thanked her associate for passing that on to her; "Great job."

Ms. Morgan and Mr. Smith walked into the courtroom together and took their seats. After the judge entered and all were again seated, the bailiff told Ms. Morgan, "Please call your first witness."

Ms. Morgan called Maribelle Robinski to the stand.

Maribelle approached, took the stand, was sworn in, and was seated.

Ms. Morgan asked, "Maribelle Robinski, what is your occupation?"

Maribelle responded, "I'm the supervisor who takes the data from the investigating team and compiles it into chronological order and links evidence taken to actual incidents reported to authorities."

Ms. Morgan said, "I'm a little confused about what you do for the FBI. Can you clarify?"

Ms. Robinski responded, "If data comes to my department from, let's say, blood splatter, telling us this blood belongs to Mrs. X., we trace missing persons reports for any reporting of Mrs. X. We notify kin, we gather all we can find regarding Mrs. X, and then we put all of that information into chronological order and deliver it to our agents in charge of the investigation."

Ms. Morgan asked, "Are you familiar with the Wilkins investigation?"

Ms. Robinski stated, "Yes, our division has been diligently working on the data to create a time line for our agents."

Ms. Morgan asked, "How long have you been working on the Wilkins case?"

Ms. Robinski answered, "Three and a half weeks, and we are still putting together more data as we receive it from the labs."

Ms. Morgan said, "Your Honor, I am submitting these three notebooks as State's Exhibit One." They were three-ring binders, each one three inches thick.

Ms. Morgan asked the witness, "Please describe the contents of these notebooks."

Ms. Robinski said, "Each one is an individual, with the evidence listed in chronological order: date of death, filed missing persons report, facts of the person prior to the date of death, their entire history."

Ms. Morgan asked, "How many of these notebooks do you have completed?"

Ms. Robinski stated, "We have twenty-three of the twenty-eight known persons completed as far as we can go."

Ms. Morgan asked, "What is the holdup on the other five?"

Ms. Robinski stated, "We have the skull, we have the papers stating where there organs were sold, and we have the blood banks who received the blood, but they don't fit the rest of the twenty-five."

Ms. Morgan asked, "What do you mean?"

Ms. Robinski replied, "The twenty-five were either farmers or businesspeople owning large amount of land or property. The missing five were not in that category, mostly everyday working people. They had no connection to any of the other twenty-five or to any of those who are arrested or are now in prison."

Ms. Morgan asked, "Why would that matter?"

Ms. Robinski stated, "It's just puzzling why they would go through all the trouble of harvesting their organs, selling the blood and saving a skull."

Ms. Morgan asked, "Could it be just that they fit a need?"

Mr. Smith rose. "Calls for speculation, and leading a witness, Your Honor."

Judge Adamson said, "Sustained; either rephrase the question or proceed."

Ms. Morgan asked, "Have you found evidence of transplant facilities calling for certain organs related to the times of their deaths?"

Ms. Robinski said, "Not so far; we are still checking."

Ms. Morgan said, "I have no further questions for this witness but do reserve the right to call her at a later date. Your witness, Mr. Smith."

Mr. Smith approached the stand. "Ms. Robinski, how are you this fine day?"

Ms. Robinski answered, "Very well. A little nervous, but good."

Mr. Smith stated, "I have gone through one of the notebooks you provided our firm a few days ago. Very thorough, I must say. How long have you been doing your job for the FBI?"

Ms. Robinski answered, "This is my fifteenth year with the Bureau."

Mr. Smith asked, "Have you always been with the division you're with today?"

Ms. Robinski stated, "My first three years I worked in research; then they assigned me to my division."

Mr. Smith asked, "How long have you been a supervisor?"

Ms. Robinski replied, "Six years now."

Ms. Morgan stood and asked, "Where is this going? Does he have a question regarding the case or not?"

Judge Adamson said, "Mr. Smith, do you have an actual question for this witness?"

Mr. Smith replied, "Your Honor, the evidence in these notebooks is very thorough but very confusing to the reader. I'm trying to determine her qualifications."

Judge Adamson said, "You have determined her qualifications. Now either proceed with your questions, or allow Ms. Robinski to leave the stand."

Mr. Smith picked up a notebook from the evidence table, opened it up to a certain section, and showed Ms. Robinski the page. He asked, "On April 23, 2000, this victim was pronounced dead; is that right?"

The witness stated, "Yes sir, that was taken from the death certificate in section three."

Mr. Smith said, "The missing persons report was filed on April 27, 2000. Are these papers correct?"

Ms. Robinski answered, "Sir, the dead person does not file a missing persons report. We just put the data together. If you'll notice, the one filing the missing persons report was not a family member or a friend. It was one of those arrested for this crime."

Mr. Smith said, "Ma'am, just answer the question asked."

Ms. Robinski said, "Counselor, you questioned how a time of death is different than the date on a missing person's report. I explained that."

Mr. Smith stated, "I have no further questions for this witness but do reserve the opportunity to recall the witness at a later date."

Judge Adamson excused Ms. Robinski and asked Ms. Morgan, "Please call your next witness."

Ms. Morgan called Joseph Stern to the stand. He was sworn in and seated.

Ms. Morgan asked, "Joseph Stern, what is your occupation, and how long have you been at that position?"

Mr. Stern replied, "I'm the FBI district director for this geographical area. We review each case to determine that there is enough evidence to proceed to trial. I've been with the bureau for twenty-five years and been assigned as the district director for seven years. I have been reviewing cases for eighteen of my twenty-five years of service."

Ms. Morgan asked, "Is there enough evidence against Mrs. Wilkins?"

Mr. Stern replied, "This case meets all FBI standard requirements to proceed to trial."

Ms. Morgan asked, "How long has your department had the evidence to evaluate?"

Mr. Stern replied, "We started receiving data two and a half weeks ago; we have had twenty investigators reviewing delivered data nonstop during that time."

Ms. Morgan asked, "Is only one person reviewing the evidence and making the determination?"

Mr. Stern replied, "No, one agent receives, let's say, this notebook full of data. They review the contents, enter a comment as to their recommendation, and pass it off to the next agent. At a bare minimum, ten agents review the contents and evaluate whether it should go to court for trial. Those evaluations are put together and delivered to one of my supervisors, who assesses the data and files a recommendation before it is delivered to our office. We review the reports and the evidence that they reviewed to determine if trial is warranted."

Ms. Morgan asked, "For that process, two and a half weeks of reviewing evidence seems fairly quick; is that unusual?"

Mr. Stern stated, "We work around the clock. The evidence we received came from top-notch investigators with a reputation for accuracy. Our protocol was followed throughout, from gathering and reporting data, to processing the collected data, to compiling the data for management to review and look for errors, and finally sending it to our team to evaluate all aspects of the process."

Ms. Morgan said she had no further questions for this witness, reserving the right to recall him later. "Your witness, Mr. Smith."

Mr. Smith stood up and stated he had no questions for this witness, also reserving the right to recall him if necessary.

The judge stated, "We will have a thirty-minute recess at this time."

The bailiff asked the court to rise while Judge Adamson left the courtroom.

The press was given a thirty-minute recess. "Use it wisely," stated the county employee in charge.

Thirty minutes later, everyone was back in the courtroom. The bailiff called the court to order and announced, "The Honorable Judge Adamson presiding, please rise."

Judge Adamson seated everyone. "Ms. Morgan, please call your next witness."

Ms. Morgan called former Police Chief William O'Brian to the stand. At once Katy Wilkins leaned over to confer with Mr. Smith.

Chief O'Brian entered the courtroom, flanked by two county sheriff's deputies, and stepped to the witness stand, where he was sworn in and seated.

Ms. Morgan approached the stand and thanked the chief for appearing on behalf of the prosecution. "Chief O'Brian, please tell the court how long you were the chief of our district."

Chief O'Brian stated, "I was chief in the district for twelve years. Before that, I was a detective for seven years and a patrolman for nine years."

Ms. Morgan asked, "Do you know the defendant?"

Chief O'Brian replied, "Yes, we have attended events together. She was at my swearing-in ceremony twelve years ago."

Ms. Morgan asked, "Did you socialize with Mr. and Mrs. Wilkins?"

The chief answered, "Occasionally, the events were attended by many people."

Ms. Morgan asked, "Only at large planned events?"

Mr. Smith stood and objected to the question. "Asked and answered, Your Honor."

Judge Adamson said, "Sustained, either rephrase the question or move along."

Ms. Morgan asked, "Other than planned events, dinner parties, or parties in general, did you associate with the Wilkinses?"

The chief stated, "A couple times a year, possibly—not regularly; we all have busy schedules."

Ms. Morgan pulled out a paper to show the chief and read the exhibit number. "This is a missing person's report dated April 27, 2000," she said, and showed it to the jury. Then she returned to the stand and handed it to the chief. "What did your department do upon receipt of this report?"

Chief O'Brian stated, "We post, the information for all the patrolmen to keep an eye out for the missing person. Our detectives are given copies to follow up with any calls regarding the missing person, and they are sent to family members and known associates to gather any available information about the missing person."

Ms. Morgan went to her desk and retrieved another piece of paper. She showed it to the jury after stating the exhibit number and took it to the chief to examine. "Chief, would you read the title of that form?"

Chief O'Brian replied, "It's a death certificate."

Ms. Morgan asked, "What day is it dated?"

Chief O'Brian read, "April 23, 2000."

Ms. Morgan asked, "Would you please read the name of the deceased."

"Jonathan Morehead."

Ms. Morgan asked the chief, "Would you read the name on the missing person's report dated April 27, 2000?"

Chief O'Brian nodded and said, "Jonathan Morehead."

Ms. Morgan asked, "And whose names appear at the bottom of the death certificate?"

Chief O'Brian responded, "Fredrick Fredrickson and William O'Brian."

Mr. Smith stood and objected to this line of questioning.

Judge Adamson stated, "On what grounds are you objecting, Counselor?"

Mr. Smith stated, "Leading the witness, Your Honor."

Judge Adamson asked the attorneys to approach the bench. "You know that is very weak. We won't have that again; do you both understand?"

Judge Adamson sent them to their tables and overruled the objection. "Please proceed, Ms. Morgan."

Ms. Morgan asked, "You directed your staff to search for a missing person who you knew was already deceased. Why?"

Chief O'Brian stated, "I'm a very busy man, I didn't notice the name."

Ms. Morgan stated, "On April 23, 2000, you attended a dinner at the country club with the following guests: Mr. and Mrs. Wilkins, Fredrick Fredrickson, Edgar Watson, Jonathan Montgomery, Stephan Delany, Mrs. Montgomery and Mrs. Delany. Did you witness the death certificate at the dinner or afterward?"

Chief O'Brian, looking at the defense table, paused for a moment.

Ms. Morgan said, "Chief O'Brian, I asked you a question. Do I need to repeat it?"

Chief O'Brian stated, "It was during the dinner."

Ms. Morgan asked, "Chief O'Brian, one further question. On April 30, 2000, you bank account recorded a deposit of one hundred thousand dollars. You had several checks of this sum during the twelve years you were the chief of police, and since you left office, no deposits beyond your normal retirement check appear. Could you explain to the court?"

Mr. Smith stood and objected. "Counsel is incriminating the witness, Your Honor."

Judge Adamson said, "Overruled. Chief O'Brian, answer the question."

Chief O'Brian stated, "I decline to answer the question, based on my Fifth Amendment rights."

Ms. Morgan stated, "Your Honor, our records show that for every victim during the twelve-year tenure of Chief O'Brian, he received $100,000.00 as a witness to the death certificate."

Mr. Smith asked to have that stricken from the record but was denied by Judge Adamson: "The documentation is already in evidence. We have all the signed death certificates and the corresponding bank statements."

This was the first testimony that put Katy Wilkins on shaky ground.

Ms. Morgan stated she had no further questions of this witness for now. "Your witness, Mr. Smith."

Mr. Smith asked, "Chief O'Brian, were you aware of what you were signing?"

Chief O'Brian stated, I'm standing on the 5th amendment.

Mr. Smith stated he also had no further questions of this witness.

Judge Adamson stated to the Chief O'Brian, you may step down, and instructed the deputies to escort him back to his cell.

Judge Adamson stated, "Court at this time will recess for one hour for lunch." He instructed the jury not to talk to anyone or to one another about the case and banged the gavel.

14

When court resumed and everyone was seated. the judge said, "Ms. Morgan, please call your next witness."

Ms. Morgan called Stephanie Mason to the stand. The bailiff swore her in and had her take her seat.

Ms. Morgan approached and asked, "Ms. Mason, tell the court your job title, how long you've had that position, and, how long you have worked there."

Ms. Mason stated, "I'm the county coroner for the last ten years and a bit more. I've worked for the county for fifteen years in the coroner's office."

Ms. Morgan asked, "When you are notified that a person is deceased, what is the protocol followed by your department?"

Ms. Mason responded, "We send our team to retrieve the body, along with the forensic team to collect evidence and secure the scene and talk to the parties who found the body to get as much information as possible. They bring the corpse to our lab for further investigation and autopsy."

Ms. Morgan asked, "When is a certificate of death issued?"

Ms. Mason stated, "We have seventy-two hours to issue the death certificate."

Ms. Morgan asked, "Is it customary to have anyone else but your office issue a death certificate?"

Ms. Mason replied, "No, and it could be considered an illegal document." Mr. Smith rose, but the judge waved him back into his seat without a word.

Ms. Morgan asked the witness, "Would you look at the death certificate in the plastic bag and give the court your opinion of the certificate?"

Ms. Mason stated, "This certificate would not be legal; our office did not issue this certificate."

Ms. Morgan asked, "Do you have to examine each corpse to issue a death certificate?"

Ms. Mason replied, "Of course, we can declare someone deceased if we never see the body."

Ms. Morgan showed her all twenty-eight death certificates in evidence and numbered accordingly. "Could you review these and tell the court if your office submitted these death certificates?"

Ms. Mason took a little time looking at each of the documents and said, "Not that I'm aware of. Some are dated before I was the coroner. I can't speak for those."

Ms. Morgan asked, "Were there any errors in how the documents appear?"

Ms. Mason stated, "Only that I'm not certain who the doctor is who is declaring the death, and of course the witnesses are not authorized by our department as valid signers. It also appears they are not immediate members of the deceased's family."

Ms. Morgan asked, "Did any of these deceased individuals appear in your coroner's office?"

Ms. Mason replied, "It does not seem we ever saw any of these corpses."

Ms. Morgan asked, "Once you receive a corpse, how is it handled?"

Ms. Mason responded, "The circumstances—natural death, homicide, accident, or whatever—determine what kind of investigation is required by the pathologist."

Ms. Morgan asked, "Could a family member or friend receive the body intact?"

Ms. Mason replied, "Not normally. Under certain circumstances, in situations involving a court order, we must comply."

Ms. Morgan stated, "Reserve the right to recall Ms. Mason, Your Honor. Mr. Smith, your witness."

Mr. Smith asked, "IS there a possibility that an attending physician can fill out a death certificate without going to the coroner's office?"

Ms. Mason stated, "Only if the deceased was under their care or hospitalized for a period are other doctors authorized to write the death certificate."

Mr. Smith asked, "So a physician can declare someone deceased?"

Ms. Mason stated, "They have to be authorized by the state. Otherwise it's illegal, and the certificate is invalid."

Mr. Smith said he was finished with this witness, and Judge Adamson called for a thirty-minute recess before the next witness. Again he warned the jurors not to talk to each other or anyone regarding the case.

When court resumed, Judge Adamson said, "Ms. Morgan, you may call your next witness."

Ms. Morgan called Dr. Samuel Cortez to the stand.

As Dr. Cortez approached the stand, Katy again fell to talking with Mr. Smith.

Dr. Cortez took the stand, the bailiff swore him in, and he sat down.

Ms. Morgan approached the stand. "Dr. Cortez, could you tell the court your specialty as a doctor."

Dr. Cortez replied, "I'm a kidney transplant specialist, practicing for fifteen years."

Ms. Morgan asked, "Are you familiar with the defendant, Mrs. Wilkins?"

Dr. Cortez stated, "I have met her at my office, and we had a few business meetings, after our first meeting."

Ms. Morgan asked, "Dr. Cortez, was Mrs. Wilkins in need of a kidney?"

Dr. Cortez answered, "Not to my knowledge."

Ms. Morgan asked, "Were your meetings personal or professional in nature?"

Dr. Cortez replied, "Always professional. We talked about my transplant business."

Ms. Morgan asked, "If she was not in a need of a kidney, and she's not a doctor, why would you take time to talk with her?"

Dr. Cortez replied, "She could supply me with kidneys if the need arises."

Ms. Morgan asked, "I'm confused. You're a transplant surgeon talking to a housewife about supplying you with kidneys?"

Dr. Cortez replied, "I had a client who needed a kidney transplant. He had a certain blood type, and she happened to have a possible match available."

Ms. Morgan asked, "How often were you in contact with Mrs. Wilkins?"

Dr. Cortez replied, "I would hear from her assistant after our initial meeting. He was also a surgeon. I would tell him the criteria for my next surgery, and if they could supply a kidney, we would make the transaction."

Ms. Morgan asked, "Did you tell them ahead of time what the next transplant would require?"

Dr. Cortez replied, "Yes, I would tell the doctor about the need for an upcoming transplant."

Ms. Morgan asked, "How many kidneys did Mrs. Wilkins supply you?"

Dr. Cortez replied, "I believe six kidneys."

Ms. Morgan asked, "Did the doctor ever tell you where they were getting the kidneys which they supplied?"

Dr. Cortez replied, "Mostly auto accidents. We could not use an alcohol- or drug-tainted kidney."

Ms. Morgan asked, "If I show you some death certificates, could you tell the court if you received a kidney from any of these persons?"

Dr. Cortez replied, "Yes, I brought my list with the donors' names and dates when I received the kidneys."

Ms. Morgan showed Dr. Cortez the twenty-eight death certificates. Dr. Cortez went through each one and set aside the ones that matched his list. Ms. Morgan asked, "May I enter that list as court evidence?"

Dr. Cortez said, "Of course."

Ms. Morgan said, "All six victims' kidneys match the doctor's list, and the date each was received was the date of that death certificate. Is that correct, Dr. Cortez?"

"Yes."

Ms. Morgan asked, "Would you read the cause of death on the death certificate and tell us what you were told about the kidney?"

Dr. Cortez read off each cause of death and compared it to what they had told him was the cause of death. He also compared each to the proposed date of his scheduled transplant operation.

Ms. Morgan asked, "Dr. Cortez, I remind you that you are under oath. Did you know or were you aware of how they were able to supply you with a kidney exactly when you required a certain blood type?"

Dr. Cortez replied in an angry voice, "No, I was not aware. I thought God was answering my prayers for my patients."

Ms. Morgan asked, "Of the twenty-two other victims, were any lining up with your kidney transplants?"

Dr. Cortez replied, "No, but two of my associates were also being supplied by Mrs. Wilkins. I gave them her phone number."

Ms. Morgan stated that she had no further questions for this witness but reserved the right to call him back at a later time. "Your witness, Mr. Smith."

Mr. Smith, after a spirited exchange with Mrs. Wilkins, stated he had no further questions for this witness, but he might at a later time.

"Dr. Cortez, you may step down," stated Judge Adamson.

Mr. Smith, still standing, asked, "Approach the bench?"

Judge Adamson said, "Counsel, please join me at the bench."

Mr. Smith told the judge and Ms. Morgan that his client had just fired him as her counsel.

Judge Adamson announced to the court, "We will be adjourning until eight o'clock tomorrow morning. Jurors, please do not talk to anyone or to one another about this case.

"Mrs. Wilkins, please see me in my chambers with Ms. Morgan"

Katy, was escorted to the judges chambers by two deputy sheriffs. .

"Mrs. Wilkins, your counsel informed us that you've fired him. Is that correct?" asked the judge.

Mrs. Wilkins replied, "Yes, Your Honor. He would not do as I instructed, and I asked him to pack his bag."

Judge Adamson said, "Ma'am you know you need sufficient counsel to continue this trial?"

Katy Wilkins replied, "Your Honor, I need an attorney with a backbone who can see these are trumped-up charges, all made-up lies to influence those mindless jurors."

Judge Adamson said, "We can give you an extra day to find another attorney if necessary."

Katy Wilkins replied, "My son will procure another attorney."

15

Jonas Smith immediately contacted his law firm to inform them that Mrs. Katy Wilkins had released him. He was told to stop work on the defense and report to the office in the morning. He was to prepare billing for services rendered, including all his research, either finished or in process, and invoice the son for reimbursement.

Natalie Morgan had had a fruitful day against Mrs. Katy Wilkins. There were a few more holes she needed to fill in to make the defense nearly impossible. She returned to her office to see how David Greenspar had done with the finishers from Smooth as Silk Concrete Finishing.

Upon arrival the receptionist handed her messages she had received during the past three days out of the office. She returned greetings by the staff and entered her office. *Nice to be back in the comfort of home.*

Mr. Greenspar entered her office, animated. On his heels, Natalie's assistant brought in two cups of fresh-brewed coffee with creamer and sugars. "Thanks," Natalie said. "I really needed this to wake me up."

She turned to Greenspar, "So tell me, David, what is the great news you have for me?"

David said, "Natalie, I was handed a human bone in a sealed plastic bag. The finishers recovered it from a concrete pour done for Katy Wilkins."

"Well, that was my next question—how your interview went with Smooth as Silk this morning. Okay, that bone needs to go to the FBI. Do they have more than one?"

"They have a bone from each location they finished for Stephan Delany. They have the license plate numbers of the vans that dropped off the bones while the finishers were taking a lunch break waiting for the concrete to set up. And one more thing—this will blow you away. They have cell phone photos of those who got out of the van.

"They have two photos of Katy and her sister pulling in while the bones are being placed in the concrete."

Natalie asked, "Are they willing to testify against Katy Wilkins?"

"Yes, they feel it's only the right thing to do at this time."

Natalie said, "You need to contact the agent Bellow. handling the evidence for the FBI. These finishers will have to be questioned by the FBI, fingerprinted, photographed, all the rest. They are disgruntled employees of Smooth as Silk Concrete Finishing, are they?"

David said, "They no longer work for Smooth as Silk ever since Stephan Delaney was imprisoned. You see, Smooth as Silk was owned by Delaney Development; he took over the company when the real owner was forced to sell."

Natalie said, "Find the owner of Smooth as Silk; this could be very interesting."

David said, "We know where he is. He's one of the five skulls they mentioned during Wildom's testimony."

"Whose are the other skulls?"

"One is the girl who did the makeup for the great granddaughter and the bank robbery, one is a former servant for Katy Wilkins, and one is a former superintendent for Delaney Development, another was a bank examiner. They're still working on the final skull."

"Tomorrow we have a new defense attorney," said Natalie. "Katy fired Mr. Smith; no backbone, she told the judge."

David asked, "She's not aware that she has no defense, that her bases aren't all covered as she thought?"

Ms. Morgan stated that the news agencies, were in a scramble this morning when the protesters failed to show up at the courthouse; "Maybe tomorrow," the reporters assured viewers, I'm certain she is well aware of her situation.'

Natalie said, "How did the closed-circuit idea work?"

"Each television company had everything set up for the reporters to tell the audience what they saw," replied David. "None of them said that there was not enough evidence to convict Katy. One reporter said she believed that Katy has no defense against her charges, judging from what they saw today and have recorded from the prior two days of testimony—in her professional opinion.

"We heard her company will not be sending anyone to the courthouse tomorrow. They'll just review the discs sent to them at the end of the day."

"Governor Bronson is on line two, to talk with Natalie Morgan," the receptionist interjected via the intercom.

Natalie picked up the line. "Good afternoon, Governor Bronson."

"Ms. Morgan, I personally want to express my gratitude for all the work you and your staff have done on this case so far; great job. Diane and I have watched the proceedings from the very first witness. We are very impressed with how you've handled the case. We know it's premature to pop open the champagne and strike up the band; we just had to tell you how impressed we both are at this moment."

Natalie said, "Thank you, Governor. We still have many surprises before we rest the prosecution. We are trying to defuse the defense as much as possible."

The governor replied, "After the trial, I'd like to meet with you to discuss your future. I know you're a rising star in the US attorney's office, but I'd like you to consider joining forces with my legal staff along with Marie—if I can convince her to return to the courtroom.

"Meanwhile, best of luck with the case. I have magnums of champagne getting chilled for the finale."

They said their goodbyes, promising to talk again.

As Natalie hung up the phone, her supervisor, the assistant US attorney, walked into her office. David excused himself to get the ball rolling for the concrete finishers to appear in a couple of days.

Edwin Zore, Esquire, the assistant DA, was on cloud nine as he sat down to talk with Ms. Morgan. "Mr. Zore, what gives me the pleasure of your visit this fine afternoon?" she asked.

Mr. Zore stated, "I'm impressed beyond belief how you have put this case together, with the precision of a fine-tuned machine, well oiled and running to its peak performance. Great job!"

Ms. Morgan said, "I owe it all to my staff. I just tweaked it enough to eliminate a grandstand by the defense."

Mr. Zore asked, "What happened to Mr. Smith? He's a top-notch defense attorney."

Ms. Morgan said, "Katy Wilkins wants an attorney with more backbone; she told the judge Smith was too weak."

Mr. Zore remarked, "She'll have a tough time finding anyone better than Mr. Smith. I was a little nervous when I heard she'd chosen him as her attorney."

Ms. Morgan stated, "I was nervous too, but I knew what evidence we've amassed. He played a card today that showed me they really have no defense. Too much evidence puts her in the crosshairs."

Mr. Zore asked, "What's planned for tomorrow?"

Ms. Morgan stated, "I have a few more nails to put into her defense, which should get her off her high horse. If tomorrow's testimony doesn't bring her down, the next day's will surely be the icing on the cake."

As they were talking, David Greenspar interrupted the meeting, apologizing. "This is important: Jonathan Montgomery, Fredrick Fredrickson, and Edgar Watson want to testify, for a plea bargain."

Ms. Morgan asked, "What are they requesting?"

David answered, "Take the death penalty off the table."

Mr. Zore said, "The governor told the populace a few months ago that all those involved in the kidnapping and murders will be prosecuted to the fullest extent of the law. We will have to confer with the governor on this."

Ms. Morgan asked Mr. Zore, "Do you believe we have all of those involved?"

"I don't believe we have everyone. We have some very serious players, but I'm not certain we have the kingpin."

Ms. Morgan asked, "If we encounter the real kingpin, could that change the outcome of the trials scheduled ahead?"

Mr. Zore stated, "That person or persons would have to have hands on everything to change a verdict. I don't believe the one calling the shots has that kind of involvement. It's more financial than hands on, I would expect."

Ms. Morgan asked, "Do you believe, even after these trials are completed, that this will all end?"

Mr. Zore replied, "I believe there is another scheme starting or others are already in operation but not yet found."

Ms. Morgan asked, "You think this just might be one branch to a much larger tree?"

"I would be very surprised if this is a fluke. It was too well organized to be a stand-alone organization. You put Katy Wilkins and her gang of twelve or thirteen away, that's the best we can offer at this point."

David reentered the room. "Sorry to interrupt again, but all of her arrested associates want to testify against Katy, according to their attorneys."

Ms. Morgan sniffed. "Very loyal friends and associates, I might add."

Mr. Zore stated, "I now know there are more players. These are just the middle-of-the-road players. They are afraid they won't be able to defend their actions and will be left holding the prison bag while the rest of the group runs around free as a bird."

Ms. Morgan asked, "Do you think they'll cooperate with the investigators?"

Mr. Zore said, "Not unless they know their own necks are protected."

Ms. Morgan said, "Thank you, David, for all you have done for this case to date. Keep up the good work, and there's a lollipop in it for you."

Mr. Zore asked, "What will be my reward?"

"A new luxury car."

Mr. Zore said, "It's getting near quitting time. I must join the herd on the freeway and say good evening to my beautiful bride. See you all tomorrow."

David walked Natalie out to her car telling her he was proud to be working with her and not sitting at the defense table licking his wounds.

Another day in the record books; can't wait until tomorrow for a new opponent. Just who will the Wilkins team bring to the defense table?

16

Oh, what a beautiful morning—sun shining, birds chirping, car started right up, all-time favorite song on the radio. Thank you, God. I needed to start this day off on the right foot, thought Ms. Morgan.

Arriving at the parking structure, she found her favorite parking space, labeled "Attorney Only." *Checked my badge—yep, I'm still an attorney. Remarkable start of another trial day.*

She entered the walkway and met again with microphones and cameras jammed in her face. Two officers pushed open a pathway for her to enter the courthouse. One of them said, "They'll never learn. Soon they'll start getting my billy club in the gut."

The other officer asked, "Who is that attorney replacing Mr. Smith? We have to escort him to the courthouse as well.

The first officer answered, "I believe they told us at the morning meeting his name is Twistling or something like that."

Ms. Morgan knew who it was they were going to escort to the courthouse: not Twistling but *Twingling,* Jefferson Twingling, defense attorney extraordinaire.

She had butted heads with him a couple of years ago. It took a little time, but she'd taken him down a peg or two from his very high perch. He used a variety of strategies to sway a jury if he felt them favoring the prosecution. Ms. Morgan was up for the challenge, hoping today's witnesses would leave him cowering.

She made it to her office where five people sat waiting for her. All were saying good morning to her.

Ms. Morgan called for her assistant. "Kelli, who are all these people?"

Kelli handed her business cards of all the visitors.

Ms. Morgan noticed they all were from the FBI. "Ladies and gentlemen, welcome to my office. May I ask why I'm so fortunate as to have five representatives from your organization greeting me during a very important trial?"

Agent Billow stated, "We have great news for you regarding some bones we received in our lab last night. We thought you would like firsthand information before going to court this morning."

Ms. Morgan said, "Agents, thank you for the information. I heard about that last night from Mr. Greenspar and instructed him to deliver the bones to your lab to be investigated. We hope they are the missing bones to go with our skull collection.

"You all know I'm going up against a premier defense attorney this morning. Please make an appointment with my assistant—and not all at one time. I'm a very busy woman right now.

"Kelli, could you please escort our guests to your desk and set up appointments for tomorrow and the next day? Thank you."

She checked the time; only fifteen minutes before the court bell.

She grabbed her briefcase and headed for the courtroom. Of course the press corps were flocking all over her, but she was known for a great elbow, and most of the reporters give her room to avoid bruises.

She elbowed one reporter, who persisted, so she shoved him with her briefcase, which put him on his knees. She'd given him fair warning, but he must have been focused on upsetting her. If so, it worked.

She entered the courtroom, and there stood her nemesis, Jefferson Twingling, Esq., looking dapper, polished, and ready for battle.

She went over and shook his hand: "I'm happy to see Mrs. Wilkins was able to hire you to defend her."

Katy Wilkins looked up and said, "Your easy potshots at my reputation have come to an abrupt end, my dear."

Ms. Morgan said, "Attorney Twingling should fill you in on what happened at our last match."

The courtroom was called to order by the bailiff. "All rise for the Honorable Judge Adamson."

Judge Adamson seated everyone and acknowledged defense attorney Twingling. "It's been a few years since our last encounter. Ms. Morgan, please call you next witness."

She called Dr. Adolph Reinberg to the stand.

Mrs. Wilkins leaned questioningly toward her attorney, Twingling, who just shrugged.

Dr. Reinberg approached the stand, where he was sworn in and seated.

Ms. Morgan approached the stand. "Welcome, Dr. Reinberg. Would you please tell the court what is your profession and job title and how long have you held that position?"

Dr. Reinberg replied, "I'm the director of transplant medicine for the state. I've been in that position for ten years."

Ms. Morgan asked, "Are you familiar with the Wilkins case?"

Dr. Reinberg answered, "More than the defendant could even imagine."

Ms. Morgan asked, "Could you please explain that comment?"

Dr. Reinberg replied, "Over five years ago we had a complaint which we were in the process of following up with our investigators. It appeared that her organization was providing organs for transplant without having the proper license or inspections required by the state."

Ms. Morgan asked, "Who filed the complaint?"

Dr. Reinberg responded, "The question is not who but how many complaints did we receive. There are five major organizations that can legally supply organs for transplant, and they were not one of those authorized by the state."

Ms. Morgan asked, "Were any charges brought against Mrs. Wilkins?"

Dr. Reinberg stated, "We filed three different charges against her organization, but all were abruptly dismissed."

Ms. Morgan asked, "Who dismissed the charges?"

Dr. Reinberg replied, "The governor of the state at that time said his attorney general's office was overloaded and could not fit another high-profile case into the docket. We appealed his decision, and that appeal was denied by the circuit judge appointed to that case."

Ms. Morgan asked, "What did you find with the denial of the appeal?"

Dr. Reinberg said, "Donations to campaigns. She is a heavy donor to both the governor and the appointed judge."

Ms. Morgan asked, "What were the charges against Mrs. Wilkins?"

Dr. Reinberg replied, "They denied us access to their lab for inspection and insisted that their chief surgeon was board-certified and authorized to perform such surgeries."

Ms. Morgan asked, "Could you not just shut them down for improper licensing and inspections?"

Dr. Reinberg stated, "We filed every form, more than required by law. We needed a search warrant, which never was issued due to lost paper or not filing in a specific time frame—one excuse after another. We finally cut ties with the doctors who perform the surgeries, stating if they used an organ from this organization they would be prosecuted."

Ms. Morgan asked, "Did that work?"

Dr. Reinberg replied, "We finally had a transplant doctor who went against our letter, and we arrested him for the illegal organ."

Ms. Morgan asked, "Could you identify for the court the doctor who violated your warning letter?"

That got Attorney Twingling out of his seat with an objection. "Irrelevant. Mrs. Wilkins is being charged with murder, not trafficking in organs."

Judge Adamson overruled the objection. "Dr. Cortez has testified that he purchased organs from the Wilkins organization." He instructed Dr. Reinberg to answer the question.

Dr. Reinberg stated, "It was Dr. Cortez who violated the letter. We took him to court, and he explained the circumstances around the purchase. The patient was in a life-or-death situation, and they had the only kidney available that matched and saved the patient's life. The doctor was not aware they had taken a life to save a life."

Ms. Morgan asked, "Did that lead you to Mrs. Wilkins's lab?"

Dr. Reinberg answered, "No, the address we were given was a home, empty, with a for-sale sign in the front yard."

Ms. Morgan asked, "Have any more organs been purchased from Mrs. Wilkins's lab?"

Dr. Reinberg replied, "They may have changed the name and location from what we were given. I can't truly answer that question."

Ms. Morgan stated, I have no further questions for this witness but reserve the right to recall the witness at a later date. Your witness, Mr. Twingling."

Mr. Twingling rose. "Dr. Reinberg, you stated that Mrs. Wilkins's organization was operating illegally. Under whose law was she operating illegally?"

Dr. Reinberg stated, "State law," and gave the number and date of enforcement. He also produced a copy of the law, which the bailiff numbered and put into evidence.

Mr. Twingling asked, "How were you trying to contact the organization?"

Dr. Reinberg stated, "Through the mails, through subpoenas delivered by the sheriff's department, by phone, though the numbers were changed often, and through doctors who performed transplants."

Mr. Twingling asked, "Did you ever talk personally with Mrs. Wilkins?"

Dr. Reinberg answered, "Never personally, since we never received a response, nor were any of the phone numbers a direct line to her. No human ever answered the phone numbers we had on record."

Mr. Twingling asked, "Are you certain you called the correct phone numbers?"

Ms. Morgan stood up and objected. "Asked and answered; the numbers got no response, and no human ever answered the phone."

Judge Adamson said, "Sustained; reporter, strike the question. Mr. Twingling, you need to stop badgering the witness."

Mr. Twingling stated he had no further questions for this witness and also reserved the right to call him back later.

Judge Adamson told Dr. Reinberg he could step down. "Call your next witness, Ms. Morgan."

Ms. Morgan called Dr. Clarence Stone to the stand.

Mrs. Wilkins shrugged when her attorney leaned toward her with a question.

As Dr. Stone was approaching the bench, Mr. Twingling rose and asked, "Who is this witness? He is not on our schedule. May we approach the bench?"

Ms. Morgan brought a list of witnesses with her and showed Mr. Twingling that on the second page, the first name listed was Dr. Stone. She said, "We are finished with the first page; you can go to the next page now."

Judge Adamson warned Ms. Morgan to keep everything professional.

Ms. Morgan approached the stand after the bailiff swore in Dr. Stone and he was seated. She asked the witness, "Please tell the court your profession and how long you have pursued it."

Dr. Stone replied, "I'm a board-certified heart transplant surgeon with twenty years of practice."

Ms. Morgan asked, "Dr. Stone, do you know the defendant?"

Dr. Stone replied, "I have never met Mrs. Wilkins, but I have been contacted by her staff and her surgeon asking for information on upcoming transplants."

Ms. Morgan asked, "How often were you contacted?"

Dr. Stone said, "At least twice a month for at least three years. They changed the name of the organization a once or twice during that time."

Ms. Morgan asked, "Did you ever purchase a heart from their organization?"

Dr. Stone replied, "Two of my assistants purchased two hearts; theirs just happened to match our patients' criteria, and we had very little time."

Ms. Morgan asked, "Were the hearts as you expected?"

Dr. Stone answered, "One heart was as expected, although the cause of death struck me as being odd."

Ms. Morgan asked, "Can you explain? What made it odd?"

Dr. Stone replied, "We had a call out for a heart to all of our normal suppliers. They just happened to have a match out of the clear blue. Then the death certificate we received after the operation gave me cause to wonder, how could an auto accident occur with the donor having the exact match for a heart? The odds had to be enormous."

Ms. Morgan asked, "Has that ever happened before?"

Dr. Stone responded, "Not to me nor my staff has that ever occurred prior."

Ms. Morgan asked, "Did you follow up with the organization that furnished the heart?"

Dr. Stone replied, "We called numerous times, left messages, sent a certified letter asking for clarification, but got no response, ever, even to this day."

Ms. Morgan asked, "How was the heart paid for?"

Dr. Stone replied, "Up front in full, which is standard practice for most of our suppliers. There was one thing my office manager noticed: the bank number where the check was deposited did not match the bank of the organization from which we purchased the heart."

Ms. Morgan asked, "The bank account was not affiliated with the organization?"

Dr. Stone replied, "No, it was deposited directly into Mrs. Wilkins's account. We thought we had made a mistake or got the wrong account number. We contacted the bank, and they confirmed that Mrs. Wilkins's account is used by the organization in question."

Ms. Morgan asked, "Did you contact the organization after that?"

Dr. Stone replied, "Numerous times; we will forward our phone records to the court as soon as they arrive from the phone carrier. We've had no answer, just a recording, no response even to this day."

Ms. Morgan asked, "Is the organization still in operation?"

Mr. Twingling stood and objected to the question. "That is not relevant, and she is leading the witness."

Judge Adamson called for a bench meeting. "Counselors, this is my one and only warning; after this warning you will be held in contempt of court. Mr. Twingling, your client is operating a business. Her business depends on the outcome of this case. If they change a name or location of operations, it is still her business. I'm overruling your objection."

Judge Adamson stated, "The objection is overruled. Dr. Stone, answer the question."

Dr. Stone replied, "We keep getting the same answering service, and they have referred us to another phone number. That too has more hurdles for the customer to jump over, and no human is manning the phones."

Ms. Morgan stated, "I have not further questions for this witness but do reserve the right to recall him later. Your witness, Mr. Twingling."

After conferring with his client, Mr. Twingling stated he had no further question at this time but reserved the right to recall the witness later.

Judge Adamson stated, "Dr. Stone, you may step down. Ms. Morgan, the hour for a lunch break is drawing near."

Ms. Morgan said, "Then may we adjourn for lunch, since the next witness would take us well past noon?"

Judge Adamson stated, "Court is adjourned for one hour. Jurors, I remind you not to discuss the case." The bailiff had everyone rise, and the judge left the bench.

Ms. Morgan headed to her office. Her assistant had ordered lunch for her and the staff. The office had no visitors, which was a relief; some real quiet time was desperately needed.

Kelli brought her a deli sandwich at her desk. It was her favorite, a grinder with Italian dressing, and her diet cola. She was ready for some nourishment to help her take on the rest of the witnesses poised to take the stand.

She was on her third bite when David Greenspar brought in a plate of food and sat across from her at her desk. She asked, "No more chairs available in the conference room?"

David responded, "I have encouraging news and didn't want the entire staff to hear. I hope you don't mind?"

Ms. Morgan continued to enjoy her grinder, saying between bites, "I'm listening."

"The foremen will testify tomorrow, with photos of those who present when the bones were tossed into fresh concrete. The other suspects detained will be on the next day's docket. We have located Mrs. Wilkins new address and phone numbers, and they will raid that location within the hour. The FBI had to obtain a warrant. We thanked Dr. Stone's office manager, who also will testify if you so desire."

Ms. Morgan said, "That is encouraging news. But one little thing is missing: who else is out there lurking in the shadows? How are they running the organization when all the main players are incarcerated? This makes Mr. Zore's theory more realistic than theory."

David replied, "The FBI has put more people on to research this organization. They ought to come up with some error in judgment by someone involved."

Ms. Morgan said, "Don't count of that. It took years to uncover this, and if it weren't for Fred Stockdale this would have never happened. He had questions about the bomb shelter; it just didn't quite fit the norm.

"Get ahold of Papa; see what they can come up with. The more eyes the better."

She looked down at her desk. "I ate too much. See what you made me do? I lost track of how many bites I had consumed."

David said, "You must have needed the extra bites, knowing the second half of your day could require the extra energy."

Ms. Morgan stated, "Nice try. This afternoon's witnesses should go smoothly; I expect few or no objections."

David gathered up his lunch plate and beverage. He told her he would dig in deeper on the items she requested and hoped to have something for her after today's session. With that, he departed her office.

17

Ms. Morgan returned to the courtroom for the afternoon session and sat down at her table, waiting for the court to be called to order.

Mr. Twingling approached her table and said he had received a revised witness list during his lunch break. He asked, "Are these surprise witnesses?"

Ms. Morgan stated, "You will receive the information required before the day has ended. You have to right to request a continuance if you choose."

The bailiff called the court to order: "All please rise for the Honorable Judge Adamson, presiding."

Judge Adamson stated, "Ms. Morgan, please call your first witness."

Ms. Morgan called Lucinda Robinson to the stand.

As Lucinda Robinson approached the stand Mrs. Wilkins was whispering with her attorney—perhaps passing along anything she knew about the witness.

Ms. Morgan approached the stand after Lucinda was sworn in by the bailiff and seated for questioning. "Ms. Robinson, could you tell the court your occupation and how long have you held that position?"

Ms. Robinson replied, "I've been an assistant bank manager for three years, after nine years as a bank teller."

Ms. Morgan asked, "Have you been employed at the same bank for the entire time?"

Ms. Robinson answered, "Yes ma'am, same bank just received a promotion."

Ms. Morgan asked, "You were working as a bank teller on June 15, 2013, when something odd occurred. Could you tell the court about that event?"

Ms. Robinson replied, "Yes, on that date Mrs. Wilkins approached my window and was depositing checks into her account."

Ms. Morgan went to her table and picked up an envelope with the evidence number listed on the label, which she read to the court. She took the evidence envelope to Lucinda, asking, "Do you recognize the contents?"

Ms. Robinson said, "Yes ma'am, that is one of the checks that Mrs. Wilkins deposited during that exchange."

Ms. Morgan took the evidence to show the jury panel. She asked the witness, "What made this check different from the rest of the deposit?"

Ms. Robinson stated, "There was what looked like a bloody fingerprint on the check. I asked Mrs. Wilkins if she'd cut herself. She responded no; her office clerk had gotten a paper cut, which happened every so often, and they didn't know how to clean it off the check."

Ms. Morgan asked, "Did you complete the transaction?"

Ms. Robinson answered, "Yes, and after Mrs. Wilkins left the bank, I took the deposit to the bank manager to make certain that I would not get in trouble for accepting the check. Our manager put the check into a plastic bag and took it over to the police station to have them run the proper tests."

Ms. Morgan asked, "What happened next?"

Ms. Robinson replied, "The bank manager received a call telling her to return to the police station to pick up the check."

Mr. Morgan asked, "Then what happened to the check?"

Ms. Robinson stated, "We had a bank audit, and the auditor said that the check needed to be sent to the FBI as evidence. We were in violation for withholding such an item from them."

Ms. Morgan asked, "Do you know what happened to the check after the FBI received it?"

Mr. Twingling objected. "Calls for speculation, Your Honor."

Judge Adamson sustained the objection. "Ms. Morgan, either rephrase or else move to your next question."

Ms. Morgan asked, "When were you notified that you would have to testify?"

Ms. Robinson replied, "Your office sent a subpoena for me to appear."

Ms. Morgan stated, "I have no further questions for this witness but do reserve the right to call her back later. Your witness, Mr. Twingling."

Mr. Twingling asked, "Do you ever see bloody prints on checks being deposited?"

Ms. Robinson replied, "No sir, this was the first I had ever seen."

Mr. Twingling asked, "Why did you take the check to your manager?"

Ms. Robinson replied, "I did not want another teller or bank employee asking who took this check and why didn't they follow procedures. I needed my job and didn't want to lose it over being negligent."

Mr. Twingling asked, "Why did you question Mrs. Wilkins regarding the blood on the check?"

Ms. Morgan stood and objected. "She was doing her job; protocol, Your Honor."

Judge Adamson called the attorneys to the bench to hash out where this was going. Mr. Twingling stated, "She was a bank teller, not an investigator. She should deposit the check as the customer requested."

Judge Adamson stated, "Sustained; she was following protocol."

Judge Adamson addressed the courtroom: "Objection sustained. The last question is stricken it from the record, and jurors are to disregard it." Then he turned to Mr. Twingling. "Please continue."

Mr. Twingling leaned over to talk to his client and then said that he had no further questions for this witness now.

Judge Adamson instructed Ms. Robinson that she could step down and thanked her for her testimony. Then he told Ms. Morgan, "Call your next witness."

Ms. Morgan called Jeffrey Dogan to the stand, and he approached. Ms. Morgan picked up the check evidence from her table.

As the bailiff was swearing in Jeffrey Dogan, Mrs. Wilkins and her attorney were whispering to each other; apparently neither one knew this witness.

The bailiff instructed Mr. Dogan to please be seated.

Ms. Morgan asked, "Mr. Dogan, please tell the court your profession and job title and how long you have been in that position."

Mr. Dogan replied, "I'm a blood specialist for the FBI, supervisor for the last fifteen years."

Ms. Morgan asked, "Mr. Dogan, can you identify the contents of this envelope?"

Mr. Dogan looked at the item. "Yes, this is a blood-stained check, something we rarely see in our department."

Ms. Morgan went to her table and retrieved another plastic envelope with some papers inside and went back to the stand. "Mr. Dogan, do you recognize these papers?"

Mr. Dogan replied, "Yes ma'am, those are my reports of the findings on the bloody fingerprint found on the check."

Ms. Morgan asked, "Could you explain the contents of the reports?"

Mr. Twingling stood and objected. "Leading the witness, Your Honor."

Judge Adamson said, "Overruled. Please answer the question, Mr. Dogan."

Mr. Dogan stated, "The fingerprint is that of Mrs. Wilkins. The blood belongs to Joseph McPherson, a missing person at that time; a few days later a death certificate was issued."

Mr. Twingling objected again. "The witness is drawing a conclusion about the actual time of death of the missing person."

Judge Adamson called the attorneys to his bench. There he told Mr. Twingling to explain his objection.

Mr. Twingling stated, "Mr. McPherson was dead; the death certificate was in the process of being filed."

Ms. Morgan stated, "How do you know this for certain? Did you witness his death?"

Mr. Twingling glared at her. "I'm not on trial here. I was informed that the timing is off."

Judge Adamson said, "Counselor, the only person who would have known the actual time of death of a missing person would have had to be with the missing person. You're aware of what you've just implied? I'm saving your bacon, Mr. Twingling, and overruling your objection." He sent the lawyers back to their tables.

Judge Adamson stated, "Overruled. Mr. Dogan, you can finish your answer."

Mr. Dogan said, "We researched the data, and the time line of the bloody fingerprint was approximately three to five days prior to the actual death certificate being recorded. That would make Mr. McPherson still a missing person or someone being kidnapped or held hostage when the fingerprint appeared on the check."

Ms. Morgan showed the jury the report generated by Mr. Dogan.

Then she turned to the witness and stated, "To pull this time line together, Police Chief O'Brian attended another luncheon, two days after the date that the blood finger print was on the check where he and Fredrick Fredrickson signed the death certificate for Mrs. Wilkins. The date of the check being deposited to the bank was also two days prior to the death certificate, to corroborate with Mr. Dogan's report for the court's records. Mr. Dogan, is that correct?"

The witness replied, "That's right."

Ms. Morgan stated, "I have no further questions for the witness at this time. Your witness, Mr. Twingling."

Mr. Twingling asked for a moment's conference with his client. Katy Wilkins was staring at Mr. Dogan, while her attorney whispered in her ear. Outwardly emotionless, she turned and whispered something in response,

Mr. Twingling then said that he had no questions for this witness but reserved the right to call the witness back.

Judge Adamson stated, "Ms. Morgan, please call your next witness."

Ms. Morgan called Elise McPherson to the stand. As she came forward, there was more whispering between Mrs. Wilkins and her attorney.

The bailiff swore in Ms. McPherson and had her take a seat.

Ms. Morgan went to her desk, picked up another evidence envelope, and approached the stand. "Ms. McPherson, Your father was Joseph McPherson, who went missing and was later found deceased. Is that correct?"

Ms. McPherson said, "Yes."

Ms. Morgan said, "I have a copy of the death certificate of your father in this evidence envelope. Would you look at the certificate and read for the court what was the cause of death."

Ms. McPherson stated, "Overdose of an unknown medication."

Ms. Morgan asked, "Did your father use prescription medication?"

Ms. McPherson answered, "Daddy never used any type of medication. He was very healthy."

Ms. Morgan asked, "How about unprescribed medication?"

Ms. McPherson replied, "My father was a very religious man; he didn't use any type of drugs or medication—didn't drink or smoke either."

Ms. Morgan asked, "How long was your father missing?"

Ms. McPherson answered, "I didn't live at home, and Mom had passed away two years prior to Daddy being reported missing."

Ms. Morgan said, "I call your attention to this missing persons report," and stated the exhibit number. Then asked the witness, "Who reported your father missing?"

Ms. McPherson replied, "Some man named Stephen Delaney."

Ms. Morgan asked, "Did you know of Stephen Delaney?"

Ms. McPherson said, "Not until his trial was reported in the newspapers."

Ms. Morgan asked, "Did your father ever talk about Stephen Delaney?"

Ms. McPherson stated, "Only one time. He said Mr. Delaney was interested in buying his farm."

Ms. Morgan asked, "Was the farm for sale at the time?"

Ms. McPherson replied, "No, my father told me he had no interest in selling the farm. It had been in our family for three generations."

During this exchange Mr. Twingling and Mrs. Wilkins were huddled in whispers. Mr. Twingling stood up and asked to approach the bench.

Judge Adamson said, "Mr. Twingling, what is it this time?"

Mr. Twingling stated, "Mr. Delaney is not on trial here. We don't see how his wanting to purchase the farm has any bearing on this trial."

Ms. Morgan stated, "Mr. McPherson's blood was on a check that Mrs. Wilkins deposited."

Judge Adamson stated, "I have to agree with Ms. Morgan. If his blood had not been found on a check Mrs. Wilkins deposited, and if Mr. Delaney had not filed a missing person's report on him, I would agree with you."

Judge Adamson stated, "Ms. Morgan, please proceed."

Ms. Morgan asked, "When did you last talk with your father?

Ms. McPherson responded, "About two weeks after he told me about Mr. Delaney and wanting to purchase the farm."

Ms. Morgan asked, "Did he say any more regarding selling of the farm?"

Ms. McPherson stated, "He just said Mr. Delaney kept calling him, and he kept telling him no."

Ms. Morgan asked, "When did you become aware of your fathers' disappearance?"

Ms. McPherson answered, "My father's longtime friend called me to ask if my dad was visiting me, since harvest time was over. I told him no and asked why. He told me he was not at the farm."

Ms. Morgan asked, "Did you go to your father's farm?"

Ms. McPherson said, "No, I live too far away. My brother lives closer, so I asked him to see if Dad was just gone that day or if anyone around knew his whereabouts. He told me he would go to the farm on the weekend; he was busy on a new contract.

"When he arrived at the farm that Saturday, he called and told me something was wrong. Dad never left the farm unlocked. Everything was unlocked, and the keys to his truck were lying on the kitchen table. He went to the police station in town and the officer in charge said they had not heard from anyone regarding his whereabouts."

Ms. Morgan asked, "Did your brother file a missing persons report?"

Ms. McPherson replied, "The officer told him to return on Monday if Dad hadn't shown up at the house by then."

Ms. Morgan asked, "He didn't return on Monday?"

Ms. McPherson stated, "No, he had to return to work, so I called the police chief to file the report. Then he told me one had been filed by Mr. Delaney just that morning before I called."

Ms. Morgan stated, "I have no further questions for Ms. McPherson; she doesn't need to relive her nightmare. I do reserve the right to recall her at a later date. Your witness, Mr. Twingling."

Mr. Twingling asked, "Did you contact Mr. Delaney once you found out that he filed a missing person's report?"

Ms. McPherson replied, "I tried at least ten or maybe fifteen times. His secretary always told me that he was out of the office and that she would give him the message."

Mr. Twingling asked, "Did he ever return your call?"

Ms. McPherson stated, "No, so I contacted my father's best friend, and he went to Mr. Delaney's office. But some construction men wouldn't let him in; they told him never to return or they would do bodily harm. I called Police Chief O'Brian and explained the situation to him. He said he would get back to me in the afternoon. He has never called me, from that day to this."

Mr. Twingling asked, "When did you hear of your father's death?"

Ms. McPherson replied, "When Ms. Morgan subpoenaed me to appear to testify."

Mr. Twingling asked, "You never knew he had died?"

Ms. McPherson said, "He didn't *die*; he was murdered to steal the farm and his life insurance policy. I saw all the forged documents from the insurance company. That woman you're protecting, ask her these questions, not me."

Judge Adamson said, "Ms. McPherson, you only need to answer the questions asked of you. Mr. Twingling, do you have any more questions of this witness?"

Mr. Twingling answered, "No, Your Honor."

"Then, Ms. McPherson, you may step down. Thank you for testifying, this had to have been difficult for you."

Then he addressed the room: "Court is in recess for thirty minutes. Jurors, please don't talk to each other or anyone else about this case." The bailiff had the courtroom rise, and Judge Adamson left the bench.

Ms. Morgan met up with Ms. McPherson and escorted her to her office, comforting her as they walked down the hallway. When they arrived, she asked Kelli to bring them some coffee with cream and sugar.

Ms. Morgan asked Ellie to please have a seat and told her that the defense lawyer had no reason to continue. "I'm glad you laid into him. I was going to jump down his throat, but you beat me to it."

Ellie said, "My brother and I received nothing, not one red cent from my father's farm, no life insurance, no farm equipment, not even the family photo albums or Mom's china or jewelry—nothing. All of our childhood memories are gone, my mom's linens, Grandma's knitted blankets and quilts, all gone. Most importantly, we have no grave site to visit our father. His body parts are scattered, and only Mrs. Wilkins knows where. His bones, where are his bones? Do you realize how this feels to all of the survivors of those twenty-eight people they dismembered?"

Natalie got up from her chair and hugged Ellie. "I'm so sorry. I did not realize how far those heartless people went to procure lands and businesses. You received nothing?"

Elise said, "Nothing. Even Dad's Social Security survivors' benefits are caught up in red tape; they're saying they were told he had no heirs. My brother and I are filling out reams of paper to prove we are his children—birth certificates, school records, vaccinations, doctor visits and exams from birth to now."

Natalie said, "We will get that all clarified for you, and you will receive a large settlement check for the land, life insurance, and compensation for the years they took away from him, the equipment, jewelry, and heirlooms stolen. She and her estate will pay."

Natalie called in David Greenspar. "Could you work with Ms. McPherson regarding all the property that Mrs. Wilkins stole from her and her brother?"

Natalie hugged Elise and returned to the courtroom, just in time to stand while the court was called to order by the bailiff.

Judge Adamson stated, "Ms. Morgan, call your next witness."

Ms. Morgan called William Short to the stand. While he was sworn in and seated, she gave the defense team a horrible look.

She stood and asked, "Mr. Short, please tell the court your occupation, your job title and how long have you been in that position."

Mr. Short replied, "I'm a local real estate broker specializing in land sales. I'm the owner of Short Estates for the last twenty years."

Ms. Morgan asked, "Do you know the defendant, Mrs. Katy Wilkins?"

Mr. Short said, "I do know Katy Wilkins. She's a good customer of ours."

Ms. Morgan asked, "How many properties has she bought from your firm over the years?"

Mr. Short said, "I believe twenty or maybe more. I can get you the exact count if you need it."

Ms. Morgan asked, "Did she purchase the McPherson farm?"

Mr. Short replied, "Yes, I believe she purchased the farm, but I would like to verify that to confirm my statement."

Ms. Morgan asked, "How did you sell the property without the family's consent?"

Mr. Short said, "Counselor, the paperwork was handled by the bank. We just marketed the land for sale, and she purchased the property through the bank. We just put the buyer in touch with the title company and get paid the commission on the sale."

Ms. Morgan asked for a sidebar and headed for the bench to wait on Mr. Twingling.

Judge Adamson asked Ms. Morgan, "What is this all about?"

"I want to know if Mr. Short could be held as a coconspirator in twenty or more murders. Ms. McPherson informed me she and her brother not only received no money from the sale of the property and farm equipment, but proceeds of the life insurance policies, Social Security death benefits, everything—it all was stolen. I want Mr. Short arrested and charged as a co-conspirator, now."

The judge motioned for the bailiff, who approached. "Bailiff, get two sheriffs into the courtroom." The judge said, "Ms. Morgan, do you want to read him his Miranda rights, or may I have the pleasure?"

Ms. Morgan said, "Your Honor, it would be my privilege to have you read him his rights."

The two sheriffs entered the courtroom, and Judge Adamson addressed the witness. "Mr. Short, please rise." Then, with the witness looking at Mrs. Wilkins with a bewildered expression, the judge read him his rights and had the sheriffs escort him to the county jail.

The judge informed the jury, "Mr. Short will be formally charged by the end of the day. Court is adjourned until eight o'clock tomorrow morning."

Once the gallery was cleared, Mr. Twingling approached Ms. Morgan and said, "I had no idea."

Ms. Morgan said, "I'm looking at a totally different perspective starting today."

She'd given him that look two years ago, and she could tell he knew what it meant.

18

Natalie Morgan returned to her office to review what was ahead for tomorrow: three foremen from Smooth as Silk Concrete Finishing, and an FBI forensic team of three. The corporate takeover with Katy Wilkins's signature for Smooth as Silk, linking Mrs. Wilkins to Stephan Delaney, should secure the defendant's fate. Natalie had to remind herself, *No "happy dance" until the fat lady sings; too many Perry Mason last-minute surprises could still pop up at the finish line. It's not over until the jury foreperson hands the verdict to the bailiff, who hands it to the judge, who asks the foreperson to read the verdict, then either the "happy dance" or the dirge. Then: "Next!"*

David Greenspar entered her office. "How did it go today?"

"Same old, same old. Twingling with his objections; most were overruled. He's in a very difficult position right now: how do you defend against truth? I'm giving him no entries into my arena. He and I have gone toe to toe before. I know what he looks for and how he can twist a tiny misplaced fact into an enormous blunder and keeps reminding the jury of that blunder, even days after it occurred."

David said, "Tomorrow should put him in a deeper hole."

Natalie said, "I want to close in the ends of that hole to make sure Mrs. Wilkins has no escape."

David asked, "So your goal is to put Mrs. Wilkins in the final resting place?"

She replied, "I only want to do the best for all of those innocent people whose family lost not only their living relative but their land, home, farm equipment, belongings, life insurance, everything. I want the Wilkins family to be left destitute, along with her cronies and the entire organization that's behind this type of behavior.

"Have you received any word from Papa?"

David replied, "He has all his contacts looking at all possibilities. Oh, by the way, the FBI raided the new location this morning; it was vacant. There was a note on the floor that read, 'Too late.'"

Natalie said, "Ask the people filming the trial to see if they have shots of those allowed inside the courtroom, and have a copy sent to the FBI to run their photos. I have a feeling that someone is a plant; they aren't who they claim to be."

David quickly excused himself so he could catch them before they left the courthouse.

Natalie contacted the agent handling the Wilkins case, asked to have a forensic team to enter the courthouse and dust the seating area for fingerprints.

Natalie called over to Judge Adamson's office to inform him what she was proposing to do. He was a little concerned, since all those allowed into the courtroom were previously scanned. "What have you found out?"

Natalie told him that the FBI had raided the new location disclosed during testimony and prior to the media being released. The place was vacant with a note that said, "Too late."

Judge Adamson said, "Tomorrow the courtroom will be cleared until we can determine who that person or persons are."

Papa called David and told him they will put heat on the telephone carriers in the area and pull up all new phone numbers related to those they already had. "It could take a couple of days, but these folks have a huge mouth to feed, can't dedicate too much time tracking phone numbers."

David returned to Natalie's office with great news: "The film crew, will send all sessions to the agent handling the case to identify all those attending the hearing."

She told him, "The judge is aware of the circumstance, and no one will be allowed in the courtroom tomorrow."

David said, "That could cause a concern to Mrs. Wilkins."

"Oh, you're saying she may not appreciate not having it her way?"

David said, "Will they cross-reference those identified to Mrs. Wilkins?"

Natalie said, "You could contact the agent to make sure upon identification that they do cross-reference, especially her children's friends or classmates in college, or fellow workers with their spouses or neighbors."

David said, "Is there no end to this case?"

Natalie stated, "They have had it their way for so long, felt they had everything covered. Then, a simple thing: where's the garage and a kidnapping of a daughter who is a defense attorney for the most powerful organization in the world. They didn't do their homework, got too caught up in stopping a successful competitive magazine, and lost their focus on the game plan—that's how this all shakes out for me."

David said, "Like that pesky dripping faucet, drip, drip, drip, or a running toilet: jiggle the handle, sit back down, and it starts up again; keep jiggling, but it doesn't stop."

Natalie stated, "That is a good scenario. Once one of the players defected, the dominos started to fall. Catching the eight together was a godsend. Freezing their assets really got the little women in an uproar; that was priceless. How dare we freeze their blood money? Just who do we think we are?"

The whistle blew. "Well, it's time to head home, have some dinner, review tomorrow's witnesses, and return to Mrs. Wilkins's dream vacation."

David said, "One her money could not buy."

Natalie said, "She gets three square meals a day, clean linen, her own bathroom next to her bed, nice neighbors, and a bath once a week. Security is top notch at no cost, she gets chauffeured with armed guards, and there's really nice jewelry, very stylish and matching, along with the bright orange jumpsuit, monogrammed. Can't see why she would complain."

David said, "She can call the hired help by banging her tin cup on the steel bars; it's better than the pesky door chimes at her mansion."

David walked Natalie to her car and returned to the office to notify Agent Billow, Then he was off to his own home.

*

The next morning Natalie returned to the courthouse, elbowing her way past the media circus to her office.

Kelli brought her a cup of coffee and a breakfast roll and three messages from defense attorneys for the gang of twelve; the list was growing by the minute.

Natalie responded, "Wait until this afternoon and this stack will triple in size. If they continue to call, tell them I'm in receipt of their prior message, and when I find time, I'll respond."

Kelli said, "The governor's office returned your call; they will get back to you shortly."

The courtroom bell was nearly ready to ring. Natalie strolled down the hallway to the courtroom, with the press all over her.

When she got inside the courtroom, Mrs. Wilkins and Mr. Twingling asked, "Where's everyone who's allowed in the courtroom?"

Natalie looked around. "I didn't notice; sorry. Maybe today no live audience."

The bailiff waited for the jury to be seated and called the courtroom to order: "Please rise for the Honorable Judge Adamson, presiding."

Judge Adamson entered the courtroom and told everyone to be seated. He announced that the courtroom would be empty today due to some technical difficulties. "Ms. Morgan, call your first witness."

Natalie called Manuel Rodriguez to the stand. As Manuel was approaching the stand, she picked up two bags of evidence. Manuel was sworn in by the bailiff and instructed to be seated.

Ms. Morgan asked, "Manuel Rodriguez, please tell the court your occupation, where you are employed, your job title, and how long have you been in that position."

Mr. Rodriguez stated, "I'm a concrete finisher for Smooth as Silk Concrete Finishing. I'm currently a foreman and have been for the past ten years."

Ms. Morgan asked, "Are you still employed by Smooth as Silk?"

Mr. Rodriguez replied, "I'm not sure, ma'am. Our company was purchased by Stephan Delaney, and he's in jail. We're just finishing up contracts."

Ms. Morgan asked, "Do you know the defendant?"

Mr. Rodriguez answered, "Not personally, ma'am. I have seen her at the jobsites."

Ms. Morgan took the bags of evidence to Mr. Rodriguez and asked him if he recognized the contents.

Mr. Rodriguez looked at them and said he did recognize the contents.

Ms. Morgan took the bags over to the jury panel so they could see the contents, and she returned to the stand.

Ms. Morgan asked, "Just what is inside of the first bag?"

Mr. Rodriguez stated, "On June 15, 2012, we were on the construction site pouring a home's floor plan, two trucks of concrete—roughly eighteen yards, about six yards more than normal for that size pad."

Ms. Morgan asked, "Is that unusual?"

Mr. Rodriguez stated, "Yes, but we had those amounts beforehand, so we weren't too surprised. Once the concrete mixer offloaded the concrete, we had time to take a break, about ten minutes, we guessed. The lunch wagon always comes at ten o'clock. As we were at the lunch truck, a white van pulled next to the concrete pour; this had happened before. Two men got out of the van and took two bags from the van, as before. Then when our break was completed, we returned to the pour to start finishing the concrete."

Ms. Morgan asked, "What were the two men from the van doing by your concrete pour?"

Mr. Rodriguez answered, "Our view was blocked by the van. We were told at another pour to take our lunch or break until the van left. Our company owner pulled in with Mrs. Wilkins and another lady while the van was there. They all walked to the other side of the van, and just before the van pulled away, they all three got back into the car and pulled away. Your second bag is the photos we took of that moment."

Ms. Morgan asked, "Is this the first time you saw Mrs. Wilkins?"

Mr. Rodriguez stated, "No, we saw her before with Mr. Delaney and another man."

Ms. Morgan asked, "What is this bone?"

Mr. Rodriguez replied, "While we were finishing the concrete, we had one spot where no matter how hard we pushed down on the concrete, there was a bump. We knew that the flooring contractor would be angry if there was any unevenness in the finish. Remember, we are Smooth as Silk; a bump is not allowed. Our supervisor said, 'That bump is not acceptable; fix it, now.' So I got on my kneeboard, took my trowel, and dug down about an inch. I came across the end of the bone and pulled it out and handed to my laborer to put in our lunch bag and put it in the truck. I had my other laborer bring me some concrete from the wheelbarrow to fill in the hole and finish the concrete before it set up."

Ms. Morgan asked, "Was that the only bone you found?"

Mr. Rodriguez stated, "That day, ma'am, it was causing problems in our finishing of the concrete pad."

Ms. Morgan stated she had no further questions for this witness but reserved the right to call him back. "Your witness, Counselor Twingling."

Mr. Twingling asked, "Who took the photo of Mrs. Wilkins?"

Mr. Rodriguez stated, "I took the photo of not only her; I'm responsible for the finished product."

Mr. Twingling asked, "Are there more photos of this project?"

Mr. Rodriguez replied, "Yes sir, the forms, the steel reinforcement, the unfinished concrete, and the finished concrete pad."

Mr. Twingling asked, "Where are all the photos?"

Mr. Rodriguez answered, "In the construction file folder with all our reports attached."

Mr. Twingling asked, "Does your company owner know you have this photo?"

Mr. Rodriguez stated, "The owner of our company is dead."

Ms. Morgan stood and asked the court for a sidebar. She and Mr. Twingling approached the bench.

Ms. Morgan addressed the judge: "This is badgering the witness. He told the counselor earlier that his owner is dead and Mr. Delaney is in jail; they are only finishing up the remaining contracts."

Mr. Twingling said, "This photo should be with the others."

Ms. Morgan asked, "Just who is looking at the file folders, your client?

"Strike that, Your Honor. I'm trying my best not to wring their necks."

Judge Adamson stated, "Ms. Morgan, I agree he was badgering a witness with his line of questioning. Mr. Twingling, refrain from such questioning. Ms. Morgan: patience."

They returned to their tables, and Mr. Twingling said he had no further questions for this witness but might need to call him back at a later date.

Judge Adamson stated, "There will be a thirty-minute recess. Jurors, don't talk to anyone or among yourselves during our recess."

19

After the thirty-minute recess, everyone was back, and the bailiff called the court to order: "All rise, the Honorable Judge Adamson, presiding."

Judge Adamson asked, "Ms. Morgan, please call your next witness."

Ms. Morgan called José Martínez to the stand.

As José Martínez approached the stand, Mr. Twingling stood and asked, "Are we going to hear from the entire crew or company?"

Judge Adamson called for a sidebar. The attorneys approached the bench, and Judge Adamson told Mr. Twingling, "Another outburst like that and you will be held in contempt of court. Ms. Morgan, please continue."

As the attorneys returned to their respective tables, José Martínez was sworn in by the bailiff and seated. Ms. Morgan asked, "José Martínez please tell the court your profession, whom you work for and for how long you have held that position."

Mr. Martínez stated, "I'm the field superintendent for Delaney Development Company. Seven years I have been employed by Delaney Development."

Ms. Morgan asked, "Mr. Martínez, do you know the defendant?"

Mr. Martínez replied, "Yes ma'am, we have completed many jobs for Mrs. Wilkins."

Ms. Morgan asked, "What was the first project you completed for Mrs. Wilkins?"

Mr. Martínez stated, "When I was a laborer, we did the forming for the bomb shelter at her home."

Ms. Morgan asked, "Was there anything that made the forming nonstandard?"

Mr. Martínez stated, "The floor thickness was double the normal thickness, and there was no reinforcement in the pour. Mr. Delaney stated that the customer did not have the funds to reinforce the concrete."

Ms. Morgan asked, "Was there anything else?"

Mr. Martínez said, "The finish was lumpy—it had what we call fish ponds all over the finished floor. That made it very difficult to set forms for the walls. There were no keyways joining the walls to the floors. We were told to hurry up and finish forming the walls by not only Mr. Delaney but Mrs. Wilkins. Our foreman tried to explain how difficult it was for us to form, but she told him, 'You're not getting paid to stand and talk to me.'"

Ms. Morgan asked, "Did you finish the forming?"

Mr. Martínez stated, "No, we tried to even the floor by chipping away some of the rough spots to fit the form, and we hit a bone under the surface. When we brought it to the attention of Mrs. Wilkins, she called our boss, and he fired all of us for being disrespectful."

Ms. Morgan showed Mr. Martínez a bag with bone fragments. "Do you recognize this bag?"

Mr. Martínez answered, "Yes ma'am, that's the bag of fragments we kept to try to get our jobs back. Our boss, wouldn't listen to us, so we found work elsewhere."

Mr. Twingling objected to the evidence, stating, "How do we know they came from that site that day?"

Ms. Morgan said, "Your Honor, "We have the forensic report as well already in evidence. I was about to show that to Mr. Martínez to verify the date and time, which should correspond to the FBI forensic report."

Judge Adamson asked to see the report. Ms. Morgan showed it to him. The report even identified who the bones were from and the approximate date of death and how long they had been in the concrete embedment.

Judge Adamson asked, "Mr. Twingling, do you have a copy of this report?"

Mr. Twingling stated, "I'm sorry, Your Honor. I did not see the report; I only received it last night."

Judge Adamson stated, "Overruled. Please continue, Ms. Morgan."

Ms. Morgan showed Mr. Martínez the FBI report after he told the court the date they were fired due to disrespect: April 19, 1997.

Ms. Morgan asked, "Please read the date listed on the report of the date of concrete embedment."

Mr. Martínez said, "Around April 16 to April 18, 1997."

Ms. Morgan asked, "Whose bones were they?"

Mr. Martínez stated, "Kathrine Borgren."

Ms. Morgan asked, "Did you ever meet Kathrine Borgren?"

Mr. Martínez stated, "Only once. About two years earlier we did some concrete work at her home. It was my first year working with a concrete crew. The foreman kept yelling at me, and when we took lunch, I sat by myself. Mrs. Borgren sat down beside me and told me to keep trying, to do my best. 'You're a good boy,' she said." He started to get teary-eyed.

Ms. Morgan went to her table and brought him a tissue. "I have no further questions for Mr. Martínez but do reserve the right to call him back at a later date. Your witness, Mr. Twingling."

Mr. Twingling said, "Very touching. I'm almost in tears myself. She just sat beside you during your lunch break. Mr. Martínez, Mrs. Borgren was a very wealthy socialite. Why would she waste her time talking to a construction laborer?"

Mr. Martínez said, "We had talked a couple days earlier. She brought us out water and a couple of cookies."

Mr. Twingling said, "Pray tell, a construction worker talking to a socialite, that would make the front page of the newspaper. Who else saw that happen, Mr. Martínez?"

Mr. Martínez answered, "My friend Miguel Gomez, who will testify today."

Mr. Twingling stated, "How convenient that you brought your friend to corroborate your story. No further questions of the witness; I supposed I should reserve the right to hear another story later."

Judge Adamson said, "Mr. Martínez, please step down. Ms. Morgan, please call your next witness."

Natalie wanted to say, Mr. Twingling, do the honors, but on second thought didn't want to be charged with contempt of court. "We call Miguel Gomez to the stand."

Mr. Twingling stood up and asked, "Your Honor, are you going to allow this one lie and another witness to swear to the lie?"

Judge Adamson stated, "Bailiff, note that Mr. Twingling is charged with contempt of court. Sentence to be carried out at close of proceedings today."

While Miguel Gomez was being sworn in, Ms. Morgan went to her table and picked up three evidence envelopes. Then she asked, "Mr. Gomez, please state to the court your job title, whom you worked for, and for how long."

Mr. Gomez stated, "I was the construction superintendent for Delaney Development for five years. I'm now with Smooth as Silk, same position."

Ms. Morgan showed Mr. Gomez the evidence envelopes. "Do you recognize the contents of these envelopes?"

Mr. Gomez replied, "Yes ma'am, these are photos that I took on the day we were setting forms at Mrs. Borgren's residence."

Ms. Morgan asked, "Who is that girl standing behind the one I'm presuming is Mrs. Borgren?"

Mr. Gomez said, "We were not introduced, but while Mrs. Borgren was sitting with Mr. Martínez, the girls called her 'Mom.'"

Ms. Morgan asked, "Do you happen to know the date this photo was taken?"

Mr. Gomez said, "I wrote the date on the back of the photo when I got them from the drugstore."

Ms. Morgan turned the photo over. "So June 2, 1995, is the date the photo was taken?"

Mr. Gomez answered, "Yes ma'am, we poured the concrete the next day."

Ms. Morgan stated, "I have no further questions for this witness. Your witness, Counselor."

Mr. Twingling asked, "Do you always take photos of customers?"

Mr. Gomez replied, "Mrs. Borgren requested a photo of her and Mr. Martínez for her photo album. I got a copy for her and delivered it to her when it arrived."

Mr. Twingling asked, "How do you know the girl behind them is a daughter?"

Mr. Gomez stated, "She called her 'Mom.' We were not formally introduced; she seemed in a hurry that day."

Mr. Twingling asked, "Was it your job to appease the customer?"

Ms. Morgan objected. "Your Honor, he's the superintendent, the spokesperson for the company. It's his job."

Judge Adamson said, "Sustained; either rephrase or move on. The reporter will strike the question, and jurors are to disregard it."

Mr. Twingling stated he had no further questions.

Judge Adamson said, "Court is adjourned for one hour for lunch. Jury, please do not discuss this case."

Natalie retreated to her office; Kelli had her cup of coffee ready.

Kelli told her, "They are in hot pursuit of the new facility. The FBI received an anonymous tip of the new location. We should know shortly what they've found."

Natalie asked, "What about the people filmed in the courtroom? Any word?"

"David has some information for you. He's out buying you lunch."

Natalie was just adding cream to her coffee when David entered her office. He had her favorite sandwich from her favorite deli down the street. The chef knew her and prepared her sandwich per her specifications—corned beef on rye with special slaw.

She was excited about David's choice. "I needed this. Wow, what a pleasant surprise. Thank you so much."

David, blushing now, said he had heard that the witnesses called today were questioned by Mr. Twingling in a less than professional way.

She said, "He knew these men were going to take away what little defense he has left. I'm expecting Mr. Twingling to either plea bargain or withdraw from the case. He's that pompous and does not want to damage his reputation."

As they were unwrapping their lunches, David said, "We now know who is feeding information out of the courtroom."

After swallowing her first bite of her sandwich, Natalie said, "Well, I'm listening. Tell me, please."

He said, "Papa was spot on about who it might be."

She said, "David, I only have an hour; I don't need much more drama in my life."

David said, "Sorry, just trying to build up some suspense. It's one of her son's college roommates, who just happens to be an investor into Mrs. Wilkins's organization. He's been sitting behind the defense desk, and twice there were notes dropped on the floor which the young spectator quickly picked up."

"Has he been arrested?" asked Natalie.

"No, we are opening up the courtroom for this afternoon session. Once everyone's seated, while you're presenting your case, you will just happen to ask if your witness has been notified of the new location for Mrs. Wilkins's organization. He has been given the new location. Mrs. Wilkins does not know the new location. We want to grab the note that is passed, and at that point he will be arrested. The two men sitting next to him are FBI agents."

Natalie took a few more bites of her sandwich, drank some coffee. Then she said, "Make sure the agents get my regards."

Lunch was the best part of her day so far. She had two more witnesses, and then the parade of Mrs. Wilkins's gang of seven would plead with the court for mercy with two days of how feared for their lives. She could almost write their pleas.

The hour was coming to a quick end. She freshened up and strolled back through the hallway to the courtroom.

She entered the courtroom, which was now full of concerned citizens. She sat at her desk waiting for the call to order. She made sure the evidence required for the next two witnesses had come to her from the evidence storage area.

The bailiff called, "All rise for the Honorable Judge Adamson, presiding."

Judge Adamson addressed the gallery: "We are sorry about any inconvenience caused you. We had to address a technical situation before we could allow you all to return. You will all receive a video of this morning's proceedings. I was told that the court had a nice breakfast for all of you."

Then he said, "Ms. Morgan, please call your next witness."

Ms. Morgan called Dr. Jeffrey Thrumberg to the stand and picked up the envelope containing evidence for him to witness. He was sworn in by the bailiff and seated.

Ms. Morgan approached the stand with her evidence envelope in hand and asked the doctor to describe his specialty and how long he had practiced it.

Dr. Thrumberg stated, "I've been a liver transplant specialist for the past fifteen years."

Ms. Morgan asked, "Do you know the defendant?"

Dr. Thrumberg replied, "I know of her but dealt with Dr. George Clybourne or Mr. Jeffrey Wilkins."

Ms. Morgan asked, "What was the nature of your call."

Dr. Thrumberg answered, "We needed a liver for one of our patients, and they were listed as a source for transplant organs."

Ms. Morgan asked, "How often did you talk with Dr. Clybourne?"

Dr. Thrumberg said, "The first time we talked for a few minutes, he asked if I had any other needs for livers and could we forward specific data to them so they could check my needs to their availability."

Ms. Morgan asked, "Is this a standard procedure?"

Dr. Thrumberg replied, "Most facilities want to be informed regarding our demands or future needs. Some patients are less common than others, and the wait could become lengthy."

Ms. Morgan asked, "Was Mrs. Wilkins's organization able to provide you livers?"

Dr. Thrumberg stated, "They did provide us with a few, even some that would have been harder to fine, which was a blessing."

Ms. Morgan asked, "When was the last time they fulfilled your order?"

Dr. Thrumberg answered, "About three months ago. We had a more recent need, but their source became unavailable."

Ms. Morgan asked, "Why was that?"

Dr. Thrumberg stated, "They claimed the source was no longer available to them."

Ms. Morgan asked, "What date did they say the source was no longer available?"

Dr. Thrumberg told her the date he had received the call.

Ms. Morgan stated, "That was the date when Delores Stockdale and Marie Albright were freed from their kidnappers. Were you aware that the Wilkinses were harvesting organs for profit?"

Mr. Twingling objected, "Leading the witness, Your Honor."

Judge Adamson said, "Sustained. Ms. Morgan, you will refrain from referring to a case still under investigation."

Ms. Morgan asked, "What happened after they told you their source was no longer available?"

Dr. Thrumberg stated, "The liver required, which they ensured me they could provide, was not common. My patient was elated until we told her the bad news."

Ms. Morgan asked, "Have you contacted them lately?"

Dr. Thrumberg said, "The phone number I have on record is no longer in service."

Ms. Morgan asked, "If you had the new number, would you still do business with them?"

Dr. Thrumberg replied, "I believe Dr. Clybourne is in custody. Has another surgeon taken his place?"

Ms. Morgan stated, "Our records indicate that they relocated to 1574 Waterfield Drive here in town."

Mr. Twingling stood to object. "Your Honor, that address is not in our records."

Just as he was making his objection, the two FBI agents had the young man stand up and put his hands behind his back. They picked up the note that Mr. Twingling had purposely dropped onto the floor for him to pick up.

The agents took the note to Judge Adamson to read to the court. It read, "They know your address; leave now." Judge Adamson called for a sidebar and asked the bailiff to get two sheriff's deputies to the courtroom.. Both Ms. Morgan and Mr. Twingling approached the bench.

The judge stated, "Mr. Twingling, you are under arrest for obstruction of justice." He read him his Miranda rights, and the deputies took him into custody.

As they were removing Mr. Twingling from the courtroom, Judge Adamson addressed Ms. Morgan: "Your witness will have to return tomorrow to finish his testimony." He apologized to Dr. Thrumberg for any inconvenience that this might cause him.

He then turned to the defendant. "Mrs. Wilkins, you will have to find another attorney, or if you are unable to do so, the court can appoint one for you. And in future, you may want to avoid having family friends sitting at the railing just behind the defense table."

20

Prosecution Continues

Judge Adamson turned to the jury panel after they cleared the spectator section of the courtroom. "What you have witnessed was going on for a couple of days. The attorney will be charged for his actions.

"You are not to talk to anyone or among yourselves about this incident. If you took notes, please strike it out of your notes. We will adjourn the court today and resume tomorrow morning at eight o'clock."

The bailiff had all parties rise, and Judge Adamson left the courtroom.

Natalie gathered up her belongings and returned to her office. She would have to shuffle her deck; since not all witnesses on the schedule had testified today, they could spill over into the day after tomorrow.

She was met by David with news: "The FBI has found the new facility and has the staff in custody. They won't disclose what other evidence they procured."

Natalie said, "The old wait and see is in play."

David said, "It appears the protesters have disappeared."

Natalie stated, "I'm very glad. They may have found a new hobby. I was getting to the point where my elbow would turn into a knee, a trick my self-defense coach taught me."

David asked, "Do you think tomorrow's court session will be delayed since Mrs. Wilkins is without legal representation?"

Natalie replied, "I hope not, but that is a possibility."

Kelli came to the door and told David that he had a call holding on line two. He went to his office to answer the call.

Natalie asked Kelli about tomorrow's witnesses. "Were they all notified and given specific times to be at the courthouse?"

Kelli assured her they were all notified and had said they would make sure to be at the courthouse in plenty of time.

Natalie said, "If we get word that the court session is delayed due to Mrs. Wilkins not procuring legal counsel, we want to make sure they are told the date when they will have to appear. Keep the time the same; just change the date."

David returned to Ms. Morgan's office and told her the FBI were questioning five more people in custody. "It seems this is a new staff. They may not have been involved with any of the murders but may be associated with new ones."

Natalie grinned. "How do you spell job security?"

21

This is the morning we have all been dreading. Mama and Papa are boarding the airplane to Oregon. It's excitement for them to be in their own home and tears for those seeing them go away, even though for just a week. Already it seems like a lifetime for the girls.

The girls were hugging them all the way to the airport. Leslie had crocodile tears rolling down her cheeks. "We will miss you so much. You'll go pet our lambs and calves; tell them we'll see them next week. Give them some of our love—please, Grandpa."

Their furniture arrived yesterday from their home in New York. Stuart and Murray had the moving company packing up their belongings with some of Papa's relatives making sure all was handled with love and care. Papa's other daughter took inventory of all the belongings and forwarded them to Marie via email. They took a photo of the moving company's trailer for their records.

Mama was excited to see her belongings; she hadn't seen them in over a year. Papa had rented their home to one of his brother's sons with a wife and three grandchildren. They would take great care of the house and promised Papa that if they chose to do any improvements to the home, they would ask permission first, with the minimum of three estimates with plans for his approval.

Papa told them that the home was in the same condition as when his parents gave it to him. He would prefer only to have modifications done in line with a restoration, nothing more. The home was built for his parents in the 1940s by quality craftsmen handpicked by his father. "It's a seven-thousand-square-foot home on a three-acre partial. The property line is fenced by brick walls ten feet tall. It has a horseshoe-shaped driveway with a circular planter and a large sugar maple in the center; the fall color is breathtaking. A formal garden surrounds the estate. The maple trees lining the driveway, with the perimeter trees dotting the landscape among ash, elm, and conifers as well as many flower trees for the spring bouquet, were all established by the landscape architect who designed the property."

Papa was hesitant about leaving his estate, but loved his granddaughters far more than his estate. Papa had a huge family with Mama, and these four girls were very special to them. They wanted to watch them grow up and be a major part of their lives.

With all the tears wiped from their eyes by Susanne—of course, she had her film crew at the airport filming the departure from Denver, "And the arrival in Oregon is scheduled live—the girls can see their grandparents arriving at the airport, showing on their program. They want their viewing audience to see Mama and Papa arrive and pick up their luggage at the baggage claim."

Silvia had the limousines ready to pick up Mama, Papa, and Susanne's assistant. The moving company had the furniture offloaded with three professional interior decorators and their crews setting up their new home. Numerous photos were taken from their home in New York, so the designers would know how Mama and Papa had their home set up.

Phillip had three full crews, one for each house. Raymond was the superintendent making sure all three projects would be completed before we arrived. They had Mama and Papa's patio and craft house nearly completed before they arrived. Murray had the barbecue and fire pit ready, with a gourmet chef from the restaurant set to prepare their first home-cooked meal, with numerous guests attending.

This was just the warm-up for next week's party, planned at least three months in advance to sure all T's were crossed and all I's were dotted. It was driving Silvia crazy trying to keep this all a secret. All the office managers and staffs were arranging flights for everyone to attend the open houses for all of us.

Angel designed the landscapes for all three homes, Juanita designed the low voltage lighting system, and Juan designed the irrigation system. Brad arrived two weeks ago so he could lay out the stream feature and build the waterfalls and streams. Phillip built the two bridges and benches to match Marie's existing setup.

Maggie was asked to be one of the servers. Sally had every room at her hotel full, arranging for all the airport shuttles to bring in the guests for this main event. Her bumper, as Sally calls her backside, was getting a workout; some guests would be there for two weeks. They would fly in the lady singer and the violins for the open house.

Murray had the spa contractor start the spa, hopefully to complete it by the time everyone arrived. The construction schedule had no room for hiccups; the crews had never been put under the gun as they were now.

When I went to Texas for three days to meet with Marjorie, Juan flew into Oregon for three days to work with Manuel, Miguel, Angel, Juanita, and Murry. The additional experience made Murray's job much easier. Phillip's crews were setting the posts so our crews could start the wall footings, the barbecues, and the spa.

Miguel was teaching Murray's crews how to prepare the steel for the concrete pour. The most time-consuming part of the raised planters was the waterproofing of the walls; it took two coats of Henry 107. We used eight-by-eight-by-sixteen-inch tan split block on the perimeter wall and heavy duty block for the planter wall along the paver edge, which will receive the stone fascia and precast concrete cap.

Since the perimeter is three feet high and the paver side wall is twenty-seven inches, the precast can will terminate into the perimeter wall. Murry had three small excavators digging the footings for the walls and barbecues. The spoil or excavated soil was to be placed into the raised planters using skid-steer loaders.

The subgrade for the pavers would be dug with the skid steer loader after being loosened by rototillers. The equipment would save time to a point; hand labor would still be needed for the final detailing.

Moving the blocks from the pallets to the wall locations would also be done with skidsteers or wheelbarrows, and all of the wall cells would be done with a concrete pump and cement trucks.

Since we were doing three houses at one time, pumping would save a huge amount of time and make for less mess and easier cleanup.

The gate contractor was scheduled to show up on Monday and stay on site, using our garage as the construction site and Marie and John's garage as the finishing site. A production line will speed up the process; seven gates and two shrouds will take some time to complete. Six front doors and six French doors were on the work list as well.

To aid in drying time they brought with them a heating system and a dehumidifier. They already had door racks to use as little space as possible and do less damage to the finished doors. They also had the jigs set up for cutting the holes in the doors and recess the hinges. They had set up workstations to keep the sawdust down to a minimum; they also wiped the doors clean before taking them to the finishing garage. These precautions had produced the mirror glass finish they perfected. The garage door at John and Marie's was never opened to allow dust particles to enter the garage.

Phillip was one day from finishing Mama and Papa's playhouse craft room and just needed to apply one more coat of polyurethane to the hardwood floor. The house looked beautiful, and Murry was jealous since the playhouse would be the centerpiece to their home. Silvia told me she was in complete awe of how it came out; the trim of the playhouse matched the home they built.

The doors being hung today made the house glow. She said, "It's the maraschino cherry on top of a banana split." She was talking to Phillip about getting me to design a babe cave for her. "Before you head home, you have one more, right, my sweetheart?"

Murry said, 'yes my love, one more banana split.'

Murray said, "Phillip, you have to please her. It will make our wedding just that much more enjoyable. She also wants the elevator and wraparound staircase for her grand entrance to the reception."

It was nearing the time when Silvia had to head to the airport to pick up Mama and Papa. She was taking one of her new assistants, Maggie, who had joined the company a week ago to help in sales. She also worked for the restaurant. She was a celebrity now and had to think of her fans.

Plus her tips had more than doubled now that she was now on the wall of fame. She gave up an event to welcome home Mama and Papa. The magazine slated a film crew with Susanne's assistant taking the MC position to be aired live so the girls and their moms, who were their invited guests for today's show, could watch and talk with Mama and Papa as they retrieved their luggage and rode to their new home in Oregon.

Their house was all decorated with the furniture in place, thanks to the interior designers and crew working on the finest details. The refrigerator was stocked with their favorite food, and cabinets were stocked. Marie had supplied a list of the groceries her parents usually purchased.

The home looked like a magazine showroom. The designers upgraded the bedding for today's showing. Marie was texted a photo from Silvia.

Marie texted Silvia, *Mama will just faint. This is my home? Papa will slip off his shoes; I know them both very well.*

Silvia wanted the designers to set up a couple pair of slippers for Mama and Papa after receiving the text from Marie.

Upon their arrival at the airport, everything went per plan. Silvia and Maggie were shaking from anxiety. The day had arrived. Silvia had waited so long for this day to get to show Mama and Papa their new home.

After what seemed a lifetime of waiting, Mama and Papa were approaching the baggage claim area, Silvia and Maggie both ran to give them the best Oregon hugs they could muster up.

Papa said, "Girls, could you do that again a little slower so my blood has time to flow to enjoy your hugs to the fullest?"

Mama slugged him. "That will be enough out of you. These are our Oregon daughters; you ought to be ashamed of yourself. Girls, you both are stunning." Then she told the other passengers, "You can only look; Papa issues the dance cards."

The chauffeur retrieved the luggage and put it in the waiting car. The film and sound crew were loading equipment into the van. One cameraman positioned himself in the limousine's front seat to film the trip to their new home. The limousine gave them about fifteen minutes' lead time to set up at the house.

Maggi asked, "Mama and Papa, when are my little sisters coming?"

Mama said, "A week from today, about the same time. They were crying the entire trip from our house to the airport and gave Papa specific instructions on loving their farm animals, telling them they will be home next week."

Susanne's assistant was giving the audience an approximate time of arrival, only so many minutes away from their new home. This was designed to alert the designers—Murry, Phillip, Angel, and Juan—about how far away they were. If they needed more time, they should tell the assistant in her earpiece, so they could do some sightseeing or take a longer route to the house.

The sound system was playing Mama's favorite songs. Marie also gave them the list of music Mama and Papa enjoyed. The restaurant chef and his staff were minutes away from having a five-course meal ready for Mama, Papa, and the staff and workers at all three sites. They even had a live six-piece ensemble tuning up their instruments. This was going to be a marvelous event.

The camera crew arrived, offloaded their equipment, and started setting up. The van moved to our driveway and parked. They were ready in a few minutes, waiting for the limousine to round the turn and head for the driveway. They were very careful not to show the livestock, since the dogs were watching the herds.

The cameraman turned to show the view from the windshield, making sure not to film Marie's and Delores's homes; they kept the camera toward the lake and trees.

Marie and Delores wanted to see their homes. Susanne said, "They're teasing you by design; no peeking, not allowed."

Stuart and Doreen were on the patio, waiting with open arms for their newest neighbors. The limousine parked in the driveway; the garage had a huge surprise for Papa. They entered the house through the front door. Marie was correct: Mama nearly fainted, and Papa slipped off his shoes.

Marie said, "Mom, it's beautiful—oh my God, Mom, I'm so jealous. Look at your home!"

The girls were all screaming. Leslie said, "Grandma, you're so lucky. Can we come and visit you every day?"

Mama said, "And spend the night, of course."

Mama and Papa were in total awe of their new home. Silvia and Murray were giving the guided tour of all the rooms. Murry said, "This is beyond spectacular, but wait—there's more. Follow me." He opened the French doors leading to the patio, and Mama nearly fell to the ground, caught by Maggi and Silvia. They supported her to the patio and took her to the elevator to show her the new craft room. The girls were very excited: "You have an elevator too, Grandma!"

In the craft room was where Mama met the three interior designers responsible for her home's appearance. She could not stop hugging them, tears of joy streaming down her cheeks.

Sarah said, "Grandma, you have your own playhouse." The girls were now hugging their moms. "When can we go to our new homes?"

Delores said, "Next week, girls, you will be in your new homes. We can't wait either."

The designers were showing Mama and the audience her new craft room, with all sorts of bells and whistles. They even had a table and chairs for the girls to learn from Grandma and ample lighting, with a pull-out lamp, to help grandma lighten up her project for better vision. She could also turn off the room lights and use only the pull-out lamp.

Papa arrived via the elevator and told Mama that lunch was ready. "The chef does not want to burn our lunch. Ladies, please be our honored guests." Just then the elevator door opened, and the ensemble started to play Mama's favorite Italian song.

Two waitresses, handpicked by Maggi, escorted Mama and Papa to the guest of honor table where the staff was bringing them the salad and beverages. They even had a glass of goose juice, with the label kissed by Maggie and Silvia.

Silvia held up the glass of goose juice with their lip prints and said, "Freddy, eat your heart out. If you're a good boy, maybe you can earn a glass or two."

Juanita was finishing up the low voltage lighting system, ready for the ultimate light show starting in a few hours. Murry would throw the switch to illuminate their back and front yards.

Susanne's assistant was planning on showing Mama and Papa the arched gateway entrances to the backyard, but Susanne said, "Hold off; too many surprises can be seen from that angle."

Lunch ended, and the band played on, entertaining the guests and crews working on the other two houses.

Murry took Papa to the lambs and calves for him to get acquainted with the livestock. He showed him the feed, and the ranch hand demonstrated how much to give them. "If you give them too much, they will stop foraging and could rely only on humans to feed them. We want them to seek out their own food so they can rejoin the herds and flocks as they get older and stronger."

Murry said, "We want the girls to experience the joy of raising some livestock and get them involved in the 4-H programs. I've watched them do the gardening chores with their moms and dads, and they really like to help."

Papa said, "They liked the opportunity to help get snacks and lemonade. Marie and Delores always have a shopping spree planned for the girls. They did keep Fred on his toes. 'Daddy, here is another pile of leaves for you. Do you want us to slow down? Are we going too fast? We know, you're old, and we should let you catch up.' They would sit at the table drinking the lemonade, and Marie and Delores would tell them how great they were doing. 'Let Daddy catch up while you cool off.'

"They worked for about ten minutes tops." Murry just laughed. "But they wore stylish, gloves, hats, sunglasses, and cute outfits, the whole nine yards."

Scooter and Lulu greeted Papa, and he petted them. The ranch hand said, "They love people; the girls will be their best friends."

Papa said, "The girls don't know about the dogs, do they?"

Murry said, "We were told not to tell them it would break their hearts, knowing the dogs are outside and could get hurt."

Papa said, "You know they are going to love these two dogs all day long with the lambs and calves. I'll tell Mama to keep it quiet."

Murry said, "Watch this." He let the two dogs out of the pasture and headed upstairs to the playhouse. Both dogs beat him up the stairs and waited on the porch. He let them in the tunnels, and they ran from one playhouse to the other.

Murry whistled, and both dogs came and sat at his feet. He said, "We'll have to teach the girls to whistle and reward the dogs with a doggie treat but only once, so they follow the command.

"They both have been trained to herd sheep and cattle, and they are extremely good. Scooter loaded up our cattle trailer a couple days ago; took ten to fifteen minutes. We closed the door, and off we went to another pasture. I opened the gate and the door of the trailer, and Scooter did the rest, leading the cattle into the pasture. We did that four times. Lulu stayed behind and watched over the lambs and calves to keep predators away."

Murry said, "I'll take the girls with me after they are here awhile so they can watch Scooter work the cattle."

Papa said, "If I'm a good boy, can I come along to watch as well?"

Murry said, "You can go with Scooter and me tomorrow morning to round up another trailer load.

"I just wanted to see how talented Scooter really is. We saw him with babies; what about adults? He shines with young, old, and in between. The trainer told me she would show me how he works sheep if we need to round up our flock.

"We will do that in the spring, to shear the sheep. The vet will be here to inoculate them for any diseases and give them their shots. Our vet will quarantine any animal that looks suspicious."

He went on, "We will section off the pens if we have some quarantined animals and care for them in the pens. If they aren't aggressive and don't charge the girls, then the girls can feed them. Scooter and Lulu will protect the girls if need be."

Papa was giving loving to the lambs and the calves with Scooter and Lulu standing by his side.

Murry was telling Papa the names the girls gave them. "But there are twice as many in the pen that the girls still have to name. Silvia is having name tags made up for the girls in case they forgot."

Papa said, "Those girls don't forget. They named an aquarium full of fish and knew exactly what fish they caught. They all looked alike to me, but they know the difference. I just smiled and tried to figure out just how they know. It's all beyond me. Those girls are gifted; Scooter and Lulu will have their paws full."

The girls were calling Murry and Papa back to the Welcome-to-Oregon party.

Papa said, "It must be dessert time. You know how ladies feel about desserts. I can't eat another bite, and zoom, it's gone in the blink of an eye. Mama will tell me, 'Just why did you allow me to make a pig of myself?' That's one question as a husband—remember, son—don't answer it. Pretend you never heard the question."

Murry asked, "Why?"

"You called her a pig—you agreed with her logic. If you tell her she's not a pig, you insulted her intelligence. Either way you lose. Your next bed is the sofa, until she feels the punishment suits the offense. Oh, if you think you are safe for a romantic evening, you can double the original sentence."

Murry said, "Silvia is different."

Papa said, "Murry, they all are the same. They may act a little different, but bottom line, it's all in sequence. They all talk and give each other ideas: 'He did what?' Or 'He said what? Here's what you do: don't ever allow him that much leverage over you. We will strip you of your womanhood.'"

As they walked through the gate, Murry got the old "You didn't tell us where you were going. We looked all over the house and yard. You better tell me next time so I don't worry."

Papa put his hand on Murry's shoulder and said, "Different?"

Later, when Papa and Murry were alone, Papa explained what her last four words really meant. He was now being a translator from woman to man. " 'So I don't worry' is to make you feel guilty. That phrase goes straight into your soul. You're her protector; she now has doubts about your protection qualities. She knocked you down one step off your manhood ladder. Did you feel a little shorter?"

Murry said, "I did feel like I let her down."

Papa said, "Bingo! That was the intent. You will be very hesitant the next time you want to go somewhere; like a trained puppy you will tell her. Do you think she was really worried?"

Murry said, "I don't know for sure."

"Different, huh? No, son, they are not different. Four words at the end of your scolding are deep seated forever."

Papa went on, "It all starts with your mother when you're a little boy. There you were afraid of getting spanked, physically. She was setting you up for the verbal spankings you'd get later—some days often."

Silvia caught up to Murry and Papa walking down the sidewalk. She heard Papa say, "The planters look very nice. Great job, Murry."

Silvia told Murry, "It's that time. Could you both follow me?"

They did as Silvia requested, joined everyone on the patio, and entered the house. As they passed through the kitchen to the door into the garage, Silvia had Mama and Papa close their eyes, Murry opened the door and turned on the lights.

Silvia had them both by the hand, led them forward a few steps, and said, "Open your eyes."

Papa and Mama saw two brand new small SUVs, one with a pink bow and one with a blue bow. Again Mama almost fainted on the spot. Silvia had a good grip on her, and Maggi was standing right behind her for support.

Papa hugged Murry. "Son, they are beautiful. What can I say? Thank you with all my heart." Stuart and Doreen joined in on the hugs. Papa was now in tears. "I'm overwhelmed."

Stuart said, "Papa, this is our family's way of saying thank you for saving the lives of so many people."

Papa asked, "Do they come with drivers?"

Stuart asked, "Don't you drive?"

Papa said, "Years ago, but with our organization, we were driven for security reasons."

Stuart asked, "What about Mama?"

Mama replied, "I rode a bicycle as a child. Ever since I met Papa in high school, he drove us to school and home; then he went to college. He received his degree, and we've been chauffeured ever since."

Papa told Stuart, "The organization had too much to lose if Mama or I got into harm's way. I'm still picked up and taken to where I need to go with at least three to five armed guards."

Susanne's assistant said, "We had three gentlemen escorting us the entire trip. Two cars were assigned to follow us to the ranch; once on the road to here, they waited until the limousine driver said we'd arrived."

Stuart said, "We never had to worry about that sort of thing."

Papa said, "With me and Marie, your ranch will be watched twenty-four–seven from this day forward. You will even have an escort; you just won't be aware of their presence. Don't change your daily routine; they will adapt to it."

Murry said, "Hop in. I'll drive you around the ranch, and when you feel the urge to get behind the wheel, just let me know."

Maggi said, "Come on, Mama. Let's get the tires dirty. The vehicle is far too clean for the ranch."

Murry, Stuart, and Papa took off in his SUV. Silvia, Maggi, and Mama took off in the other SUV; the decorative bows were taken off before they left the garage.

They all arrived back in plenty of time to watch the light show; Juanita was getting a little worried that they would not return in time.

Angel assured her that Silvia and Murry were looking forward to showing Mama and Papa the view from the craft room playhouse.

The stage was set, and the band was playing Italian love songs for the occasion. Angel was given the microphone with cameras running to present the light show on cue.

With everyone in position, Angel had the crew and guests start counting down from ten. "... Three, two, one. Turn it on," said Angel. The band was playing Mama's favorite song when all the lights lit up their backyard and front yard. The tunnel was lit, the playhouse was lit, and the patio and the whole landscape was lit.

Mama told Angel, "It looks like Marie's house. You made it just like home." Mama gave Angel and Juanita huge hugs, and the tears were running down her cheeks.

Mama's phone rang. She picked up, and Marie said, "Mama, it's beautiful. I can't wait to share our first night standing with you on your balcony. Even the girls are choked up with joy. I just gave your designer a huge kiss and hug; should last him a few days."

All the girls wanted a chance to talk to Mama and Papa. Emotions were running off the charts.

When the girls were ready to go to bed, Papa, Mama, Silvia, and Maggi all said prayers with the girls and made sure they were tucked in. The air was full of murmured "I love you"s as the lights were turned off.

22

They all promised to call the girls every night to say their prayers. "Can't wait for seven days to pass. See you all next week."

Marie and Delores told the girls that they had to start packing up their bedrooms the next day. They would help them organize the boxes so the movers would know which room each one needed to go to. On Monday the movers would arrive and load up everything, and it will all be waiting in Oregon when we arrive. "Make sure you box up the playhouses as well," said Marie.

Sarah asked if Leslie and Kim could spend the night. "We'll all make breakfast and pack up our rooms and playhouse after breakfast. We can spend the next night with Leslie and Kim so we can help them with their rooms."

Marie and Delores agreed, that would be a great idea. Boxing should be easier and more relaxing for everyone. With all the girls tucked in, foreheads kissed, and night lights on, "Love you, sleep tight; see you in the morning, my loves."

Marie and John headed home for a planned rendezvous. Marie said, "We can use the eight-second clock for the first time."

Delores gave her a hug, saying, "It's only eight seconds; you can do it, my love."

Marie got a five-dollar bill out of her wallet put it on the kitchen table. "If he makes eight seconds, it's yours; if not, you match."

John pulled out a five-dollar bill and laid it on top of Marie's. "Double; I could use twenty dollars.

Marie said, "I will shoot the time on the eight-second clock to confirm."

Being inquisitive, I asked, "Are you counting the entire event?"

Marie said, "Look at me. Not the entire event. I have to have time to start the clock; I don't want to take unfair advantage."

John put a ten-dollar bill on the table and said, "The entire event. She'll be worn out by tomorrow morning, rubber knees and all."

Delores pulled out a twenty and laid it on the table. "Under eight seconds. Come on, sis. Be easy on him, or he'll be wiped out before he hits the sheets."

Marie said, "That lady was right to ask if the clock can record less than a second on the clock."

Delores said, "When she asked that, I almost wet myself laughing so hard."

Marie said, "You know, another lady asked if the clock could time a blink of an eye."

Delores said, "I missed that; I must have been laughing too hard."

I told John, "I'd match all the money on the table, but that's my Happy Meal money for next week; too risky."

Marie told Delores, "Side bet, my eight-second clock to yours? Twenty dollars?"

Delores looked at me. "Before I spend my laundry money on your stability, come here. Look into my eyes." She turned to Marie. "This is a real gamble. Okay, laundry or no laundry ... so risky. Here's my twenty."

The next morning we all lost. The girls beat us to the table and pocketed the cash. They were yelling, "Finders keepers," as Delores and I were descending the staircase.

"I forgot, I told Delores.

"Yeah, it takes a while for you to become normal. Wait, I said that on our wedding night; still waiting."

I smacked her backside, and she gave me a look. "You know, that just took tonight's rendezvous off the table."

Marie and John arrived, Marie looking forlorn. She said, "Six seconds; how about you?"

Delores said, "It doesn't matter; the girls won all the money that was on the table." Then she told Marie, "You would have won; nowhere near that time."

Marie came over to me. "What happened?"

"Too many previews before the show."

Delores said, "Nothing mentioned about previews being illegal."

Marie put her arms around Delores. "That was cheating, but you gave me a great idea before we do that again."

The girls were already starting the breakfast. "Come on, slowpokes. We have work to do, you know?"

Marie and Delores were making coffee and hot chocolate. John was setting the table with Kim. Toast was in the toaster, Leslie was stirring the pancake batter, Sarah had the sausage cooking in the pan, and I had to fly to get the Albright scramble ready on time.

Bacon chunks on high; no medium heat this morning, or the girls would say, "Come on, Dad, we're starving." I had the onions and bell peppers cut and ready for the heat. The bacon was nearly ready when Leslie had her pancakes completed. She came over to me and asked with a smirk if I needed some help.

She was becoming more like her mom every second.

Marie's favorite tease to me is putting her hands on her hips and asking, "Do you like it?" I'll respond affirmatively, but then she says, "Sorry, Charlie, too late, already spoken for," and sashays away.

One time she walked over to Delores with her palm up and said, "He failed."

Delores pulled money from her pocket, shook her head, and said, "He'll pay dearly later," as she put the money in Marie's hand.

The best part about having your wife being best friends with your best customer ever: they can be themselves, no holds barred. Marie has equal rights to mess with my head; Delores has the same privilege with John. Both ladies take full advantage of the situation and create new ways of stripping our egos to the bare bones.

Albright scramble was completed, bowled, and placed on the table just in time, or the girls would have been loaded for bear. All I heard by the time I turned around was the clinking of the spoon in the empty bowl. "Thanks, Dad" was the general saying around the table; "So good. Make some more, please, Daddy?" said Marie in her little girl voice.

I got more bacon and started frying, cut up some onion and bell peppers ready for the heat, and got the eggs from the fridge.

Marie said, "Daddy, is it done yet? My tummy is screaming at me. You don't want to hear my tummy screaming, do you, Daddy?"

I walked over to her and kissed her cheek. "Just a few more minutes, honey, give me a few more minutes." That was the wrong thing to say. I regret every syllable now; at the time I thought I was a genius.

John put his head in his hand. "Dear God, give him wisdom next time, please."

Marie asked Delores, "Was that his question last night?"

Suddenly I knew why John put his head in his hand.

Delores said, "Nope, he didn't ask for more time. He was spent before all the time on the clock ran out. He told me that was his goal, to beat the clock."

John asked, "How much do they pay you?"

Hey, right on cue, the Albright scramble was finished in record time.

Everyone took a smidgen, leaving me with multiple helpings. Delores said, "Enjoy, dear. I didn't have the heart to empty the bowl."

I went to the fridge, got the jar of mayonnaise, and made an Albright scramble sandwich with my toast. The girls wanted a bite. I knew where this was going, so I got up and made two more pieces of toast—then two more pieces of toast, then two more. I got back to the table to an empty bowl. "Great idea, Daddy," said Marie.

Delores leaned over and kissed my cheek. "You're such a lapdog. I love you."

The girls helped with the dishes, grabbed a two pack of cupcakes from the snack drawer, and headed upstairs to start packing boxes. Moms were only a couple of steps behind them. John and I had the list of packing materials required from the ladies. Marie said over her shoulder, "Don't take all day, do you hear me?"

"John, don't let him drive the cart," Delores added.

Marie said, "If you two aren't back in what we would consider an allowable time, we will unplug the eight-second clocks and pack them until Oregon."

John and I were in high gear. We found about 85 percent of the list and returned home in impressive time.

Or so we thought. The girls and their moms were sitting on the living room sofa, arms folded, looking at the clock on the wall. The girls were shaking their heads side to side, saying, "Tsk, tsk, tsk. Nice try, Daddies, but you're late."

We thought we were gone less than an hour, tops. Nope, we were gone for an hour and a half. John chose the shortest checkout line, but it was short for a reason: the cashier had to know everybody's business before waiting on the next in line. Two snails passed us while we waited, and we had a twenty-foot head start. If she hadn't used the scanner to ring up a customer order, we would have missed dinner, having waited to get in line till nine o'clock in the morning.

John said it was his fault. He thought that checker would be the fastest, until it was too late. "Fred said, 'Get behind this guy,' but he left and was drinking his second six-pack by the time she waited on us. She called for a price check on three of our items; she thought they were in the ad and didn't want to overcharge us."

"John told her about the eight-second clocks," I said. "She stopped and had to know all the details. I was loading the cart, so I stopped and got a hamburger across the street. When I got back, he was just finishing up the story."

Delores asked, "John, honey, who drove the cart?"

John told her I drove the cart.

Marie asked, "Did either of you stop and ask a clerk where the boxes and packing material were located in the store?"

Delores asked, "Who made up the cockamamie story?"

John said, "We stand on the Fifth Amendment."

Marie said, "You both should have drunk the Fifth, not stand on it."

Delores said, "You both take the boxes upstairs and then come and sit on the sofa until Marie and I figure out what your punishment will be."

Marie said, "I know what to do with them."

Delores said, "Forget it. We don't have a tree that tall or a new rope."

We did as we were told. The girls and moms filled the boxes, while John and I watched the clock on the wall. We were summoned to the bedroom to carry the boxes back down and stack them against the living room walls so the movers could load them quickly. They had all but three filled in a very short time.

John suggested we would return to the store to purchase more boxes.

Delores said, "Nope, you're both on restriction. Marie and I talked and determined that what Fred's office wives did to him was perfect punishment, so for the next week, you go to work, come home, cook us a meal, and sit on the sofa until bedtime. The eight-second clocks will be kept boxed until we find two real men who can last to the buzzer and even longer."

The girls were instructed, "Keep an eye on your daddies. We will return with more boxes and packing tape."

Delores and Marie got into their vehicle and returned within the hour with lots of boxes and rolls of packing tape and bubble wrap.

John and I brought the items from the vehicle into the house. Marie said, "Could you two start our lunch or early dinner?" We both agreed to do our best, and John told the sofa that we would return to keep it warm.

The grill was brushed clean, oiled, and fired up to cook the culinary delights to please our ladies. While I was preparing to grill our meat offerings, Marie, Delores, and the girls all started on the sides and salads. John was the runner between the kitchen and the grill.

John told me he was truly sorry about out outing earlier. We should be ashamed of our actions, and he was going to ask for forgiveness. I told him, "Make sure you stand outside striking distance."

As John entered the kitchen, the phone rang. It was Mama and Papa, calling to talk to the girls. Papa wanted to tell them he fed and gave loving to the lambs and calves. Mama said, "He spent over an hour in the pasture, walking around with them and following them. He told them you will be here in six days."

The girls asked him many questions. Papa answered as many as he could, telling them the calves and lambs all came and surrounded him, wanting attention.

Papa told Marie that they were each given vehicle, and her mom was learning how to drive. "Maggi and Silvia are taking turns riding with her on dirt roads, away from any outside vehicles or obstacles."

Marie was shocked. "Mama's driving? I had to walk to school every day. She never wanted to learn how to drive. Her mother, grandmother, and great grandmother never drove a vehicle. She would not cave in, just to be like those other floozies.

"How is she doing, driving?"

Papa said, "She hasn't crashed the car yet! I started driving again with the help of Murry and Carlos. They both have patience beyond my belief. Tomorrow we will go into town so I can adjust to driving in traffic."

Marie said, "Dad, you be really careful. Don't take any chances. We'll be there in six days. Enjoy being in your home and playing with the farm animals."

Papa said, "We sure miss being with all of you. I didn't realize how much you have filled our lives full of joy and happiness. Oregon is really special, and you'll fall in love with it immediately."

He went on, "I actually went to see the farm animals twice today; don't want them to feel alone."

Mama told Papa, "Let me talk to my daughter. Don't be a phone hog."

Mama said, "Marie, this is your mother. I'm a driver now. You'd better watch out. I'm getting really good at steering, giving it gas and braking. Silvia has aged a few years in a day, but she'll get used to my sudden stops."

She mentioned something about seat belts. "Maggi got out of the vehicle and kissed the ground, thanked God for returning her to my garage. I asked her if that was her family's tradition. She hugged me and said no; she just felt the urge to give thanks to our Savior."

Mama said, "I always had a gift of bringing out the best in people."

Marie said, "I'm getting excited to go for a ride with you, Mom. I'll say my prayers before getting in, while riding, and when we return. It will become quite spiritual."

Mama said, "Like going to church?"

Marie said, "I'm sure even more spiritual than church, Mom." Then she laughed; I never knew she was that religious.

They talked to the girls for about another fifteen minutes. Mama was telling them about her playhouse; she spent a good part of the day looking out the windows at the lake and pine trees and the birds flying around. "It's so pretty here."

The girls told Mama that they would be happy to spend time in her home as well as theirs, if she would spend time in their houses as well.

Mama said, "I will spend time in your houses, I promise."

The goodbyes were difficult to watch; tears were flowing freely.

When the call ended, the girls and moms carried out the sides, salads, plates, utensils, condiments, napkins, and candle with candleholder.

The girls stated that since John and I were on restriction, their moms would join them for dinner or late lunch, and told their speech.

John and I knew our invite would come once we were in Oregon. Maybe competition will be much tougher.

The dinner was better than expected. The girls all came down and gave me hugs, thanking me, and of course cleaned the grill of any extra meat offerings. They took them upstairs and shared them with their guests.

Dessert time, and since Mama was not here, we had chocolate cupcakes with the white squiggle on top or a snowball, your choice.

I told John, "Enjoy," and we clinked the cupcakes together—lightly of course.

On Sunday I started packing up the garage, while John packed up his garage for the movers on Monday. Our living room was full of boxes, and the garage was packed. Juan would be here in the morning, when we would load the items going to the shop and warehouse.

I finished just after lunch and headed over to help John. When I arrived, his garage door was closed, so I went into the courtyard found the whole gang sitting at the patio table. The girls were on their balcony. Sarah said, "Daddy is here!"

I said, "Good afternoon, ladies. How is packing coming along?"

Leslie said, "We're all finished; taking a lunch break."

Delores said, "You'd better be finished with your garage; John finished over an hour ago."

I told John, "Great job. I came over to help."

He asked, "Are you hungry?"

I told John, "I could eat. Got any extra?"

Marie said, "Haven't you learned anything? Your daughters have for months tried to show you how to convince someone you are grateful and proud of their efforts to please those who are your guests."

John told me he had one burnt hot dog. "The girls said it's got wrinkles, not how Daddy makes them." He placed the dog in a bun and handed it to me. "Sorry, but the condiments were cleared off the table so we could enjoy our cupcakes."

"Plain allows for the true flavor of the meat grindings to come to life in your palate," I said; "no surprises when it hits the tummy. No separating of condiments and dog; all flows in a natural rhythm."

23

The girls still had some packing to complete, so John and I became the box carriers and stackers, making sure all boxes were labeled. If the box was heavy, we labeled it so the movers would put the heavy boxes on the bottom row. Fragile boxes were on top. John and I separated them as we stacked them in the living room.

The girls were keeping their friends out of the boxes until the last few boxes, all labeled "our friends, be careful, don't make them cry," written on the box sides and tops.

The ladies were filling the wardrobe boxes with outfits that they would not wear this week. John and I were sent to purchase three large suitcases with specific instructions. "This is a chance for you two to get off the sofa, but that's all."

When John and I were in his vehicle, I told him, "They're softening; the punishment was too harsh."

John said, "No, they don't want to do all the work while we just sit on the sofa. The punishment is too light. Think about what's left to box up: the kitchen, the den, the walk-in closets, the girls' closets, the storage closets—most just-crammed-in-and-shut-the-door closets."

We returned with the three large suitcases. The girls had us remove the items from the shelf above the clothes rods and bring them to the bed so they could separate the keeps or donations. There were a couple responses of "Oh, so that's where those went."

Then I heard Marie say, "He won't need them anymore."

John asked, "What did you find that I won't need anymore?"

Marie, with a gleam in her eye, said, "Honey, those days are over."

I told John, "I think the sofa is calling us."

Marie said, "Not so fast, gentlemen. Help pack up these boxes, and then help the girls with the top of their closet. Then you can work on the hall storage closets. After that, get the ladder from the garage and a bucket with Spic and Span and scrub this closet, the girls' closet, and the hall closet. Your sofa break is over."

As we headed to the girls' room, I told John, "How did you know?"

John said, "As they walked up the stairs, they both turned and looked down at us just sitting on the sofa. I knew the sofa would not be our safe heaven any longer."

By the time we emptied out the girls' closets, in came Marie and Delores to help the girls load up boxes and go through stuff for donations. John and I returned to the master bedroom and started shuttling boxes to the living room.

When that task was done, we started emptying out the hall closets, sorting as we went. The girls and moms came to start packing up the boxes. We in turn went and hauled the boxes from the girls' room to the living room.

We were not a well-oiled machine, trained carriers of boxes. We finished just in time to shuttle the hallway boxes to the living room. Marie and Delores were emptying out some of the bathroom drawers of items like curlers that were not being used and cleaning chemicals, which went straight to the garage for the next movers to haul to Oregon.

More boxes were going to the garage now than the living room; these were the items not needed right away.

"They finished upstairs, now the kitchen," Marie told John. It's pizza time; we will be eating pizza or store-bought dinners until we get to Oregon. Pack up everything in the kitchen and put it in the living room. Paper plates and plasticware go on the countertop."

Marie was labeling the boxes as fast as the girls and Delores could load them. John was assembling the new boxes and taping the tops. I was the shuttler to the living room. Marie got on her cell phone and ordered two large pizzas with salad and a pair of two-liter bottles of sodas.

In a half hour we were dining college style.

Marie said, "You know store-bought pizzas taste even better than these. Not a salty, tomorrow lasagna, but pizza Supremes, bagged salads, bottle of Italian dressing, and breadsticks. Delores, you go shopping with me in the morning."

Then the warning: "Boys, your grilling duties will be suspended for at least a week. We will have new duties for you."

We had a couple more closets to be boxed, then it would be back over to Delores's house to do the same with the closets.

The girls told us, "The playhouse is all boxed up; could you make sure they are with the other items in the living room."

John and I cleared the boxes from the playhouse, stacked them in the living room, and prepared for the next round of "here, carry this." The day was moving by quite fast now, since we had been assigned special duties. In about an hour we were all at our home doing the same routine, boxing and carrying to the living room.

Delores and Marie decided to head to the grocery store for tonight's dinner, but while en route they came upon a Chinese restaurant and decided to surprise everyone. They returned with three boxes of food, chopsticks, fortune cookies, egg rolls, fried, steamed, and brown rice, soy sauce, sweet and sour sauce—so many choices, it was a very enjoyable meal.

The girls loved the variety of different dishes. Dinner took a little longer, as the girls gave up on chopsticks and resorted to forks. John and I were having a chopstick fight until both Marie and Delores yanked them from our hands. "Men, I swear," said Marie.

John and I each had the other one and started up again. This time Delores not only yanked them from our hands but told us where she would put the next chopstick if we did that again.

As we finished our Chinese meals, we discussed the next task to be completed. With a game plan in place, everyone was excited to get finished to avoid a mad scramble tomorrow morning.

We continued until the girls were getting ready for bed. Leslie and Kim planned to spend the night, changing from their original plan, since the moving company would be at our house first. They had their pajamas on, teeth brushed, and were under the covers when the phone rang. Mama and Papa were calling to say prayers with the girls.

Papa told them, "The lambs and calves now know me and came to me when I entered the pasture. They all love being petted and talked to with words of encouragement. I'm trying to be like you girls so they get used to lots of attention. Twice today I went out to them."

The girls told Papa that they, with moms and dads, had spent the day packing boxes for the movers. "Our babies are all boxed up, and some of them were crying, Papa. We were crying along with them. We hope they are all right. We can't wait to put them back on the shelves at their new home."

Papa assured them, "They will be fine, and they'll tell you about their journey to Oregon."

Mama joined in said, "My mixing bowls are all ready for your little hands to do their magic."

After prayers were said, foreheads kissed, and lots of "love you"s were exchanged, then came the tears as everyone said goodbye. Everyone had tears; no way to avoid them.

John and Marie left with kisses and hugs. "See you two in the morning for breakfast," I said. "Cold pizza and Chinese food are on the menu, and I'll scramble some eggs and make some toast and hash browns."

Delores and I headed upstairs. When we got to the bedroom, she said, "Don't you dare say a word tomorrow morning. Yes, silly boy."

24

Morning came awfully early. The girls pounced on our bed and scooted under the covers to get warm. "Daddy," said Sarah, "our hunger pains are strong this morning. That Chinese food doesn't last long."

"Up and at 'em. Girls, you keep Mommy warm while I make the coffee and hot chocolate. Then we'll start the rest of the breakfast."

It wasn't long before my pancake flipper, toaster operator, sausage turner, and blushing bride arrived. They all got into position and proceeded to complete the task at hand.

The doorbell rang, and my entire crew vanished to get hugs and kisses from Marie and John. Marie asked Delores if all went well.

With a glow in her eye, she stated, "Very well."

Marie asked, "Very well?"

Then Delores whispered into her ear. Marie said, "Same here."

I had to get ready to go to work. Breakfast was as good as ever. The girls would head to studio to film today's show. Delores and Marie were sticking around the houses to make sure the right items got loaded. John had to head to his office; he too is relocating some employees to Oregon, using Colorado as a branch office.

I'm, all ready. Kisses for the missus and the other missus, hugs and kisses for the little misses, and a high five to John, and I'm off restriction. In my truck and off to work, getting ready to greet my office wives. I got my Happy Meal for a later nibble; in case my snacks are forbidden. I arrived and made coffee just in time to hear, "How was your weekend?" from Charise. "I hope the coffee is better than ever; I need extra caffeine."

I poured her a cup and one for me, and off to my office we went.

She was dressed in high style office attire; *dazzling* would be putting it mildly.

I booted up the computer and asked, "Why do you need a jolt of caffeine?"

Charise said, "I heard on the news this morning that Mrs. Katy Wilkins hired a top-notch defense attorney, poised to take on Ms. Morgan. She takes no prisoners, hates to lose."

Ms. Morgan had Mrs. Katy Wilkins on the ropes, throwing punches and waiting for the knockout.

Charise said, "They are talking her up, Jasmarian Davidson, as if she'll be a savior of the incompetent news media.@

I said, "There isn't much she can defend. Ms. Morgan has covered all aspects of wiggle room."

I started checking my messages, and some of the repeaters were on steroids. One organization had sent ten messages only a few minutes apart. As we were enjoying our first cup, in walked wives two, three, and four. All looked poised and fresh, ready to take on any task at hand. Soon all four were seated, waiting for my explicit instructions, sipping my freshly brewed coffee.

Janice said, "We all talked on Friday about how sitting in your office is a major part of our day, and we'll miss it and be saddened when it comes to a halt."

I told them, "You can always put me on speakerphone, still sit in my office, and tell me what you tell me daily."

Charise said, "It won't be the same, but it'll have to do."

The four ladies finished their coffee and filed out. Charise refilled my cup and put one chocolate cupcake on my desk. "You finish the rest of those messages, and you'll earn another."

Doing the rest of the messages was a little daunting, but I endured the pain and earned my second cupcake. Phillip called me and sent me some photos of the playhouses with the tunnels connected, along with a few inside photos to show the girls. Phillip told me he got the okay to build a playhouse for Silvia. "She will send you the plot plan of her rear yard. Could you get that to me by this afternoon?"

I told him my astute staff would be excited to crank out another playhouse. "You thinking the same size as the girls' house?" It appeared that was what they had determined; too small would cramp her style.

After I hung up with Phillip, I talked to Janice. "Using the same dimensions as the girls' playhouse, Phillip will need a drawing once Silvia sends the plot plan of her backyard."

Janice said, "We just received the plot plan, with some photos for you to take a look at."

"Could you send me a copy so I can see the surroundings?"

Janice said, "With a click and a kiss, it's on your computer." She clicked it and blew it a kiss toward my computer.

I looked at the data to determine the best location for the playhouse. Her property was tree-lined, and I wanted to do a little damage to the trees and not give squirrels access to the playhouse. I called Silvia. "You have to measure the distance from the trunks of the trees to your home. Could you do that as soon as possible?" She told me Murray was close to her house; she would call him to provide the information.

I also asked her to give her colors to Phillip for the trim and siding. "Or he could match your home."

Silvia said, "Phillip just pulled in. I'll talk to him. Talk to you later; bye."

*

It was nearing the eight o'clock hour. Natalie Morgan was heading down the hallway to the courtroom. She knew she had to face another attorney, highly skilled at defending her clients. She entered the courtroom, greeted Ms. Davidson, and returned to her desk, waiting for the call to order. She did a quick check to see if all the evidence bags ordered were on her table.

The bailiff called the court to order. "All rise for the Honorable Judge Adamson presiding."

Judge Adamson stated, "Please be seated. Welcome, Ms. Davidson. Have you had time to review the case documents?"

Ms. Davidson stated, "I have, Your Honor."

Judge Adamson asked, "Are you ready to continue?"

Ms. Davidson stated, "I am, Your Honor."

The judge turned to the prosecutor. "Good morning, Ms. Morgan. You may call your first witness."

Ms. Morgan replied that her first witness had a scheduling problem. "He will be my second witness, and the schedule second witness will testify first."

Judge Adamson asked, "Ms. Davidson, would that be acceptable to the defense?"

Ms. Davidson conferred with Mrs. Wilkins and then responded that switching the two witnesses would be acceptable.

Judge Adamson stated, "Proceed, Ms. Morgan."

Ms. Morgan called Fredrick Fredrickson to the stand. As the witness approached the stand, he avoided eye contact with Mrs. Wilkins, turning his head toward the bench as he walked past the defense table.

The bailiff swore in Mr. Fredrickson and told him to be seated.

Ms. Morgan asked, "Mr. Fredrickson, could you tell the court your occupation and how long you have held your current position?"

Mr. Fredrickson answered, "I'm the owner of Willow Tree Country Club for the past twenty-three years."

Ms. Morgan asked, "Mr. Fredrickson, how did you become the owner of the Willow Tree Country Club?"

Mr. Fredrickson replied, "Our family owned the property that the country club occupies. My father was the original owner until he passed away. When he was in ill health, I was asked to take over as the president, and upon his passing I became the owner."

Ms. Morgan asked, "Do you know the defendant, Mrs. Wilkins?"

Mr. Fredrickson stated, "I do know Mrs. Wilkins. She and her family were among our original members."

Ms. Morgan asked, "You were arrested along with Mrs. Wilkins and seven others at the cabin owned by Jonathan Montgomery. Were you all there for hunting or a relaxing getaway?"

Mr. Fredrickson was about to answer when Ms. Davidson rose and asked for a sidebar. Ms. Morgan met her at the bench.

Ms. Davidson stated, "Just what does that question have to do with the charges against Mrs. Wilkins?"

Ms. Morgan answered, "You have eight prominent people at a mountain cabin in the middle of the week. All of them just happened to be notified by the chief of police to get out of town and hide until the heat is off."

Ms. Davidson stated, "That puts my client in a very bad situation. If she just happened to be at the cabin and they all arrived, she now becomes a coconspirator, being innocent."

Judge Adamson said, "Ms. Morgan, rephrase the question. Ms. Davidson, the court needs to know why they were together in the middle of the week."

Judge Adamson excused the attorneys and stated, "Objection sustained. Ms. Morgan, please rephrase the question or have it stricken from the record."

Ms. Morgan stated, "On August 15, 2019, you were arrested at the Montgomery cabin with eight other people. Why?"

Mr. Fredrickson replied, "On charges of murder."

Ms. Morgan asked, "Why were you all together at the same location?"

Mr. Fredrickson stated, "We were notified that local authorities had warrants for our arrests."

Ms. Morgan asked, "Who notified you of the warrants?"

Mr. Fredrickson answered, "Police Chief O'Brian."

Ms. Morgan stated, "Police Chief O'Brian had been in FBI custody since August 10, 2019. Are you certain it was the chief?"

Mr. Fredrickson stated, "Yes. I have the email, and my attorney has the copy."

Ms. Morgan stated, "Who determined that the cabin was the best location in which to hide?"

Mr. Fredrickson stated, "We were all in a panic. With arrest warrants out against us and the police chief in custody, we decided that the cabin was far enough away to give us time to figure a better plan."

Ms. Morgan stated, "Were you aware that two women were kidnapped and taken to that exact cabin and had been held hostage?"

Ms. Davidson objected, "The question has no bearing on this case."

Ms. Morgan, "Your Honor, I would like the court reporter to go back to last Thursday's testimony with Doctor Jeffrey Thrumberg and read the answer to the question regarding the liver." The court reporter read back the testimony aloud.

Ms. Morgan stated, "The kidnapping is already linked to this trial. The kidnapped women were freed from captivity aborting the liver transplant."

Judge Adamson stated, "The connection has been established. Mr. Fredrickson, please answer the question."

Mr. Fredrickson stated that he read about it in the newspaper.

Ms. Morgan asked, "Mr. Fredrickson, remember you are under oath. This isn't a country club social gathering. Were you aware that the cabin was used to hide the kidnapped ladies?"

Mr. Fredrickson replied, "Yes."

Ms. Morgan stated, "We have been notified by the governor's office that no plea bargains are on the table. Are you aware of that?"

Again Mr. Fredrickson replied, "Yes."

Ms. Morgan asked, "What is your involvement with Mrs. Wilkins?"

Mr. Fredrickson replied, "She is a longtime member of our country club."

Ms. Morgan went to her desk and picked up an envelope. She brought it to the stand and showed it to Mr. Fredrickson and the jury panel. "This envelope shows bank deposits of several hundred, of thousands of dollars. Each deposit is dated, and those dates correspond to the dates when the death certificates of all twenty-eight murder victims were signed by you, Mr. Fredrickson, as a witness. She was more than a longtime country club member. One other thing, Mr. Fredrickson, those funds never were deposited into the country club's account.

"Let me ask again: what is your involvement with Mrs. Wilkins?"

Mr. Fredrickson replied, "I was in financial trouble, and Mrs. Wilkins was kind enough to help me and my family."

Ms. Morgan asked, "So you were in financial difficulties twenty-eight times, on the exact dates when you signed a death certificate for someone named on a missing person's report?"

Mr. Fredrickson stated, "I want to claim my Fifth Amendment rights."

Ms. Morgan stated, "I have no further questions for this witness at this time but do reserve the right to call him at a later date. Your witness, Ms. Davidson."

Ms. Davidson conferred with Mrs. Wilkins and then stated, "We have no questions for this witness, Your Honor."

Ms. Morgan asked for a brief recess since her witness has a half hour before he is scheduled to testify.

Judge Adamson stated, "The court will recess for one hour. Jurors, you know your guidelines." The bailiff told the court to rise, and Judge Adamson left the courtroom.

Natalie headed to her office. As she arrived, Kelli had a cup of coffee ready for her, and David was a couple of steps behind her.

Ms. Morgan sat down, and David said, "Wow, every one of the others arrested said they do not want to testify to get a plea bargain."

Kelli came into Ms. Morgan's office and said, "Judge Adamson has summoned you to his chambers."

Ms. Morgan entered the judge's chambers, where she was greeted by Mrs. Wilkins and Ms. Davidson. Judge Adamson said, "Mrs. Wilkins is changing her plea from not guilty to not guilty by reason of insanity. The trial will be put on hold until we get psychological reports confirming her as criminally insane."

Ms. Morgan said, "This is a sudden change. What is the time frame necessary to conclude the findings?"

Judge Adamson said, "Ms. Davidson, would you provide that information to Ms. Morgan? She has other cases on her docket."

Ms. Davidson stated that her firm used a certain clinical psychologist. "I will contact you either later today or tomorrow morning."

Natalie left the Judge's chambers and returned to her office, where Kelli brought her a fresh cup of coffee. Dr. Weinberg, her next witness, was in the lobby, as the receptionist informed her by phone. Natalie told her to send him to her office.

Kelli brought another cup of coffee for the witness.

Ms. Morgan greeted her next witness and had him sit down. She then told him that the case had just been put on hold. "Mrs. Wilkins is changing her plea to not guilty by reason of insanity.

The witness just laughed. "She will have to do one amazing performance to pull that one off. I'll buy her an Oscar and present it to her and the psychologist as best actress and best supporting actor or actress. That woman is no more insane than I am."

Natalie said, "Well, the coffee is wonderful."

Dr. Weinberg stated, "I was hoping to be the final nail in the coffin. Well, I guess there still is a chance if they can't find her insane."

They both finished up their coffee, and Dr. Weinberg said, "Let me know the outcome of this insane notion they just sprang on you." They shook hands, he departed, and Natalie started checking her docket.

David returned. "So what do you think?"

Natalie said, "I'm numb right now. I was feeling my oats in the courtroom and didn't expect Mr. Fredrickson to stand on the Fifth. That took me by surprise. I guess the answer to my question would incriminate him so badly that he could not lie his way out of a conviction."

David asked, "So what's next?"

Natalie said, "The old 'wait and see' now comes into play."

David asked, "Will this delay cause problems down the road for your court schedules?"

Natalie answered, "It just depends on how long they will require. If it's more than a month, there will be a rescheduling issue with my calendar."

25

Relocating to Oregon

There is a break in the trial of Mrs. Katy Wilkins, and our moving company arrived right on time. They loaded the furniture from our house first with all the well-stacked boxes and took our velvet paintings off the walls. The truck was loaded in about two hours, and they were very happy to see we had taken the extra effort to put the boxes close to the front door. They used a hand truck to load them into the trailer, saving even more time.

They arrived at Marie and John's about three hours earlier than expected. They did the same procedure to load the Albrights' belongings. All the unnecessary furniture was loaded; the beds would remain with the house. The kitchen table and chairs along with a sofa and end tables would also stay behind. Stuart told Marie and Delores, "If you're not happy with the furnishings you own, leave them for the next renters, or those people will find a happy home for the items."

Stuart was making this move far too easy for the ladies. They couldn't wait to go shopping for furniture, clothes, and kitchen gadgets. The credit cards are being oiled up for easier sliding in the machines. Stuart also told them not to worry about cleaning up the houses. He had scheduled a home detail company to completely clean up the houses beyond model site specifications.

Silvia had two separate crews scheduled to detail the homes—a very reliable company whose employees were excellent and very thorough. "They detailed the new houses that Marie and Delores will move into," she told me.

Mama was beyond words to describe how her home looked. She told Marie, "Please, you are nowhere near as thorough as this company."

Marie and John's items were loaded and on their way to Oregon, to arrive by Thursday or late Wednesday. The designers were poised and ready. With Mama already in Oregon, she would be a great help on how things should be set up.

Just before our lunch break, Silvia sent me an email giving me the data required. She and Phillip went to her home and figured where the best location for the playhouse would be. I saw the approximate location Phillip suggested. It wasn't bad, but he forgot about the tree branches. I didn't want to remove large branches unless we had no other choice.

I moved the playhouse over about eight feet, which worked to save the large branch. It also gave her more privacy, just in case she had a neighbor with a camera with telephoto lens or something else to improve their vision.

She did have that capability to attract onlookers. "Eye candy" was her specialty.

I sent the data back to Janice with a kiss from my computer. She and Melanie had nearly everything ready for the exact location of the playhouse. I asked Janice to print me the location of the playhouse so I could draw in the planters and other amenities for the ambience I had promised Sylvia months ago.

I want to surprise her when I arrive in Oregon, and I will give her my personal touch, to make sure her yard stands up in comparison to our homes. I know, I'm such a great guy, always thinking about others' well-being, Nobel peace prize knocking at my door. I may have to push away some other notable people to squeeze in the nomination.

Janice brought in a clean base sheet for me to create my masterpiece of ambience for Silvia.

Property lines are in place, tree line drawn in to scale of the home's footprint including the drive and walkways. She even has the playhouse in place. I know from Silvia's last masterpiece she wants areas to sunbathe, so I will increase the south side of the playhouse with a patio deck large enough for a couple of lounge chairs and a table.

In her playhouse will be the playhouse bar and fountain. The French doors will be facing the southern deck; the bar is on the northern wall. You will enter the house from the western side backward from the girls' homes. This is to allow the optimum sunbathing house, which I know my beloved and Marie will frequent on sunny days.

I will incorporate Silvia's bar adjacent to her kitchen with a pass-through window. The bar will have a patio cover overhead to shelter the bar and customers drinking at the bar top. Enough room for at least six people at the bar. We need electrical, water, and a drain for the sink into the main sewer line. The drawing shows the sewer cleanout very close to the bar location.

"Merrily I draw the lines, draw the lines, draw the lines; merrily I draw the lines all through the day." I totally forgot about the time. Charise and the girls are back from lunch with a pleasant surprise, my Goose under Glass.

Charise said, "You're back. When we left, you were in a zone, and we knew better than to up your anchor and cause you a severe heart attack. We brought you some lunch, with a Post-it note kissed by your favorite waitress. We stuck it to a 7 Up can, not quite the same but extremely close to the real goose juice. Oh, by the way, the goose is without feathers; your daughters plucked your goose, your wives cut down the amount of French fries, and we ate your garlic toasted bread roll. It smelled so good, we couldn't help ourselves."

I opened the Styrofoam box and found a few bites from the bird were missing as well.

Charise said, "You can't have a garlic roll unless you supplement it with some chicken cordon bleu, in rule number thirty-five, paragraph three, section four.

"Since all three of us had some garlic roll, we of course had to follow the rule book, and that is why you have a couple small holes in the goose."

"I am out of my zone, correct?"

Charise said, "Yes, you are back on planet Earth as we speak."

"Great. Since reality has returned, I can eat the remaining pieces of my lunch. How much do I owe for partial lunch?"

Charise said, "Do you think we bought you a lunch?"

"Well, let me think. Rewind what you said when you entered my office. Was it *bought* or *brought*? Big difference, isn't there?"

Charise said, "I'll refresh your memory. *Brought*, not *bought*, so to answer your question, it's you owe us nothing. Just enjoy your 'free bird' before the vultures arrive. Oops, too late. Hurry, eat quick; they're here."

"Daddy, we're home," shouted Sarah. The four girls and moms were now standing in my office; bird in the box was fair game. Fries were attacked first.

Delores said, "What, no ketchup?" Then she washed down the fries with my goose juice. Marie cut a good chunk from the bird and shared it with the girls on a paper plate fetched by Charise with some plasticware. To my utter shock, the bird flew the coop, the fries vanished like a drop of water hitting the sun, and goose juice now had lipstick on the lid as well. I did what I could to cause a burp, but nope, not even a hiccup; it was all gone except the container.

"Well, it was nice to share my lunch with all of you. Give the chef my regards."

Delores gave a little burp and wiped her lips with my napkin. "Do you have anything else that you can share with your wives and daughters?"

I opened my desk drawer, revealing a pair of two-packs of chocolate cupcakes with white squiggles on top. The girls grabbed them. "Dibbies on the cupcakes," said Leslie.

The girls were sitting on my sofa, and the cakes were toast. "They get that from their moms," I noted.

Janice brought me a cup of coffee with a warm hug. "Here, Hubby. You will need some energy trying to keeping us all satisfied."

I was told they just stopped in to say hello and build up my spirits—"and keeping me slim and fit," said Delores.

She told Janice, " 'Keep us all satisfied'—not by a long shot will that ever occur."

Marie said, "One a day, maybe. All? I agree: nope."

The ladies all went to their office for their last visit for a while. They uncorked the three bottles of champagne in the fridge. Then, with Dixie cups in hand, they toasted the ladies' club, did some type of chant, and chugged the champagne until all the bottles were empty. Then they had a belching contest; I thought only guys did that.

They do one thing that guys don't do, that's pat each other's behinds; not a guy thing. With three bottles of champagne gone, and six ladies feeling less pain than when they arrived from lunch, it was time for the office to say good night.

I was of course the last to leave the yard and office. I had the duty of locking up the joint. On the way home, yep, I stopped for two small hamburgers and a small diet soda at McDonald's and ate them before I entered the cul-de-sac of Marie and John's. Thank goodness for eating ahead of time, because I was met by Delores as I parked.

She hopped in the truck and said, "Take me for a ride to the grocery store. I'm driving the shopping cart. The girls have hunger pains."

We walked up and down aisles, grabbing groceries for breakfast, lunch, and dinners for three days. It was nonstop "Grab that—no, not that one, the other one. No, you grabbed the same thing." "No sir, I grabbed the one next to it."

Delores grabbed my shirt with two hands and got inches from my face. "There are two rows of the same item. Pay attention, or you will get hurt real bad. Hear me?"

Let's try it again: the other one. Now the dilemma, the product on the right or on the left? I'm going to get kneed for sure.

Delores asked, "Now what? The store, does have a closing time, and the girls are getting hunger pains. It's the one on the left."

Now I forgot. *Which is the one that got me in trouble?* She pushed me aside, got the one she wanted, and showed me the product inches from my face. "This one, honey, the one on the left. Do you know your left from your right? Am I going too fast for your itty-bitty brain?

"Come on, follow me to the next product. I'm going to buy a leash, the kind I saw a lady using on her child. I'm hoping they carry a choke collar; that would be ideal."

Another aisle bites the dust, and another one, then another one, and another one bites the dust. Delores said, "Hello, is anybody home? It does not matter one bit if you're pushing the cart or free to roam—you zone. How do you get anything accomplished? Lord, help me, please!"

At the check stand, finally, Delores was greeted by the cashier. They both turned to look, and Delores told me, "Honey, the lady needs to ring up the groceries. Put the items on the conveyer belt before I put you through the window." She told the cashier, "He just needs a little encouragement at times."

I put one item at a time on the belt and waited until the cashier picked it up before I put another on the belt. The gentleman behind me said, "Buddy, hurry it up before I help your wife put you through the window."

I explained I didn't want to have the cashier pinch her fingers with an item colliding with another item. Then the gentleman suggested, "Why don't you race two items to the cashier, and we both can cheer on our favorite item? See how easy that was? Now empty the damn cart while you can still breathe."

As I emptied the cart, the man behind me was applauding my efforts, which got a couple of other customers behind him to applaud. Then a couple of clerks walked by, and they were applauding; I was a celebrity. We loaded the groceries into the truck and headed home.

Delores said, "You were very close to getting your clock cleaned. I had my can of mace in my hand waiting for your new friend to grab you, to cause you bodily harm."

We arrived at Marie and John's in the nick of time. The girls were having hunger pains—"Real bad, Daddy." John and I were the invited guests to dine with the girls. Since our restriction was lifted, they felt it was our turn.

Delores was telling Marie about our shopping trip.

Marie said, "Keep walking. If he lags behind, find a clerk to announce on the loudspeaker that you have a lost husband."

John was preparing his grill. The girls came out of their house to help their moms make the side dishes and salads. They had on their hard shoes for clogging the tunnel; they will surely miss that tunnel.

I brought out the meat offering to John. He looked at the platter, looked at me, and said, "Are we all dieting?"

I told him, "We have fewer mouths to feed, and half of our eaters have small tummies."

John told me, "They out-eat us at every meal."

I said, "They run from place to place; we waddle from place to place. They burn calories; -we, not so much."

As John was grilling the meat, the girls were bringing the sides and salads to the table, along with the candleholder, candle, and matches. They gave John and me hugs along with our cans of goose juice.

Leslie said, "Daddy, we only have two more meals after this one at our home. Our new home will be just as nice—right, Daddy?"

John, holding her tight in his arms, told her, "Even better. You will have what you have here with your sisters, Mama and Papa, Silvia and Murray, Jessica and Mickey, Stuart and Doreen all visiting us every day. You'll be five minutes from your home. I know it seems like you're giving up a lot, but I've been assured that our new home is far better."

Leslie looked up at him. "Mommy said she won't have her staircase to perform on anymore?"

I told Leslie, "The studio being built has three staircases modeled after the one in your home. Stan is building them right now."

Leslie asked, "Does my mommy know?"

"It's our secret—her surprise from me, Stan, and Mr. Beans. Promise not to tell?"

"I promise. I feel much better now. Thank you, Daddy." She hugged me, and tears of joy were flowing down her cheeks.

I told John, "Find that on social media or on any television program."

John said, "That kind of emotion is not allowed to be shown. You have to be a mold of what they believe the populace wants. Hurting others sells; rape sells; one actor and actress breaking up and then the months of their personal issues spread across the screen so the viewers get riled up over make-believe."

I told him, "There are no more true friends, only imaginary friends. Those are the ones you have to impress, or else you're left out. We used to collect and trade baseball cards; they trade personal data.

"We were always told to go play outside, and be home before the streetlights come on. Today you rarely see kids playing outside unless it's a soccer match. Different times and different teaching of our young; so sad."

John said, "We were taught it's okay to fail as long as you try."

"Do you think the classrooms have chalk boards anymore?"

John said, "I'm sure the dangers of chalk dust have stopped its use."

I told him, "I used to clean the erasers for the teacher after class. She always thanked me and a couple of times gave me a hug."

John said, "I think they can get fired or put on leave if they hug a student."

The girls and moms were coming to dinner. Each one picked up a plate from the patio table and formed a line. John was putting the burnt offering on their plates.

The girls reminded us we were eating with them; the ladies were not happy but figured it would be the last time we got preferential treatment. John and I of course gloated as we ascended the staircase to the girls' house. Marie threw an ice cube at us. "Begone, you peasants," she shouted.

Sarah asked, "Are our moms mad? We only want to be fair. They were our guests last night. Did we do wrong, Daddy?"

I told her, "No, honey. We caused them to be upset. We were rubbing it in, like we are more important to you than they are. It was wrong for us to do that, and we will apologize to them after dinner. You girls treat everyone equally. We are so proud of all of you!" I gave Sarah and the rest of the girls huge Daddy hugs.

The side dishes the girls prepared were again better than the meat offering, but John had advanced his cooking talents beyond beginner and even beyond assistant cook. He would earn his chef's hat on his birthday.

The girls really enjoyed eating our grilling, much better than meat grilled on the stove in oils, they say. They have learned from helping with breakfast that cooking their eggs in some bacon fat gave a far better flavor than cooking them in oils.

We had a great conversation with the girls. They loved to express themselves over burnt offerings. They assured John he is a master at burning the hotdogs just right.

We finished our meals, and they were ready for dessert—store-bought pie, a little letdown from actual homemade pie from Grandma; in fact, no comparison.

We had pumpkin pie with whipped cream piled high to enhance the flavor, with chocolate shavings on top and the girls' favorite maraschino cherry.

Marie took a photo with her phone and sent it to her mom: *See what you caused? Store-bought, we're lowered to store-bought. Three more days of this, seventy-two hours, two more store-bought desserts. I hope the girls don't have nightmares.*

Mama texted back: *Trials and tribulations we all must endure, my dear. I have had two grilled meals from your father, so we're not even yet, my love. He wants to practice, so you get to enjoy your first meal in Oregon from his grill. Come hungry, so you can have my portion. I'll call you after my antacid kicks in, I hope soon.*

Marie told us what Mama had sent her, and we all laughed. "Poor dear," said Delores.

Marie said, "Hey, my dad's cooking is better than what we have been trying to digest in the past few months."

I told John, "You know they are sticking a knife into our meat offerings."

John said, "It was a great idea making three barbecue islands; every third day sure beats every other day."

The girls will dictate who is the guest chef for each night, along who dines with them and which playhouse will be their dining room.

We all ate our store-bought pumpkin pie with store-bought whipped cream. It was fairly good, though not Mama's by any stretch, and the girls wanted a cupcake to lessen the pain the pumpkin pie caused.

The girls already planned to spend the night with Leslie and Kim, so we all said prayers, tucked them in, and kissed their foreheads. "Love you"s exchanged and night lights on, the checklist was complete.

Delores and I headed home for an evening of rest and relaxation, but since we didn't have to keep our close encounter quiet, the thrill was gone. "Not tonight, dear; maybe tomorrow. That pumpkin pie did me in."

Oh sure, blame it on store-bought treats. That must be number twenty-eight on the excuse list.

The night passed faster than normal. Delores texted Marie, *Here or there?*

Marie texted back, *Your choice?*

Delores texted, *Here. I don't feel like getting dressed in street clothes this early in the morning.*

As she finished texting, the doorbell rang. Delores said, "Who could that be?" I scurried down the stairs to find the Albrights and Stockdale's at the door. I opened the door and was hugged by all the girls and Marie, and I shook John's hand.

Delores said, "Did you get my last text?"

Marie said, "We all were standing on your porch."

The girls were still in their pajamas along with Marie; John came in breakfast attire.

Off to the kitchen, where everyone had their job down pat, the right pans, the right utensils, everything according to the breakfast book. Stir, stir, flip, flip, turn, turn, pour, pour—all like clockwork, better than a five-star kitchen.

The girls were whistling, "Whistle while You Work," all-in four-part harmony. I used the wooden spoon to play the skillet drum. John was tapping his spoon on his coffee cup until Marie's hand snatched it from him. "Too early, honey, and you were off beat."

Delores thanked Marie. "He was making me dizzy. It was worse than singing off key."

John said, "I haven't had my coffee yet. Takes longer to get into rhythm."

Marie said, "Honey, we only have one pot of coffee. We don't have a tanker truck full."

The girls felt sorry for John, and they all went over and gave him a breakfast hug. "We love you, Daddy. Mommy is being mean."

"Daddy, should we make her stand in the corner?" asked Leslie.

John said, "No, make her sit on my lap."

Marie said, "Okay, I accept the punishment." She plopped down on his lap. "I hope I didn't hurt you."

In a high-pitched voice John said, "It's okay; it will heal," and gave a little cough.

Breakfast was cooked and getting served. Again there wasn't quite enough of the Albright scramble, so I had a nice slice of toast to dunk into my coffee. I learned years ago it's better to feed the ladies; your life is much more enjoyable.

*

We all sat around waiting for the light show. We never get enough of watching the lights illuminate the landscape. We like to go over to the waterfall, sit down, and listen to the water falling and the soft music playing. I was hoping we could duplicate just that one final *ahh*, to end a perfect day.

The girls joined us this evening, enjoying a conversation with moms and dads, even though light and frivolous. *Building memories is one memory at a time for your book of life.*

Marie said, "I'll hate shutting off the waterfall when we leave. It gives the backyard so much life. I'll call Stuart in the morning and see what he thinks about letting it run."

I told Marie, "It would do the fountain an injustice to turn it off. It's designed to be the heart of the landscape; it has to keep pumping or the ambience will fade away."

Delores said, "That was beautiful. Another word, and I would have started to cry."

Marie's phone rang, and it was Mama. "Her antacid has kicked in, and she feels like a million bucks" Marie told us and then turned on her speaker.

She told Mama we were all at the waterfall. "Lights are on, music is playing softly in the background—it's so peaceful. How is Papa?"

Mama said, "He now goes to the lambs and calves three times per day and spends at least a half hour with them. They see him coming and stand by the gate. *Baa-baa-baa, moo-moo-moo* I hear from my balcony. I love my house; I have never had so much happiness. What a wonderful gift to give an old lady."

Delores said, "Will you have time to be Grandma again?"

Mama said, "I'll squeeze in some time for all of you, or we all could have a cup of tea in my house every day."

Marie asked, "Do you have curtains and a throw rug?"

Mama said, "It was all decorated for me. I can just walk in, sit down, and listen to soft music, watch the birds and butterflies, read a good book, or do some crafts."

She said, "Silvia came by, and we went to the fabric store. I picked up some patterns that the girls can make. I can't wait; three more days! This is killing me and Papa."

Marie said, "We know how you feel. Today seemed like two days in time."

Mama said, "On the news a while ago they mentioned that the trial is being delayed. What happened?"

Marie said, "We heard from the attorney that she wants to plead not guilty by reason of insanity, so they have to evaluate her."

Mama said, "Insane? She thinks she's *insane*? Not insane, but a pathological liar, a manipulator, godless, hateful, greedy, yeah. Insane? No way."

Marie said, "She has money to pay the psychologist to say anything."

Mama said, "Papa and I have watched some of the case. That Ms. Morgan, the prosecutor, is a smart cookie. She reminds us of you, when you were in the courtroom."

Papa said, "She had one more nail to put into that woman's coffin; she's left no wiggle room for the defense. It's amazing to watch."

Marie said, "Insanity was her only out, from what I saw of the trial."

Papa said, "Fredrickson's testimony was laughable. He left his lawyer in a hopeless position. I don't think he'll be able to plead not guilty by reason of insanity; stupidity maybe."

Mama said, "They should get life or death, just from the arrogance they are displaying."

The girls wanted to hear about their day, so Marie invited them closer so all could talk and hear.

Sarah questioned Papa about the lambs and calves. "Are they eating okay and drinking plenty of water? Is it getting cold at nights? Do they need blankets or a heater? Do they respond to their names?"

Papa said, "I believe they are extremely happy. Tomorrow morning I'll asked Murray if they need blankets or a heater. They all lie down together, so I think they keep each other warm. I'll talk to them and they respond, but I haven't called them one by one to see if they respond to a name. They all want feed more than cuddles; I'm saving the cuddles for you girls."

Mama said, "We will call you back at eight o'clock our time to say your prayers. Love you; talk to you soon." And the call was over.

We all got up and went into the house to get some hot chocolate and coffee—with a breakfast roll, just to keep that hunger pain from getting out of control.

It was getting to be that time, and the girls all got their pajamas on. They would stay with John and Marie, and they will be at our house tomorrow.

The phone rang, and Mama and Papa were ready to say prayers with the girls. They were all tucked, in teddy bears in their arms, and the prayers began. Afterward the girls got their foreheads kissed, and with night lights on, they were ready for needed sleep. "We'll be at our house at the same time tomorrow morning," said Sarah. "Set your alarm so we don't get cold standing on the porch."

We were off to the house. "Tonight's the night"—Delores confirmed she would be okay—"but no more until Oregon."

26

Early the next morning I saw the headlights of Marie's vehicle pulling into our driveway. I gathered two throws off our sofa, opened the door at the exact time and surrounded the girls with the throws. They all were shaking. "It's so cold outside. Thank you, Daddy," said Leslie.

Marie asked, "Where is my throw?" I wrapped my arms around her and gave her a hug. "Nice try, but I'm cold all over," she said.

"Wait a second." I found a bath towel and wrapped it around her shoulders.

Delores came downstairs with the blanket from our bed and wrapped it around Marie. "Here, sister. This one is warm."

Then she gave me a look. "Were you born in a barn? Close the front door. Men. No common sense, even in their pinkie finger."

I took my helpers to the kitchen, still wrapped up in the throws, still shivering. I made some hot chocolate and coffee to get the blood flowing again. They kept the throws wrapped around them while they sipped the hot chocolate, I got the pots and pans ready for the breakfast feast to begin.

Delores and Marie came into the kitchen with our blanket wrapped around both of them. I poured them each a cup of coffee, and they both were shivering as they thanked me for causing them to be cold.

I thought a nice pat on top of the head and a kiss on the cheek would make them feel better. Nope, that got me an elbow in the stomach.

The girls were starting to warm up and shed their throws. They earned lots of points from their moms when they put their warm throws around their moms.

They also gave them a kiss on the cheeks and didn't get an elbow. They got an "I love you" and a hug.

Everyone manned their battle stations, ready to fight the hunger pain growing inside of them, wooden spoons at port-arms, pancake turner poised to flip the first pancake, sausage turner at the ready. Soon the toaster was toasting, and we were on schedule to rid the girls of hunger pains.

Marie got out from under the blanket and throws, grabbed the coffee pot, and refilled hers and Delores's—but not mine. Then she got back under the throws and blanket and shook. *The house is seventy-five degrees, and the girls are starting to perspire, but moms are shaking; go figure.* Sympathy was written all over that move.

By the time the girls were serving the breakfast, the ladies had shed their blanket and throws to get into serious eating. Knife and fork were gripped for digging into the prepared meal placed in front of them. We even made hash browns today as a special treat.

Breakfast was delicious, very filling. I headed up to get ready for work, while the ladies and girls cleaned up the kitchen. When I was ready to meet the world, the girls were about ready for the limousine ride. Marie and Delores were also ready for their limousine ride; they would be teaching their class two more days, then their assistant Eileen and Denise, the waitress from their favorite eatery, would take over the class.

Marie and Delores had taught their substitutes very well. They were ready to take over as instructors for all classes afterwards. They were booked solid for six months with a waiting list.

With hugs and kisses, all of us with our warning devices, I got into my truck to face the office wives. Of course, I will stop for my morning snack at McDonald's, just in case my office snacks are held hostage.

I arrived at the office and put on a fresh pot of coffee. My day began when I heard "Good morning, Boss Man" in Charise's voice.

She said, "You know the girls will be disappointed when the coffee isn't finished when they walk in. You have spoiled them beyond belief."

"I do what I can to keep you girls on your toes, in tip-top shape."

Charise said, "Well, they will just have to go through withdrawals. I'm not coming in ten minutes earlier to please them."

"We could purchase a timer," I said. "You set up the pot when you leave the office, and as you and they walk into the office, your coffee is ready."

Charise said, "A little whine from prim and proper girls will be enjoyable."

We headed to my office with our coffees in hand. We talked about what they needed to complete today. Charise would have to hire a sales department. Janice could be the salesperson, and we could move Melanie into Janice's desk, and hire an assistant for Melanie.

Charise said, "Didn't we do that with Denise? She went to sales; then Marjorie grabbed her for Texas, left me with two rookies and no one pounding doors. You have three appointments this morning. Will they become new work?"

"I hope so. Remember, we have three restaurants on the boards, and they all are coming very close to starting. You will also have the Dunley residence; the plans are nearing completion. Stuart and I will talk on Saturday. Do you want me to take Janice with me this morning?"

Charise said, "If you want to make her the salesperson, this would be a great opportunity for her to learn your magic." She looked at her calendar and said, "You have five appointments tomorrow. We girls will not be here the entire day. You have to remain silent. It's a surprise for Marie and Delores."

"I'm good at being quiet. You can count on me not to spill the beans. And thank you for adding another layer of can't-dos to my list."

Janice, Melanie, and Marsha all came into my office with cups of coffee in hand.

I welcomed them all to my humble abode and sprang the news on Janice that she would be escorting me today.

Janice said, "You want me to be an escort?"

"Not that type of escort. You will get to help measure the properties and take some notes from the customers so you can create a plan for them. Then you reschedule an appointment in two weeks and give the presentation of the final plan drawn."

"So you want me to become the salesperson?" asked Janice.

"I'm offering you that position if you are willing to accept the additional responsibility."

"What about the position I now have?"

"Well, my precious office wife, you will have the honor of training Melanie to assume your position and also train her assistant. Are you up for the challenge?"

"What if I mess up?"

Charise said, "Honey, we all mess up. We just have to fix up the mess. There's nothing you could do that we as a team can't fix."

I told her, "You give me 100 percent, as you have done so far, and I'll stand behind you. Just take your time; double-check every measurement, make sure to write down the customer's likes and dislikes, and send me your data. We will guide you through each project until you feel comfortable. Make sure Juan sees what you propose, to make sure they can reproduce your vision. You'll do wonderful!"

I also told her, "Denise and Silvia can help you too. I'll have Denise come to the office to help you with the presentation. She has the talent to sell just about anything."

Janice said, "I'm so nervous right now. Are you sure you want me to be the spokesperson for the company?"

I looked at Charise. "Are you sure I'm making the right decision?"

Charise said, "You know, at first I thought she would say no. I looked into her eyes and posture, and they both said, 'Yes, but can I do what they want?' Honey, we are here to help you and guide you. You'll do wonderful, I assure you."

Melanie asked, "So you are moving me to the design desk?"

I told her, "You will have the support of Janice, Denise, Silvia, and Gloria. With those backing you up, how can you go wrong?"

Melanie asked, "They won't mind helping?"

"If they do, you send your data to me. Let me analyze your design and send back suggestions to make your design sing with ambience.

"Did you see the photos of Mama and Papa's new home?"

Janice said, "I have not seen the photos."

Charise said, "You girls sit at your desks, and I'll forward you the photos. Get ready to be inspired. Your boss created this from his desk, while he was on restriction from cupcakes. You both can be this good at designing from your heart as he does on a daily basis."

After their coffee prework break, Charise forwarded the photos for the girls to absorb the progression from bare dirt to ambience.

It was time for Janice and me to head to our first appointment. She was still a little nervous, so I told her, "You're with me to observe. You won't get questioned. I introduce you as our new salesperson learning how to prepare their home for a landscape plan."

Our first customer was extremely nice and helpful and so pleased to assist her in every step of the interview. As we ventured into the rear yard, the homeowners pointed out what they would like to have removed and what to keep. I realized this was what they felt would improve appearance or take away from the design.

I did my usual thing, look at different angles of the shrubs or trees, taking in the shape. If we were to install a new irrigation system, would it make the installation harder or have no bearing? I looked for overhanging wires; were they in the way of what the customers' dream landscape could become?

I told Janice what to write down so that when we drew the plot plan, those items would be recorded. I told her to put a small dumpster on site to remove the majority of the existing landscape. We examined the existing irrigation system; "Too old to keep" was my response to the homeowner. "It would cost more to modify the existing than it would to install a new system to fit the new landscape."

The homeowners had some concerns, thinking I was trying to make the job more lucrative.

I pointed out, "The existing valves are no longer manufactured, and the new valves aren't interchangeable with these. The controller is outdated too, and again no one has parts to repair. I could take it to one vendor have them give me a price to have one of their controller repairmen give us an estimate and compare the cost to a new controller."

I asked the only question that caused the two to disagree: "Is the old system watering automatically?"

He said yes, and she said, "Why do you hand water part of the yard?"

He responded that he has dry spots.

I said, "This may sound silly, but do you have the extra time to water the dry spots?" Then I asked, "Can I turn on the valves by hand and see the coverage?"

The homeowner said, "You can turn them on by hand?"

"Yes sir. Didn't the installer show you how to operate your system?"

"That was years ago," said the homeowner. "I may have forgotten what he told me."

I took him to the valves and showed all three spectators how to manually turn on each valve and had them turn on a valve.

The valves which had dry spots had nozzles that were plugged.

I told them, "I could have one of my irrigators return this week and detail your old system. We charge you by the hour, but it will get you to stop hand watering until our plans are completed."

The wife said, "That is a great idea. What about parts?"

"We won't replace any old parts unless absolutely necessary. If we do replace, let's say, a sprinkler head due to excessive damage to the old head, we will replace it with a head we will use on your new system."

The wife asked, "Do we have to be home when your irrigator arrives?"

"Not necessary unless you have a dog. You can tell your neighbors that we are working on your irrigation system; that is always helpful."

"Our neighbors are at work during the day," said the husband. "They probably won't care to know."

"Our irrigator has a uniform, and the truck has signage. If you do get a call from a neighbor, could you tell them, 'It's okay, he's working on our sprinkler system'?"

"How long before the plans will be ready?" asked the wife.

"We like two weeks' time, but it could be finished sooner. If we can have a daytime phone number, Janice will call you when the plan is completed."

They both were excited to see something they could use and invite their friends and family over to enjoy. They even gave Janice a not-to-exceed budget number.

I told them, "We will design your dream. Each item is stand-alone, so you can pick and choose without affecting any other number in the estimate. Janice will not get an overactive pencil; we do believe in a quality project, not a quantity project that you have to replace in a couple of years."

They were very happy. Janice and I measured the house and perimeter of the yard when completed. Then Janice rang the doorbell, told them we were finished, and set up a return appointment date and time.

She got into my truck and was on cloud nine. "How did I do?"

I told her, "Perfect. You were polite, you made them feel at ease, and they both liked you. You weren't pushy, and they were receptive about you handling the presentation of plans and budget numbers. I couldn't ask for anything more than that from you."

"They had so many questions that I didn't know how to answer," said Janice.

"Write them down, take a photo of the items in question, and forward them to me, or call Juan on his phone to come to the address if he has time. Otherwise, you will get back to them tomorrow with their answer. If it is something that Juan must take a look at, schedule a time you and he can meet with the homeowners to discuss the issue."

"How did you know the dry spot was caused by a plugged head?"

"I didn't know for sure, but since the areas around the dry spot was green, it was either an irrigation issue or an insect issue. Cutworms cause areas that look like the area isn't getting watered."

Janice said, "This is thrilling but scary at the same time."

I told her, "Once you get a burning in your tummy, that is what you're striving to achieve. Like when you first did the grand entrance—that feeling."

Janice said, "That scared me, until Marie hugged me and said, 'Welcome to the Ladies' Club.'"

We arrived at the second home and rang the doorbell. The homeowners invited us in, saying they had waited for three weeks for us to come there. "Are you that busy?"

I told them, "We are that busy making each customer happy; that is our goal. We are sorry about the delay; we have a large backlog of customers waiting, due to the magazine and cable networks showing our work."

The husband asked if we could add more crews.

I told the husband, "Unfortunately, it's the nature of the beast, caused by forces beyond our control. We can't find enough people wanting to work with their hands. Most people want big paychecks without much effort.

"I don't want to cheapen my finished product due to untrained or unskilled personnel. I want you happy enough that you tell your friends and family about your experience as our customer."

The wife asked, "Do you advertise for employees?"

"We have a running ad in all local papers, in trade magazines and supply houses. Not one sniff; most companies hang on tight to what they have. We and they know replacement is nearly impossible."

I asked, "Have you called others to give you an estimate?"

The husband said, "Four other companies. Three never showed up, and one said six to nine months before they could take on any more work."

I told them, "It will only get worse for the construction industry as more and more employees go to electronic or manufacturing jobs."

The wife asked, "Why is that?"

"The work is easier, it pays more, and it's not as physical."

I went on, "The owner of Hostess, the company that made Twinkies, gave a news interview when the bakery union demanded more money per hour for their employees. 'You can only charge so much for a Twinkie,' he said. 'I'm selling the business.' He did just that. Now you find the Hostess name on the product packages, but the product is smaller, the price is high, and they don't make them in our country. But don't hold me to that; my memory isn't as sharp as it once was.

"So what do you need done to your home where we could be of help?"

The wife said, "Follow me. It's too hard for me to explain."

We followed her to the rear yard. "Oh, Lord," said Janice. "What happened?"

The husband stated, "We gave up over a year ago and closed the curtains so we didn't have to look at it any longer."

"You know, this will take some time just to clean up so we can start with a fresh canvas," said Janice.

The wife asked, "Could you just dynamite the entire yard, blow it to smithereens?"

Janice laughed. "Wouldn't that be nice? But I'm certain the neighbors and the police might not share the same interest."

I said, "That for sure would draw some attention and some healthy fines, and I'd lose my contractor's license. On the bright side, I would get three square meals a day for quite a few years."

We went back into the house, and I asked them, "What is your dream for your backyard?"

The wife said, "Serenity, peacefulness, and a place to unwind that would make me less grumpy."

The husband said, "Ditto, make her less grumpy."

"So do you like to barbecue?"

The wife said, "Do you mean burn the meat into jerky?"

"The new barbecues are much better than the old charcoal grills, just like cooking on the stove but much more efficient."

The wife said, "Can a woman cook on them?"

I told her, "If your husband is willing to share."

"I would feel safer if I did the cooking," she said.

"How about a patio cover to shade you while you cook up the lunch and dinner?"

She asked, "He does the dishes?"

"That would only be fair. You would be less grumpy, correct? Do you like concrete or pavers for the decking?"

Janice show them some catalog pages of the two choices.

The husband asked about a wood deck.

Janice gave him a catalog of wood and composite wood decking, to compare with poured concrete and pavers.

The homeowners were now confused and were asking about maintenance costs, durability, and replacement costs, all at the same time.

I told them, "With the patio cover shading all the types of decking, longevity is comparable. Concrete does crack, wood does deteriorate, and pavers can loosen and break due to excessive wear or heavy equipment traveling across the surface. There are pluses and minuses on every form of decking. The sun's ultraviolet rays are the major factors of deterioration."

The wife asked, "What would you recommend?"

"We have had good success with pavers. Certain manufacturers make a more durable product, but that might not be the answer to your landscape."

The husband asked, "Can you give us three separate bids? That will make our decision easier."

"Do you have children or grandchildren?"

The wife answered, "One grandchild and one on the way. Why do you ask?"

Janice showed them the playhouse. "Would you consider having a playhouse or craft room for yourself? Air-conditioned, heated, with electrical power, even gas, if you choose, all custom built to fit your specifications.

"We have placed them on the ground and on top of the patio cover. Both approaches work very well. We even installed an elevator in one for my mother-in-law. She has bad knees, and climbing stairs is difficult for her."

The wife asked, "You can price that separately?"

"Yes, each item is stand-alone. If you want to have the playhouse, we check the box yes. If you decide maybe later, we can make adjustments so that when you're ready, we won't have to tear up your landscape to install the playhouse."

The wife said, "I hate to ask, but could you draw the playhouse showing it on the ground and on top of the patio cover?"

"The reason we started to put the playhouse on top of the patio cover is that it saves space so you can enhance your dream backyard."

I called Juan. "Do you have a crew who could start a cleanup either this week or next week?"

Juan told me he had a cleanup crew ready to start either tomorrow or the next day. "Do you have another job ready for them?"

"Hold on; let me ask."

I told the homeowners that they could start the cleanup either tomorrow or the next day, whichever would work for them.

They told me, "That is a godsend. Please be our guests."

I told Juan, "I'll give you the address when I see you tonight at the office. I'll have Charise arrange for a dumpster and a Port-O-Let for tomorrow morning."

Janice and I measured the best we could and decided to leave it to Juan to measure the yard on Friday or Monday.

On our way to the next home, we stopped at the fast food restaurant for some freshening up and a soda to wet our whistle.

Janice was now feeling more at ease and looking forward to the next disaster.

I told her, "Some we visit you think to yourself, *The place is immaculate; why am I here?* Then the wife informs you that this is the previous wife's landscape, and the faster it all goes away, the better. I didn't ask any questions or comment about how the landscape looked; we removed everything in two days. She called me and said, 'Good riddance; thank you for being so prompt. When will I get my new landscape?'

"I told her it'd be a bit longer than two days.

"She told me, 'Start as soon as possible. Even the bare dirt reminds me of that woman.'"

Janice said, 'Do you, get into many of those situations?'"

"Once or maybe twice a year. More often the wife says yes, and the husband says he wants to think about it for a few days. Marjorie was one of those situations; she had her husband get on the phone and call at least three landscapers to see how long before they could start a new project. 'We'll wait,' she said.

"He left the room, and by the time he came back, Marjorie had finished three margaritas. 'Well, we're waiting. What did you find out, genius?'

"He said the earliest would be three months. 'They only do landscape and irrigation systems.'

"Marjorie told me to start. She was tired of looking at dirt and weeds. 'Make it happen as soon as possible.' Her husband left the room, and she said, 'Thank you. He'll pout for at least a week and try to find every little thing wrong. Tell him to go inside and tell me his troubles.'"

We finished our sodas and headed to the third residence, rang the doorbell, and introduced ourselves. I handed the guy a business card. He looked puzzled but then said, "Oh, you're the landscape guy. I'm sorry, you both looked so familiar. Please come in. Honey, it's those landscape people from the magazine."

The lady of the house came out of the back room and said, "I sent that magazine a check last week. Phone calls aren't enough; they send bill collectors to our door."

The husband said, "They're not here to collect any money. They're the landscapers who do the projects shown in the magazine."

She looked us up and down. "Why are you here then?"

"Did you call our office wanting an estimate?"

"I didn't." She looked at her husband. "Did you, genius?"

Her husband said, "I thought they could help solve some of our landscape problems."

She looked at me. "Do you know how to get Genius here off my sofa and behind the lawnmower and pull weeds?"

I told her, "Can we see what your landscape looks like?"

She said, "Be my guest. Genius needs a map to find the backyard."

We went into the backyard. Grass needed mowing, and weeds were at least two feet tall, in bloom and ready to drop seeds.

Her husband said. "Don't listen to the old bag. I mow every other week and pull weeds two or three times a year."

I told the husband, "Mowing every other week is hard on the lawnmower; it plugs up the chute. Grass gets too long; the machine is not designed for that kind of mowing. You need to hire a gardening service; that will keep the little woman happy."

"They want too much money," he said.

"Well, do they see it in this condition or after you have it mowed?"

"This way, usually. I don't want to spend that much money per month."

I asked him, "How much did you pay for your lawnmower and gardening tools?"

He said, "Exactly, I couldn't tell you. Ballpark, almost a thousand dollars."

"How much are they proposing to charge you per month?"

"One gardener wanted a hundred dollars; another wanted a hundred and fifty."

I asked how often they proposed to provide the service.

"One said every ten days or three times a month; the other said every week."

"Well, you know you could have had a gardener for nearly a year. You wouldn't have to store the lawnmower or the tools, have a gas can sitting in your garage, or have the lawnmower serviced.

"Call them both back, and ask about irrigation repairs, fertilization, and spray for insects that are damaging your shrubs. Take Mama out to dinner, buy her flowers, pamper her for a couple of weeks, and enjoy not having to do the landscape maintenance. You might be able to use the lawnmower and tools in lieu of a monthly bill until they meet your price."

The little woman came out of the house to join us. "Well, genius, what did the gentleman tell you?"

"Get a gardener, and have them maintain our yard."

She looked at me. Then she hugged me and kissed my cheek. "Thank you. I've told him that for years. He's not geared for yard work. You can't sit in front of the television, expecting the grass to mow itself."

She and I strolled through the high grass and looked at the flower beds. I wrote down some ideas for the gardener to enhance the flower beds' appearance. I showed her how and where to have the gardener prune and thin out the trees to allow more light on the turf, which was thinning due to lack of light. "Have them check the irrigation coverage once the grass has been mowed twice."

She said she was sorry about when we entered her home. "Genius said the magic word, *magazine*, and that threw me off target." Janice was following us, taking notes. When we were finished, she handed the notes to the homeowner.

The husband said the one gardener would be there in an hour. "He seemed pleased that I called."

His wife said, "If I were a few years younger and we were alone, I would tip you, but since that won't ever happen—" She gave me a hug, gave Janice a hug, and told me to bill them for our time. "I promise not to come unglued."

On our way back to the office, Janice said, "Why didn't you just tell them you weren't interested?"

I said, "You saw the classic situation of homeowners not communicating. I knew if we walked away, she would get on the phone before we were gone and bad-mouth us to everyone she could. I wanted to see what she was so angry about.

"He was proud of himself about mowing every other week, like he was beating the system. He might even get a kick out of making her angry. He may have acted that way since they purchased the home, I don't know. But I didn't want to walk away without at least knowing just what was going on.

"She had to have been listening to our conversation from inside the house. She knew I was solving her problem and his problem in one fell swoop."

I told Janice, "You've seen three totally different customers in one day. You're very lucky to have had that experience."

Janice said, "I'm amazed that you never got frazzled, showed emotions, or got angry. I was almost ready to punch that lady."

I told her she was clearly frustrated at the situation, more than likely had yelled at him earlier to get off the sofa and mow the yard, which he had no intention of doing. "That can wear on even the calmest, most even-tempered person."

I had her call Charise and ask if they were going to lunch.

Charise told her they were waiting on her so they all could eat together.

"Tell her we're about ten minutes from the office. I'll run a couple of red lights if they're in a real hurry."

Janice said, "I'd rather you not do that." She told Charise, "We're about ten minutes from the office, but if we hit all green lights it could be quicker."

I love that positive thinking; all green lights alone would be a miracle.

When Janice rang off, I told her, "They'll all want to know how your first day with the boss went. Have fun telling them of the experience you received; don't hold anything back. You did great, and I'm very proud of what you did under the circumstances we encountered."

Ten minutes just flew by. When we walked in, the ladies all had their purses on their arms, and Charise told me they would bring me back lunch—"Crow, of course. Be prepared to share as always."

I had a burning sensation to call the girls and my real wives. I called and got the receptionist, who put me through to the small studio. There the girls were telling the crew, who wouldn't be going to Oregon, how much they would miss working with them and how much they had all helped them through some tough times, especially when their moms were kidnapped.

Susanne had her assistants get cases of tissues. "Hurry, this is going to be tough on all of us." The tissues arrived and were placed on every table. Susanne stayed with the girls as they went to everyone with hugs and kisses, telling the audience what each person had done for them since the beginning. They asked for the hairstylists and the makeup and wardrobe personnel to join with the lunch.

Makeup was fixing Susanne. After every hug, she was having a hard time keeping tears bottled up. It had been like this ever since the girls had her stay with them for the light show with the governor and his wife, seeing the courtyard lit up the very first time.

They had changed Susanne from a pompous, stuck-up person to a warm and loving individual. They had taught her to be real and honest, sincere, loyal, and trustworthy all in one evening. She'd always been told she was beautiful and could use her beauty to get everything she ever needed or wanted. "Good looks and a nice body can buy more than your wallet. Their wallets will open up just being around you," she was told over and over again.

Her talk with me got her thinking, *What if the girls blacklist me? I've never been blacklisted. They'd better not even attempt such a thing.* She told herself, *I'll teach them a lesson they'll never forget. I'm beautiful, with a great body. I dress to the nines, and people go out of their way to be near me. They don't know what they're dealing with. They are just little girls; what do they know?*

That attitude melted away. She was humbled after one invitation, shedding tears as she never had before. She even hugged the girls—giving warm embraces like never before, not even caring who was watching. She watched the video of herself starting to cry and her hugs, over and over again. She cried every time. *Why?* she would ask herself. *Why are you crying? You have seen this video hundreds of times. Get ahold of yourself.* None of these talks to herself worked, and they still didn't work.

"These girls have a way of tearing down even the staunchest stubborn person into a warm and loving soul," she told Marie. "If they spent even one hour with Mrs. Katy Wilkins, the girls would melt her like frozen butter bathed in microwaves. She'd be on her knees begging for mercy, spilling out all the reasons why she did what she did."

Marie said, "You know, I have to have a meeting with Ms. Morgan. We could have a hidden camera and show the world the transformation, from evil to good. In fact, here's a wonderful idea: we will show her all the episodes the girls filmed while we were held captive, nonstop in her cell, over and over and over again. We'll see just how crazy this woman is.

"Of course, we will have it filmed behind a two-way mirror and watch her reactions. We could even show a physician removing an appendage, over and over and over again."

Marie texted herself with her thoughts to call Ms. Morgan to have that arranged to see just how crazy the defendant was.

The girls only had a few more staff members to bring to tears. Susanne was nearly out of fluid now. The caterer and his staff were nearly ready to serve a marvelous lunch. They also had enough cupcakes to feed ten people ready to bring to the tables with each person's name inscribed on the top with white icing.

The girls were finished with all of the staff. So Susanne said, "Let's eat and celebrate."

The entire staff rose to their feet and applauded the girls, thanking them for allowing them to help them from the beginning.

Mr. Barns told the staff, "We will have the girls make appearances every so often at the studio so you can help them with the magic they bring." He then said, "We'll also bring back the Wiloby children on occasion to be filmed in this studio. We are working on having another set of girls to put in this studio, giving us three hours of programming."

We are working diligently with numerous talent agencies, nothing close, yet. My girls are ones of a kind, we love them with all our hearts, said Phyllis.

The lunch was being served. Marie and Delores both talked to me for a few minutes before their meal superseded me in importance. "Goodbye, see you at home tonight," said Delores, and *click.*

I started to earn my cupcake, being a good boy, responding to the calls, deleting those of no importance. Some vendors were relentless: *Let's do lunch; let's get together for dinner.* My response: *Send me a catalog with current pricing. If I'm interested, I'll send you a purchase order. No time for lunch or dinner, but thanks for the offer.*

I must have sent that fifty times in a week to at least twenty vendors. One vendor got *My bandwagon is full; no room for another vendor, no quotes, and no riding on the bandwagon; that is company policy.*

Boy, did that stir up the hornet's nest. I was bombarded with at least ten emails with various quotations of useless data on items we would never use. I gave them to Charise. "Respond stating we are landscapers, not interior decorators."

I ridded my stack of emails to less than ten that I needed to answer. *My lovely Gloria wants some loving, Marjorie is lonely, and Silvia can't wait for me to coddle her. Not one needs help with a landscape issue. Office wives can be just like my wife at home: "Hold me. Can we just talk tonight? How was your day?"*

You know, a few days of talk is not a cure-all for males. We don't do feelings very well. We're hunters, not gatherers; we bring home the bacon and then go out and hunt some more. Sitting around talking about how that poor animal must feel is not what we want to hear, we want the happiness of filling your tummy.

While on the daily hunt, we don't want to have to doubt what we do; just do it, and do it well is our main concern. When we're in a deep zone, last lap, leading the race, getting challenged, turn by turn, finish line just ahead, do we win the race, or do we surrender to a competitor? Never once do I consider how he's feeling or else I'll never win. There's nothing wrong with competition; getting to the finish line is like bring home the hunt. It's dinner or starve; talking about feelings is not on my list of things to do.

I heard a little voice. "Hey, hello. We're back," said Charise. "Oh, good grief. Leave you alone for an hour, and bingo, into a zone. Here is your lunch. We took those pesky chocolate feathers from your crow, you don't need the calories."

"We also sampled the bird and fries to make sure there was no poison in your food," said Janice.

"We were all looking out for your best interest," said Charise.

They all left my office, and I got a message from Charise: *Wow, you're such a good boy today. Momma will bring you in a treat. Now eat your lunch so you will grow big and strong. Bye-bye.*

With plastic knife and fork in hand for some carving and a goose juice standing by, I cut my first piece of bird and was taking a bite when in came my cupcake on a dessert plate. Charise saw I had carved a couple of bites off the bird and of course had a plastic fork under the plate. She dove into my bird and fries and took a health swig of goose juice.

"Something about eating your food gives me thrills inside," said Charise. "I'm not hungry, but I can't help myself. Boy, this is really good."

I could see McDonald's in my future—drive-through dashboard dining before I pulled into the driveway. It's a vision I get regularly, being an office husband.

27

The day ended, girls all headed home stating that they would not be in the office tomorrow. "Don't you dare say one word," was the general consensus. I gave Juan the address of the cleanup. Charise ordered a dumpster and Port-O-Let for the house, to be delivered before ten o'clock.

Juan told me they would start clearing tomorrow at seven o'clock. "When the dumpster arrives, we'll then start the loading process."

I told Juan, "Make sure they all have gloves and dust masks and that they wear hats and eyewear. Take some hoses to keep the dust to a minimum. I don't want the neighbors to complain. And bring business cards to hand out to onlookers."

Juan was anxious to get started on a cleanup; they always found treasures buried amid the debris.

I just told him to be cautious. "Take your time, and document everything with notes and photos for the homeowners."

I headed home and texted Delores to make sure I would be at the right location.

She responded, *I'm where you think I should be.*

Great job of a nonanswer, you should be a politician. Seriously where is everybody?

We are here where we should be, stated Delores.

Fine, I'm heading home. If you're there, then you're there. If not, then you're elsewhere.

Delores texted, Now you're getting it: here, there, everywhere.

I looked at the roof of my truck, saying, "You couldn't give me one who answers without riddles. Thank you."

Before I arrived home, I stopped and picked up some hunger pain medication and some treats for the wives. Better safe than sorry; better than having to turn around and fetch them, with a strong warning about not being thoughtful.

Great thinking. I was met at the front door by four girls with severe hunger pains. "We love you, Daddy," said Sarah as they scurried off to their house with a box of cupcakes and devoured a two-pack.

Moms did serious damage to the bags of high-end chocolates and champagne. I told them, "Enjoy, since there are no such stores near our home or office in Oregon."

That little sermon didn't seem to faze them. "Maybe your bunk buddies can bring some of theirs."

"You know, I will never live that down—a constant reminder of something that didn't happen and never will happen. But thank you for instilling that into my brain, etched there forever."

Marie told me she'd contacted Ms. Morgan with her idea. "Ms. Morgan will run that by the judge and opposing counsel, to keep the playing field level. She will even have three psychologists or psychiatrists present behind a two-way mirror as observers. She will let me know the decision."

I told her, "The defense attorney will more than likely object. If she loses the insanity plea, where will she go to defend her client?"

Marie said, "We really don't care if she has no defense. She needs to pay for what she did to all those people, not sit in an insane asylum for life on our tax dollars."

"So is it time to fire up the grill?"

Delores said, "Honey, you're an adult. You have the authority to proceed with making us and the girls happy, or you can choose to bring us to anger. Either way, the final result will rest on your shoulders."

"Well enough said. I'm totally confused. I'll fire up the grill; it keeps me busy."

Delores told Marie, "A hot collar might work better."

Marie said, "My glass is empty. All that hot air is evaporating my champagne."

Peace and quiet now, with the grill heating up, well oiled, ready for the meat offering. Oh, the platter of bovine was fast approaching, with a little sway and a come-and-get-it smile. *They're trying to kill me slowly.*

Delores said, "Here, dear, would you like some more?"

"Some more of what, might I ask?"

Delores said, "You might ask."

She swayed back toward the kitchen, look over her shoulder and waving an index finger side to side—*not now*—and walked inside.

She's killing me. She knows what she said last night; males don't forget those things. Is she changing her mind or driving me out of mine? I decided this was too many questions; *Just cook the meat and earn some hugs from the ones who really show true emotions.* She returned with a can of goose juice, swaying even more than the first time, purposely moving every step with precision to entice.

"Here, sweetie. I knew you would need some refreshment to cool you down a couple of degrees. I'll be back in a few minutes to sample your grilling."

She is making this grilling very difficult; my concentration is out the window. If I don't get focused, I could grill my own skin. I watched her every step from the grill to the French doors; she even opened them with sensuality. I told myself, *This is a setup; you're going to make a fool of yourself. You know she knows how to drive you crazy.*

I started to flip the meat and saw the girls scurrying down the staircase, heading to the kitchen door to help moms. *They are so full of energy, always smiling and willing to give hugs at the drop of a hat.* Only two more nights of guests for them at their old house. They were getting excited about a new house as their moms were encouraging them every day.

John showed up with the news that he and Marie were dinner guests. "Sorry, pal. I know how it is to be second. Hey, look at the bright side of being second: no one ever remembers who was second."

"John, remember: come Saturday we will never know whether we're second or third or fourth, we aren't first picked. We will more than likely come after the farm animals on the list of guests."

John said, "You know, that is really sad to think of but so true. Now I'm depressed."

The girls started bring out the sides, salads, dinner rolls, condiments, plates, and plasticware and told me, "We will choose our own pieces of meat tonight, Daddy."

All the girls and moms were approaching the grill, each bringing a plate. I opened the hood of the grill. Leslie was the first to choose and picked a pork chop and a hot dog, Sarah picked the same as Leslie; Rebecca and Kim chose hamburgers and hot dogs. Marie chose the steak and hamburger, Delores chose the steak, and John and I had a hamburger and hot dog. Once all were served, the grill was put on simmer, with still a couple of pieces of meat left on.

John and Marie made the trek up the staircase, being cautious since tomorrow they will be the ones at the loser table.

Delores and I had a nice candlelight dinner. Talk was sporadic; in between biting and chewing, our conversation was short and sweet. I told her she looked ravishing; what was her secret?

"Three margaritas while riding in the limousine put me in the right frame of mind. With what the girls did today for the staff, there wasn't a dry eye in the house. Susanne was a wreck; I can't imagine if she weren't moving to Oregon to be with the girls."

Delores said, "I don't think she could love any children more than she loves our daughters. She told everyone how she was transformed the night of Marie's open house. She got every eye in the house pouring in tears. I never knew her old self; I thought she was always sweet and charming. I don't know how those girls pull that off, sure glad they can.

"Susanne said you told her the governor was lucky to accept them. He would have been blacklisted by the girls if he shoved them aside or belittled them."

I told her, "She and I discussed the matter after she delivered the note to the governor. The girls trusted her with the note; that was huge. They saw that Susanne possessed something they trusted. She told me she hoped to be asked to dine with them. She was so sad when they asked Mama and Papa to dine with the governor and his wife. She came to me and said, 'I guess I'm on the ask-later list.'

"I told her, 'So is everyone else at the party. The space is small, and their budget is small; you heard Leslie's apology to those attending.' She was about to start crying I could feel it inside. She found her husband and they dined together. When desserts were served, she helped the girls deliver the desserts to their guests. That was when they did the most encouraging thing for Susanne, asking her to join them for the light show on their balcony.

"She came to me, told me what they'd just done for her. 'They like me; they truly like me.' They made her life complete, accepting a woman who's lived on her looks, body, clothes, and makeup. They saw through the plastic appearance and took her for just being her, stripped of all the social acceptance. This was the first time she'd been picked without social boundaries."

Delores said, "You know quite a lot about Susanne. How did you find that out?"

"After the light show when the guests were starting to leave, she and I talked at the waterfall, from the heart, not from idle chatter. She thought you, I, Marie and John had something to do with the girls and how they behave. I told her no; we are learning how to be better parents from them.

"She had overheard the governor and Diane talk about how the girls act so mature that the parents must have a lot to do with them or they are playing a part that they rehearsed. I told her, no script, no parent teaching of these girls; the playhouse has changed them.

"I asked the girls over a week ago to make sure Annie and her friends get packed into a box. 'Tell them we are moving to a new home and they will always have a home with our families.' They confirmed that Annie and her friends were packed and secured in their stuffed animal box, so they would be with their friends. They would keep them company, and they promised they would show them their new homes."

Delores said, "You know, that is pretty scary, our daughters speak to spirits."

I told her, "If we weren't so into other things and took time to listen from the heart to little voices, we could do the same."

Sarah and Leslie approached the chef. "Daddy, you know your grilling is the best, we can't get our fill of how good your grilling has become. Would you be so kind as to allow us to share the final pieces of your grilled meat with our guests? Their hunger pains aren't quite cured. We will make sure that Mama gives you the biggest piece of cake on Saturday."

"Well, girls, I can't say no to such demands. Are you sure I'll get the biggest piece of cake?"

Leslie said, "Yep. Remember, we do the serving. Mama just slices and puts the slices on the plates."

As I opened the hood on the grill there were three pieces left, two steaks and a pork chop. Their eyes widened; "We thought it would be a hamburger and hot dog." They were very excited to see the real meat still on the grill. I put them on their plates, and they gave me the best girl hug a daddy could ask for.

When I returned to the table, Delores said, "You know their husbands will never replace you and John. You both treat our daughters like little queens; not easy for any young man to compete with that."

The flame was flickering in the slight breeze, glistening in Delores's eyes and glowing off her red lipstick. She said, "What are you staring at? Do I have something on my lips?"

I told her, "Red gloss lipstick; the flame reflection is glistening."

Delores said, "Eileen and Janice are doing a wonderful job on teaching the ladies. Marie and I just watched today, giving them all encouragement. We were a little nervous until we saw Eileen in full form taking on the hardest student. She worked with her until she got loose and put her own style into her moves. Eileen has far more patience than Marie and I do put together."

Time for dessert; we hear the little one descending the staircase. "Let's go, Mom," said Rebecca. "We have desserts to serve."

They all headed to the kitchen. Marie and John were on the balcony, complimenting me on only burning one side of the meat. I told them I'd do better next time; half burnt makes it almost look like I know what I'm doing.

Marie said, "The girls want to spend the night tonight; they got too cold this morning. That will be okay with you two?"

"That's fine with us. They always pounce on our bed before dawn, snuggle under the covers, and shiver, getting all our body heat. Then we cuddle them until their tummies now have hunger pains. I head to the kitchen and get the breakfast started, and they come down and help. All is good.

"When they are sleeping at your house, I miss the pouncing on the bed and having them all shivering until they get warm. They like lying between Delores and me; the bed's the warmest there, where we both were lying. Now we are on the cold mattress, and they are nice and warm."

Marie said, "Now I know why they do that to us as well. They scared us really bad the first time they did that. I must have jumped a foot off the bed."

"Are you two ready for Oregon?" I asked.

Marie said, "Yeah, I'm ready. I'll hate leaving our home; we went through so much. But Oregon is so pretty, and the weather is milder, wetter but milder. Mom told me the mornings are absolutely gorgeous. Sunrises and sunsets are breathtaking; the damp cold chills you to the bone, she was saying."

Our desserts were arriving—pie with vanilla ice cream with chocolate shavings and of course our cherries. The girls always seem to get our cherry with their puppy-dog eyes and irresistible smiles. The *pleeease*, the long-drawn-out version, helps them as well.

The desserts were wonderful, and the light show was top-notch. We went inside for coffee and hot chocolate for the girls. Tomorrow night we have hot apple cider for the girls giving the chocolate a rest for a while. We bought a gallon of apple cider; we will just heat it up and put in a cinnamon stick, for additional flavor.

It was nearing Papa and Mama calling time. The girls all got in their pajamas, climbed into bed, and shivered while the bed was warming up, Delores had put two heating pads on top of the covers to lessen the chill, the girls noticed right away the bed was warmer than two nights ago.

While we all were just talking about the girls saying goodbye to the staff, I told them, "That was so nice of all of you to do that. The staff must have been surprised."

Leslie said, "We all talked with Susanne the day before yesterday about what we wanted to do, and she liked the idea. I think they were surprised."

Marie assured her, "The staff was very surprised and so thankful for all of you. They all told me they will miss you very much."

The phone rang. It was Mama; she was all excited about how gorgeous the day was. No rain, and the sun shining between white puffy clouds. The lambs were talking all day long. Papa told them in two days the girls will be here, and they all were calling you from that time on. The calves were mooing, and it sounded so nice. The birds were chirping. I saw a blue jay sitting on my hand railing. Papa fed him peanuts in the shell, and he will be back tomorrow morning for sure."

Papa told the girls, "I went and saw them four times today. I thought they were lonely; they called all day long. They like attention."

The girls told Mama and Papa that they told the staff goodbye today had a huge party. "Everybody cried; we went through a case of tissues."

Mama said, "I'm sure they will miss you; Papa and I miss you, and it's only been six days—some of the longest days in my life."

Then she asked, "You girls in bed?"

"Yes, Grandma," they all said over the speakerphone.

Mama asked, "Are you ready for prayers?"

"Yes, Grandma, we're ready," said Leslie.

They all said their prayers, thanking God for everyone and for their lambs and calves and the fishes in the aquarium—"We forgot them last night, and our little frog." They said, "We want to make sure God will be with us on our flight to Oregon, we can't wait to be in our new home. All three families, together, thank you, God, for blessing us."

The prayers lasted longer than normal but were worth the extra effort. After kisses on the foreheads, all were tucked in. Then with "I love you" across the board, night lights on and lights out, "Sleep tight," said Papa, and everyone hung up.

*

Mama and Papa were joined with all the Oregon ladies for the flight to Colorado. They would arrive around eleven o'clock to be taken by limousine to the hotel where they always stay. Gloria and the Utah ladies arrived at nine o'clock and all of the Texas ladies are to arrive at any minute. The hotel was full of beautiful women. Charise, Janice, Melanie, and Marsha all left the office and set up all the rooms, making sure they had enough rooms for all the ladies. They also had fruit baskets in all the rooms; all the amenities were open ready for use.

Susanne was there also organizing the arrival of all the ladies. She is the company hugger—a new title.

The Wiloby children arrived with the Texas ladies, the boys were well taken care of emotionally—hugged and kissed so much that Matthew asked Marjorie if he had any skin left on his cheeks.

28

We were awakened by four little girls pouncing on our bed. They hurried up and snuggled up under the covers, shivering like always.

"Good morning, Mom and Dad," said Sarah.

"We want to spend the night again tonight," said Leslie. "It's too cold in the mornings in our house; this is much better."

Delores hugged her. "That's fine with us; we love having you spend the night."

Sarah said, "Daddy, we all have hunger pains. Is it time to start the breakfast?"

I told them, "I need one more shiver from all of you."

They all shook. "How's that, Daddy?" said Leslie.

"Well, that did it. Time to get the fires started," I told them.

I slipped out of bed and tucked my side in, went around to Delores's side and tucked that in, and headed downstairs to get the coffee and hot apple cider going. I got out the pots and pans and put the bread in front of the toaster. Then, with some oil in the sausage pan, we were ready for some action. The girls joined me once the hot apple cider was ready and sat at the table with a throw from the sofa wrapped around them in pairs. I asked them, "Are you still cold?"

Leslie said, "Only for a couple of minutes. Once we drink some apple cider, we'll be warm enough to help make breakfast."

Delores joined us with four robes for the girls, "Just in case you get chilled."

The pans were warming up, and I was finishing the batter for the pancakes when our doorbell rang. Delores went to open the door to allow Marie and John to enter.

Everyone had either apple cider or coffee in hand, and the girls were getting loving from moms and dads. Marie asked if they'd had a good night's sleep. Rebecca said her teddy bear kept making noises, little noises, whimpers. "She misses her momma."

Marie gave her a hug. "They'll be together in another day. You just have to tell her that her momma's safe, and Annie is watching over them."

All of the girls were performing their jobs: pancakes being flipped, sausages being turned, and toast being made. Marie and Delores were chatting about what they would teach the ladies this morning.

My Albright scramble has improved so much that Leslie told me, "It's better than the restaurants. Could you make salsa when we get to Oregon?"

I told her, "We can make the salsa. That way, you can give the recipe to the restaurants to perfect their dishes."

Leslie's eyes lit up. "You mean you will teach me how to make salsa?"

"Honey, you have mastered pancake flipping, making desserts with Mama, and making side dishes. You're more than ready. I will be proud teaching all of you if you're willing to try."

All of the girls said, "We're ready, Daddy."

"Perfect; we have a salsa date. Moms can get us the ingredients, and they can be the taste testers. How about that?"

Delores said, "Only if we can have margaritas and an Albright breakfast burrito to make the meal complete."

I told Leslie, "They want your scramble to become a breakfast burrito. What do you think?"

Leslie said, "The restaurants will expand their menus, and that will make them happy. Sounds like a great idea."

Leslie said, "Mom, can we invite the chefs to our playhouse on the set to have an Albright breakfast challenge?"

Marie said, "We will ask Susanne today what she thinks."

I told them, "Susanne will be jumping for joy to have the three chefs return to the playhouse. What a gift you'll give your audience."

Breakfast was ready to serve. The girls took the dishes to the table, and they all dug in. Soon, not a crumb was remaining.

I must admit, our breakfast was the best we cooked. The girls are so good at their jobs, that makes my scramble secondary.

They all said, "Salsa will make the scramble retake the lead."

Sarah said, "Daddy, we won't make it hot, just flavorful."

I told her, "We will make both, not hot, just a little bite, not nose-running hot."

I headed up to get ready for the day. The girls put the dishes in the dishwasher and turned it on.

All ready for work, I gave kisses and hugs and was on my way to the office wives. Then I remembered: *I'll be alone this morning. I can get my McDonald's Happy Meal without the pressure of sharing.* My smile was ear to ear.

I arrived at the office, made a fresh pot of coffee, went to my desk, booted up the computer, and took a couple sips of brewed coffee. I opened up my messages, every office manager told me, *Good morning. We are all watching you. Don't disappoint us by ignoring all of our desires. Your punishment will never end.*

I responded by telling them, *God is watching you. Be on your best behavior. I earned five cupcakes already this morning; so filling. I'll make you proud of me with five new projects.*

I called Juan to see if the cleanup had started.

He told me, "What an absolute mess. Do they do nothing in their yard?"

I told Juan, "They gave up over a year ago, just closed the curtains."

Juan said, "We may need a second dumpster, depending if we can crush down the debris."

I said, "Just tell the homeowner to call the dumpster company for another one if needed; it is what it is. You have to measure the rear yard and give those numbers to Janice to make the plan. Take good notes and photos; I'm curious as to what lies underneath all the debris."

Juan said, "I believe it's been longer than a year since they have done anything. I have to go; the homeowner just came out of the house, and I need to talk to them."

He called back about fifteen minutes later. The homeowners had bought them two dozen donuts and two large coffees. "She is so excited. We had about ten feet of area removed and piled up. She said, 'I forgot what our backyard looked like.' The husband asked if it would stay like this? I told him it would become a landmark for the neighborhood.

"I took shots as you entered into the backyard and before we cleared any debris. Now I'm getting shots of an hour into removal for the photo album. This project will become one you can hang your hat on, trust me."

I finished my Happy Meal and had another cup of coffee. I got a call from Delores. "All is well. We're getting styled and made up now. It should be a fun day with our ladies' class."

Susanne called and told me, "All the ladies are hidden from Marie and Delores. Eileen and Janice are getting the same treatment as Marie and Delores, so they are not aware of today's event. I'm so excited and—you know—tearful. I have ten cases of tissues at the ready. The governor and Diane are due to arrive in an hour. Can you come today?"

I told her, "I have five new customers to visit this morning."

Susanne said, "Check the address of the first customer."

I looked at the address. "Are you kidding me? Charise set me up."

Susanne said, "Not Charise; I did. See you soon. The limousine will be there in about fifteen minutes."

Office wives are nearly as bad as housewives: sneaky, very sneaky. I went to the little boys' room to freshen up and returned to my desk, polished off the second cup of coffee, turned off the coffeepot, and prepared to leave the premises.

I talked with Phillip's receptionist. She said she would go to our desk to watch the offices; "No need to lock up the office." She was so excited about what was going to happen today for Marie and Delores. Marsha would send her photos all day long.

Phillip was planning on being here this morning, but with the new playhouse for Silvia starting today, he too would get hourly photos of the event.

I walked her down to the other desk, where she told the staff that she would be downstairs; one designer told her he would join her in our design area. He felt she could use the company, and if anyone tried anything funny, he would be there to stop any intruders.

Our complex was looking fantastic. The cul-de-sac was fenced off to the public; the gate guard would allow deliveries, but no one else could enter the site.

My limousine pulled in. I told the receptionist, "If you don't receive any photos, just text me, and I'll send you mine."

The ride to the studio was faster than I had anticipated, I was met by one of Susanne's assistants, who took me to a door I had never pass through before. Very sneaky they have become.

She put her finger to her lips telling me to be quiet, very quiet, and we tiptoed to the waiting room. She took me to the holding area with fifty of the most beautiful women on the planet. I told God, *Thank you; is this heaven?*

We all had very quiet hugs and kisses, making no noise; silence was the name of the game. We were all behind a velvet curtain in a large studio with plenty of room for all of us. We heard Susanne tell Marie and Delores that their class would be held in here today since the small studio where the ladies' class was normally held had another event scheduled.

We then heard Mr. Barns and Phyllis enter the room. They got their hugs from the ladies. Our daughters were brought in; they would help moms with their class, showing the ladies how to get their way using Leslie's and Sarah's techniques. It's one of the hardest things the ladies will have to learn. No videos; the girls are live.

They brought in a male volunteer who has no idea what he will be in for with these girls. Susanne told him they needed a male, a father figure for four little girls. He had three daughters all about the ages of our girls; "Perfect," said Susanne.

The stage was set, Susanne, being the mother hen, asked Marie and Delores, "Where are your ladies for the morning class?"

Marie and Delores looked at their watches and shrugged, saying, "They are normally here; they are never late."

Susanne said, "Let me go ask the receptionist. Maybe they don't know where the large studio is located."

Susanne left the room but waited just outside the door, figuring how long it would take to go to the receptionist's desk and return. Then she went back in.

"She said she sent them to the large studio and gave them directions." Then she asked the stage attendant, "Could you open the curtain? Maybe they're behind the curtain." The attendant opened it just enough for the new class of ladies were standing. Susanne said, "There you are! We have looked all over for you. They all entered the studio where Marie and Delores were standing, they were all hugging when all of a sudden, music started to play. Susanne said, "Who turned that on?" As she turned to exit the studio, the parade started from behind the curtain, led by Juanita.

Marie and Delores both started to tear up, and Susanne had the tissues ready. Mr. Barns said, "Marie and Delores, this is your life." Each lady performed their grand entrance into the large studio, about ten to twelve feet apart. Their class all started applauding the ladies entering the studio, one after the other, giving it their best, showing Marie and Delores what they created. Soon all of the ladies were in the studio, when the sliding doors from the small to the large studio opened, with the ladies forming two lines about six feet apart like at our grand opening. John, then Mama and Papa, then I, and then the huge surprise of the day, the governor and Diane came into the large studio.

Marie and Delores were a wreck. They each went through a box of tissues. The small studio had the caterer all set up, and tables were scattered throughout the area.

Mr. Barns took a microphone and said, "We have another surprise for you two. Stan, open the other curtain." There standing in all its glory was an exact replica of the staircase.

Marie said, "Stan, it's beautiful." They showed the ladies the back access to the staircase via an elevator and platform, to the staircase entrance.

The girls were all given numbers. That would be their order for descending the staircase. They were each given a glass of champagne as they entered the elevator; if they happened to down the champagne while riding in the elevator, there were waitresses on the platform to fill up their glasses. The film crews were filming the entire event live on all cable networks.

Behind the curtain, another curtain hid the orchestra poised to take over from the preprogrammed music being played. The first ladies were poised and ready, and Juanita had the honors of being the first to descend the staircase. The lights were dimmed and a spotlight put on the lady, elbow bent, champagne glass poised. Let the show begin! The crew had lined the studio with velvet ropes with brass stanchions for the girls to follow.

Juanita was thrilled to be selected to lead all the ladies. As she reached the bottom step, the next lady started her descent. There were nearly eighty ladies, counting the new class, who were getting the ultimate makeover; their numbers were fast approaching.

Each lady making her descent was better than the last, each trying to outdo the leading lady who performed flawlessly, so graceful, poised, sophisticated, glamorous—all of the adjectives one could put on such a performance, stunning and breathtaking,

The new class was now filing in with the experienced ladies all getting pointers from those who had descended many staircases.

When Angel appeared in her chauffeur's uniform, the applause was so loud you could not hear the orchestra play. I never thought I would see my Angel blush. She was overwhelmed with all the attention. Then Denise appeared, and there was not one male in the room who didn't have improper thoughts running through his head. This lady could cause men to run into each other, fall over trash cans, walk into walls missing the doorways, fall onto moving sidewalks—you name it, she had videos. Eileen was next to descend. She and Denise walking through the airport could cause a pilot to run the plane into the terminal; they are that attractive.

I swear the orchestra missed some notes while playing. I couldn't fault them. Most men would forget what they were supposed to be doing.

Following Eileen was another vision of mine: Gloria. She looked even better than the last time I'd seen her. She absolutely glowed. She'd asked for "The Girl from Ipanema" to be played, and she fit that song note by note.

Following Gloria was Charise, followed by Marjorie, Susanne, Diane, Phyllis, and then Silvia. Then my lovely wife, Delores, put on the best descent I have ever seen her perform. She was descending to "Sway." Behind my bride was Mama. Mr. Barns announced, "This is the lady responsible for bring our number one lady into our world, what a blessing she bestowed on all of us." Mama performed her grand entrance with Marie standing on the approach to the staircase.

Mr. Barns stated, "Without her none of this would have ever become a reality. She followed the vision of Fred Stockdale on the morning when he presented John and Marie his vision to adjust their landscape to perfection. You all have seen the video of the beautiful courtyard; we all wish we might be so lucky."

As our beloved and cherished Marie made her descent, the orchestra played "Return to Me," sung by her favorite singer, brought in for this occasion. As she approached the bottom step, Delores went to her and they hugged.

Mr. Barns said, "This is so fitting, the two who started the program. But, ladies, we have another surprise." The spotlight was put on the staircase entry for the appearance of Janet and Brad, then Jerome and his escort, then Jonathan and his escort, then Matthew and his escort, then Leslie and her escort, followed by Sarah and her escort, then Kim and her escort, and finally Rebecca and her escort. All three moms were a complete wreck as each child descended the staircase.

Susanne told everyone that lunch was being served followed by the large studio being turned into the ballroom.

As everyone was being served, Maggie donned a waitress outfit to help serve the tables. Sally also donned her hotel outfit to help serve.

Everyone was seated and being served beverages, salads, and then the main course. Of course you would think steak and lobster; nope, crow with chocolate feathers, French fries and goose juice. Maggi was busy teaching the waitresses how to make labels, and soon the entire staff of ladies were making labels for the guests.

The entire party of ladies were applauding Delores for her contribution of the meal. Mr. Barns asked Delores to explain the meal to all attending.

"Well, first, you all know my husband. He's quite the character; he has the ability to put his foot into his mouth and step into piles deposited on the ground.

Through the years of married life, I have retaliated creating crow sandwiches. Once in a while I throw in a pigeon or two for good behavior.

"He teases me about my cooking, so I have found ways to pay him back. One afternoon while he was grilling our dinners to a nice blackened state, I brought him a can of 7 Up with a label calling my creation goose juice. I added a couple drops of lime juice in the can to disguise the flavor.

"He felt the obligation of sharing his reward with the rest of the family. He would sprinkle our grilled meat with the goose juice just to see if there was a reaction. Just trying to digest the blackened meal, we did not notice the difference in flavor until we saw what he was doing from our kitchen window.

"When we confronted him, he decided to have a taste test. Some he would sprinkle with goose juice and not sprinkle the others. We didn't believe him. We thought he might be cheating, so we said, 'Go one night with goose juice and one night without.' Marie and I controlled the goose juice.

"We all agreed that the meat with a splash of goose juice did have a better flavor. That's how all of this started.

"Our chef at our favorite eatery is the one who designed your meal today. Please enjoy his creation. We steal, my husband's french fries and feathers each time; that's how he keeps slim and trim. Ladies, feel free to borrow your spouse's things—or your boyfriend's or any man's things. That's what makes us different from them: we have goodies, they have things."

All the ladies stood up and applauded Delores; "Our hero," they chanted.

The estrogen levels were redlining about now.

Susanne said, "We have a surprise prepared by all of our chefs today for the girls' main treat. Each table has a three-layer chocolate cake with chocolate icing with your names inscribed on your own piece of cake. Thank you, girls, for giving us hunger pains with the proper medication to put those at rest.

"The waitresses will cut and serve you your private piece of cake."

Once everyone had dined and desserted, the orchestra was replaced with the dance band that performed at the governor's ball. As couples approached the dance floor, each lady was given a corsage to be either pinned to her outfit or worn on her wrist. There were hired escorts for each single lady and any whose spouse was not able to attend.

The escorts had been given a lady's name as their partner for the day. The dance floor was filling up fairly fast the songs were easy to dance, some fast some slow but all danceable. The kids were having a great time; their escorts were the ones they'd had at the governor's ball.

Janet and Brad were making up for lost time apart. Marjorie knew that when Janet turns of age, she will be married to Brad; they had talked to Marjorie regarding their plans. Jason came with the ladies; he and Denise were as one and forever. We all knew her moving to Texas was very important to that relationship.

Everything was going smoothly. The governor and Diane were dancing with everyone. They spent a good bit of time with the girls; they will miss them immensely and on visiting them at least once every month or two. His schedule is the only restriction. The girls can't wait for them to see their lambs and calves. They will show them how to feed them and introduce them by name. The girls, the governor, and Diane were all in tears; they truly loved one another.

As the day passed on, Mr. Barns and Phyllis asked for Marie and Delores to approach the stage. When they arrived, Mr. Barns announced, "One of our biggest events featured a total surprise for these lovely ladies, and we want to reenact that moment in time. Gentlemen, open the doors."

As the assistants opened the doors to the studio, in strolled two white horses pulling a carriage with Prince Charming riding inside. The staff brought in two lavish mid-century chairs for Marie and Delores, and the stylists set tiaras on their heads. These were real; no zirconium found on the tiaras. The horse-drawn carriage came to a halt, and Prince Charming emerged carrying two shoeboxes from Christian Louboutin. This time he knew which shoe fit which lady; the staff had put their names on the lids.

Clearly an actor, he read his brief script off one box. Then he placed the shoes on Delores's feet first and escorted her to the carriage; then he did the same for Marie. Then in a motorcade of police cruisers, the carriage was taken to the nearest five-star resort hotel, a mile away on of the most traveled highways in town.

The police escort blocked off traffic from both sides of the boulevard to allow the carriage to enter into the resort hotel to deliver their passengers. Of course, the entire trip was recorded live for all channels to air. They came to the portico, where Prince Charming helped the ladies from the carriage and delivered them, one on each arm, to the hotel manager and waiting staff who escorted them to their waiting suites.

Prince Charming kissed the ladies farewell and returned to the carriage, which returned to pick up the girls and their husbands. The traffic from the main street was detoured around the event.

When we all arrived, the ladies were toasting each other with champagne. They told the camera they both wanted to have all the ladies come to the hotel for more dancing and dining; Susanne passed the message back to them.

This was one grand event. Marie and Delores were in complete awe of the entire day. Marie asked Delores to pinch her nicely, so she could know this was really happening.

They both were starting to weep. Marie said, "I never imagined this would occur from having my home re-landscaped. The most spectacular landscape, a friend for life, so many lives changed over something fun—how do I ever repay you, your girls, your husband?"

Delores hugged her and said, "You have repaid us many times over. You, your girls, and your husband filled a void in all of our lives. I thank God every night for bringing all of you together with us."

Marie said, "We both needed this. Prayers do come true!"

Delores said, "This just wasn't by chance?"

Marie said, "No, dear, this was destiny, from our prayers."

Our families were being summoned to the lounge; "We have numerous guests wanting to know where you are," said the messenger.

Marie looked at Delores. "Well, sister, showtime."

They arrived to a full lounge, where everyone was standing and applauding them as they entered. The girls and boys were swarming them with hugs and cheek kisses.

Susanne announced, "The two most fantastic women I have ever met and had the privilege of getting to know personally. Let the party begin, maestro: 'Return to Me,' for my lovely friend Marie and John." As the spotlight was on Marie and John, Delores and I, Mama and Papa, and all the kids joined in with the dance.

Then anyone who wanted to dance found room on the dance floor, between tables in the aisles, in the lobby, wherever they could dance freely.

Even some of the hotel guests joined in, a marvelous sight to behold. After the third song I got tapped by the governor, but I told him, "I don't know how to follow; I can only lead."

The governor said, "My dear friend, your wife is who I wish to dance with, if you will allow."

"Governor, she is all yours; just messing with you. Oh, don't step on her twelve-hundred-dollar pumps; we may have to return them for groceries."

The governor told Delores, "He's a remarkable man; you're a very lucky woman. Good husband, great daughters, great career—you have to be on cloud nine."

I was heading over to the bar when someone grabbed my sleeve. "You owe me, mister," said Gloria.

I told her, "Honey, there isn't enough money in the bank to ever pay the debt."

Gloria and I danced. She told me she had looked forward to the night for weeks, ever since she heard they were putting it all together for Marie and Delores.

"I couldn't sleep last night. They both have given all of us so much—money, joy beyond our wildest dreams, great jobs, the clothes, wow. Then you come along and change my life forever. Do you know how many proposals I get every week? If I accepted all the requests for dinner, I'd weight five hundred pounds. How did you know a simple hair style and color would take me from 'ignore' to 'hey, babe'? My daughters are getting angry; I'm stealing their thunder. Men their age are asking me out on dates."

"How do you politely tell them no?"

"I tell them I'm old enough to be their mother. One young man said, "If you were my mother, I'd never leave home.' My daughter went out with him. Guess what."

"I don't know. What?"

"He does."

"He does what?"

"Lives with his mom."

We both started laughing. Then Gloria got tapped; it was Marjorie. Gloria turned and started dancing with Marjorie. I told them, "Enjoy the dance. I'm going to get a goose juice."

I had a few more dances with my bride and Marie; Marjorie got her one dance, and Silvia snuck one in. She was terribly excited; one more day, and she and the girls would have endless fun together. Phillip's crew had started her playhouse; posts were in, and beams would be placed tomorrow with the joists. Murray and Stuart planned to pick us up at the airport with three limousines.

As Delores and I danced, she said she was getting tired. "Could we and the girls all head up to our suite?"

"Of course. You must say good night to all the ladies; you won't see many of them for some time."

Delores found Susanne. "Do you have more tissues?"

Susanne replied, "I do. What's up?"

"I have to say good night to all of my ladies. This won't be easy."

Susanne said, "I'll be beside you. Come on, you'll do just fine."

When they approached Jennifer, she told the band to play a good line dance song. The band knew of one, the best line dance song in history, "Boot Scootin' Boogie." Delores handed me her pumps, John got Marie's, and the escorts got all of the other ladies' pumps. "Hit it, maestro," said Jennifer.

Jennifer turned to Marie and Delores. "You taught us how to do what you do; it's our turn to teach you." Before the song ended, the film crew was having as much fun filming the ladies as the ladies were dancing.

Some of the moves the ladies were doing skyrocketed the viewership. All of us shoe holders put the pumps under our arms so we could applaud them. The band kept the song going at least twice more. Our daughters and the Wiloby children all joined in with the ladies.

The manager of the hotel told the crowd, "If all you ladies could perform every night, we would have a waiting line just to watch you. Drinks on the house for one hour as a thank-you. What a pleasure to have you in our establishment."

Susanne told him, "We filmed the dance, and we'll give you a copy in a few days. We'll also give you a wall of fame. All of these ladies have autographed photos for you to display."

He asked Susanne, "Could you show me a wall that is fitting for such lovely ladies?"

The two walked around the club and determined the best walls lined the entrance for guests walking into the club. Susanne also told the manager, "We'll have our subscription people set up a rack for your guests to have copies of the most current issue."

Marie, Delores, Mama, and the girls were all saying goodbye. Boxes of tissues were being passed out. We saw lots of hugs and heard, "I love you"; "Have a safe trip home"; and "Send us photos of your new house."

Gloria was the toughest parting for Marie and Delores, some serious crying along with the hugs. She told them, "Please visit me for a weekend or a week. Stay at the house, use the spa, enjoy the sunshine, and bring what's-his-name so he can use my grill. We need nourishment, you know."

We finally got to our suite. The girls all wanted to spend the night together in one suite, so we elected our suite, since I would go to the lobby early and get supplies for the hunger pains. The limousines were scheduled to return us to our homes by nine-thirty so we could get everything boxed up and completed for our two o'clock flight for Oregon.

That would give us two hours to put stuff into the garage for the movers on Monday. Juan would let them into the garages first at our home then at Marie and John's. The truck should arrive at our Oregon homes on Wednesday or Thursday at the latest.

29

All of us said our prayers with the girls, kissing their foreheads and tucking them in. Delores had brought the night lights so the girls were very happy with her. She even brought their teddy bears, knowing that the bears miss their moms, who are in Oregon with Annie and her friends.

We all gathered in the living room area and talked about tomorrow's adventure. The plan was to reunite with the Oregon staff, who would be on the same flight. Murray and Stuart texted us with the details. We of course would all dine at his restaurant and then head over to the homes. "Can't wait for my new neighbor to arrive," said Stuart.

Mama told Marie, "He is really a great man. He stops by every morning to make sure we are okay, and a fresh cup of coffee waits for him. I've made breakfast rolls for him to enjoy. He doesn't act like a multimillionaire, more like a good old boy, so willing to help, even with the littlest things. He carries his plate and cup to the sink and throws his napkin into the trash can, things like that."

Marie asked, "What time in the morning does he arrive?"

Mama said, "Between nine and ten o'clock, not with the chickens."

Papa said, "You know, I missed being with the lambs and calves today, I kept thinking about them all day."

Mama said, "I told you, you were getting attached to the affection they give you. You know, you'll have to be with the girls nearly all day long, or you'll feel left out."

Papa said, "That would be my dream come true. I'm looking forward to having them right next door."

Mama told me, "Your idea of connecting tunnels from one playhouse to the other is fabulous. Rain, snow, and wind won't bother us." She told Marie and Delores, "It's heated and air-conditioned just like the house, same temperature. Papa and I have been to all the houses; it's great exercise for us."

She went on, "The floors are wood, and clogging sounds wonderful."

We all said good night, went to our suites, and slept soundly until the four girls pounced on the bed, squirmed under the covers, shook off the chills, and got their morning hugs. I headed down to the lobby for coffee, hot chocolate, breakfast rolls, and a hug from my favorite vision.

Gloria was getting her rolls, tea, and hugs.

While we were chatting, another hotel guest was pouring a cup of coffee. Oops, he missed his cup. The desk clerk was freaking out: "Sir, sir, you're pouring coffee on our floor, sir. Please, sir, watch what you're doing."

I told Gloria, "Tell Denise you just caused a major pouring mishap."

She answered, "Honey, if I told Denise about all the mishaps I have caused since you corrected my appearance, she would be depressed."

I hurried back to the suite, knowing the girls' hunger pains were nearing their peak. I arrived at the room to find the entire clan sitting at our round table with utensils poised and ready for caloric consumption.

"What took you so long this time?" asked Marie.

I told them, "I ran into Gloria. While we were collecting our goodies, another hotel guest was pouring a cup of coffee. One little problem: he missed his cup and poured the entire pot of coffee on the floor. His focus was on Gloria, not what he was doing. I told her to tell Denise that she often causes such mishaps."

"He poured the whole pot on the floor?" asked Delores.

"The desk clerk was yelling at him while he was pouring, and he didn't seem to notice or even hear her screaming."

"We were with her once when she dropped a piece of paper or napkin on the floor," said Marie. "Two men banged their heads together trying to pick up what she dropped. You created a hazard for your fellow men."

Delores said, "By the way, where are Marie's and my redo's? We want men to fall into trashcans and miss the doorway and bang their heads."

"You have to have a re-landscape project."

Marie said, "We both have had what Gloria has, before Gloria has what we had."

I told Marie, "Once I figure out what you just said, I'll be pushing up daisies. By the way, you two have John and me. What more could any woman ask?"

There was a knock at our door. I opened it to Silvia, Juanita, Angel, Sally, Maggie, Phyllis, Mr. Barns, and Susanne. I picked up the phone, called the desk clerk, and told her my dilemma. She said, "We'll bring up two carts full of beverages and breakfast rolls, stat."

Not five minutes later, the hotel had three carts with coffee, tea, hot chocolate, and rolls galore. One cart was being pushed by Gloria. Well, not Gloria per se; the gentleman who had poured the coffee on the floor was now helping out since he had caused so much ruckus.

Gloria introduced him as Mr. Missed the Cup. "Okay, his real name is James. He will join us for breakfast, and we'll make sure the waitress does the pouring."

John asked him, "What happened?"

James stated, "I have never seen such beauty so early in the morning. I was mesmerized, not paying any attention, and didn't realize I was actually pouring the coffee. I heard the desk clerk yelling, but if you don't realize it's you they are yelling at, you don't respond. I realized what I had done when a janitor brought a mop and bucket and asked me to step aside.

"As you can imagine I was so embarrassed that I apologized to everyone. I had to talk to Gloria. Still embarrassed, I asked for her forgiveness for such a foolish act. I was ready to leave when she invited me to join you all for breakfast.

"I told her I couldn't face the gentleman she was talking to earlier. She told me he was her boss, and he found it humorous that she could cause a gentleman such a mishap.

"So I just came to apologize to everyone."

Marie walked up to him and said, "No need. We enjoyed the story. Please join us; we'll be happy to have you. Gloria needs an escort; keeps her out of trouble."

Gloria handed him a cup of coffee and a roll. By the time our scheduled breakfast time down at the restaurant came about, he was nearly back to normal.

We all made it to the restaurant.

Leslie told the waitress that she had a special order request: the Albright scramble, as shown on their television show. If she could write it down and present it to the chef, they would like eight servings and maybe more if the other guests order the same.

The waitress returned with the chef, who talked with Leslie and me about the ingredients. He added a three-cheese blend and put some homemade salsa into small bowls for Leslie to sample. Leslie took a bite and passed the plate around to her sisters, the Wiloby children, and me. "What do you think?" asked the chef.

We all agreed that it was very close, and could we all have an order, with pancakes, hash browns, and link sausages? Leslie had the last bite, which she put salsa on and said, "Perfect, that salsa makes it sing." Then she asked, "Could you make a breakfast burrito using the Albright scramble?"

The chef said, "My dear, we can make anything you wish."

Leslie told him that we had talked about making breakfast burritos yesterday morning, and we'd love to try one today. The chef said, "I'll be right back." He told his staff how to prepare the Albright scramble, and twenty plates were required. He personally made the burrito, one wet, one as ordered.

The chef returned to the table, where he cut the burritos into bite-size pieces for all of us to share. The order grew from twenty Albright scrambles to include fifteen burritos—eight were wet—plus salsa all around. The entire group of diners were now eating the Albright scramble and Albright breakfast burrito.

The manager we had met last night came to the table. "Good morning, everyone. I have heard you ordered your breakfasts without using our gourmet menu."

Leslie said, "Sir, my daddy makes an egg dish we crave. It's so good, your chef was kind enough to make it for us. We hope you don't object. Can you ask the chef to allow you to sample our egg dish? He also has salsa that he has offered to provide our group."

The manager said, "I'll be right back." He came back with a breakfast plate in hand and sat at our table, asking all to forgive him while he sampled the dish. After a couple of bites of the scramble, he turned to Leslie. "Mademoiselle Leslie, may we add your egg dish as our breakfast special for today?"

Leslie said, "We would be honored to have our dish as your special."

The manager returned to the kitchen to tell the staff to make the dish the special for today. "This is very good."

The breakfasts all started to arrive. The waitresses were also serving a bowl of salsa, and they excused themselves to put the salsa in a larger bowl for all to share, They didn't have enough to give everyone their own bowl. "The staff is busy making more salsa."

As the dishes were being served, new customers were asking what we had ordered. They hadn't seen that dish served here before.

The waitresses told them, "It's the daily special. Would you like a sample?" The staff made up three sample plates of the daily special, and before we left the restaurant, nearly every table had ordered the special.

The head chef brought the girls their favorite: all the kids got a chocolate cupcake with chocolate icing with their names in white icing on top. Susanne had called the day before and ordered the cupcakes for the kids.

Breakfast was fantastic, and making the Albright scramble into a burrito was beyond our expectation. The key to upgrading the scramble using salsa was phenomenal. Everyone who tried the burrito was in heaven; "the best tasting breakfast burrito" was the theme of the day. Those who were not a part of our party had nothing but praise for their meal.

The manager said they were making the Albright scramble part of their menu. They handed out hats for all the kids and T-shirts for all the ladies to promote the establishment.

As we all departed the restaurant and headed back to our suites, the staff gave the ladies hugs.

We got all packed up and headed to the lobby for our limousine ride to our homes.

30

Back at home we scrambled to get our belongings to the garage. Both families worked, starting at our house and then moving to Marie and John's. Juan would take my truck to the yard and use it; his truck would go to our new superintendent, whom Juan is training.

We all loaded into Delores's vehicle and Marie's vehicle, which they'd left in our driveway the night before.

When we arrived at John and Marie's, we had to hurry. John and I operated the forklifts, while the kids, Mama, Papa, Marie, and Delores were all packing the boxes. We finished with about ten minutes to spare. The two limousines pulled in and whisked us off to the airport to get searched, of course we informed them we were wearing warning devices and not to put us through any type of X-ray devices or magic wands.

They had all of our names on the computer system showing that we were safe to enter an aircraft. They pulled us from the line and guarded us so we couldn't wander off until we were confirmed by officials.

At the terminal, we met up with all those flying back to Oregon. Across the terminal were the ladies from Texas, who started hooting and hollering Texas lady slang: "Y'all," "Howdy," and so on. They started to line dance, which got all the passengers for their flight dancing too—along to elevator music, no less. It was pretty funny to watch a line dance in slow motion, not as exciting as one would pay money to view.

The ladies all had enough time for one last hug and met in the middle. Denise showed how to make men forget what they were doing. Jennifer hugged her and said, "You have to stop that, or some poor soul will get seriously hurt." She got two guys to run into each other watching her.

Jason of course told her, "Be nice, you're nearly a married woman."

They started calling all the first class passengers and business class to board; that was our entire group. Both aircraft had only coach seating left after we'd all boarded.

The flight attendant asked if the ladies from Texas were the Dallas Cowboy cheerleaders. Marie told her, "Not one of those girls are cheerleaders at this time; they're our ladies," and handed her a business card.

"You all are associated?"

Marie told her, "That's only half of the Ladies' Club. If you're talented and like to make serious money having fun, contact the phone number on the card. You can talk to the lady a couple of seats behind us and arrange for an interview. Her name is Susanne; we will put you through the test."

The flight attendant talked with Susanne.

They arranged for her to meet with Eileen on Tuesday at the studio.

We had the best service ever on the airplane ride to Oregon. We landed and had no delays getting off the plane from first class. We had very few carry-ons and headed over to the baggage carousel and waited patiently. Murray and Stuart were there to greet us, and the hugs from the girls were well received.

The girls asked Murray about the lambs and calves. "Did you give them hugs today?"

Murray said, "We have three farm hands caring for your animals, and they gave them love. The lambs are very playful with humans; your grandpa has them spoiled."

Stuart informed Marie and Delores that all of their belongings had arrived safe and sound, in good condition.

The girls asked whether their stuffed animals were crying. Doreen said, "They were happy to see daylight and looked all over for you four. I think they are a little sad; you may have to give them some special hugs in the next few days."

Our luggage was starting to get a ride on the carousel, and soon the limousine drivers were gathering the bags onto carts and heading outside to load them up. They made sure all luggage was accounted for and escorted the ladies to their vehicles. Angel was tempted to wear her outfit but knew that if she did, one of the drivers might have a mishap. Besides, the cameras were packed, so no one would know.

Everyone in the vehicles went on to the restaurant for nourishment. We arrived in about an hour. The girls were excited to be in Oregon, most importantly to see their stuffed animals and the real ones as soon as possible. They had no hunger pains; at least they didn't express that to us.

The restaurant staff were all ready for us, and we were seated in the banquet room where all sorts of banners, balloons, and streamers welcomed us to Oregon. Everyone got the rib eye steak deluxe lunch meal. The waitresses had my goose juice ready, and there were five pitches of goose juice for the rest of the guests, each of whom had a glass.

Susanne announced, "Everyone, pour a glass of goose juice so we can toast the inventor and the man responsible for all of this."

Stuart, Doreen, Delores, and I were told to stand once everyone had a glass ready for the toast. Susanne had Mr. Barns offer the toast.

He began, "Without these four wonderful people this would not have occurred. Marie, please stand as well. This lady took the bull by the horns, didn't just ho-hum the vision presented to her, and developed the most sought-after program ever. I thank you; my employees thank you all for everything you have done, not only for us but for our subscribers and our viewers around the world. Please, all stand now; this is for all of you and what you do on a daily basis. Cheers!"

The salads were starting to arrive. There were five different homemade dressings for the salads; the waitresses were asking which dressing each one wanted and putting it in a small dessert cup for them.

Before we could finish the large salads, here came the rib eye steaks, baked potato, steamed vegetables, and grilled Texas toast, utterly mouthwatering and so delicious that each bite melted in your mouth.

Marie asked Stuart if his chef could teach her husband how to grill steaks like these. Stuart said, "Our chefs have years of experience; this is not found in a grilling cookbook. You know those Texan ranchers building the theme park? I bought their entire herds, over ten thousand head. They will go through our inoculation before joining the existing herds."

As lunch drew to an end, the chef brought out the cupcakes for the girls, who had almost forgotten about them. The dessert tray was full of thousand-calorie delights. Most everyone passed on redoubling the multi-thousand calorie meal just devoured. The girls asked for boxes for their cupcakes; they wanted to see their animals before dark.

All vehicles were loaded and everyone buckled up, and off we went to see the new homes, animals, and playhouses, in that order.

The limousines entered the farm gates and headed to the new homes; the girls were on the edges of their seats with excitement. The saw their new homes and gave out a "We're home, Mommy and Daddy, we're home!"

"Look how beautiful," said Leslie.

We rounded the corner to see the walls of the arched gateways all finished. The landscape was completed; all the plans that I'd drawn were now reality. The girls ran through the house, not even noticing that the homes were both furnished. They had one goal, their lambs and calves.

Papa tried to slow them down. "They don't know about the dogs! The dogs don't know them." John and I ran after the girls along with Papa.

The girls were about to open the gate to the corral when they met Scooter and Lulu—who more startled than angry, but their job was to protect the animals. A couple of quick barks got the girls' attention, and they turned to get their Papa. The two youngest were visibly scared.

Murry had heard what happened and ran outside just a few steps behind everyone. He settled down Scooter and Lulu, giving them love. "Come on, you two, let's meet the girls." He had them sit and stay. Then he had one girl at a time approach them. "Don't be scared; they are very friendly. You just startled them. Their job is to protect the lambs and calves, and that's what they were doing."

Murry first had Kim and Rebecca kneel down and pet their dog friends. He told them their names and had Leslie and Sarah join their sisters. Now Scooter and Lulu understood: these were the girls that everyone was talking about. Scooter started licking Kim's cheeks as she was hugging him, and Lulu was doing the same to Rebecca. Then all four girls were getting licked and hugging the dogs.

Murry said, "Come on, girls; the dogs will follow you. You're now their friends and soon to be their masters."

The sheep were scared from hearing the dogs bark and hid by the trees until they knew it was safe and came out to see the girls. The calves came after all had settled down.

Murry explained to the girls, "Did you see the animals hide by the trees until they knew everything was safe? The dogs taught them that. These are very smart dogs, Border Collies, one of the smartest breeds of dog, used for herding livestock."

We all were now in the corral, and Papa got treats for Scooter and Lulu, telling them, "Good dogs."

The girls asked Papa, "Why didn't you tell us about Scooter and Lulu?"

Murry said, "It was Silvia's and my surprise for all of you. We didn't want you to be sad. If we'd told you earlier, you would cry, and we don't want to see you cry."

Leslie said, "That's okay. We're tough; just ask our moms."

We all decided to go see our new homes. First the girls raced each other to the stairs to the playhouse. Murry let Scooter and Lulu follow the girls up the stairs to see inside the playhouse and tunnel.

Murry reassured us, "The dogs are housebroken; not to worry. If they head to the door, let them out, so they can go potty or check on the livestock."

Silvia was giving Marie, Delores, Mama, and all the staff a tour of the houses. They of course came into the playhouses, greeted by Scooter and Lulu. Sylvia pointed out that herding dogs don't bite to hurt but to warn people to back off until their masters come to their aid.

Scooter and Lulu greeted the ladies before in the tunnel entrance to the playhouse. Silvia called them by name, and they wagged their tails. Then she introduced them to all the ladies with her.

Delores got on her knees and started petting the dogs. "Who do they belong to?"

Silvia said, "You, Marie, the girls, Mama, and Papa. They are your family dogs who are trained to watch over the livestock."

Marie got on her knees and started petting both dogs with Delores. The girls came to the tunnel, got down on their knees, and petted the dogs as well.

Leslie said, "This is Scooter and that is Lulu. We love them, Mom, they are so nice to us."

Marie said, "They are so well mannered and loving, how did you find these great animals?"

Silvia said, "We have, sources for such dogs. We made sure they were just as the owners described before we agreed to purchasing them. Scooter is five years old, trained to handle sheep and cattle; he herded them for two ranchers. On Wednesday he loaded two trailers of beef so our ranch hands could move them from one pasture to another without doing a roundup on horseback or ATVs. Lulu stayed at the corrals to protect the sheep and calves. Lulu is also trained to herd sheep and cattle.

"Most important thing we looked for was that they were friendly to children. Proof is in the pudding: they love the girls—see, they're giving them kisses. Oh, by the way they are housebroken.

"Their job is to watch over the livestock. They barked at the girls because they didn't know them, and they were protecting the sheep and calves until Murray told them it was okay."

Silvia went on, "They would not have bitten the girls, but they would not allow them near the sheep and calves either. They would have herded them away from the livestock."

The girls said, "Come see our new house!"

"We are so happy, Mom," said Leslie, with tears forming. "Thank you and Daddy for our new house."

31

The New Playhouses

The ladies followed the girls into the new playhouse for Sarah and Rebecca. Once all ladies were inside the new playhouse, they were in awe. The pitched eight-sided ceiling was painted with primitive artwork like the original. A chandelier hung from a ceiling fan, and there were speakers for the sound system. A window in the panels let the girls watch the corrals and see the house and the French doors leading to the patio. It had a light above the front door, just as on their other house. This house was as big as the one at the office, with cabinets and seating above the cabinets—everything they had before but bigger.

Silvia said. "The temperature of the tunnels and playhouses is the same as inside your home." Scooter found his spot; his watchful eyes were glued to the entry of the playhouse.

They all wanted to go see Leslie and Kim's house. As they headed to the door leading to the connecting tunnel, Scooter and Lulu led the way, checking over their shoulders to make sure everyone was following them. The door to the next playhouse was closed, so Scooter and Lulu sat down by the door, waiting for someone to open the door for them.

Leslie opened the door, and both dogs checked the place while the ladies and girls followed. They were not sniffing like a house dog; they were looking to make sure there were no intruders.

Silvia told Marie and Delores, "Before you enter your home if you have been away for some time, have the dogs search the house first. They will alert you if something is not right. They are that good; we have tested them at our house."

Leslie and Kim's house was just as glorious as Sarah and Rebecca's. Scooter found his perfect spot to keep an eye on the tunnel door. The girls are very happy with their new houses.

Leslie said, "We can't wait to have you all as guests in our houses. Can we see our bedrooms now?"

Marie said, "I don't know—well, okay let's go."

The ladies, Scooter, Lulu, the girls, Mama, Papa, and the rest of us dudes all trooped in to see the girls' bedrooms.

The girls now got to see how the house was decorated. Leslie said, "Mom, this is so pretty. How did they know how to put your things in just the right place?"

Mama and Papa said, "We helped some. They had their own ideas; they're professionals, you know."

They arrived at Leslie's room. "Is this my room?" asked Leslie.

The girls were all jumping up and down and hugging each other. Scooter and Lulu had no idea what to do. They knew they weren't in trouble, but they had never seen the girls do that before. Looking puzzled, they put their paws on the girls, maybe to try to hold them down.

They went to Kim's room and had the same reaction as with Leslie's room. Sarah asked, "Can we go see ours?"

Off they all went through the tunnel to the playhouse, down the tunnel to Sarah and Rebecca's playhouse, and through the tunnel into their house. All the way down the hall to Sarah's room, the girls were jumping up and down. This time Scooter and Lulu just lay on the floor watching the festivities.

I asked myself just what must be going through their heads. *Humans don't act like sheep and calves. They're more loving; they feed us. Strange bunch of beings.*

They entered Rebecca's room, and the same jumping up and down and hugging each other ensued. Then their moms, Susanne, Silvia, Mama and Papa, and finally their dads got some recognition.

Murry told the girls, "Scooter and Lulu have to return to their family. Let's take them to their home, and you can watch them put their family to bed."

The girls called Scooter and Lulu to follow them: "We'll take you home." They were giving the dogs lots of love. They returned to the rear yard gate and opened it, and Scooter and Lulu herded the sheep and calves into the shelter that Phillip and the ranch hand built for them.

The girls were hugging and loving the lambs. Lulu stayed with the lambs while Scooter gathered up the calves and herded them into the shelter. He waited at the ready until all of the calves were lying down; then he too lay down, watching the calves.

The lambs were still wanting attention. Lulu made sure they did not leave the shelter while the girls told them all good night.

When the girls and Murray joined all of us in the kitchen, Murry told Susanne, "You have to film this tomorrow. I have never seen such a rewarding scene in my life. My dad will be utterly amazed."

The girls were asking, "Is there any hunger pain medication? Or do we have any dessert?"

Mama said, "I know exactly where the designers put the hunger pain medication." She opened the snack drawer, and there sat two boxes of their favorite snack. Mama gave them each a two-pack to hold them over.

The girls got into the elevator with Murry's instructions on how to operate it. They were going to their house to have a very important meeting.

We all guessed that this was their meeting with Annie, making sure she was doing well. In the kitchen we adults were having our coffee and sweet rolls and planning our day for tomorrow.

Murry had a couple of meetings to attend in the morning. Silvia was volunteered to take me to her house to see the playhouse and then to two other ongoing projects and finally to the office or lunch, depending on the time of day.

She drew out a map on paper, to the grocery store for Marie and Delores. Tomorrow she would take them to the furniture stores to fill in for the furnishings they'd left at our homes in Colorado.

We all strolled outside to look at our patios and barbecues, the spa, the walkways, and the water feature. We had the sound system on soft soothing music, we were watching the waterfall when the girls came down the staircase, crying.

Marie and Delores hugged the girls asking, "What is wrong? Why are you all crying?"

Leslie said, "Annie wants to go back to her house, our old playhouse."

I got down on my knees. "Tell Annie we will bring her house here. I will have Phillip dismantle the playhouse and rebuild a new one on the patio cover. We will build her house in the corrals where you all can visit one another. Tell her she is our family; she'll break your hearts if she returns. She can have your house while we bring hers here."

I called Phillip and had him send a truck. "Be extremely careful of the old shed and rebuild it on our property. Can you start tomorrow?"

Phillip said, "I will talk to Raymond. He'll dismantle the playhouse and rebuild a new one on top of the patio cover. Then he'll ship the shed to your house. Didn't the girls like the one we built?"

"They love the playhouse that you built. Someday I'll explain everything to you."

The girls returned to their house and came back about a half hour later, in a much better mood.

"Annie agreed to stay in their house while her house is being rebuilt. She doesn't want to hurt us, Daddy. She loves us, as we love her," said Sarah. "She wants the old table brought with the house and the two chairs—please, Daddy."

I told them I would tell Juan to make sure the table and chairs were brought with our other belongings. With that, the girls returned to their house.

We all settled down watching the waterfall listening to the music. Delores said, "This is almost as nice as Marie and John's original setup." We went to both water features to see if one had more ambience than the other; "about the same" was the general consensus. They loved how the bridges connected the two decks and the angles of the bridges across the streams; the bridges were arched just enough to add that special touch.

Marie and Delores told me that I'd done good. They both gave me a hug but informed me that this didn't give me a one-up; they just liked the design and how it felt; no bonus.

As a male for many years, it is extremely difficult to get the female to feel she owes you one. They know something sacred that we males will never fully understand.

We continued to stroll all three properties. The light show was now on full display. What a difference the lights made to the landscapes. The pathway lights illuminated the walkways perfectly. Juanita was walking with us, and I told her, "Great job."

Angel said, "I taught her everything I know."

I told her, "You did a marvelous job. You can train each branch office to have a Juanita.

"That just reminded me. Juanita, you have to go to Texas next week to install Jennifer's lighting system. I'll have Marjorie make sure all the materials are there, and she'll have someone help you, someone willing to learn."

We all returned to the kitchen, where we'd started. Sarah asked if all the girls could sleep in the same bed tonight at our house.

Sarah's bedroom had a king-size bed, so we all saw no harm. Susanne asked if she could sleep in our guest room or in Rebecca's room tonight. The girls know there are doors that adjoin the two bedrooms.

Delores said, "Of course, but when lights are out, it's sleep time. You have to be up early to feed your animals."

It was about an hour before bedtime, and the girls wanted to spend some time with the stuffed animals and play a board game.

Marie and Delores went to Kim and Leslie's room to get pajamas for the girls. Marie told Delores, "You know, living next door to each other, we don't have to get our street clothes on. We can use the tunnels back and forth; this is so nice."

Delores said, "Our husbands are remarkable. They knew we were both afraid of rejection, and they got us to tell our true feelings."

Marie said, "It was one of the best days of my life, becoming your sister."

The two returned to the girls' bedroom to give Leslie and Kim a pair of pajamas.

Susanne was playing a board game with them; she was not winning. She was in fifth place; that was the good sign.

Susanne said, "Good thing there aren't more playing."

Sarah gave her a hug. "That's all right, Susanne. We're not playing for money."

Marie said, "Now that is the bright side."

Delores said, "You have about fifteen more minutes; then you have to get ready for bed."

Marie told Susanne, "Good luck; maybe you'll finish fourth."

Susanne said, "Nope, I had to borrow from the girls just to stay in the game."

We had everyone come up to Sarah's room for prayers and kisses and to tuck them in.

When we all arrived, the girls were already under the covers. Susanne was reading them a story from one of their books.

Marie asked, "Is that your reward for finishing fifth?"

Susanne said, "One story per night for five nights, to pay off my debt."

I told her, "Good thing it isn't *War and Peace*; that could take a while."

Susanne said, "Tomorrow night is *Rules of the Game*. I just lost, if you care to sit in."

Delores said, "That is a real page-turner. I had to endure that a few years ago."

We all gathered around the bed and said prayers with the girls, kissed their foreheads, gave them the stuffed toy they wanted from the shelf, and turned on the night lights. John and I tucked in the girls.

We all departed to the kitchen area then said our goodbyes. After this long day, we were all tired.

Mama, Papa, Marie, and John departed by way of the tunnel connecting the playhouses to each home, they all said how wonderful not having to drive or even endure the climatic conditions outside. The homes are all at the same temperature with the tunnel and playhouses. The lighting is controlled by each home. As they left our home, we waited until John and Marie turned off their lights to the playhouse; then we shut off ours. We could see that John and Marie waited for Mama and Papa to turn off their lights before they turned off theirs. The tunnels are in sync with the playhouse.

Delores and I took the elevator to the top floor, the master bedroom. Wow, what a room! A new bedroom suite with a king-size bed, decorated like a Victorian farm house. We had dimmers on the light switches for the ultimate in ambience.

The bed was incredibly comfortable. The bedding was soft and luxurious and smelled newly laundered and fresh. We even controlled the lights from under the covers. We played with the handheld remote: off, on, off, on, off, on—then "Stop it, or you will sleep on the couch," said my dearest to me.

Before the cock crowed, the girls all came up, pounced on our bed, and quickly squirmed under the covers. They commented on how much softer our sheets were compared to theirs. The girls were all shivering until they got their hugs and stole the warmth, we had generated throughout the night. Delores and I were on the coldest part of the mattress.

I knew the next demand: "We have hunger pains, Daddy. Is it time to make breakfast yet?" asked Leslie.

"Say no more; I wasn't sleeping anyway." I got up and headed down the elevator to the kitchen, where I started my normal routine. Only one slight problem: *Where is everything? This is not as automatic as yesterday morning.* I found the coffee but couldn't find the pot; found the hot chocolate mix but could not find the pot. I looked in all the cabinets but found no pots or skillets.

Soon I was joined by Delores and the girls, all with throws wrapped around them. They all sat at the table watching me open and close all the cabinets, scratching my head.

Delores asked, "What are you looking for?"

"The pots and pans; do you know where they are?"

Delores said, "Yes, we know where they are." The girls all started to giggle, and Delores had a huge smirk on her face.

Fists on hips, I said, "I don't have time for games. Could you please tell me?"

The girls in unison said, "Look above the stove."

"I looked in those cabinets. There are no pots and pans in those cabinets."

Delores stood up, walked to the kitchen island, took a pot off the hook, and said, "Not in the cabinet. Are you blind, too?"

"Okay, I'm not as bright as I look. Would you happen to know where the coffeepot is located?"

Delores said, "Girls, if we want to eat before the sun sets today, let's have Daddy sit at the table and watch. He's hopeless today."

Delores opened a small cabinet door and slid out the coffee maker. She made the coffee, and the girls made their own hot chocolate. Our elevator bell rang, and in came Marie and John, followed by Mama and Papa. Then came Susanne. She had slept in; too comfortable in her new bed. "I didn't even move during the night, I've never done that before, ever," she said.

The coffee was hot, and Marie poured, knowing I had gotten into enough trouble this morning. She didn't want to give Delores more ammo.

Delores was making the Albright scramble, following tips from Leslie as she flipped the pancakes and Sarah turned the sausages. Rebecca and Kim made the toast and hash browns. We had a kitchen table and a stovetop counter with five stools. The girls and Susanne took the stools, giving us old folks the table and soft, cushioned chairs.

It was pretty nice to sit back and watch my masterpiece being created by my wife and children. *My job is done.*

Dream on, buddy; your nightmare is only begun. You just think you're running the show. Fooled again; you will never run a three-woman show, not in the cards.

Breakfast was nearing completion. Marie and Susanne got the condiments on the table: butter and jelly for the toast, ketchup, and a jar of salsa. Yeah, salsa in a jar—not very thrilling, but it would have to do until we got the proper ingredients to make homemade salsa.

Breakfast was really good. Delores's Albright scramble was very tasty; even our Albright scramble connoisseur remarked how good the scramble tasted. Of course, all the females agreed with Leslie.

I told them, "Then we all have a new Albright scramble chef?"

They all laughed. "Not quite, Charlie," said Marie. "You don't get off the hook until we free you from that hook, this isn't catch and release. If you're out of town or ill, we might give you a pass."

Delores said, "Or if you can't find the pots and pans hanging in front of your eyes." She turned to Marie. "You know he had to duck the pots and pans to talk to me? You know, I almost peed my pants when he asked where the pots and pans were, while ducking his head to talk to me."

The girls all went upstairs via the elevator to get ready for today. The sun was peeking just above the horizon; it was almost time to feed their babies. Papa told them in about a half hour he would go out to visit the lambs, the calves, Scooter, and Lulu; "Let's give the dogs a break."

Papa went home and got some scraps from their lunch steaks for the dogs, knowing they would love the meat. He told the girls that they could give the dogs some of their dog food and make sure they have fresh water. He did see Scooter drinking from the calves' water trough.

The girls were all set with boots, jeans, plaid flannel shirts with T-shirts underneath, and work socks. "No frilly girl stuff this morning; we are farm girls today. All set, Grandpa. Let's head to the pasture and do some chores."

They reached the corral gate, met by Scooter and Lulu who had the sheep and calves on their feet ready for some breakfast.

Papa showed the girls how much hay to give the calves and sheep, how much food to put in the dog's bowls. He gave them each a piece of steak to give to Scooter and Lulu. The girls instructed the dogs to sit, which they did. Then they gave each dog one piece of meat from each girl.

Scooter and Lulu took each piece from the girl's hands very gently, almost licking the meat from Kim's and Rebecca's hands. Papa was amazed how nicely they took the meat. They waited until the animals were finished eating, but then the girls got to give them all hugs and pet them. They told them they loved them, and if they needed anything more, they could just give them a call.

Scooter and Lulu followed the girls into their playhouse. At first they seemed unsure whether to follow Papa or the girls. They decided on the girls since Papa was going into the house.

After about a half hour, Murray and Silvia arrived. Murray wanted to check on the animals. Scooter let the girls know there was someone in their yard, so they let him out of the playhouse. Then he saw it was Murray and settled down. The girls and Lulu soon followed Scooter, and into the corral they all went.

Murray said, "You have already fed the sheep and calves?"

Leslie said, "Yes, and Scooter and Lulu as well."

Sarah said, "Papa showed us how much, telling us not to overfeed them."

Murray gave the girls a hug. "Great job, girls; we're so proud of you. You all look like my ranch hands. I almost didn't recognize you. Wow, only your first day, and you're professional ranch hands."

Silvia came from the house and asked the girls how they liked caring for the sheep, calves, and dogs, while giving them hugs.

Kim said, "We got up early so our family could have some breakfast with us. We love them."

Silvia said, "Since the lambs are surrounding you, I have to say the feeling is mutual."

Murray told Silvia, "My dad will not believe what he sees this afternoon."

Three of the calves were walking toward the girls to get some attention; then the rest followed, Scooter was not herding them. They did it on their own.

The girls gave the calves hugs and petted them, telling them they loved them. "If you need anything, let us know." The girls headed to the corral behind Leslie and Kim's house. The calves and sheep followed them, while Scooter and Lulu checked the ground for critters.

Murray told Silvia, "I'm telling you, my dad is in for one treat. He will not believe his eyes."

Silvia was ready for our road trip; she would chauffeur me around her part of Oregon. I gave the girls hugs and kisses and did the same with their mothers. I hugged Susanne, who would be filming our home and spending the day with the girls on the farm. She had wardrobe on site to aid in the proper attire for the situation at hand.

The ladies were heading off to the grocery store. I asked to drive the shopping cart, but that would not happen anytime soon. I know if I had won the Indy 500 race, they might be more inclined to allow me to drive the shopping cart. Losing was my downfall.

32

I asked Silvia if there would be a quiz at the end of our tour. She asked, "What type of quiz?"

"How did we get from my house to your house?"

Silvia said, "You will learn the directions soon enough. I don't want to cloud up your mind today with driving directions; that's what Google Maps are for."

She told me, "Murry is so happy to have the girls around; he is so impressed by them, as we all are. How did you, Delores, Marie, and John manage to get them to be like they are?"

"You have that backwards. We didn't do that to them; they did it to us."

Silvia said, "I'm confused. You're the parents."

"It's a long story, somewhat unbelievable. Someday I'll have Delores and Marie disclose the real events, which will answer your questions."

We arrived at Silvia's house; I remembered the house from my last visit to Oregon.

We entered her backyard, where Phillip's crew was covering the joists with plywood sheeting, getting ready to install the subfloor. The staircase was constructed, just unfinished. They did not have hand railing on top and asked us not to climb to the second floor until the decking was completed.

The posts and beams were primed with two coats waiting for the color coat to be painted tomorrow, since the weather was too wet; it had rained the night before. I looked at the location of the playhouse; then I looked up and saw the bedroom windows. I asked Silvia, "Can we go take a peek out of those windows?"

Silvia said, "Follow me. You can peek, but you can't touch."

Soon we were standing at the windows looking out; it was the master bedroom. "Would you like to walk out of your bedroom onto a deck and into your playhouse?"

Silvia said, "That would be one huge step; two feet maybe, but fifteen feet? Murry and I would fall short."

"Let's connect the house to the playhouse. Your upper deck will allow you to sunbathe on lounge chairs in the sun, not in the shade. We could even give you a bar if you so choose."

Silvia said, "You know, I picked a man who does not drink alcoholic beverages. Go figure; how did I miss that when choosing a man to marry? A bartender to marry a nondrinker; knock me over with a feather."

We went back outside for me to take a picture to send to Phillip. I talked with the foreman and told him our idea. We shot a couple of elevations and found it could attach fairly easily. They would remove a couple of siding boards to install the header beam.

Silvia said, "My fiancé designed and built this home; he has the blueprints you can use. We will need to see how the window is installed and what's between the outside and inside walls of the house."

"Do you have another bedroom you can stay in while the construction is taking place?" asked the foreman.

Silvia asked, "How long will the walls be exposed to the elements?"

"We possibly could have it opened and closed in one day. Depends on the French doors and the necessary door casings. Phillip would fly in his wood worker to custom make the casing and French doors, using your garage as the wood shop."

"Will this delay the construction of the playhouse?"

"No, the posts are staunch enough to support the weight of the deck. The materials required are readily available; we could start making that happen tomorrow. Fly in the woodworker tomorrow, cut out the door opening the next day, and put in a temporary plywood door while he makes the casing and doors. Our woodworker makes these in his sleep; he is very fast and accurate. While he is making the doors and casing, the deck will be completed. He can make the hand railing as well."

I took some wonderful photos of the window and siding and the playhouse structure. Silvia wants a photo album just like Marie's.

Silvia forwarded the photos to Murry, explaining what she wanted for their home. Murray responded that he would send his superintendent, who had built the house, to confer with Phillip's foreman. "We don't want our house structure or weatherproofing to be damaged. Our crew will install the header for them to attach the structure. I'll call Phillip to explain; thank you for alerting me."

"Perfect," I said; "let's take some measurements and send them to Angel. She can correct the construction drawing. The supplier. can adjust lumber sizing to forward to Phillip." Once we were done with the measurements, we left for the next project.

We arrived at one of Silvia and Angel's designed landscapes. Silvia introduced me to the foreman and superintendent on the jobsite. I had never met either one before; both were hired by Murry.

The superintendent showed me what they had accomplished, unrolled the drawings, and told me their game plan for the week. As we were walking the project, I was asking questions of both Silvia and the superintendent, making sure there would be no hiccups causing a tear-apart and rebuild. The barbecue area needed the gas line and, electrical conduits before the pouring of the footings. "Can I see the details you are following?"

The foreman joined us and explained they were digging the footings first; then they would run the lines into the barbecue through a sleeve. I asked the superintendent how deep they would lay the gas line and electrical conduit.

"The electrical is twenty-four inches, and the gas line is eighteen."

"What is the depth of your footings?"

The foreman said, "Twelve inches."

"Then the gas lines and electrical conduits will be run and inspected before you pour the footings. You're setting us up for failure by the city inspector, which will escalate all through the project."

The foreman told me that was how his past employer would build their projects.

I told the foreman, the superintendent, and Silvia, "Not for me, never. We build per building codes, with permits in hand. Everything is inspected, or all projects will stop and be corrected before moving forward. I don't want any court battles; that's what kills the company in the future.

"Silvia call the rental company, call Dig Alert, get the trencher delivered, and have this job flagged by Dig Alert before another thing is started.

"The footings for the structure—where is the permit?"

The superintendent said, "Phillip has the permit, I think."

I called Phillip. "Do you have the permit for the patio structure?" and gave him the homeowner's name and address.

Phillip said, "Let me call you back. I have to contact my foreman who was on that project."

I took Silvia aside. "You need to have all permits in our files. Phillip is a subcontractor. We pull the permits, not the sub-trade. If that permit was not pulled and the footing inspected, the structure comes down and gets rebuilt to code."

She went and told the superintendent what I'd just told her: he needs to pull the permits from now on; no excuses.

The superintendent came over to me and said, "I have to pull the permits?"

I told him, "We could have the office staff do that for you—after the meeting in our office at one o'clock today. Please both of you be there; no excuses will be honored."

Silvia and I went to the next project. During our drive I told her, "This is not right, and I won't tolerate projects being built with 'lawsuit' written all over them.

"Where is Murry?"

"He's at a new project getting ready to start tomorrow."

"Text him to be at the office at one o'clock, required."

Silvia said, "Wow, one day, all foremen and superintendents to report. What about the crews?"

"They can go home unless there is something they can do without supervision, which I only allow if I know they are truly capable."

At the next job, I wanted to see the permit card. The foreman said, "It is with the superintendent." We spent about five minutes at the site. I told the foreman, "Send the crew home at lunch. You be at our office at one o'clock."

We arrived at the office, and I told Silvia to go on the computer and pull the city, county, and state requirements for permits.

I went to see Angel. "Could you call Dig Alert and get the requirements? Go online and print the form required when you call in." I asked Juanita, "Call Juan for me, and tell him to call me when he gets a chance."

As the girls were completing their assignments, I had them sit down in my office chairs.

Silvia texted Delores. *Your husband called meeting at one o'clock to our office. He seems a little distant. What's up?*

Delores texted back, *Does he seem normal or agitated?*

Silvia texted back, *Agitated.*

Not good. What did you not do?

He had a foreman tell him that he would put the utilities in a sleeve through a footing.

Delores texted, *You're in for one horrendous meeting.*

All of the girls were seated in my office with all the required forms and data.

I welcomed them to my office. "Now I want you all to know, things will change this afternoon. The forms you are holding are required for every project. Look at these forms. Does every project you have started and completed have these forms? Silvia, please bring me a completed job file."

Silvia brought in a job file, and I opened it up. "Let's take a peek, shall we? Front page, name of the client, check; address of the client, check; funding, missing; start date, missing; completion date, missing; check roster, missing.

"Okay, ladies, how would I know if the project was paid? No check numbers, no copies of the checks submitted for payment. How about a progress payment request to verify the check matches the billing amount?

"Let me be frank, if a judge looked at this file, he would award any suit to the customer. Where are the signed-off permits for the project? Where are the permits, period? Where are the Dig Alert forms? Where are the requests for materials with the matching purchase orders? Where is any correspondence to the homeowners? Were there any change orders required for this project?

"I want to make something perfectly clear. The field works for us; we do not work for them. You tell them what to do via the superintendents; if that does not occur, then they dictate to you what they will do and how long it will take them. That's not happening anymore.

"Ladies, you need to get tough. If there's no paper from them requesting materials with a signed authorized purchase order, you do not purchase the materials, period.

"I want a starting and finished inventory from the superintendent for materials. The extra materials will be re-warehoused, not left on the foreman's truck."

Silvia said, "We have ten jobs going on right now."

"I saw two of them with you a few minutes ago. Silvia, this file folder of a completed project is horrible, it has 'lawsuit' written all over it. We could get sued by the homeowner for more than what we charged to do the work.

"Angel, go to the nearest store and purchase three *Remodeling* magazines. Call them first to make certain they have them in stock." Angel did as she was asked to do.

I told Juanita, "Go to your favorite restaurant and purchase five lunches with beverages, please.

"Silvia, you need to stay here and talk to me."

Once alone, I asked her, "Did Marjorie instruct you on how to manage an office?"

"We had several meetings on procedures to follow," said Silvia.

"Did she show you a completed projects file folder?"

Silvia said, "No, we just went over hiring procedures, making payments to vendors, and making payroll."

"Did anything I was talking about make any sense to you?"

Silvia said, "No, I was not aware, of any of those forms." She went on, "Murray was handling the field. Since he hired them, he's in charge of them, and I'm in charge of the office staff."

"No, Silvia. You are in charge of the entire operation. He has a budget to follow and scheduled dates to be met. The superintendents get direction from him, that's all. Murray will have to step up to the plate. This is going in a lawsuit direction, and I'm not going to tolerate it any longer."

Silvia asked, "Are you upset?"

I told her, "*Upset* is not the correct word. I'm worried that everything I worked for lies in the hands of a few superintendents and foremen who have no vested interest in the well-being of the company."

Angel returned with three copies of the magazine. "How come you wanted copies of the magazine? Can't Susanne send us copies?"

"Yes, she could, but she's at my house. She could have them here maybe by tomorrow; I need them now."

Juanita returned with five wonderful Mexican lunches: enchiladas, rice, beans, salad, salsa, and iced tea. Angel helped her bring everything into the conference room.

As we had our delightful lunch, we chatted about changing our procedures and rules to follow, enforced in the field by the office. We talked about what they had to have completed before handing off a project to the superintendent, who assigns the project to a foreman. "Without a field request, the job will sit until the form is completed."

Silvia asked, "What if the homeowner is complaining about no work being started?"

I told her, "If you're missing a form from the assigned foreman, you call the superintendent and ask where the form is. It will go back to the foreman on the project. If you process the order for the foreman, good luck getting any more forms from anybody.

"We will have a game plan established today. One warning will go to the foreman, which also counts as a warning to the superintendent. A second warning puts them on a fifteen-day restriction, and the third means termination."

Just after I gave that little speech, Juan was on my phone. I told him, "I'm putting you on speaker. I have Silvia, Angel, and Juanita all sitting at the table.

"Juan, remember a few years ago when we had a foreman and superintendent meeting in the garage of my home?"

There was a short pause. Then Juan said, "Yes, I remember. What happened?"

"We're having another one today, at one o'clock our time, in the office."

After another pause, Juan asked, "I can't be there. Is that why you had me call?"

"No, I need you to tell the girls in the office what you got from that meeting."

Juan said, "I got promoted from laborer to foreman."

I asked him, "Why did you get promoted?"

"Four foremen quit. They said they would never do what you asked them to do," said Juan.

I asked, "What did I ask them to do that they said they would never do?"

Juan said, "Paperwork. Request forms for materials, mostly."

"What happened to those foremen who quit?"

"Within two months they returned to work for us under me," said Juan. "The paperwork was not as bad as they had imagined. One of them is a superintendent in Oregon."

I asked Juan, "I need you for a couple of day to come to Oregon, to meet with our superintendents to enforce the issue of paperwork before starting a project. Could you do that for me next week?"

Juan asked, "You want me to be the bad guy?"

"Not the bad guy, Juan. Their *paycheck savior* is the term I would use, including Murry."

Juan said, "Yeah, maybe on Wednesday if all goes well Monday and Tuesday."

"I'll have Charise make all the arrangements, and we'll fly you home the same day."

We had fifteen minutes before showtime. The girls were making copies
for each foreman and superintendent of the forms they had in hand. They also
made a purchase order form as an example. Silvia said she would have a printing
company produce a multi-form carbonless purchase order: white to the vendor,
pink to the office, yellow to the field.

The foremen and superintendents were all arriving for the meeting. We set
up the conference room with a nice bottle of water for each one and yellow pads
and pens for them to take notes.

Murry arrived with his dad. "Stuart wanted to hear what the meeting was
all about, hoping to get some insight into how I operate."

We had all but one foreman. "We'll wait," I told the superintendent. "He
knows to be here by one o'clock?"

"Yes, I told him."

"Silvia, call him, and see where he is."

Silvia said, "He is leaving the fast food joint on his way here."

About ten minutes later, the foreman arrived with his soda in hand.

"Thank you for joining us. Such a pleasure waiting for—what's your name?"

"Reg. They call me Reg."

"Do you happen to know who I am, Reg?"

"No, sir, we have never met before."

"Well, allow me to introduce myself to all of you. I'm Fred Stockdale, and I
own Stockdale Landscape Construction. I'm your boss, Reg.

"As of today, your past procedures are gone. I don't care where you worked
before or who you worked for. You are now my employees, and you will follow
the company's procedures.

"In the center of the table are three magazines, *Remodeling* magazines, to
be precise. If you thumb through the issues, you will find a few of our projects
currently being built. The reason you are employed is because of that magazine.
Do you all understand?"

I dropped the completed project file on the table with a loud bang. "Who was
the superintendent of this project?"

John MacDonald stated, "I was."

"Mr. MacDonald, who taught you how to manage a project?"

Mr. MacDonald said, "My prior employer."

Mr. MacDonald, "I don't want to single you out; this just happened to be
a nearby project folder earlier today. I will tell all of you right now: we in the
office tell you what to do. I never want to hear from a member of the middle
management or a laborer how they will perform a task in the field. What I was
told today would get me sued. We get sued enough, and you gentlemen will be
standing in the unemployment line, is that clear? If I get sued for any reason—see
that magazine, over twenty million are distributed across the globe, and it will

no longer have Stockdale Landscape Construction as the primary company they photograph.

"As you all can see, the way you all have performed paperwork is horrible. You will all as of today be held accountable: no papers, no jobs."

Murry asked, "How will we make money if there are no jobs?"

"The same way your ranch makes no money without cattle."

"We don't make money without cattle," said Murry.

"And we don't make money without the proper paperwork. No court in this land would award us squat with the papers in this folder. You all need to forget what you did for you prior employers. They more than likely had someone else covering for you. I don't want to hire assistants unless you all want to work for less money to share your paycheck with your assistant.

"Right now I want each and every one of you to fill out today's work completed on your yellow pad. Then tell me what you will accomplish tomorrow, how many men, what each one will be doing on the jobsite, and what will you do the next day and then the next day. Superintendents, you get with the foremen to complete each job you're responsible for.

"Murray, you're in charge of the field. You work with the superintendents to fulfill the contractual work on each project. You will check the amount of payroll spent compared to the budget for each project. You and I will meet tomorrow to go over what you have determined has been completed compared to the remaining budget for each project to see if we will lose money or make money. You will also check daily for all paperwork required for each project per superintendent. If any paper is lacking, you will notify Angel, and she will let each superintendent know the paper they are missing; that's warning one. If it's not completed that day, that's warning two, and there is no warning three. I'm dead serious, and I'm going to allow my other three offices to support this office.

"You all know now who you are working for and what I require of each of you. If you feel you cannot perform these tasks, you can decline your position and step back to allow someone else who will fulfill the required work. Superintendents, you would become foremen; foremen, you would become leadmen or laborers.

"Silvia will have a paper for you all to sign, starting tomorrow, with the exact tasks that you will perform. If you fail, I'm telling you right now, failing is not an option for gainful employment.

"We have over seventy jobs on going in four locations—soon to be five and possibly six. Manuel is one of my Colorado foremen who moved here to become a superintendent. We are proud to promote from within before we search the job market. You all could be moved up the ladder by doing what we asked.

"Just to let you all know, I started as a laborer and moved up the corporate ladder, reached the top, and decided to start my own company.

"Work on your projects, and have your reports on my desk by tomorrow morning. No work on any job if you have not contacted Dig Alert, period.

"Let me tell you a quick story. A grading contractor doing some brush clearing for the transportation department did not contact Dig Alert before he started clearing a parcel. He was told by the state transportation department that there were no utilities located in the parcel he was to clear. He has a D8 bulldozer, so he dropped his ripper tooth into the soil to drag out existing shrubbery. He pulled the first area of shrubs out of the ground, and in the process, he hit a fiber optic cable and tore it in two. Eighty-five thousand dollars later came out of his own pocket to pay for the damage. But if he'd made only one simple phone call, and if the locator failed to locate that cable, he would have paid nothing.

"Oh, by the way, he was under contract to complete the clearing in a certain time frame. His contract stipulated four weeks from start to finish and assessed fifteen hundred dollars liquidated damages for every day beyond that deadline. It took eight weeks to repair the broken cable. The department of transportation enforced the liquidated damages on top of the eighty-five thousand for the repair.

"Murry and Stuart, could you join me in my office?"

After the conference room was emptied and we were settled in my office, I said, "Gentlemen, I'm sorry about this meeting. I have only had to do that one other time. As I stated, the project file is horrible. I talked to the office staff earlier, and the entire operation is backwards. The field does not dictate to the office. If that was the setup, we'd have each superintendent get a contractor's license, and they could work as a subcontractor for other general contractors."

Murry said, "We build houses and office complexes with little or no paperwork. I don't understand why this business requires so much paper."

"Okay, let me ask you some questions. First off, the houses you are building—who are they for?"

Murray answered, "Friends and family mostly."

"How about the office complexes?"

Murry answered, "The same."

"How many of our contracts are family and friends?"

"With your three houses, that was it. All others are customers," said Murry.

"Would one of your family or friends take you to court? Stuart, how many customers are family and friends who eat at your restaurants on a daily basis?"

Stuart answered, "Maybe ten percent would fall into that category."

"Any of the other ninety percent you serve, could they sue you?"

Stuart said, "We make certain each and every customer is fully satisfied before they leave our establishment."

"That's not an answer, and a court of law would reject it."

Stuart said, "Well, we've never had a lawsuit, but I suppose someone could sue if they could say we caused some illness."

"I'm trying to teach everyone how not to get sued. If we do the paperwork correctly, follow the purchase orders to match the bids, do a proper job costing, and track if our proposals are a direct reflection of how our projects are built, our profit margins will increase. I want to make it clear: with no profit the business can't grow, but too much profit leads to higher taxation. If we purchase unwisely, we will pay taxes for that mistake.

"The paperwork gives us a clearer picture of reality. We can also find out if we are financing an employee's personal projects. The office will make a blanket purchase order to the vendor covering our materials in our bids and ship that to the construction sites. This eliminates the foreman or superintendent going to the supplier and waiting in line for their portion to complete the item on the proposal, leaving the crew unsupervised. You only have so many man-hours to build the project. Once you exceed the hours in the proposal, where do you get the money for payroll to complete the project?"

Murray said, "From prior projects' profits."

"So your idea is if you made, let's say, fifteen hundred dollars on project A, you can use the fifteen hundred dollars on project B for payroll that you allowed to overrun the budget. But what happens to project C if it has a budget overrun? You spent the fifteen hundred dollars on B; where does C get the funds?"

"We have to watch the suppliers also. If your employee goes to the supplier and buys over the counter something that was or was not on that vendor's quote, the employee won't receive the quoted price. Vendors have multiple price charging mechanisms. Remember, when you pick up a part off their shelves, there's a bar code on that product. Is that bar code represented in your quote?

"This is not a maintenance situation; we are building a project from costs quoted by suppliers who know that most companies have foremen or supervisors who don't ask them to follow the quoted price. You do know our quotes are only valid for thirty days, and prices are 'subject to change without notification.' Win that one in court. Fine print is there for a reason, and not to favor the consumer.

"The only time I have found the quoted price honored is upon a return of that item back to the supplier. Then they charge you for restocking, which could reach twenty-five percent of the current price, not the purchase price. They won't give you cash back unless you're a cash customer. They credit your account for the original purchase price, not the restock change they just added to your account.

"Murray, you have to get your superintendents to understand that if we lose, they lose: no bonuses, no raises, no promotions—they could even lose the forty-hour work week."

Stuart said, "How do you know all this, or are you just trying to make a point?"

"Let me tell you, this is from my project management experience. I had to do job costing for multiple projects that I was in charge of completing. The owner of the company had a meeting with one of our suppliers the next day, and it was going to get heated over something the owner did. I started checking invoices against the bids and found that were increasing the linear foot price on all sizes and schedules of piping across the board. We are talking truckloads of pipe, not a few sticks. It came to over twenty thousand dollars which our accounting department overlooked, since they were checking line pricing. So if there were five hundred feet of pipe at ten cents per foot and the total price matched their calculator, it was good to them. Our bid was eight cents per foot; they overlooked the two-cent difference in price. Many feet of pipe was purchased over the course of completing the irrigation system. This was ammo for the owner's gun, so when the supplier came to the office in a bad mood, he left in a worse mood. They were caught in price gouging. The owner of our company was no saint, but neither were they.

"I went to our office manager and showed her the discrepancy. She had the accounting department go through two months of invoices for three separate jobs and found we were getting overcharged by all vendors, because the field would run in to purchase a quoted item over the counter. We were charged the counter price, not the quoted price; we lose."

Two of our superintendents came into the office with their yellow pads. Manuel showed Murry his reports. He was in charge of four projects, and he and his foremen had drafted up what we requested. Murry looked at the report and asked, "How many men are on each crew?"

Manuel stated that he had three on one crew and five on the other. "That crew will lose two men in two days to join another project that has two men, and the final crew is just starting the job, and my foreman has one man.

"Juan, taught me to move men from one job to another so no job has people standing around waiting for something to be completed so they can do what they are trained to do. I also learned from our boss that if a job is nearly completed and needs a push to complete tomorrow, instead of going back for two or three days with a small crew, add the manpower to complete it on time.

"I heard him call Marjorie and tell her to run a payroll report to see if we could add the additional men without overrunning the budget. Marjorie told him how many men and for how many hours, so we followed her advice and completed two projects in the same time period."

I told Stuart and Murray, "Marjorie keeps a close eye on materials and labor and informs me if a crew is not keeping up with a proposal. I need Silvia, Gloria, and Charise to follow her advice and learn from her. Right now we will have to teach Silvia to crawl, then walk, and then run on job costing."

The final superintendent came in with his report. He was still somewhat confused, not certain that they all were correct.

I said, "Juan plans to be here next Wednesday. He will spend the majority of one day teaching all of you how he keeps the office informed on each project."

Manuel said, "I will be glad to see Juan again. He's he helped me a lot."

Murry said, "I'll review these reports and have the girls type them up for your records and the job folders. Thank you, gentlemen; see you tomorrow morning."

All of the superintendents shook my hand. "Hope we did what you needed. We'll call Dig Alert tomorrow to upgrade our markings."

"For the rest of this week," I said, "call in to Silvia. Tell her what phase you are on with each job so she can get purchase orders to the suppliers; just tell her what day you need the materials."

33

The room was emptying out, and Murray went to another office to talk to the superintendents.

Stuart asked, "Do all of your offices follow this procedure you just put in place?"

"I made a mistake," I told him. "I did not have Marjorie work with Silvia in the early stages of the opening of the Oregon office. We had so many projects starting and no crew, no office, no suppliers, but start dates fast approaching. Silvia was working with me taking measurements and talking with customers; she has a knack at being personable. The magazine was pushing over two hundred prospective clients wanting what Marie received now.

"Marjorie did all the footwork for Silvia. It wasn't until I opened the Utah office that Marjorie was getting burned out. She was on the verge of quitting, which would have devastated the company. I had all the cards in the deck ready to deal but not enough players sitting at the table who knew how to play.

"I have to have Marjorie come here or send Silvia to her to establish just how all of this works. I have to have the office control the field. Your managers of the restaurant control the chefs. I'm guessing if it were the other way, you'd tear up your menu if the chef has a migraine today, and your customers get tomato soup from the can. How would that make you feel?"

Stuart said, "I'm starting to understand the principles of your business."

I told him., "Imagine one of your waitresses had a bad night the night before, so she writes on the ticket for table twelve 'Food' and hands it to the chef to prepare for your customer. He asks, 'Food? What food?'

"Your waitress snaps at the chef, 'Food. Are you so dumb you don't know what food is?'

"That's what I got today; that's what triggered this whole mess. A foreman is telling me how he is going to get me sued, sleeving a footing for utilities and not calling for inspections. I don't care how his past employer taught him. I have a superintendent standing there beside me not even opposing what the foreman said and Silvia standing beside both of us going right along with what the foreman said, as if that was okay."

Stuart asked, "Who is to blame for the foreman's actions?"

"I gave them too much free rein; I should have looked at the files every time I arrived in Oregon. I should have interviewed every new employee; he would not have been hired in the first place. Now that I'm here, either the players adjust to the game called by the dealer, or they get up from the table to make room for a player who has the same desires to achieve the greatness put in front of them."

Murray came into the office and said one of the superintendents had given his two-week notice.

"Is he still here?" I asked.

"No, he just pulled out of the parking lot."

"Have him turn around right now and return to the office."

Murry texted the superintendent to turn around and report back to the office. I told Silvia to run the superintendent's final paycheck.

He stormed back into the office. "What do you want? I have a dinner date with my family, and I'll be late."

He entered my office. "I'm here, I gave you the paper you wanted. What do you want?"

I said, "First off upper management talks to upper management. I don't accept two-week notices. You need to surrender the company cards, your company cell phone, and the keys to the company truck right now."

He said, "How am I going to get home?"

I looked at him. "You do know that I own this company; you own nothing of this company. If Murray is nice and wants to take you home, that's his choice, not mine. There are cabs, and there's your family to pick you up. I'm sorry to tell you so, but I don't tolerate insubordination, nor do I want to give you two weeks to poison the crews. That little foreman on your crew today, you can have him; he will no longer be employed as of tomorrow morning."

The superintendent looked at Murray and said, "Can you take me home?"

Murry told him, "We need the phone, the credit cards, and the keys to the truck." Silvia brought in his final paycheck and handed it to him and then simply turned and walked out of the office. She had interviewed him and then asked Murry to interview him. She was his door opener.

When we had the keys to the truck, the credit cards, and the cell phone, Murray told him, "Let's go. I'll take you home."

Silvia came into my office as Stuart was heading out the door. She plopped down in my office chair and said, "So, boss, what's scheduled up for tomorrow?"

"Well, I'm calling Marjorie. Either she comes here or you go there to learn how to set up the project files, issue reports, and hold the superintendents' and foremen's feet to the fire. If you allow what I saw today to continue, this office will close in less than a year."

Silvia said, "So what the foreman said on the job walk made you upset?"

"Silvia, you do know that I'm the owner of this company?"

Silvia said, "Yes, I know you're the owner."

"Any employee who thinks I'm not aware of building codes and believes they can install landscapes without calling for inspections or acquiring permits is sadly mistaken. I will not tolerate sloppy construction, corner cutting, or hiring their friends so the work is completed on their time frame. Nope, it's not happening. You will cut the paycheck for that foreman in the morning and give it to Murray. He will usher him off my project and return the truck to the yard, and we'll hire a new foreman.

"Oh, by the way, do the same for Mr. MacDonald; last check tomorrow. I will not allow the middle management personnel to run anything. I don't want people working for me with an attitude or thinking they are entitled. You earn that; it's not a given."

Silvia said, "I have never seen you like this, you are normally so laid back and easygoing. One bonehead move really changed you. Has Delores ever seen you like this?"

I told Silvia, "You know, you have to learn from today. If you're doing your job to the best of your ability, the waters are calm, birds are chirping, the sun is shining, and you will see me as I am. If you do not do your job to the best of your ability, cop an attitude, or think you're entitled to look down on the owner, you will get what you got today."

Silvia said, "I texted Delores earlier and explained what was going on. She said, *Not good.*"

"I have to go see my little darlings. Can you take me home, or should I take the superintendent's truck?"

Silvia said, "I want to see my little sisters. I missed them today."

I told her, "Let's go see some sheep and calves."

We arrived at our house to find the girls in the corral giving the animals love. Silvia ran to the corral to get her fair share of loving. Scooter and Lulu met her at the gate, wanting to make sure she was authorized to be near their family.

The girls all hugged Silvia and told her about their day showing their audience their new home and their farm animals. They introduced each one to her and even introduced Scooter and Lulu. They all had a fun day and planned on doing it again tomorrow. They wondered if she and Murry would be their guests on Friday's show.

Silvia asked me, "Can I be their guest on Friday's show?"

"If you do all the work assigned today and tomorrow, then you could earn a visitation with the girls," I answered.

Delores met me at the corral gate. "Honey, are you all right?"

I told her, "Why do you ask?"

Delores said, "A little bird told me you were not having a Freddy-type day."

"Do I know the little bird?"

Delores said, "Yes, you know the little bird."

"Is she close by?"

Delores said, "She told you we texted, didn't she?"

"Honey, it was a day I should have had when we first opened the office. We had so much new work starting, no employees, no office, no vehicles, no phone, no insurance, no license. We had work under contract."

I went into the corral, knelt down, and petted the lambs and Scooter and Lulu, giving them all kinds of love. Then I stood up and went to pet the calves. They were a bit apprehensive since I was much bigger than the girls. They drew back until I petted one; then the others came to me. Scooter stood beside me while I petted the calves, apparently curious about how the calves would react to an adult.

After about ten minutes the girls asked, "Mom, how long before dinner?"

Delores told them that John was grilling the meat. "We should go help Mama and Marie with the sides and salads." She asked Silvia, "You will join us tonight, won't you?"

Silvia said, "I'd love to dine with you, thank you," and joined them to help with the dinner.

I strolled through our yard with Scooter and Lulu beside me. As we entered Marie and John's yard, the dogs smelled the meat cooking, which got their full attention. Papa had been giving them meat scraps for nearing two weeks, so they were getting a craving for scraps.

Scooter and Lulu saw Papa and immediately went to his side for loving and to check whether he had some scraps. Papa told them, "Not yet, a little while longer."

Marie and Delores came outside with the goose juice.

Marie told me the transportation company called her this afternoon. "Our vehicles will be here tomorrow around ten o'clock; will you or Delores be home?"

I told her, "I won't be here. Do you have anything planned?"

Marie said, "We'll be here tomorrow with the film crew; they had a great time with the girls, Scooter, Lulu, and he lambs and calves. Susanne needs to get a little tougher; a calf came up behind her and licked her elbow, and she shrieked. It scared the lambs, and Scooter and Lulu almost started a stampede with the calves. The calf behind her was wanting the alfalfa in her hand. He does that to the girls and they giggle; his tongue tickles them.

"Murry sent the ranch hand to the Outfitter store to get her the appropriate Western wear. Her high heels, short skirt, and city slicker blouse just do not impress the livestock. We had her all farmed up by lunchtime. The girls told her she looks like their ranch hand now."

She gave me a searching look. "I heard you had a tough day at the office. Silvia has never seen you like you were earlier."

I told Marie, "You haven't seen me like she saw me either."

"Silvia said you were agitated. Would I like to see you agitated?"

I told Marie, "I don't like to see me agitated. No, you wouldn't like it, and neither would the girls."

Marie asked, "Are you violent?"

"No, not violent. Agitated."

"Would you do well on the stand in a courtroom if an attorney kept repeating the same question to you, trying to make you angry?"

I told Marie, "If you're doing your job and doing it well, you will never see me agitated. If you lie to me or disrespect me or belittle me, you will get the wrath of agitation, and you'll never forget the verbal barrage I will throw in your direction.

"Marie, I'm not sure what you're trying to get me to say or tell you, but I would prefer to drop what occurred today. I need to fix this office before it gets out of control, and there is no fixing how it has evolved."

The girls were nearly done bringing the sides, salads, condiments, plates, plasticware, and candle and candleholder.

The girls announced that Mama, Papa, Susanne, and Silvia would be joining them for dinner. "We have a bigger space, but the budget is still small. We would love to have all of you; please forgive us," said Leslie.

Marie said, "I wonder who will be left out tomorrow night."

I said, "John and I wonder, but don't count your chickens before they hatch."

I told John, "Maybe tomorrow night we can use a shop light instead of the candle."

John said, "You don't give us much hope."

"Be serious, John. We're males; we're doomed."

Dinner was excellent, our first meal in our new home. It just felt right. We got to experience flying creatures, but they didn't land on our food. We had a slight breeze and a beautiful sunset, with soft soothing music to dine by.

We did have the sheep start to baa and the calves started mooing, so they must enjoy the music being played.

John asked Marie if they could find farm animal sounds on a CD at a child's department store.

Delores started singing, "Old MacDonald had a farm, E-I-E-I-O." The girls heard and joined in, so we had the first floor serenading the second floor and vice versa. Scooter and Lulu just shook their heads in disbelief: *Humans—can't live with them, and can't live without them.*

I thought Scooter and Lulu wanted to hide in the other playhouse until snack time.

Delores said, "You know someday the dogs will join in singing as well."

Dinner was delicious. The girls did come down the elevator to get the leftover meat, so their guests wouldn't have hunger pains. Papa showed the girls how he gave the dogs snacks, showed them they waited until he said okay before they ate. Papa gave the meat scraps to the dogs on the deck, not inside while eating. He had brought their dish with him from earlier in the afternoon. Both dogs waited until the meat was evenly divided between them and gave Papa kisses. Then he said "Okay," and they devoured their snack.

John of course caved in to the girls, as we both do, and the girls took their meat into the elevator and back up to the playhouse.

Papa told Marie and Delores, "You could never ask for any better trained and behaved dogs; you barely know they're here."

Dinner was so good and we ate so much that we decided to stroll the yards before having desserts. Silvia made the ladies margaritas, Goose Juice for me, and nonalcoholic margaritas for the girls. They gave a little to Scooter and Lulu, who sniffed it and walked away; not their cup of tea.

The girls led the dogs up and down their stairs to their homes, and then they all decided to see the lambs and calves. It would be more fun than playing board games. They asked Susanne if she would join them.

Susanne in her farming outfit agreed to be a farmer's daughter for a little while. She received some alfalfa from the girls to feed the calves, and the girls fed the lambs. They were all getting lots of love from the girls and Susanne.

As everyone was returning from the petting zoo, the light show was just coming on. So impressive. The girls were pointing out the different lights to Susanne; they know the difference between pathway, up lights, down lights, and wall washers. They all will make wonderful outdoor lighting experts.

Mama had made peach cobbler and served it with vanilla ice cream topped with the girls' favorite maraschino cherry. We had coffee for the losers table; the girls had hot chocolate, and their guests had coffee and hot apple cider.

Papa and the girls took Scooter and Lulu back to their family, where the girls made straw beds for Scooter and Lulu and laid two blankets on top of the straw. The dogs stretched out on their beds for the night.

Leslie asked Phillip to make them a doghouse "so they don't get wet from the rain." He promised that once they were done with Silvia's playhouse, they would build them a doghouse with two entries, one for each dog.

Phillip and I talked about tying in the old playhouse with the girls' new playhouse. Since the octagon panels were larger than the original playhouse, we just weren't sure how to make the attachment.

Annie's house should arrive tomorrow; our second truck should be here as well. They were delayed by bad weather yesterday.

34

We all set the girls up in Sarah's bed. They all felt comfortable sleeping there; they just like pouncing on our bed in the morning. Getting some extra loving and hugs never hurts. Delores and I enjoyed being awakened by them; we get as much out of them as they do us.

Plus we were closer to the livestock for right now. There was talk about putting the calves on one side and the lambs on the other. Calves from the herd were coming in from Texas, being loaded up tomorrow; Stuart told me at least twenty head were coming. The girls were all excited; more babies for them to feed and love.

Silvia gave everyone hugs and told me she would pick me up around six thirty to go into the office. We would create a game plan for the day once she had some fresh brewed coffee in her.

Susanne was going to sleep in Rebecca's bed; having her close to her girls made them feel safer.

Marie and John and Mama and Papa ventured off to their homes. Delores and I finished our coffee and headed up the elevator to our grand suite. Delores said, "Do you feel better now?"

"You know, I hate what happened today, but tomorrow is another day."

"Will you have a similar day tomorrow as you did today?"

"I don't know. The project files are a disaster, and the field dictates to the office. I want all suppliers put on notice not to honor any orders without management's approval. I really need to forget about today so I can sleep tonight. Could we change the subject?"

I gave Delores a smooch and rolled onto my side, not facing her, trying to wind down.

The next thing I remember is the girls pouncing on the bed. "Good morning, Mom and Dad," said Sarah. "We slept so well, but we have strong hunger pains. Daddy, can we start breakfast right away?" They all had on robes, not wanting to snuggle. *They're on a mission.*

I jumped out of bed and put on my robe, and we all got into the elevator. Downstairs, we headed to the kitchen. I went to the snack drawer and got them each a two-pack. Then I fixed up the coffee pot till it was making the proper noises, got the pan from above the stove—lesson learned—and poured in the milk to heat up for the hot chocolate.

The girls devoured the cupcakes. They seemed to be gone in two bites, faster than a speeding bullet. Then Momma Bear joined the girls at the table. Delores said, "Is the coffee ready yet?"

Our elevator was moving up to the second floor and then back down. The door opened, and Marie yelled, "Surprise, it's your neighbor. Is the coffee ready yet?"

I went to the snack drawer and gave each lady a two-pack. Within a couple of minutes Susanne joined the ladies at the table. The girls were manning their posts, ready for the cooking to begin.

I checked the time; it was five o'clock. I told the ladies, "Once breakfast is cooked, I have to get ready for work. Silvia will be here to pick me up."

Delores said, "She can wait. You're the owner; you give the directions, and she follows."

Marie said, "Your wife is correct. We want to see you eat, just in case you slip something into our food. You take the first bite, and we'll follow your lead."

I got the girls to start in on "Whistle while You Work," and whistling put them all into a great mood. It was so contagious, even the ladies were tapping their silverware to the music.

Just as breakfast was ready, from the elevator came Mama and Papa. They were each carrying a baking pan full of sweet rolls made last night by Mama.

Forget about all the blood, sweat, and tears it took to cook the meal they were about to eat; the girls wanted the sweet rolls. We put our foot down: "Once you finish your breakfast you can have a sweet roll."

While the girls inhaled breakfast, Papa went to the corral and brought in Scooter and Lulu. They happily wagged tails; getting loving from everyone brought a twinkle to their eyes. I made six extra pieces of bacon for the dogs and broke them in half so each of the girls and Papa could give the dogs a treat.

I reminded them not to feed the dogs from the table. Delores had purchased two bowls for the dogs and put them on a small rug so the girls wouldn't have to go outside to give the dogs a treat.

They started giving them dog bones, as rewards for being good. I gave everyone hugs and then went up the elevator to get ready for work. Once that task was competed, I returned to the kitchen, where Silvia was looking at her watch. She was five minutes early, so I made her wait.

She had a cup of coffee and a sweet roll; "Just like old times," she said. "Oh, wait a minute, not quite. There's no bed in your kitchen, and everyone has clothes on. I guess not exactly like old times, right, buddy?"

While driving to the office, I called Marjorie. My office wife said, "This better be good. I was painting my fingernails. What's up?"

"Well, sorry to interrupt your nail painting. I need you here in Oregon to straighten out the job folders and show Angel how to job cost."

"Today?" asked Marjorie.

"Nope, next week."

"Will I stay at your favorite hotel?"

"Nope, my house. I need someone who can cook breakfast."

Marjorie said, "Let me check my schedule and see if I can fit in chef duty. Nope, no time for chef duty; sorry."

"Can you set up a flight for Wednesday of next week?"

"Would you be able to send Silvia to me?" she asked.

"I can do that; can you arrange for hotel accommodations?"

"I could use a bartender for a couple of days. My margaritas are horrible."

"You and she talk," I said. "I just need to have her trained in putting together job folders, how you keep the jobs on track. Can you teach her job costing as well?"

"You know, sir, I do have an office to run. My only free time is painting my nails, which you interrupted. Oh, by the way, you know that Jennifer's party is next weekend. Can Silvia stay for the party?"

"Well, since she is a lady, and all ladies are required to be present at scheduled events, I suppose I could allow her that opportunity. What's the theme for her party?"

"Hmm; I don't truly know that answer. I will talk to her in a few minutes and get back to you on that issue."

We pulled into our office parking lot. Sylvia was truly ready for a cup of coffee. She made a fresh pot of coffee, ready for Angel and Juanita to show up for work. Juanita would fly to Texas this afternoon to help illuminate Jennifer's landscape and train two employees on how to install low voltage lighting. Juan planned to meet her in Texas to put the finishing touches on the project.

I got a phone call from Marie while waiting for the coffee. "Ms. Morgan just called to say that Mrs. Wilkins and Attorney Davidson agreed to what she had proposed. They're going to put her into a room and show various phases of what she is charged with—amputations, kidnapping of women, and they will use the girls' cable show appealing for their moms' release, and all the letters the girls received. All of this will be monitored by three reputable psychologists to evaluate her reactions to all videos shown to her. The videos will run nonstop for over four hours, no breaks."

I asked, "Will you and Delores be asked to appear before her?"

Marie said, "The magazine will have us live on closed circuit from our studio here in Oregon. Ms. Morgan will ask us questions along with Ms. Davidson, with Judge Adamson presiding."

"Your Q&A will be shown to Mrs. Wilkins, while she's being observed?"

Marie said, "Yes, this is very important. We were the only ones who escaped, and they want her reaction to that."

"Will Ms. Morgan prompt her to become agitated?"

"She wants to press her on how she allowed us to escape her network of safeguards put in place for many years."

I asked Marie, "Wouldn't her attorney reject that type of question?"

Marie said, "Ms. Morgan and I will establish alternative questions if necessary. I want to make the questions so no matter how she answers, she admits guilt."

"This will all be filmed for future showing?"

"You have to be careful about that, or an appellate court could overturn the conviction. I want that woman to endure the greatest penalty allowable by law. I want her execution to be slow. She should have no one feeling sorry for her; she showed no remorse to her victims."

I told Marie, "That is great news. I feel that's the fairest way to conduct her sanity hearing; it keeps money from buying her a comfy cell."

"Ms. Morgan said that if she's found not criminally insane, she wants Judge Adamson to impose the extreme penalty the law permits."

"The governor said no plea bargains. Would an appellate court rule death too severe?"

Marie said, "If the death penalty is her sentence, anything is possible. Ms. Morgan also stated that Ms. Davidson has filed for an appeal already."

Silvia looked at her wrist; she wore no watch, but I got the message. I told Marie, "Silvia and I have to leave to visit some jobs this morning. Can we continue this discussion later today?"

Marie said, "Of course. I'll be at home writing questions, waiting on the furniture, playhouse, and vehicles with your lovely bride."

35

Silvia and I waited a few more minutes for Angel and Juanita to arrive. She found a couple of two-packs for us to enjoy with our coffees.

She asked, "What did Marie want?"

"You know there's a trial going on that involves Marie and Delores?"

Silvia said, "Yes, they keep me up to date since our television stations are too caught up with the Me Too garbage going on. Every day it's something else that some group thinks we should dish out money for their cause.

"Murry and I are so tired of every type of perverted person crying in front of a television camera, whining, 'What about me?' with their hands out.

"The last straw for us was the push for unisex restrooms. We both feel they should have only one restroom for all positions. One restroom for the entire building, have them wait in line, no partitions, two toilets, one sink, rolled linen towel so they can enjoy the moisture from the previous lawmaker. They have those conditions until they reverse the law; no company complies until six months of use by the government officials.

"That would be only used by those who voted for the bill. Everyone else uses the normal restrooms."

Angel and Juanita walked in, so we had the opportunity to escape the office.

We headed to the first project that Manuel was responsible to build. We pulled up to the residence, where we met Manuel standing in the driveway. He explained that his foreman did not show up this morning. He was waiting for one of his leadmen to show up to the jobsite.

Silvia asked, "Who is you foreman?"

He said, "Steven MacDonald, John's brother."

I told Silvia, "If he has no apparent reason for not being at work, cut his final check. We have to stop this nonsense right now."

I told Manuel, "I had to release an entire crew one time, run by the vice president of the company after the corporate owner fired the president for embezzlement. Not a fun day, but very necessary for the company's survival.

"The vice president said I didn't have the authority to fire him; he said, 'I have the authority to fire you.' As he was mouthing off, the owner and senior partner of the firm pulled up in his Cadillac, got out of his car, and told the vice president to give him the keys to the jobsite and the vehicle. He had the payroll checks, which reflected the dates the crew actually worked from the superintendent's calendar.

"Let me explain. The general contractor's superintendent kept a daily record of the crew's appearance to the jobsite. The owner had the foreman with him change the locks on the construction bins, locked up all the tools into the bins, and in a couple of minutes there were three trucks full of our employees. They took the trucks when the rest of the vice president's crew arrived. There were also two squad cars pulling into the jobsite; the construction's superintendent had called, thinking there might be some trouble."

Manuel asked, "Did anything happen after that incident?"

"No, nothing else happened. We did a cost analysis on the project, and the entire crew could have been arrested and jailed for grand theft. Found out later the vice president and past president of the company moved to Texas."

Silvia asked, "So you have been through this sort of thing before?"

I told both of them, "I hope this is all I find. If we do a job cost report and find there was theft, remember: Marie is an attorney, and Papa is a prosecutor with lots of connections. Putting people behind bars is nothing new for them, and crooks will be prosecuted if necessary."

The leadman showed up, and we proceeded to walk the project. There were a couple of rough areas but fixable. I thanked the leadman for showing up and told Manuel, "We'll talk later today."

Silvia and I headed toward her vehicle. Once inside, she said, "Ready for the next project?"

I told her, "No, take me back to the office, and bring in all the files that John MacDonald was responsible for. I want the names of each of his foremen, and then I want your fiancé to be in my office after lunch."

Silvia said, "I think he is taking Scooter to Texas to load up cattle trucks to bring the calves to the girls."

"Okay, once we go through the file folders, make a determination if Mr. MacDonald and his brother are clear of any wrongdoing. If so, we won't need to bother him."

We arrived at the office, and I had Angel and Juanita join us in the conference room. "Make sure to bring in a beverage for yourselves and a coffee for me, please."

Silvia brought in the file folders, and I had her call all our major suppliers and tell them not to honor any orders from John or Steven MacDonald. "In fact, they're not to honor any orders scheduled for delivery on any project today. You'll call them before the day ends about proceeding as scheduled or holding up until further notice.

"Also have them email or fax pending orders for delivery this week so we can review them."

While Silvia was making the calls, I instructed Angel and Juanita to pull up the estimates for the first project, then pull up all invoices for the project, signed purchase orders, and delivery tickets and note who signed for the deliveries.

Angel had the materials for the project estimates, and Juanita was pulling out purchase orders and invoices to compare to the bid.

I quickly made some worksheets for us to use: date, invoice number, amount of the invoice, quotes used to put the bids together, compare quantities and product numbers.

After fifteen minutes of comparing the quotes during the bidding process compared to invoices and compared to shippers, the girls had found a few discrepancies. We compared all phases to the job and saw that, a little here and a little there, the bottom line on the project that MacDonald's brother was running came to a variance of a couple thousand dollars.

We had begun checking another project when Stuart walked into the office. Silvia met him and told him we were in the board room.

Stuart entered the conference room and surveyed file folders spread out and the girls pulling papers from them. He asked me, "What are you all doing?"

I explained, "We're doing a very basic job cost on all of MacDonald's jobs."

Stuart asked, "Why are you doing that? He quit yesterday."

I told Stuart, "His brother Steven did not show up to work today. Manuel had to shuffle employees to have a foreman on the project."

Silvia showed Stuart what they had found on Stephen's project, over two thousand dollars of the proposal spent on invoiced items that were not on the drawings.

On the second job they found another three thousand in materials that didn't match anything on the projects. These items were purchased as a will-call, not delivered to the jobsite.

The third job MacDonald was supervising had nearly five thousand dollars of materials not accounted for on any project he was in charge of.

I asked Stuart, "Do you know John MacDonald?"

Stuart said, "He worked for my building company a few years ago. He was looking for employment and called Murry, who needed people since he had too many jobs for him to handle."

"What did he do for your building company?"

Stuart said, "He was a project manager and did a pretty good job, overall."

"Did you ever do a job cost on the restaurants he was managing?"

Stuart said, "No, we opened the restaurants right on time, and we were more concerned with having the restaurant staffed with the right people."

"Are any of his foremen or superintendents still working for you?"

Stuart said, "I believe we have a superintendent who used to be a foreman for him."

"Can we go see him for just a few minutes?"

Stuart said, "Let me call him; he might be close by your office."

Stuart called and asked where he was. After he answered, Stuart said, "Sounds like you just passed here. That's about a mile from our new office. Could you stop in here for a few minutes?"

A few minutes later, the superintendent arrived. Grady Allen was his name. We decided to meet in my office, for privacy.

Stuart asked if he remembered John MacDonald. Grady responded, "Yes, we did a couple of restaurants, but he left the company. You gave me his position."

Stuart asked Grady, "Tell us about the working conditions while you were under MacDonald's supervision."

"We had a few items which took longer to arrive than normal. Two were walk-in coolers. In the other restaurants the coolers were delivered on a scheduled date right on time. We had to wait a considerable time before these coolers arrived. One was the wrong model number that showed on the plans. I showed John, and he said, 'Just install it; make it fit,' and walked away from me."

Stuart said, "I was never informed that the walk-in coolers were a problem." He called Doreen. "Honey, do me a favor; pull the files on the restaurants with John MacDonald's name. Call me back when you have them. Thank you, my beauty."

We got coffee while we waited, and Doreen called back in about ten minutes. She found the three projects which John MacDonald was responsible for constructing. Stuart asked her to put them on his desk to look at when he arrived home.

Silvia came in with two more projects; both had discrepancies of thousands of dollars.

I asked her to make copies of their worksheets for me to go over later at home. "Are you all finished?"

She said, "I think we have three more. Do you want the completed projects as well?"

"The day is young; might as well do those so we have a complete picture of what was going on."

Stuart said, "Silvia, please don't tell anyone about what you all are doing, even Murry. I will deal with him when he returns, if necessary."

Stuart told Mr. Allen he could leave. "Please don't say a word to anyone about this little meeting, not even my son."

Mr. Allen said, "My lips are sealed. This meeting never happened, blacked out of my memory."

Stuart turned to me and asked, "How do you do it? Just how do you know what to look for? You find mass murders, stolen money, laboratories where many people were mutilated; how? What is your secret?"

"When MacDonald's brother didn't show up to work today, that stirred up old memories of an incident that happened years ago. They reeked of the same issues."

Stuart asked, "How did you know to ask me if I knew MacDonald?"

I replied, "You looked at the paper, the top of the paper with MacDonald's name written in the title block."

Stuart said, "I was curious about the form."

"Stuart, you may have thought you were looking only at the form; your eyes were focused on the name. You may have thought we were checking papers with Murry's name; you may have wanted to defend your son."

Stuart said, "You created some homework for me to do tonight. Can we meet again tomorrow to go over a plan of strategy?"

"Of course. We can compare notes. I'm certain many will run parallel."

The girls were getting hungry, so we all decided to order in Chinese food; Silvia knew of a great place. She had a menu, and they delivered.

We all picked out what looked the pleasing to our eyes; hopefully our tummies would agree. In about a half hour our meals arrived with chopsticks and beverages. I ordered hot green tea, and the girls all ordered sodas.

We all took our lunch break—so nice, peaceful and quiet. The clatter of chopsticks makes less noise than plasticware, although before we were finished we all switched to plasticware. The food was getting cold, and we weren't the most talented at using chopsticks. Stabbing your food with the chopstick is not very courteous to the other diners. I was still in the learning stage, and you can't improve if you only eat with chopsticks a couple times per year.

Lunch was finished, but knowing we would be hungry again before the day is done, Silvia went to the grocery store and bought a box of hunger pain medication for our afternoon break.

As we reviewed the results of our investigation, job costing Mr. MacDonald's projects, we saw a distinct pattern. Silvia told me when she called the vendors telling them what I told her to say to them, she got some pushback from a couple of them.

I asked what the vendors said. Silvia answered, "They said I don't have the authority to override the superintendents."

I told her, "Let's go pay those vendors a visit. You drive. Do you have the names of those you talked with on the phone?"

She said yes. "Why do you ask?"

I told her, "You'll see, once we have one of them in front of us."

The first vendor was the irrigation supplier—not our biggest account, but we did purchase some items if our jobs were close to their facility.

We walked into the will-call area, of course. Silvia was eyeballed by the counter salespeople and the customers sitting on barstools.

I walked up to one of the counter salesmen and asked to see Stephen Jones. He of course asked, "Do you have an appointment with Mr. Jones?"

I told him, "Please get Mr. Jones, or I'm canceling all pending orders and the account. If he's too busy, your corporate office might have some concern since we have locations in four states."

As I finished talking to him, another salesperson entered the will-call area. The one in front of me said, "Here is Mr. Jones."

Mr. Jones, being somewhat arrogant said, to the salesperson, "I'm too busy to talk to anyone right now. Get a business card and I'll call them back when I have time."

I told Mr. Jones, "Excuse me. You don't have time to talk to a customer after you told my office manager, she has no authority or override a superintendent?"

Mr. Jones looked at me with disgust. "We have a company policy. An appointment is required to talk with me; do you have an appointment?"

"Hold on a second." I called his corporate office and asked for the president of the corporation, Mr. Bishops. He took my call and asked how I was doing. Mr. Jones acted as if he was going to leave. "Sir, your branch manager is too busy to talk with me. Just a moment." I handed Mr. Jones my phone and said, "Tell the president of your company that you're too busy."

Apparently, Mr. Jones had never talked with the president of his company. He took the phone and snapped, "Just who are you, one of this idiot's friends?"

The look that came over his face was priceless when the president told him to get the company magazine off the counter, turn it over, and look at the back cover. "You see that person? That is *this idiot's friend*. I will be at your office in two days to discuss just how busy you are. That friend is one of our biggest accounts. We have done business together for over twenty years. You take time now, or else you can go home."

He handed back my phone. Mr. Bishops apologized for his branch manager's rude behavior and said, "I'll straighten out the confusion they create; no one is that busy. It's great talking with you. Can we meet for lunch while I'm in town?"

I told him, "I'll be in Texas; how about next week? I'll be back in Colorado for a couple of days."

Mr. Jones, still acting arrogant, said in a put-upon tone, "Just what is it you want?"

"You know you'll find out from Mr. Bishops when he arrives in two days. I don't need to discuss anything with you or your counter help. Stop all orders for Stockdale Landscape. Silvia, we pay for nothing from this day forward."

Mr. Jones said, "Excuse me, who gives you that right?"

Silvia said, "He owns the company. Your career in this industry is toast; have a nice day."

As we got back into the vehicle, my cell phone rang. It was Mr. Bishops. "Long time no hear. How are you?"

Mr. Bishops said, "What just happened?"

I said, "You need to talk to Mr. Jones when you arrive in a couple of days. Be sure you call and make an appointment, or he may be too busy."

Mr. Bishops said, "He told me you stopped all orders as of today and won't pay for anything shipped."

"You know me. Nobody pushes my buttons, and nobody plays the arrogant game with me. If they're so high and mighty that the customer is their puppet, you know I don't need a puppet master."

Mr. Bishops asked, "Are you canceling all orders?"

"Only from that branch until we finish our job costing. You see, we had a superintendent quit yesterday, and his brother didn't show up for work today. We started doing job costs on his projects, and he's been stealing regularly from the jobs. I will let you know if Mr. Jones is involved."

Mr. Bishops said, "I'm flying in tonight for a surprise visit to Mr. Jones tomorrow morning. Will you know by then whether he's involved?"

"We should have a good picture by this afternoon. I'll forward you our reports if he is involved."

Mr. Bishops again apologized. "I will confirm that the orders will be stopped until you tell them to ship."

We headed to the next vendor on Silvia's list. This vendor met us with open arms. "Please be seated. What gives me the pleasure of your visit?"

I told him we had a superintendent quit yesterday, and his brother didn't show up to work this morning. We started to do job costing and found some discrepancies in the superintendent's purchases compared to our proposals. It came to a good deal of money, so we were alerting all the vendors that no order would be allowed without our authorization. "We're trying to keep the foremen from heading to a supply house, leaving the crew without leadership, and purchasing items that are neither in the proposal nor authorized.

"Silvia called this morning to alert vendors and received some pushback about her not being authorized to stop shipments requested from the field."

The vendor said, "We were told by Murray that the superintendents have the final say as to what is shipped and not shipped."

I told the vendor, "Part of this mess is my fault. We had so much work scheduled with no crews, no trucks, and barely an office, that we were in a scramble to get things in place so we could start building the work we scheduled.

"My office manager helped Silvia get her feet wet but did not teach her how to set up project folders, verify permits and inspections, do job costing, write purchase orders, and get the materials to the field so they can build the projects.

"She's now learning how all of this works, but meanwhile we had an employee who decided to take full advantage of the situation."

The vendor said, "Will this jeopardize the purchase orders we have that are pending shipment?"

"Our immediate concern is who wrote the purchase orders. If you have copies of the purchase orders, we'll compare them to our materials listed during bid time. If they match, then all is good, but if there are items that aren't a part of the project, then those items will not be shipped."

The vendor said, "I have items pending from my sources which I had to put a deposit down on to have the items made."

"If you would give me the list of those items, with the customers' names, then I will check if each one is indeed required."

The vendor thought that was fair. Some would be coming in any day now; "I've waited for a couple of months for these items."

"This afternoon we will send you a list of authorized personnel who can sign purchase orders. We appreciate your time, and we'll work with you on items that don't match our plans."

We headed back to the office; Silvia was nearly in tears. I asked her, "What is wrong?"

She said, "Is this my fault, all of this that's happening?"

"No, it was mostly mine for not having all of this given to you by Marjorie. If you had been told how to set up projects and failed to listen and allowed the responsibility to be shifted from your control to the field with no recourse, yes, you would have been at fault. Would I have reprimanded you? Maybe, maybe not, but you would have lost most of my respect for you."

Silvia said, "That would hurt more than getting fired. Would I have regained your respect?"

"In due time, with no more hiccups, if you did as you were asked, the respect would return. But that's not our situation."

We pulled into our office parking lot and went to see how the rest of the job costs were panning out.

Angel and Juanita had issues with quite a few of Mr. MacDonald's projects. They had lists of items not shown on the plan or on any materials list prepared during the bidding process. Two had addresses that weren't even one of our jobsites.

Silvia looked at the names and the addresses shown on the invoices. She remembered asking Murray about these; "He told me the vendor put the wrong address on the invoice, and they were okay to pay."

"Okay, I will need those invoices put into separate file folders. Credit the jobs for the amounts of the invoices. When I meet with Stuart tomorrow, I'll address these with him."

I put my arm around Silvia and gave her a hug. "Please don't fret over this. It hurts me to see you near tears. You're doing a great job for the company; all of you are doing a great job for me. We just have to regain control of the purchasing and the hiring of employees to put the train back on the track."

"Why did Mr. Jones act that way with us?"

"Don't worry about Mr. Jones; Mr. Bishops will deal with him and his hired counter employees. He does not tolerate arrogance any more than I do. I saw him one day, after we returned from lunch, fire the entire staff. He had heard that they were treating the customers as if they were stupid. You know the old saying: if you point your finger at someone, there are three pointing back at you.

"He fired one counter salesman on the spot and finished the customer's order, thanked him for stopping by, and said 'Hope to see you soon. Next!' and two other contractors rushed to his station. He took care of both of them, said, 'Next,' and within fifteen minutes all customers were served and on their way.

"He looked at the rest of the counter salespeople and dismissed them. 'Thank you for not taking care of my customers. I truly appreciate the lack of concern and disrespect you just showed me.'

"The branch manager asked him why he fired the counter salespeople.

"Mr. Bishops looked at him and asked, 'Are you still working here?'

"Well, girls, great job today. I hope you all learned something and are willing to carry this forward with a new set of responsibilities. We will adjust your pay scale. Have a great evening. Have a safe flight to Texas. Give my Marjorie a hug, and tell her there are more coming her way."

As we locked up the office, Silvia was still fairly shaken up about the entire situation. I told her, "Lock the front door."

She locked it, and I said, "There, your troubles are securely safe. Let's enjoy some good dinner, soft music, waterfalls, lambs and calves, Lulu, and my girls and wives. They all need our love, and what you give, you will receive back tenfold."

36

Insanity Plea Questioned

During our drive home, Silvia said, "What if some of the items we found that were not a part of the home MacDonald listed as the customer, but he was purchasing items for another project that he was assigned?"

"By looking at the materials purchased we can see whether something was missing on another project. For example, the Blossom residence has eight remote control valves, but MacDonald purchased twelve remote control valves that were charged to the Blossom account. On the Petals residence they have eleven remote control valves, and the invoicing shows only seven were purchased. There is a chance, if both projects were in the same mode of construction, that those four remote control valves were just charged to the wrong account.

"So while MacDonald was at the supply house, he remembered that he was missing four remote control valves, so he just picked them up while he was there but forgot to tell anyone. I can give him reasonable doubt in that case."

"From what I have seen so far, that I doubt that was ever the case."

Silvia asked, "What if Murray asked him to pick up the remote-control valves and bring them into the office, not knowing where they were going to be used?"

"Here is what I would have and have done in that situation: purchased what I needed for the job I was in charge of constructing, and purchase the items a superior asked me to pick up on another purchase order. Since the superintendents were authorized to carry purchase orders, that would not have been a problem; he could have told the supplier to contact the office to verify which project those items belonged to."

Silvia said, "I'm starting to see how your system works: everything is accounted for, leaving no doubt in the accounting process where to apply the invoices."

"Marjorie will explain all of that to you when you go to Texas. In fact, you could hook up with Murray while you're there."

Silvia said, "What if Murray knew about all of these excess charges?"

"It will make our jobs much easier," I said, "but he will have to tell us which projects those materials belong to. Then there's the question, how well did all of those projects do financially? If you show a profit of let's say five thousand dollars, but you have seven thousand dollars of items charged to another project that belongs to this project, I would ask why they were charged to another project?"

Silvia asked, "Do you think Murray may have been involved?"

"For his sake and yours, I'm hoping he did not know, if he wasn't looking for any wrongdoing but just trying to get projects completed so he could start others. Keeping our word with the customer is priceless; he could have been stretched too far to keep accurate tabs on the purchasing."

Silvia asked, "What is his dad looking for on his projects?"

"The same as what we are looking for: a pattern. How often? Near the end of the month, when rent is due, that sort of thing? Was he doing drugs, gambling, having an affair, or is it the thrill of eluding capture? He quit because of extra paperwork and losing purchasing power—making the office the approving party, not themselves. Something triggered him; possibly knowing he would get caught worried him. The game is over; find another company that's too busy to notice or has no procedures in place, no field rules."

At the house we were met by the girls, very happy we were home. They had hunger pains something awful. I saw our vehicles; *So they've arrived.* I asked the girls if the other two trucks came today.

Sarah said, "Annie's house came, and all the stuff in the garage came today as well.

"Susanne helped us put away our belongings, and four ranch hands helped moms with the furniture and dishes; it's all put away. Annie got her table and two chairs for her house; she is so happy now."

Silvia said, "Is Annie the girls' friend?"

"Come on, let's get these girls some vittles."

We arrived in the kitchen, where all the ladies sat at the kitchen table with their glasses full of frothy refreshment.

Delores asked Silvia, "Thirsty?"

Silvia picked up the pitcher and downed about half of the contents. "Ahh, I needed that; thank you, it was perfect timing. Can you make more?"

Delores asked me, "Just what did you do to our little Silvia?" She was giving her a motherly hug and kissed her forehead. "Poor girl. If he was mean to you, let me know. I have ways of breaking him."

I asked, "Why is it always the guy's fault?"

That got everyone to say in harmony, "Oh, please, are you serious?" "Asking women why is it always the guy's fault?" "Just when is it our fault, Mr. Know-It-All?"

"You know, I hear the grill calling me. 'Fred, Fred, Fred'—did you hear that?"

Marie said, "Even if we heard that, we wouldn't admit it. Why ask?"

I snuck four two-packs from the snack drawer while the ladies were busy listening to Silvia tell them about her day. The girls were just about to head upstairs to their house with Lulu following them. I called them and showed them the cupcakes. I motioned them to be quiet, so they silently took the cupcakes to their house and blew me kisses.

I oiled up the grill and applied some heat, waiting for the meat to create a burnt offering for our diners later on.

It was only a few minutes till Susanne and Marie brought out the platters with specific instructions: "Do not burn anything; read my lips," said Marie. "Burn nothing."

"It's nice you give me so much credit. I thought I was doing well; you all ask for seconds."

Marie said, "That is so we can give the dogs a treat. They seem to like your cooking for the time being. Pretty soon the thrill will be gone, and they'll dig holes and bury the treat—not for later but to feed the fungus and bacteria in the soil. They too will get tired of your cooking and force the meat out of the hole."

Susanne said, "That is quite an accomplishment having fungus and bacteria reject your cooking."

"Yea, they are used to eating rotting items. My cooking is good; they kick it out so the sun and air start making it rot."

Marie said, "Quick, Susanne, we need to get to high ground. It's getting really deep in here." She looked at me. "We'll be back in a few minutes. Oh, by the way, we saw what you did. Those girls have you wrapped around their little fingers. They have had six cupcakes today, just so you know."

I started whistling "Whistle while You Work," and the girls joined in from their patio above me. Even Lulu joined in, with a couple of high-pitched howls. She was either having fun, or the whistling was hurting her ears. I gave the girls two Milk Bones for Lulu; she gets treats too.

The girls came down the stairs with Lulu. "Daddy, Lulu is so sad without Scooter," said Leslie. "How do we make her happy again?"

"Just give her lots of loving, play with her, and make her the highlight of your day. He'll be home in a couple of days. He's just loading up cattle trucks, bringing home your babies."

Sarah said, "We miss Scooter. Can Silvia call Murry so we can talk to Scooter?"

Good idea, "Go ask her. Take Lulu so she can talk to Scooter too."

They all ran into the house and talked to Silvia. She pulled out her cell phone and called Murry. She told him to put his phone on speaker. "Call Scooter. The girls and Lulu want to talk to him."

Murry said, "Great idea. Scooter seems down in the dumps, not perky as normal."

For about five minutes the girls and Lulu talked to Scooter. Lulu howled her high-pitch howl, and Scooter did the same. The girls got a huge thrill out of seeing the dogs communicate."

While the girls were talking with Scooter, the ladies brought out the sides, salads, plates, and silverware. This was a special night: no plasticware; real plastic glasses, no throwaway glasses; the candle and candleholder. They all sashayed back into the house, tempting me, every one of them. *Something is in the making, this is not normal practice; I'm doomed. Where's John? I may need male support. Great, now I'm starting to panic. As if today was not bad enough, now this. Why, Lord, why?*

The girls and Lulu returned, and Sarah asked, "How much longer, Daddy?"

I told her, "About three minutes. Tell your moms dinner is nearly ready."

They went inside, and the ladies all came out to the patio. Mama and Papa came through the tunnels into the house, down the elevator, and onto the patio. John was with them; he must have been hiding somewhere in the house.

Everyone had plates in hand, and the grilled meat was being dispersed to all diners. The girls announced that Mama and Papa, along with Silvia and Susanne, would join them this evening for dinner.

Marie and Delores were giving each other high fives; *Loser!*

John said, "I've never seen them that happy about not being chosen."

"It's only temporary. By next week, there'll be a table for two down here, while the others dine in the upper room."

John said, "Me and my candle, flickering in my bride's eyes, giving her a luxurious glow as she forks my steak, saying, 'You weren't eating that, were you?'"

"Well, at least you got to have the candle burning before she stole your steak. Mine would be gone when I struck the match to light the candle."

John said, "We should write a book."

I told him, "By the time the reader got to the second page, he would have to call the shrink for therapy.

"I asked them a simple question: 'Why are men always at fault?'"

John said, "You didn't ask them that. Did you really?"

"I thought I was safe. They were on their second pitcher of margaritas. Silvia picked up the pitcher and drank nearly half. Then she said, 'Ahh, make some more.'"

"Delores asked her if I had been mean to her as she was giving her motherly hugs and kissing her forehead."

"So that generated the question. You're much braver than me."

"I don't know if it was bravery or if they caught me with my brains down, fully exposed to the elements."

John said, "Lesson learned."

We joined the ladies for dinner. They lit the candle and also took half of our steaks. "We are on the wife diet, you know."

Marie asked, "About today, better than yesterday?"

"Boy, these steaks are delicious, just the right scorching, almost burnt."

Marie said, "You aren't going to answer me, are you?"

Delores took my steak, holding it hostage. "Honey, answer Marie. Be a good boy, and Mommy will give you back your steak. If not, Lulu will get a huge treat."

"Didn't you get the rundown on the day's events from Silvia?"

Marie said, "We just want the male's viewpoint before turning it over to the jury."

"Well, okay then. You see, we were out of chocolate cupcakes, and our hunger pain was something horrific. We decided to order in Chinese food, we started with chopsticks, but our food was getting cold, so we changed to forks and knives. Our hunger pains were not quite satisfied, so Silvia went to the store and bought more cupcakes.

"That was not quite good enough, so we went and devoured two vendors; they weren't very tasty, so we went back to the office and decided that the only other thing that would cure our hunger pains was to give them to the ones we love the most. So here we are, dining by the flickering candlelight with those who deserve our hunger pain, which we are gladly sharing."

Marie said, "That was a lovely dance. Wrong answer; didn't even address the question. Are you sure you're not part politician?"

"You know, my dad traveled quite a bit while I was young. He may have caught a politician gene in his travels and gave it to my mom as a special gift."

Marie said, "You're amazing; no script to follow, right off the top of that brain of yours. Delores, give him back his steak; no goodies tonight."

John said, "I liked his answer. It's what I hear daily from the girls at work. 'Is it done yet?' One has a meat thermometer and sticks it on the paper she just printed from the printer. 'Nope, still has some more cooking to do; come back later.'"

I told John, "That is priceless. Don't tell my office staff. It will mess up their routine about their nails aren't dry yet. 'Oh, dear, time for my break; took too long painting my nails. That blasted phone kept ringing.' There were so many interruptions, I waited two days for one letter: the phone, their cell phones, and the texts they have to answer every minute of the working day.

"One of my office girls asked if another could help her because she's 'a little behind.' I asked her to stand up and turn around slowly, and she did. I told her, 'Nope, I think it's getting bigger.'"

Our dinner went smoothly for a couple of bites, but then the girls returned with empty plates in hand. Before they started their speech, I told them, "Let's look under the hood." There were four pieces of mouthwatering meat left, so no need to throw them away. *Let's make sure your guests are filled to the brim.*

The girls took the elevator to the upper floor. The guests thanked the chef, along with Lulu. She's happy now; she got to hear from Scooter.

Murry did tell Silvia they had one more trailer to fill, and they would be heading home, just in time to board a plane to return to where they just left.

He needed to get Scooter back since the first truck of calves would be there on Saturday morning, too much for Lulu to handle by herself.

Two ranch hands would be there for a little while to settle down the calves, they would return to feed them their dinners, then breakfast, and make sure they had enough water. They said to keep one corral for the calves and lambs the girls were caring for; the other corral would have the herd from Texas: fifteen calves in the first truck, and twenty in the second. Black and red Angus and white-faced calves. There were a few females in the herd.

The girls were all excited to have more little friends to watch over. Leslie asked the ranch hands if they needed to talk to the calves a certain way.

The ranch hand was a little confused by her question. "What do you mean about talking to them in a certain way?"

"You know, like say 'howdy' and 'you-all,' things like that," said Leslie.

"Oh, you think you have to talk cowboy to them?" said the ranch hand.

"Yes, cowboy. I didn't know the correct terminology; sorry," said Leslie.

The ranch hand said, "Girls, just be yourselves. The animals pick up your body language and tone of voice. That puts them at ease, knowing you are at ease and happy."

The girls were ready for dessert, so moms got up and headed to the kitchen and started to prepare the desserts. The girls took them to their guests. Lulu got a Milk Bone, and she was very happy. Milk Bone and hugs; what else could a dog need?

After dinner and dessert, the ladies headed over to the waterfall, taking a couple of plastic chairs.

I needed to have Phillip make two more benches and a table like Marie's first fountain and stream.

The girls headed up to their house to have some quiet time from adults. Lulu followed the girls, she loves being around the girls; it must be a female thing.

It was nearing light show time. The girls were on their patio with Lulu as the lights came on. All of our yards were illuminated, and from the decks of all three yards the view was extraordinary. Juanita did a fabulous job. The waterfall and stream feature lights gave a certain ambience that would only get better as the plant materials mature.

I was time for Lulu to put her family to bed in their shelter. She brought the lambs for the girls to cuddle and hug, while she gathered the calves. When all were in the shelter, she laid down in the bed the girls had made for her. She received pets and cuddles from all the girls. Papa brought her some meat scraps from our dinner and gave her some loving as well. They all wished her a good night. "See you in the morning," they all told her.

After a short time we all retired to our final destination under the covers for rest and relaxation. The girls were spending the night at John and Marie's in Leslie's bed with her stuffed animals. We all said prayers with the girls and then headed for our own bedrooms.

37

It was the first night's sleep that Delores when we were awakened by the alarm clock. I'd forgotten we even had an alarm clock. Scared me half to death when it rang. We could see the lights were on at Marie and John's.

Delores needed some caffeine and hugs. She told me, "You know, I really like the girls waking us up in lieu of that alarm clock. Having them snuggled under the covers makes me all warm inside. Let's go have some coffee and hugs."

I told her, "The last one there is a rotten egg."

She did one of those hip checks on me, like the roller derby skaters do to cause the opponent to lose balance. She bumped me into the door jamb and got in the elevator to the second floor. I ran to the stairs trying to beat her to the tunnel, but nope, she was in the tunnel and locked the door. I had to go into the rain and use the other door into the tunnel. *No winning this race, she'll more than likely lock the other door just to slow me down.*

By the time I entered the kitchen of John and Marie's, I was soaked, and my feet were freezing. Meanwhile, Delores was sipping her fresh cup of coffee.

"Good morning, dear," she said. "What took you so long? Didn't your mother teach you to take off your clothes before getting into the shower? Use a towel to dry yourself off. Mothers, I swear; they toss their boy birds out of the nest without proper training."

Marie walked over to me. "You designed the tunnels so you would not have to get into various climatic conditions. What happened?"

"She locked the door which allowed me access into the tunnel. I had to use the other door, but to get there, I had to go out into the rain."

Marie told Delores, "Sister, good job. That will teach him to want to race you to our fine eating establishment."

I gave the girls all high fives; I didn't want to get them wet. They were enjoying their hot chocolates and told me they slept really well, "But we missed sleeping next to Susanne."

Oh, no—Susanne! That door is still locked. I raced toward the tunnel, and there stood Susanne, soaked.

She said, "Very nice and considerate. Thanks a lot." Her hair was dripping wet, and her robe and jammies were soaked. I was already wet, so I gave her a squishy hug. Then we returned to the kitchen area.

The girls all got up and gave her a hug. "What happened to you?" asked Leslie.

"The tunnel door was locked," said Susanne. "I see your mom is dry so I'm guessing she locked the access door."

Susanne went over and gave Delores a nice wet hug. "We are not even by any means."

Delores said, "I didn't want to be the rotten egg."

Susanne shook her head. "Whatever that means. You succeeded, I'm sure." She looked at me. "One of your games? Did you two play 'last one there is a rotten egg'?" She asked Delores, "How did you take the lead?"

"I knocked him into the door jamb, got into the elevator, headed down to the second floor, got into the tunnel, and locked the door. He chose to run down the stairs to surprise me, but the elevator is faster than taking the stairs. He had no choice but to go on the deck to the other door and run down the entire tunnel. I was going to lock the door to the playhouse, but I was laughing too hard by that time."

Susanne said, "I hope you both are proud of yourselves." She asked Marie, "How big is your dryer?"

Marie said, "Not big enough. You'll dry fairly soon."

Delores asked, "How many fabric softener sheets would it take to keep the static cling from her hair?"

Marie and Susanne both started laughing. "Could you imagine your hair standing on end the entire day?" said Marie.

Susanne said, "Great, you would look like you stuck your finger into a wall socket."

I told them, "You wouldn't have to worry about the wind messing up your hairstyle."

Delores asked, "Is breakfast ready? I'm starving from all that exercise."

Marie said, "You could help, you know. Just because you won the race, that alone doesn't give you a pass on cooking."

"Okay, much older sister," said Delores, "what would you like your much younger sister to cook for you?"

"Help your daughter with the sausages and hash browns. Then help set the table. Albright scramble is nearly completed, thanks to Leslie. She supervised my cooking. It has to be perfect; her reputation is on the line."

The pancakes were all stacked on the table. Hash browns were on one side of the platter with sausages on the other half. Toast, beverages, and salsa in a bowl were all set out; we just needed the final dish so the dig-in bell could ring.

Marie had a huge bowlful of the Albright scramble with a bowl of three cheese blend. Everybody was in their eating position and passing the food. Delores told Susanne, "Try not to get our breakfast wet."

Susanne gave her an elbow in the ribs. "Oops, I had a dry spot on my elbow. It felt odd."

Breakfast was delicious. John, Papa, and I sat at the stove countertop, allowing all the hens space to roost. *I enjoy the farm life. You can say things that city folk only dream about.*

The new rule was to rinse and put your dirty dishes in the dishwasher, leaving space to your fellow eaters. I finished first, rinsed off my dishes, and was planning on sneaking to the elevator and returning the favor to my lovely bride. But the lock was reversed. *So our door is backward; that's how she got away with what she did.*

I turned around, and standing behind me was the earlier winner. "What were you trying to do, mister?" said Delores.

"I was making sure that everything was secure in case the rain man tried to sneak into the house while we were enjoying our breakfast."

Delores said, "The rain man? Come with me; you have some explaining to do to justify that comment."

She asked Marie, "Is Oregon famous for a rain man burglar?"

Marie said, "You know, I'm not certain if there is such a thing."

Delores said, "Were you going to make me, Susanne, and the girls all go out in the rain to get back into our home?"

"That did cross my mind, but only you, my dear. The others did not cross my mind. That would be very hurtful; I would feel horrible if that occurred."

"You wouldn't feel the same way about your loving wife? It would be okay for me to get soaked as a get-even?" asked Delores.

I told her, "You're pulling the same thing you pulled yesterday: men are always wrong, and women do no wrong."

Delores said, "You didn't learn from that lesson; maybe a couple more times, and you'll get it right."

"Well, I have just enough ego left to head home and get ready for work. Have a great day, everyone; love you all. Great breakfast, thank you."

38

When I entered my home, I went down to the kitchen and put on a pot of coffee, set out some hunger pain medications, went back up the elevator to the third floor, got my clothes set out, and started my shower. Once that was completed, I got dressed and headed back to the kitchen, to find the pain medication was devoured and the coffee pot emptied. I did get one thank-you from the girls, but not the older ladies. I did get a couple of ladies holding up their empty coffee cups for a refill.

"Relax, ladies. I'll make another pot of coffee."

Susanne said she was going to get out of her wet clothes, take a shower, and try to do something with her hair. "Thank you for breakfast, coffee, and breakfast roll. I almost forgive you."

Marie said, "I just received a text from Ms. Morgan. They want us to be ready either today or Monday for our interview. I have a few more questions that I'll send her in about an hour. She needs to review the questions with the judge and defense attorney before going for Mrs. Wilkins's response."

I asked Marie, "What's the game plan for you two for this interview?"

Marie said, "We are the only persons who escaped her web. Ms. Morgan wants the psych people to watch her expressions when we ask her specific questions. I made sure our questions will get a response from her so they can see if she really is insane."

"They can tell by certain types of questions?"

Marie said, "If a normal person is confronted—let's say you were caught stealing an apple, you would be embarrassed because of the wrongdoing. You know it's wrong, and you should not have done what you did. A criminally insane person would not feel guilty.

"She has shown no signs of insanity. If she is ruled insane, we are all insane as well.

"Ms. Morgan told me they will run her through a battery of mental tests—some we would think childlike, but they are designed to determine if a person is truly insane.

"Ms. Morgan said she will be found sane, and the case should continue through sentencing. Remember, there are no plea bargains available for those accused. "She also said Mr. Fredrickson's attorney has stated he is ready to plead guilty; just waiting to see how Mrs. Wilkins's fate turns out.

"Finally, if I can get the questions to her early today, she will start the process of distribution. She said she's eager to see what I have in store for her and the opposing attorney."

Marie was busy on the computer generating questions. Delores was beside her making suggestions.

I gave the girls a hug and kiss goodbye once Silvia showed up to take us to the workplace. I'm looking forward to putting closure on the MacDonald fiasco.

Murray was about two hours away from being home when Silvia showed up to be my chauffeur.

I want my truck; I have GPS. My new truck should be ready by this afternoon. I will call when I get to the office. I can't do surprise attacks if I'm being chauffeured. There are a few foremen I have not visited to see the quality of work they perform.

Silvia seemed a little apprehensive, not warm and huggable as normal. She and I talked while heading to the office.

I asked her, "Silvia, please don't feel like you did anything wrong. None of this was yours or Murray's doing, MacDonald was doing this while employed by Stuart. He's a compulsive liar and user."

Silvia said, "He would be still doing it today if you had not made the statement that the office is in control; no more purchasing by field employees."

I told her, "He can thank that foreman he hired. You know, it would have happened anyway. I would have wanted to look at the job folders, and I would have seen the discrepancy. I would have fired him on the spot. He just saved me the trouble."

We pulled into the office parking lot, where the field construction superintendent for Stuart was waiting our arrival.

He stated that our new office location will be completed in another week and asked if we would have time to do the preliminary construction walk tomorrow morning.

I asked, "Could we do it later today? We fly to Texas tomorrow morning."

He said, "Of course. I just didn't want to spring a walk on your busy schedule."

Silvia asked, "How about two o'clock this afternoon?"

"Perfect, we'll be ready; do you have hard hats and safety vests?"

"We do," said Silvia, "and they are very stylish."

*

Marie was finishing up her questions, getting ready to send them so Ms. Morgan would have them for distribution.

Susanne entered the office and asked when they needed the studio. Marie said, "Either later today, tomorrow, or Monday. More than likely, Monday would be my guess, since we leave for Texas tomorrow morning."

Susanne said, "We have a preliminary job walk this afternoon at the construction site. If we need the studio early, the construction superintendent will have to have it ready for occupancy."

Marie said, "They are that close to finishing our studio?"

Susanne said, "You can plan on starting up classes in two weeks. Mr. Barns will be flying in the middle of next week; his home is near completion. My home is only about a week from final, and my husband is in panic mode. He's a Chicken Little—you know, the sky has been falling around him for years."

The girls entered the room. "Mom, can we have Lulu come play with us? She's outside in the rain, and we feel so sad for her."

Marie said, "Honeys, of course. Bring her in; she's housebroken. She probably misses being around you. Put on your raincoats, and dry her off on the stone flooring, not on the carpet, please."

The girls were out the door before Marie finished speaking. Soon they heard the girls calling for Lulu. She met them at the gate and was happy to see them. They dried her off on the stone floor and took her into the elevator and into their playhouse through the tunnels.

They of course had her Milk Bones along with their hunger pain medication. They were all set for an afternoon of playing.

Within a half hour they saw Murray's truck coming toward their house. They all got up and headed down the tunnel to the elevator and down to the first floor as Murray and Scooter walked into the house.

Lulu and Scooter were ecstatic to see each other. They had their special greeting howls. The girls quickly got Scooter some treats and gave him some love. "Follow us, boy," they told him.

Then all six were onto the elevator and on their way to the playhouse. They were asking Scooter about his trip: "Did they feed you well? How are our babies?" Scooter wanted more loving from the girls and stayed right by their sides, nuzzling up against them for reassurance that he was still their friend. Lulu and Scooter lay on the floor next to each other for quite some time.

Soon the rain subsided, so they all went out, wearing their raincoats just in case, and opened the corral so Lulu and Scooter could play with their family. The lambs were sniffing Scooter, their way of showing their love; the calves were mooing their appreciation. Papa was amazed watching how the animals reacted to each other. He brought Lulu and Scooter some meat treats for them, and Scooter was rubbing up against Papa, showing his love for him.

By lunch time Marie received word from Ms. Morgan: "It appears that Monday will be the earliest we can confirm the meeting of all parties concerned."

She went on, "Some of your questions were approved, but some are going to take a meeting of the minds to determine the true meaning of the question."

Marie asked, "Which questions would cause concern?"

Ms. Morgan stated, "You know, I liked all of them as written. But Ms. Davidson felt her client, no matter how she answered or responded to the question, would prove beyond a shadow of a doubt she was guilty as charged."

Marie said, "They were written that way for the exact reason—no wiggle room. I don't want to give the defense an easy out, nor a reason to question the truthfulness of the question."

Ms. Morgan asked, "How do you assess Mrs. Wilkins's chances of not getting the guilty verdict?"

Marie said, "You have boxed them in with your prosecution witnesses. Tying in Mr. Fredrickson to payments received with the death certificate date filled in one loophole I felt the defense could argue to the jury was incidental. When you demonstrated that it happened twenty-eight times, that is not by coincidence. The look on Fredrickson's face was his doom; he was shocked that your office took the time to match the death certificates to the bank deposits."

Ms. Morgan said, "We looked at the most resent occurrence then backtracked each death certificate to the deposit date; after the second time they all fell into place. My staff did the reverse, working from each large deposit to the death certificate with the matching date. They even compared all those arrested with the dates and tracked the deposits right into the Wilkins account for withdrawal."

Marie said, "So you have her linked financially?"

Ms. Morgan stated, "One thing we had to take off the table: Mrs. Wilkins stating that she just rented out the basement area; she did not know what they were doing."

Marie said, "So if she was not so arrogant or confident that all bases were covered financially, she might have escaped arrest?"

Ms. Morgan said, "Her biggest mistake was being arrested with those in the cabin; that sealed her fate. We know beyond any doubt that none of the others arrested would have brought her into the equation. Even if it meant that they would all get the maximum penalty, they would have kept her out of the crosshairs."

Marie asked, "She has that much power over all of them?"

Ms. Morgan replied, "If they gave her up, she would have attacked their families, spouses, children, businesses. I look forward to seeing her expression when she sees both of you, as you're the only two that ever escaped her web. You two and Delores's husband have to be on her get-even list, if that exists."

Marie asked, "Will we be able to speak at her sentencing?"

Ms. Morgan responded, "What would that do?"

"Give us some closure."

"Do you really think that her sentencing will be your closure?"

Marie asked, "So you think this is not the end of the ordeal?"

"Not one bit. She is hiding something; she knows this isn't over. We caught one big fish, but that's not the end to all the big fish in her pond."

"Well that should make us both sleep really well tonight."

Ms. Morgan said, "Make sure you and your girls always wear their alarms."

Marie said, "It's so good talking with you on the phone. I can't wait to meet you in person. Have a wonderful day; we know you're really busy."

"We should have a meeting with the governor and Diane and bring the girls. Talk to you later," Mr. Morgan said. "I will let you know the actual date of the questioning." With that she ended the call.

Delores said, "This isn't over?"

Marie said, "It appears not. Ms. Morgan must know something—maybe from the last arrest they made a week ago."

Delores said, "We captured the head person, correct?"

Marie said, "I can't answer that. I don't know for sure what we caught in this organization. She doesn't have a job title like CKO, chief killing officer."

Delores said, "I'm worried about our girls, let's go visit them."

They got into the elevator, went into the tunnel, and knocked on the girls' front door at the tunnel entrance.

Sarah said, "Who is it?"

Marie said, "The big bad wolf and her sister."

As they opened the door, there stood Scooter looking at them. He knew their voices and scent, so he wasn't surprised.

Leslie asked, "What brings you to our humble abode?"

Delores said, "We were lonely and wanted to spend some time with our lovely daughters."

Leslie asked, "When is Phillip going to build Annie's home?"

Marie said, "He will start on Monday; he wants to finish Silvia's house first."

Sarah asked, "What time is our flight tomorrow?"

"Our flight is at nine o'clock in the morning," said Marie. "We have to leave here at seven thirty in the morning."

"Can we wear our cowgirl outfits?" asked Rebecca.

Marie said, "You may, but your mom and I are going to take you to the Western Outfitter store with Jennifer and some of her friends tomorrow."

Leslie said, "We get to go shopping?"

Delores said, "Yep, and to lunch and dinner, all planned."

Kim asked, "What's the theme for Jennifer's party?"

Marie said, "Come as you are; be ready for lots of fun, food, and prizes."

Delores said, "It's a carnival theme, with games to play where you can win stuffed animals, shooting gallery—with BB guns, not bullets—and bull riding. You girls will be the judges, just like at Gloria's event. Jason will again be running the bull."

"It will be televised as part of the 'Buck Off' series of events," said Marie.

Delores said, "You know, I love your house. It's so cozy but spacious. Do you girls love the new houses?"

Leslie said, "At first we missed our old house, but now we like the larger house. There's more room for everyone, and we can invite more guests. Annie likes our new house but really wants her old house built."

Sarah said, "She told us a secret. She painted the animals on the ceiling when she was a little girl; her daddy put her paintings on the ceiling once she was finished."

Marie said, "Were you supposed to share a secret?"

Sarah said, "Annie said, 'Tell only your moms, dads, and Mama and Papa; no one else.'"

Delores said, "Semi-secret. Our lips are sealed."

Marie asked, "Are you girls getting hungry?"

Leslie said, "We're starving, Scooter needs some breakfast, and Lulu needs a snack."

"Well," said Delores, "last one to the kitchen is a rotten egg."

Marie said, "Not this time, little sister; we're keeping our eyes on you."

Delores said, "Older sister—but three days don't make me much older. Watch it."

The girls took a detour to get Mama and Papa to join them for lunch. Mama was happy to see Scooter; she gave him lots of love. Soon they were all heading to the kitchen for their next meal.

The menu was hot soup, grilled cheese sandwiches, salad, and dessert. All the ladies were busy cooking while the girls set the table. Papa made the hot chocolate and apple cider.

Scooter and Lulu had guard duty. Then they startled at an unfamiliar noise and ran to the French doors, barking.

Marie and Papa followed them saw the tractor trailer hauling the first load of calves to the corral behind their house. Two ranch hands were opening up the corral gates when Scooter and Lulu ran inside it to make sure all was well.

The ranch hands knew Scooter and asked him to get the calves into the corral for them. The calves knew Scooter from a few days ago and obliged at his direction, and soon all were offloaded into the corral. Lulu made sure they didn't circle back and escape out of the corral gate. In a few minutes all fifteen calves were in the corral, and the ranch hands gave Scooter and Lulu love as they closed the gate. Scooter and Lulu returned to Papa, knowing lunch was nearly ready.

Back in the kitchen, lunch was on the table and in the dogs' bowls, and everyone was happy.

Papa taught the girls how to crumble crackers into their bowls of tomato soup; they added a touch of milk to soften the acidity of the tomatoes. The girls were telling everyone how good lunch tasted and wanted to know if this would be the normal lunch they could expect every day.

"Maybe not every day," said Delores. "We normally don't have lunch guests. This is special, a welcome home for Scooter and our special guest, Susanne."

Susanne said, "This is as good as the caterer makes for the girls every day."

After lunch the girls played with Scooter and Lulu and then put them in the corral so they could go with their moms to see the studios. As they pulled into the office complex, Silvia and I pulled right in behind them. The superintendent had hard hats and vests for the girls and the same for the ladies. Everyone was set for the tour.

When the magazine had the surprise gathering for Marie and Delores, they had a staircase. This studio had three staircases, all connected by a second-floor walkway with the same balusters and hand railing as the staircase. The rises and treads were biblical stone, exact replicas of the staircase Phillip had built for Marie for her courtyard.

Their studio was absolutely stunning, with maple flooring just like a professional basketball court. The girls could clog on the court in another week; the finish still needed to cure, so it was all roped off for now.

We toured the offices upstairs, and I told them, "We will never see you at home; this is breathtaking." They had each office professionally decorated, with photos from various events of all the ladies in different poses in all sorts of venues; this was to inspire all new lady wannabes.

Their boardroom was the most exquisite room I have ever seen: plush furniture and a mahogany table with a mirror finish—no particle board or veneer here, but solid wood—with an ogee routed edge, The workmanship was exquisite.

One of the decorators was present to tell the ladies just what they did to enhance the marvelous construction. They had recessed lighting and special illumination for the photo walls. Marie in her gown for her grand event held center stage on the wall; she was gorgeous in that photo, with the diamonds sparkling and the bubbling champagne.

The ladies were grabbing tissues as they caught sight of the photos on the wall.

I told the superintendent, "We can see the other areas; it will take them a while to move from this spot."

He took Silvia and me over to our new office. Our jaws dropped in a unison "Wow." It was laid out exactly like our office in Colorado—a little larger per room, but the same floor plan. Phillip will have the same layout, so we weren't sure whether to take the bottom floor or the second floor. Because of the elevator, Silvia was drawn to the second-floor location.

She told me, "Since I'm wearing almost after-five attire, walking upstairs could be revealing, so no free peeks. The elevator makes perfect sense to man the second floor."

I said, "It's up to you. I will honor whatever you, Angel, and Juanita choose."

The decorator did mention that they needed to know by Friday, so the photos of both businesses would be in the proper locations. The reception area was to have both companies represented by photos.

I took a pen and wrote down on her small copy of the floor plan who would occupy each office. She appreciated what I had done for her.

Silvia liked our office furniture, so she contacted the rental company to get the final cost of the furniture and asked them if they would relocate it to our new location. She would give them a check for the purchase price. They threw in the relocation of the furniture; it was all the same for them to pick up the furniture and store it in a warehouse for the next customer, if any. Otherwise they would sell it to a wholesaler who deals in used office furniture.

The manager of the rental company actually thanked Silvia for saving them money. The stored furniture would have to be sent out, cleaned, and then covered with plastic to be displayed for future renters to view it. He offered to clean the furniture if we could live without it for three days.

Silvia declined the offer. "We have a professional cleaning company that does our office every week. They do a marvelous job; the furniture is just like new."

I asked, "Did you tell him my chair has had a lot of teardrops fall on it?"

Silvia said, "No sir, the real problem is cupcake leavings on the cushion. We have had a couple of complaints from the cleaning staff: 'Give him a napkin, please!'"

We finished our tour and met the ladies where we had left them. They were trying to figure out where some of those photos were taken. The girls were taken to their studio, where there playhouse was set up ready for them on Monday.

Sarah came over to me and the ladies. "Come, everyone, see our new studio. It's so pretty."

We all followed her. The other three girls were sitting in the playhouse as we entered the studio. Leslie pretended to have a microphone. "Please, guests, please join us for some hot apple cider and conversation. What brings you all to our home this fine day?" she asked.

Marie said, "We heard you were giving away free chocolate cupcakes with chocolate icing and white squiggles on top, so we had to try one."

Leslie said, "Oh, I see. You're from the homeless shelter down the street."

Marie said, "No, we're your new neighbors from the studio next door."

Leslie said, "Did you get permission from our director to barge into our studio, demanding that we feed you?"

Marie said, "It's only a cupcake; not like it's a huge meal."

Leslie said, "Our space is small, and our budget is limited. If we spent our treats on our neighbors, then our invited guests would receive nothing. That alone would make us feel horrible. You would not want us to be put into that predicament, would you?"

Marie looked at Delores. "You told me they were sweet, innocent little girls whose moms are celebrities and sought after all over the world, well-mannered and respectful. Are you sure these aren't just actresses trying to fool us?"

Delores said, "Let me see the brochure we were handed when we entered the building." She opened up a folded piece of paper, looked at it, and looked at each girl. "They appear to be the same girls, but makeup can fool you."

Leslie said, "May I see your brochure, please?"

Delores handed her the piece of paper.

Leslie called for Susanne. "Look at this brochure. This is over a year old, and we look like babies. We're older now; this is not acceptable."

Then all the girls started hugging Susanne and their moms.

Leslie asked, "How did I do?"

I told her, "If you were a foot taller, I'd swear that your mom was playing you."

Marie got inches from my face. "You know, you can be replaced at any time."

I told her, "I'm one in a million, you know. My mother told me."

Marie said, "She was referring to the sperm count and how that one succeeded. Delores and I have talked about that for hours, and we can't come to a conclusion. She thinks you got knocked into the egg by the real deal; you just got in the way."

The tour had ended. The girls were having way too much fun. We all thanked the superintendent for showing us the place; we saw nothing that needed fixing.

Silvia asked if we could get some keys to the office to duplicate for the office staff. He told her, "Once the building is signed off by the inspector and approved for occupancy, then I'll bring them to your office and show you how to set the alarm."

Silvia asked Delores if they could take me home; she had a meeting to attend with Murray. Delores said, "Yes, I think I have room on the rear bumper—or wait a minute, the roof rack. Marie can duct-tape him to the top of the SUV."

I told them, "I'm buying a bumper sticker saying, 'Free Katy.'"

39

We arrived home just in time to see the second truck offload the calves. It was amazing to watch; Scooter got the calves out of the trailer while Lulu kept the other calves in the corner of the corral. It took no more than ten minutes. When all the calves were offloaded, Scooter kept them back from the gate while the ranch hands closed it.

The girls were extremely excited. They all ran into the house, put on their farming outfits and boots, and headed to see all the new babies. The stopped at the hay stack to get a flake of alfalfa so the babies would come to them.

Scooter kept the calves back while the girls entered the corral. This was one of the most amazing sights you would ever want to witness. Each girl had at least seven or eight calves surrounding her as they fed them some alfalfa. They allowed the girls to pet them and love them, totally unafraid.

It seemed that Scooter might be fluent in bovine. Papa turned on the water at the trough to fill it up; he had also brought four dog bones in his pocket. We all joined the girls in the corral to see the new calves, but once they saw we did not have food, they walked away from us.

Delores and Marie went to see the lambs and the other calves. The new babies and those already here were mooing to each other; some of each were on the fenceline getting to know each other personally.

Murray showed up with Silvia, who wanted to see the calves.

Delores said, "Hey, what's up with this? You made me take him home and then you show up? I know he showered this morning."

Silvia said, "Just as I was getting ready to leave, Murray pulled in the parking lot and told me that two trucks had offloaded some calves. He said, 'Wanna go see the calves?' So here I am. We'll be on our way to the meeting in about five minutes."

Kim handed Silvia some alfalfa. "Come on, Silvia, feed a baby," she said. Silvia followed her to where the calves were waiting, and they came over when they spotted food. Before you knew it Kim and Silvia were surrounded by calves.

One calf licked Silvia's elbow, and she jumped. Kim and the girls were all laughing. Leslie said, "They do that to us all the time; they're just saying hello."

Delores and Marie were feeding the calves and lambs. Lulu was next to them keeping everything nice and calm. Scooter was lying down, keeping a watchful eye on the new calves.

The girls went to see the lambs and the other calves; their moms were having too much fun with their babies. The lambs were loving every minute of all the attention they were getting.

After about fifteen minutes everyone had to get ready for dinner. "Make sure you wash your hands," I reminded them.

Marie said, "Only after we handle your food; then we'll wash them."

The girls called Scooter and Lulu, who came to them. The girls closed the corral gate and headed to the playhouse, where both dogs had their special spot to lie down and watch the girls.

I manned the grill. Oiled and heated, it was waiting for the sacrificial meat offering. My beloved and Susanne came out with two platters of assorted meats.

Susanne said, "I bring explicit instructions for you: 'Don't burn the meat.'"

Tell her, "Only on one side. I'll flip it over for her surprise."

Susanne smiled. "She has a knife and knows how to us it, Mr. Bobbitt."

I told Susanne, " 'Hot dog,' free at last. No more pressure.

"A-grilling we will go, a-grilling we will go—" Then the girls sang, "Hi, ho, the dairy-oh, a-grilling we will go." Then they started whistling, "Whistle while You Work." *Those girls really did like working in the yard; a lemonade and a chocolate cupcake for fifteen minutes of labor made for pretty good pay.*

"Are you ready for the sides and salads, Daddy?" asked Leslie.

"I'm ready when you are. If not, you can help your moms; they'll appreciate the extra help." I heard them in the tunnel, clogging all the way. They arrived in the kitchen to help their moms, Susanne, and Mama get everything ready for dinner. Mama brought over the dessert she'd made earlier in the day. It was covered, so no peeking.

The meat was grilled to perfection, with just enough goose juice to add some needed flavor. Sides and salads were in place, with plates and silverware—what, no plastic?

Out to the patio came all our guests. The girls announced that Mama, Papa, Susanne, and Marie were to join them tonight for dinner.

John said, "Allow me to light the losers table candle," which he did while I dished out the requested piece of meat and placed in on each plate. The girls, being wise for their young age, counted the remaining pieces of meat.

Marie and Delores would salt and pepper each side before bringing them to me. Once—*one time*—I double seasoned it, and from that day forward they took it upon themselves to salt and pepper each piece.

"You only grill," Delores had said; "we will handle the prep. If you mess up the grilling, you can only wash the dishes; we'll inspect while we dry the dishes."

"There are no lesser jobs we can entrust you with," said Marie.

We all started talking about our upcoming Texas trip. Marie and Delores have been in contact with Jennifer, and Marjorie has all the arrangements in place for all the ladies.

The girls were gathering up meat scraps for their special guests and asked about desserts. "Grandma made us a surprise, you know." That was the girls' way of telling their moms, "Dinner may be finished, but there is an unknown dessert stirring up hunger pains deep inside our tummies." They would not want that to escape unnoticed.

That took the discussion into the kitchen with Susanne and Mama joining in. Jennifer told them, "The carnival planned is more like Mardi Gras, not a typical parking lot carnival with kiddie rides. She has beads for the ladies to toss from the playhouse and a band that will parade around the property, leading all the guests in the parade. She has Cajun cooking—jambalaya; the caterer is coming in from New Orleans. You will feel like you are at a Mardi Gras."

The ladies' biggest concern was for the girls. Would they be influenced by some bad behaviors of adults?

Mama said, "If the Mardi Gras starts to get out of hand, Papa and I will take the kids from the event to the hotels. I don't want Papa to get the wrong impression either. This is my temple, not a pleasure palace."

Susanne said, "I know Jennifer fairly well. This event will be done in good taste; she just wants everyone to let their hair down and enjoy the event. Silvia will be the head bartender, and she'll keep the alcohol under wraps. Remember, most of the guests are professional sports figures, all under contract. This is being filmed and aired live, so there won't be any shenanigans going on."

Marie said, "Descending the playhouse staircase should be a moment we will all remember. We can get a little crazy with the music beat."

Susanne also said, "Jason will have the mechanical bull with the girls giving each rider scores. That was so much fun last time that some of those riders are returning from Utah; they were hilarious to watch.

"Denise told us that they have done three other events with a panel of wives as judges. She nearly peed herself laughing so hard. She told us one young man was bucked off and landed awkwardly, but then he got up and bowed to the crowd while he swung his hat side to side. He got no points for his ride but tens from the ladies judging, for his actions, after he got up from being bucked off.

"The judges told Denise they thought he was really cute doing that; 'We know from how he landed that he had to have been hurting, but still he made everyone laugh.' He got a free dinner for four from the restaurant sponsoring the event, all expenses paid."

Marie asked, "Is One Buck Short going to be there?"

Susanne said, "He and ten others from that group are regulars; they've been at every event so far. They have actually started a fan club, and people are following them to the events, cheering them on. None of them have ever come close to winning; they like the attention they're receiving."

Marie said, " 'Groupies'; they must have received a group of ladies following them."

Delores said, "Are you one of One Buck Short's groupies?"

Marie said, "No, my dear. I have my own set of groupies to contend with; I just liked the name; it fits him. His wife did well in choosing the name."

Denise said, "The last time, a guy tried to mount the bull like the cowboys did in the television show—put his hands on the rump of the bull and sprang himself onto the slippery bull. Great in theory, and cameras were snapping. The first attempt, he was short of getting onto the bull. On the second try he cleared the bull but landed on his back and slid into the handhold and fell off in agony.

"His wife ran to him and said, 'Well, I won't have to say, "Not tonight, dear; I have a headache." ' The ladies were roaring with laughter.

"His wife changed his name to A Fool Never Learns. He'll be there showing his skills."

The girls all came into the kitchen. "We're waiting; what's the holdup?" said Leslie.

Marie said, "We were talking; sorry. Let's see what Mama made us."

Marie peeled back the aluminum foil and there sat—"Raspberry cobbler," Leslie said. "Girls, let's get the vanilla ice cream with chocolate shavings and our cherries. Thank you, Grandma." The girls were all hugging Mama, saying, "You're the greatest grandma ever."

Marie was cutting the cobbler into equal pieces and putting them on dessert plates. Delores was scooping out the vanilla ice cream, Susanne was spreading on the chocolate shavings, and the girls were putting on the cherries and delivering the desserts to the gentlemen waiting at the patio table.

Everyone was commenting on how wonderful the desserts were. That sealed the deal; Mama had a permanent invitation for every night's dinner with the girls.

The girls decided to sleep in Sarah's bed tonight—"So Mom and Dad don't lock the door on their best friend and get her soaking wet, from the game they're playing." They wanted us both to be put on restriction. Annie suggested a week sleeping on the sofa in separate rooms.

Marie said, "One can sleep on our living room sofa, and one can sleep on your living room sofa."

*

Susanne informed everyone that the entire team would be there to assist in wardrobe, makeup, and hairstyling. "This should also be a great event."

We gentlemen were watching the girls with the lambs and calves. The dogs at work getting the new calves to adjust and mingle with the earlier calves was a sight to watch; Lulu stayed with the girls and the lambs. Scooter had separated the lambs from the calves in only a couple of minutes; near bedtime he separated the calves again, bringing the original calves back to the shelter.

We did not close the gate between the two herds; that way Scooter could watch both herds keeping predators from attacking. We have not seen any predators for some time—no howling coyotes or wolves.

It was time to say good night to Scooter, Lulu, and the lambs and calves, head up to bed, and get tucked in with prayers and kisses. The girls were getting tired; they'd had a great day, with a new studio, new babies, and a big trip planned for tomorrow. They looked forward to getting another Western outfit and a huge party on Saturday; they're ready.

The girls were in, and night lights were on. They made sure moms didn't forget; it was very important that the night lights have the Whispering Pines Resort logo, reminding them of their first fishing trip.

Tonight's prayer included their fish. "We can't forget about our fish," said Leslie. On their calendar, they have that weekend circled for season opening. We get reminded frequently that it is extremely important that we all appear for that event; our audience is expecting us to do well and add more fish to the new aquariums.

Once the girls were a settled down to sleep, we old folks went our merry ways to slumber. Delores and I knew our sleep time will be shortened with our morning pounce. We hope they want to snuggle for a few minutes, Delores really enjoys sharing the bed while I make the coffee and hot chocolate; she gets to have girl talk with them.

*

It seemed like minutes had gone by, but it was hours before the four girls entered our bedroom for snuggles. They squirmed under the covers and shivered until Delores and I hugged them, sharing the warmth of our bed.

The girls had lots of questions about this day. "Who will take us to the airport? Who will meet us at the airport? What time will we go to the Western store? Where will we stay? Will we spend time with Janet and her brothers? Will we get to eat at the nice steakhouse?" After about the fifteenth question I decided to leave the answers to Delores, and I got up to make the coffee and hot chocolate.

Not long after I had started the coffee and hot chocolate, Delores and the girls were exiting the elevator and joining me in the kitchen. No sooner did everyone have a cup of their favorite brew than we heard the elevator returning to the second floor. In a couple minutes, Marie, John, Mama, Papa, and Susanne came into the kitchen with their morning hugs and kisses for the girls.

Susanne told us, "There will be three limousines arriving at seven thirty this morning to take all of us to the airport. Is everyone's bag ready?"

Marie said, "Almost. A few more items, and I'll be ready." We all chimed in on similar lines.

I started to get breakfast ready. The girls were at their posts with flipper, tongs, and butter knife at the ready. Let the cooking begin.

Like clockwork, pancakes were being turned, sausages were being rolled, and hash browns were being flipped. Papa went to the corral and brought in Scooter and Lulu. Delores and Marie were setting the table, and Kim and Rebecca were making the toast. I started the Albright scramble, smooth as silk; timing was perfect. Even Scooter was howling his approval of what he was watching.

Leslie made four small pancakes for Scooter and Lulu. Sarah made them two sausages each, and Marie cut them up on a plate to let them cool off. She added the four small pancakes to cool as well. As we were finished with our cooking, Marie took a spoon and put some scramble on top of the rest of the breakfast for Scooter and Lulu. When it was cool enough, she put half in Scooter's bowl and half in Lulu's bowl. They both waited until she said, "Okay, you can eat."

When Marie sat down, I asked her if she would do that for all of us. Marie said, "So early in the morning, everyone but him please enjoy your breakfast. You go sit in the corner until you can behave yourself."

Once breakfast was consumed and dishes were finished, everyone got their bags ready for the trip. We all gathered and waited for the limousines to arrive.

Murray and Silvia arrived to join the group. Murray was going to stay in our home while we were away to feed the calves, lambs, and dogs. Another truck full of calves will arrive later in the day. His ranch hands will build another corral since the two we now have are not big enough for all the calves. They want them to forage instead of having hay and alfalfa forked in. If they rely on people for food, they will starve to death or be victim to coyotes and wolves.

The girls were giving Murray instructions on how much love to give their lambs and calves. "They really like a lot of attention. If you don't give them enough, they cry, and Lulu has to mother them," said Leslie.

"Can you call us tonight, tomorrow, tomorrow night, and Sunday morning so we know they are all right?" asked Sarah.

Murray got a notepad from Silvia and wrote down the specific instructions. Then he told her, "You stay here, and I'll go with them. This is a lot harder than I planned."

Leslie told him, "Scooter and Lulu like being in our house during the day. They stay with us; we're their friends, you know. Oh, by the way, thank you for getting them for us. We have never had a dog before; we are all so happy."

As they were wrapping up the instructions our limousines arrived. Marie said, "Time to go, girls. Our limos are here."

The girls gave Murray hugs and petted Scooter and Lulu. "We'll miss you two. Keep Murray company," said Leslie.

40

Mardi Gras Event

At the airport, we checked our bags at the counter and headed over to be examined, warning the agents, "We all have warning devices placed by the FBI." We met the usual skepticism by the staff telling us to move aside to allow other passengers to get scanned.

The supervisor came to us after a delay, equipped with an attitude. He obviously thought we were telling a major lie, or else we had disrupted his morning coffee break. I luckily had my warning device attached so I would not have to disrobe in front of the staff or the other passengers.

He was not impressed and said, "I could get such a device at Wal-Mart."

I told him, "Okay let's put your theory to the test." I pressed the alarm, and within less than a minute three FBI agents were upon him, guns pulled.

The agent who'd kept us from moving forward was now impressed and embarrassed. They took him and two other TSA agents aside to say that they had just blown their cover. "There are no other agents nearby who can be swapped in. We now have to fly to Texas with all the passengers knowing we are protecting these families. You better hope that there's no one else aboard who wants to harm these people."

One FBI agent called his superiors telling them what just occurred. We now know that the TSA supervisor will be less arrogant when others being protected with warning devices don't impress his staff.

Airport security escorted us to our gate. The three FBI agents just blended in with the crowd of passengers waiting to board the plane; only a couple of the passengers in line behind us had seen the incident, so the agents talked with them. If they had the wrong idea, they would not be able to board the flight. Those who saw the incident were allowed to board the flight, a bit shaken by the presence of the FBI agents.

They posed no threat to us. In fact, they sat with our group and talked the entire flight about the magazine. They were subscribers and own some of the videos. Susanne got their information, promised to send them some signed photos and a couple of videos, and told them to watch tomorrow for the live showing of another home that we had completed.

We landed in Texas. The girls were all excited now; they get to go shopping for Western outfits. We all wandered over to the baggage carousel, where we were met by Jennifer, Marjorie, and of course Denise. She does not want to miss out on having some poor soul fall into a trash can or walk into a wall instead of a doorway. She was not disappointed, two guys walked into one another pulling their bags on wheels. Our girls just laughed and asked Denise, "How do you do that?"

Jennifer said, "Girls, in due time, you will do the same."

Leslie said, "Do you mean we will have men do that?"

Denise hugged the girls. "Yes, girls, you will have men do that. We ladies will make it our goal to help you."

We got our bags, loaded them into the waiting limousines, and headed to our steakhouse. The girls reminded us that their hunger pains were coming back. "The breakfast was fantastic," said Sarah, "but it only last so long."

As we entered the restaurant, Silvia's cell phone rang; it was Murray. He sent her a photo of Scooter offloading the third truck of calves. She showed the girls the video he had shot for them. He showed Lulu keeping the other calves back so there would be no escapees among the herds.

The girls were all excited to see some different types of calves other than black and red Angus. He even showed the lambs standing at the fence line watching the calves being offloaded.

Murray texted Silvia, *They looked like they were waiting for more lambs to play with, not more cattle. They were all expressing their opinions.*

We were all seated when the Texas camera crew showed up with the hairstylist and makeup crew to make the ladies look their best for the luncheon filming.

The makeup crew saw Denise and shook their heads; "Can't improve on perfection."

They went to Silvia, who told them, "Make me look like her, and I'll be happy."

The makeup artist said, "How about better than?"

Silvia said, "Better is good. I like that positive attitude."

Everyone ordered steaks, some rib eye and some T-bone. All ordered the baked potato, loaded with goodies; steamed vegetables; goose juice; and salads, with an assortment of dressings, along with Texas toast—so much food, so good.

After lunch the ladies and girls went to the Western Outfitter store, with cameras and crews in tow. This was a shopping spree aired on cable television as a special event. The store was very happy to have them all return; their parking lot was full, the store was full of customers, and the cash registers were in full swing.

They tried to get the customers to join in on deciding what outfits the girls would choose and offer a matching outfit for the one or ones who picked along with the girls. Some were a little reluctant until Jennifer and her friends starting choosing numbers of the five outfits the girls put on the dressing room doors.

Then the entire store's customers were bidding on certain outfits. The proceeds of the bids went to the local homeless shelters, providing outfits for the homeless children.

The girls were trying on the outfits with the help of the wardrobe department, they were moving around the store gathering up accessories for each outfit. Each girl had an assistant who used her talents to make each outfit perfect. When the girls were ready, all dressed and accessorized, they went out the dressing room onto the round stage to model each outfit. The store department manager introduced each girl and told the crowd which manufacturer the girls were modeling and which accessories had been chosen by the wardrobe department of the magazine.

After all of the twenty-five outfits were modeled and all choices were made, the magazine produced a video of each outfit and allowed the crowd to cheer on which outfit they thought each girl would choose.

Susanne was the Mistress of Ceremonies, interviewing each girl before the winning outfit was picked.

Leslie said the outfit she thought she would choose changed once she saw the accessories that were chosen for another outfit.

Marie told Delores, "There go my chances of winning. I know my girls, but not when they change their minds; now I'm lost."

Delores said, "Whisper me your choice."

Marie did as Delores asked. Then Delores said, "Look," and showed Marie her number.

Marie said, "We will get the candle table tonight."

Susanne said, "It's time, girls, to pick your favorite outfit so some of our customers can let us know who won."

They started with Kim, who took outfit number three. Rebecca selected outfit number two, Sarah took number five, and Leslie went with outfit number one. Marie looked at Delores, Mama, Susanne, Silvia, Gloria, and Jennifer; none of them picked the outfit the girls picked. Marjorie, Denise, Nadine, Angel, and Juanita each got one outfit. They teased the rest of the ladies, "You have to know the girls better," but they expressed sorrow for the moms. Since none of them had little girls they donated them to the homeless shelter. Only three additional outfits were taken by customers; the rest were also donated.

Marjorie's kids were next to pick outfits. Then the ladies had one choice from the racks which were modeled. The crowd had to guess which outfit belonged to which lady. The kids were a dollar a pick; you could only pick one outfit per child.

The ladies were five dollars per pick, and you could select three numbers per lady. You would have to put top pick, middle pick, and last pick for each of them. The prizes were set so that only the top pick won an outfit; the middle pick won fifty dollars, and last pick won a dinner.

They started a raffle like last time. Last time the prize was a Corvette; this time it was a new pickup truck from the same Chevrolet dealer just a couple of blocks down the street.

Janet picked out five outfits and was trying them on in the same dressing area.

The boys were in the boys' department, and a stage was set up for them. The customers had all moved to that area, where Jason was the master of ceremonies. He made sure to announce the Buck Off scheduled for tomorrow's showing. "Folks, this is the most enjoyable event you will ever witness."

They showed a video of the first one at Gloria's home, and people were laughing so hard they were shedding tears. The rider who fell off even before the mechanical bull started got the most laughs. When they showed Kim giving him a single point, and she was asked why she gave him a point, Kim said, "Well, he didn't get hurt." She was so sincere and her expression so sweet that her answer was priceless.

Jason mentioned, "The girls will judge again tomorrow, and you have to watch. The bull riders' names are given by their wife or girlfriend; we don't give them names."

The boys were ready to start showing their outfits, and the department manager was describing the manufacturer of the outfit and most of the accessories the staff had collected for each outfit.

The customers were watching the boys and posting which outfit they thought the boys would choose. Lots of dollars were being spent.

The boys teased the customers, asking them, "Is it this one, or is it this one, or maybe this one?"

Janet came over and told them, "Hurry up. We only have ten more minutes, and I need to show my outfits." She walked over the dressing rooms and picked up four outfits. "Here, stop playing with these lovely ladies. You're all too young." She already knew what outfits they would choose; the wardrobe assistants had told her through an earpiece.

The boys said, "Sorry, everyone; she's our boss."

Janet said, "Follow me, ladies. I'll make it easy for you, not really."

She put on the five outfits, any one of which would be perfect for her. It was really tough; even Marjorie had no idea which one she would choose. The dollars were stacking up quick. After Janet had modeled all the outfits, she told Brad which outfit she'd chosen. Being an actor, he played up to the crowd, walking past each outfit, checking the palm of his left hand over and over.

He looked at the number of the outfit and looked at his left palm, shook his head, and knocked on her dressing room door. He told her his number had faded from sweating under so much pressure. "What number was it again?"

She gave him a math quiz: "My age, less my younger brother's age, minus my brother's age next to Matthew's age, plus the grade in high school I'm in, minus your age."

He looked at the crowd. "I remember now." He picked up outfit two and handed it to the wardrobe assistant.

Janet told the assistant, "Nope, that's not it. Try again, dear."

"I was just teasing you, honey; I knew all along it was this outfit." He handed her dress number four.

Janet said, "Are you serious? You really don't remember? You have five fingers, correct?"

Brad said, "Yes, I have fingers on one hand, take away the two outfits you selected, that leaves you three; minus two, leaves you what number? Ladies, help me out. What number did she select?"

Janet came out of the dressing room wearing dress number one. "Ta-da, you're pretty smart for an actor," she said.

At least three ladies yelled, "Yes, we love you, Janet!"

"There are forty-seven Ladies' Club members here today," said Jason. "Our ten models wore all the dresses for you to see. Your job was to decide which lady would wear what dress. Whoever matches the most ladies to the right dress wins the pickup truck. Are you ready, ladies?

"We will start with dress number one and go through all forty-seven. Ladies, as you pass me tell everyone your name. Number one was Nadine, two was Angel, all the way down to forty-seven which was Gloria. They didn't want there to be an obvious outfit—for instance, that Marie would by forty-seven."

Marie was number twelve, and the country music being played changed for "Return to Me," and when number twenty came on, it changed to "Sway" for Delores. They played "Imaginary Lover" for Denise, who was thirty-one.

After the ladies had paraded through the store, Denise told Marie she wanted that to be her song from now on.

The ranchers showed up and said the same as last time: "We want to help the homeless; count us in."

Susanne announced the winner of the pickup truck. "She picked twelve dresses correctly—not quite as good as Christine 'Jingle Bells' Clause, with sixteen picks correct last time. Our new winner of the brand-new Chevrolet Silverado is Julia 'Can't Burn the Bacon' Chowders."

Julia was jumping up and down. "I can't believe I won. Oh, my God, our other vehicle stopped running yesterday, and we have no money to fix it." Now she was starting to cry. The Chevy dealer, the store owner, Susanne, Marie, and Delores were hugging her.

Susanne had three boxes of tissues and was handing them out to anyone who needed a tissue. She said, "It can't get any better than this. Wow, we want to do this again. Would you all want to know about the next event?"

The crowd inside and outside were screaming, "Yes, do this again, we love it!"

Jason standing next to Susanne said, "We will have a Buck Off at the same time. No parking lot; all vendors and the corral for our mechanical bull. Ladies, bring your riders, with their name pinned to their shirts. A great time will be had by all."

Jason asked the girls, "You'll be our judges?"

Leslie said, "We would love to judge the riders."

Jason asked Kim, "You will give them a point just as long as they don't get hurt, correct?"

Kim said, "If he doesn't get hurt and he's funny, I'll give him a point."

Jason said, "So, everyone please be sure to watch the Mardi Gras Event tomorrow on your local cable network. You'll be glad you did. Now back to you, Susanne."

Susanne, standing right next to him, said, "Thank you, Jason." She put her hand on his shoulder. "Great job.

"As Jason just informed you, we will be shooting the Mardi Gras Event live tomorrow at Jennifer's home. Jennifer, please join us on the platform."

Jennifer came onstage in her new Western Outfitter garb. She was getting wolf whistles and applause, with two offers of marriage.

Jennifer said, "You are all so kind. I can't marry anyone; I'm spoken for. I love the outfit. Thank you, Western Outfitter; you make me feel like a million dollars. Oops, that's what the price tag says."

Susanne looked at the tag. "It says, 'If you want to look like a million, why not spend a million?' Oh, honey," she said, looking at her husband, "can I get one of these?"

Susanne asked, "So Jennifer, tomorrow, at your house, a huge event. You chose Mardi Gras as your theme. What made you think of Mardi Gras?"

Jennifer said, "My husband and I and a few friends went to the Mardi Gras a couple of years ago, and we had such a great time, we even danced with the people in the parade. We got lots of beads, the food was fantastic, and the music was loud and festive. We will try to bring that atmosphere to our glorious backyard, thanks to Stockdale Landscape Construction."

Susanne asked, "What can our viewers watch out for that will inspire them to head to New Orleans this Mardi Gras?"

Jennifer said, "All the ladies you see here today will attend, plus five more. They will be dressed appropriately tossing beads to the guests from my playhouse balcony. And the light show at sunset—wow, I mean wow. Every night I sit among the lights in total awe. We will have great food catered by a New Orleans catering company; we have three bands scheduled to play the entire event. *Remodeling* magazine will video the entire event, and all subscribers will receive the video in next month's issue.

"Oh, one other thing: my dearest friend, Jason, will be hosting the Buck Off, All of my guests are bringing their better half, with some great names for their riders."

Susanne said, "That is all for today. Thank you, Ladies' Club; my darling girls; the Wiloby children; and all of our staff and sponsors. See you tomorrow at the Mardi Gras."

The store was very busy with customers talking to the Ladies' Club, the girls, and the Wiloby's, asking them all sorts of questions. The girls told everyone about their lambs and calves and their two dogs, Scooter and Lulu. "They are our best friends," said Sarah. She told them how Scooter herded the calves from the trailer to the corral, and Lulu stood guard, allowing no calf to leave the corral."

Rebecca was telling some gentlemen about their fish and how they had caught enough trout to fill an aquarium at the Whispering Pines Resort. "Please join us when the season opens; we will attempt to catch enough fish to fill up the new aquariums being built."

It was time for the Ladies' Club, the girls, the Wilobys, the entire staff, and invited guests to caravan over to the restaurant for a steak dinner. More than a hundred people were going to attend.

Susanne got on her telephone and got permission to video the dinner for a future showing. The camera crews—one at the store and one at the restaurant—were ready. They filmed the ladies getting into the limousines. They were pouring their favorite beverages, mostly margaritas, blended with salt on the rim. The girls and the Wiloby boys were in one limousine with sodas and cupcakes, a two-pack each. They didn't survive beyond the parking lot for the boys. The girls took their time, mostly to tease the boys. They took little bites, saying, "Ummm, so good."

The boys told the girls how much they loved living in Texas. The girls told them about the lambs, calves, and dogs they were getting to raise. The girls told the boys, "Have you and your mom come pay us a visit. All our playhouses are connected by tunnels, so rain or shine, we don't get wet, and we have air conditioning and heating in the playhouse and tunnels."

Our group filled the restaurant, there were a few tables available for other customers. We had the banquet room filled; the place had two other small party rooms, which we filled; then we filled the main dining room.

We sat at the main table with Mr. Barns and Phyllis, the five ranchers and their wives, Mama and Papa, Susanne, Jennifer, Marjorie, our girls, the Wiloby children and Brad, and the Western Outfitter store owner and his wife. To keep the restaurant from going stir-crazy, we all received the same meal, and what a meal it was: soup, salad, rib eye steak, baked potato, tequila beans, and home-style potatoes if you decided you didn't want the baked potato, or you could order a baked sweet potato. Of course, it also included a dessert.

You better come to this restaurant starving; there is no way you will finish the meal without loosening your belt.

While we were finishing our soup, Susanne was talking with the restaurant manager. It seems that Murray and Stuart are being filmed at their house, and it will air live on the restaurant's big screen television.

Susanne asked for everyone's attention. "We have Silvia's fiancé and future farther-in-law, live on the big screen television. Everyone gathered around to view what was being videoed. They were shooting the scene from the corral with the lambs, calves, and dogs surrounding them.

Murray said, "Girls, your animal family want to say hello, they are all fed, watered and petted as you requested. And we have a surprise for Jennifer."

Phillip came on the air. "Good evening, Jennifer. I just want to let you know my Texas crew will be at your home early tomorrow morning to install my surprise for you. This is my thank-you gift for being such a good customer, so easy to work with and such a joy for me and my crews. Have a great Mardi Gras. Sorry I can't make your event but promise to make the next one. Love you all; have a great meal."

Murray and Stuart told everyone have a great dinner. "Enjoy our beef; the entire meal is on the house. See you on Sunday."

Jennifer came over to me and asked, "Do you know what the surprise is?"

I told her, "If I knew, then it would not be a surprise. He and I did not discuss this matter." I looked at her. "But I think he's sweet on you."

Jennifer said, "First off, I'm married. Second, he's old enough to be my father."

I told her, "His wallet is only five years old, with a hidden compartment."

Jennifer asked Delores, "Do you ever get a straight answer out of him?"

Delores said, "I gave that up years ago. I find not asking him a question is far easier."

The meal was being served. "Wow, the aroma," Delores said. "Why don't our cookouts smell this good?"

I told her. "I cook outside, and the breeze carries it away."

"No, the breeze carries away the smoke from the burnt meat."

41

The meal was unbelievable, so good and filling. Then came the dessert: a choice between peach cobbler with vanilla ice cream, apple pie with vanilla ice cream, or either boysenberry, raspberry, or blackberry pie with vanilla ice cream. The kids got chocolate cupcakes with chocolate icing and their name spelled on top with white icing.

The chef did say if you desire a cupcake like the children are receiving please let the waitress know. Give them your name, and you will receive the cupcake.

About twenty adults wanted the cupcake with vanilla ice cream—homemade vanilla ice cream, fresh, made this morning. You could top your ice cream with coconut, chocolate, fresh whipped cream, not out of a can or plastic tub, with the cherry on top.

One of the ladies wanted hot fudge put on her ice cream. That got several other people requesting the hot fudge.

I tapped my spoon on my water glass. Susanne brought me the microphone. "I just wanted to remind the Ladies' Club, let's not have another incident like the one at my company's grand opening. Enjoy your desserts."

Marie raised her fork and pointed it in my direction. "Watch it, buster, you only get one warning."

Delores said hello to my rib cage using her elbow. She said, "Just in case you became deaf, that's sign language."

I gathered that reminding them was of no importance to them. *Eat your peach cobbler, and be happy you can still breathe.*

Once dinner was completed, we all headed for our limousines and were off to the hotel for well needed rest after another long, grueling day. The girls received stuffed animals from the store. Each got a lamb. Just try and get that out of their hands; the girls had tears in their eyes when the store owner presented the lambs to them.

During the dress modeling, Kim told her lamb, "I'll be right back. I have to go to work. We'll play when I get home from work."

I told Delores, "There went my Christmas gift idea out the window."

Delores said, "Well, there is always a stuffed calf."

"Great, there went the birthday gift idea."

Delores asked, "What was your idea for my Christmas gift, a cow patty?"

I found a piece of paper in my pocket and tore it up into little pieces. "My entire list is gone in just a few minutes."

Delores said, "What were you going to give Marie?"

"Well, if she put on some more weight, a cowbell."

Delores said, "I'm telling her what you said. Don't you deny it, or you might want to consider a sex change."

When we stopped at the hotel lobby, we got some needed coffee and some breakfast rolls. The girls got cupcakes; the hotel knows their guests.

When we arrived at our suites and were just about comfortable, Delores told Marie what her Christmas gift from me would be.

With her head slightly cocked to her left side, she said, "Cowbell. A cat has nine lives. You don't have any to give up. As for getting even, that would never work; you'd still be breathing. I'll get back to you once I fit the punishment to the crime."

The girls all decided to sleep in one room. The master bedroom had a king-size bed, and the other bedroom had two queen beds. We asked if they would like to sleep in the king bed and we would take the queen beds. They thought that was as splendid idea; more room for their lambs to stretch out. I'd forgotten; we now had eight kids.

The girls were watching a program on the television but getting bored. "Is there nothing to watch on television?" asked Leslie.

Marie and Delores ran through all of the hundred stations trying to find something suitable: a kids' program, or programs from the fifties or sixties, or a farming program showing kids in 4-H, but nothing, absolutely nothing.

Marie said, "Tomorrow morning we will find a store and purchase a nice, wholesome program for you girls to watch.

They ended up with the cable network special, borderline acceptable. Marie and Delores held on to the remote to flip the channel if the program became unacceptable.

It was nearing bedtime, so John and I went down to the lobby and gathered up some goodies and beverages for our going-to-bed celebration. In the lobby we ran into some of the Ladies' Club with their spouses doing the same as we were. We all told each other, "Have a good night's sleep; long day tomorrow."

Back into the room we were nearly tackled before we crossed the threshold. John asked me, "What happened to our blockers?"

"The ladies broke through the line; we're going to get sacked."

John and I got what the ladies and girls called "Ew," maybe a third choice or fourth choice, not the first choice.

I told John, "If you dunk the roll into your coffee, it softens it enough to chew and swallow without getting lodged in your esophagus." We went through a pitcher of coffee for one roll; so fresh.

The girls were happy with a breakfast roll and a cup of hot chocolate. They were talking about tossing beads to the adults and judging the Buck Off. They were hoping some of the funniest riders from Utah would be riding tomorrow.

Delores said, "Should we have our husbands ride?"

Marie said, "People still look up to us as intelligent; that would prove them wrong."

Delores said, "You're right. I was thinking about all the money we could rake in. You know, talk it up like 'Eight seconds, they can do that standing on their heads, no big deal.' We'll bet heavy on under a second realistically; money will be on nine or ten seconds or more."

"We'd have to coaxes our husbands to hop on the bull," said Marie.

Delores pretended to unbutton her blouse's top button. "Enough coaxing will get them to do miracles."

It was time for the girls to go to bed. They were bored anyway; the program they were watching was putting them to sleep. "So exciting," said Leslie.

Sarah said, "We have already watched paint dry; it's about the same as this program."

They were all in their pajamas, teeth brushed, faces washed, and lambs in their arms. This will be the lambs' first prayer night; the girls would help them in case they started crying or got scared. Soon all the prayers were finished, kisses were finished, tucked in, and night lights were on. Mama and Papa, John and Marie, and Delores and I all said, "See you in the morning; sleep tight, our angels. Love you."

Mama and Papa were tired and decided to head to their suite. We usually got up too early for them, so they needed to get a head start. Hugs and kisses finished, they headed down the hall past John and Marie's suite.

There were two semistale rolls left with four cups of coffee in the pots. We all sat down at the round table and cut the two rolls in half to share, just like Momma told us all when we were toddlers: "Share with your brothers and sisters or I'll take all of the goodies away."

I told John, "That's what Delores tells me every night; I have to share."

John asked, "With who do you have to share, and what are you sharing?"

I told him, "The covers, with her. She already has far more than what I have; you know, her half plus my half equals hers."

We all finished our roll and cup of coffee. With nothing else exciting to talk about, it was time to get some sleep. The girls were already resting up to pounce on our mattress.

Hugs and kisses were shared. We set new rules, same as for the girls; we are all family. John and Marie were heading to their suite, and Delores and I went toward the master suite before we remembered we'd been demoted to the other bedroom. I told her, "Let's share one queen bed for half of the night then separate into both beds so the girls can pounce on two beds."

Delores gave me that look. "What are you up to, sir?"

"Well," I told her, "this is 'national hold your wife in your arms until she falls asleep' day."

Delores rang Marie's room and told her what she'd just heard from me. "Is he lying to me?"

Marie said, "Tell him that ended fifteen minutes ago. Sorry, you'll have to wait until next year. Make sure you hang up your stockings on the mantel, waiting for lots of luck to come down the chimney to fill your stockings. Oh, enjoy those queen beds, just like when you were first married, honeymoon."

Delores said, "Honeymoon, just like our honeymoon? That was in the bed of his pickup truck. He threw two tarps over the pipe rack, anchored them on the tie-down brackets and the rear bumper, and we backed the truck up to my parents' garage door. We laid down two sleeping bags and got two pillows off my bed and a blanket. The second night we backed the truck up into my parents' garage. Then we didn't have to tie the tarps to the pipe rack; the wind had blown them off during the night.

"I'll tell you the rest when we return to Oregon over a couple of margaritas; remind me," said Delores.

We decided that snuggle would be enough for tonight. We'd better hurry getting to sleep, as the girls had an hour head start.

About an hour and a half after we were asleep, nature called. I forgot we were not in the master suite, so I had to go through the living room to the bathroom for guests. Oddly, the light was on in the bathroom. I first thought that one of the girls might be in the restroom. But as I approached, I could see a lady dressed in housekeeping uniform. She was going through Delores's overnight case.

I needed to startle her, so I yelled, "What are you doing in our rooms," and shut the bathroom door so she could not run out.

I shouted for Delores to call the police, which she did. Just that fast, the girls were all up and scared. "Mommy, what's going on?" asked Sarah.

Delores said, "Wait a couple of minutes; the police are on their way."

There was a knock on our door. Delores asked, "Who is it?"

"Police department, ma'am. "He showed his badge so Delores could see it through the peephole. She let them in. The officer said, "You called us?"

Delores said, "In our restroom—my husband ran into an intruder."

The officers told me to open the door, which I did. They approached the housekeeper, handcuffed her, and set her down on one of the chairs at the round table.

"Tell us, ma'am, what are you doing in this hotel room at this hour of the morning?"

She told them she had to finish her housecleaning. "The boss is inspecting in the morning, and I could lose my job.

One officer told the other, "Go down to the lobby and bring up the desk clerk."

I told the officer, "She has no cleaning items with her, no cart, no mop, nothing."

The officer said to the housekeeper, "Where is your cleaning cart?"

"I only had to clean the mirror and countertop, I was using a bath towel to do the cleaning."

I told the officer, "She was going through my wife's overnight case which has jewelry inside."

The officer had one of the other officers look in the bathroom. "Don't touch anything; see if there's a towel off the rack."

The officer called in to headquarters and asked to have forensics come to our suite. "Robbery, unarmed … don't know … yes … don't know …. Okay, thank you."

In about ten minutes another team arrived. They had a lady officer with them who asked the housekeeper to stand so she could search her. In her pockets she found some of Delores's jewelry. She read her her Miranda rights. The other officer had brought the hotel desk clerk to the room, and they interrogated her with the suspect.

A detective and the desk clerk went to the office. They checked the employee files, and the lady being arrested was not employed by the hotel.

They returned to the suite, where they read the desk clerk her Miranda rights and cuffed her. They would take them both down to headquarters to straighten out this matter. The housekeeper had the hotel pass key in her pocket.

The arresting officer went back down to the lobby and talked to the assistant hotel clerk, had Forensics take fingerprints, and got the girl's name, address, and phone number. Then they all returned to the suite to continue collecting evidence.

Marie and John, and Mama and Papa were questioned and fingerprinted as well.

"We had to verify who they are to allow them to enter the room; don't touch anything."

The ladies asked if they and the girls could return to the master bedroom to go back to sleep. The detective on the case told Forensics to see if there is any evidence in that room.

Within a half hour the forensics officer said, "You're okay to use the bed. Don't touch the doorknobs or use the restroom counters or the cabinets."

So all four girls and their moms climbed into the master bed and fell fast asleep. Mama and Papa got the room Delores and I had been sleeping in; John got the sofa, and I got two chairs pushed together.

John asked me, "How do you do this?"

"What do you mean, John? Do what?"

"You found bones buried in concrete in our staircase, a bag full of stolen money, buried chests and steel cans in our yard, a serial rapist in Oregon, a crime scene extraordinaire in another home in our town, and now a burglar stealing your wife's jewelry. You know, most people can't find their car keys; you're a one-man crime stopper." John said, "They'll have to build a prison just to house the people you catch breaking the law."

The detective looked in and asked, "Will you be out of the room today?"

I answered, "We have the entire day planned from breakfast until late in the evening; Why do you ask?"

"We're going to have to finish investigating this room. What are the other suite numbers where your family are staying?"

John told them, "Next door and the next unit beyond that one."

The detective said, "We will check those two rooms now, and I'll let you know if they are clear. If we find no evidence which matches this suite, then please, all of you use that suite until we can get you relocated tomorrow morning, when the hotel manager comes to work."

It seemed like we were asleep for five minutes before there was a knock at our door. It was Marjorie and her children. I told them, "Could you all please wait for us in the hotel lobby? We had a break-in here last night, and we can't have your fingerprints contaminating the crime scene." I hurriedly slipped on some street clothes and joined them in the lobby.

Marjorie said, "I don't know how you do what you do, but I'm so glad you are on our team."

I explained to her what happened. "If I hadn't awakened when I did, Delores would have lost all her jewelry and lord knows what else. My big fear is that since they got into our suite, they could have kidnapped the girls without our knowledge. I couldn't handle another episode of kidnappings; that would push me over the edge. I would wipe out every one of those imprisoned."

The detective saw me talking with Marjorie and said, "Mr. Stockdale, can we have a word?"

I told him, "This is my office manager for the branch in Texas. Please be seated unless you want to talk privately?"

The detective said, "It's not necessary to talk privately if you don't mind answering some questions in front of your employee."

"She's one of my office wives."

The detective, puzzled, asked, "Office wives. You have multiple marriages?"

"No sir. You see, as the boss, I hire people to run the office under delegated authority. They are no longer employees according to that terminology; they are more like my wife away from home. I know this sounds odd, but there is little difference, except that the relationship is not physical, just verbal."

The detective said, "Yes, that is different. You have made me think about my situation at work. My staff is assigned to me and are subject to relocation without my consent."

He went on, "The housekeeper has told the officers that she was hired by the housecleaning company to do what you caught her doing. We will investigate that company in a couple of hours. From interrogating the desk clerk, it appears that she was in financial trouble, so to earn extra income she worked hand in hand with this housecleaning company, passing them information about guests in the hotel suites."

Marjorie said, "I booked these rooms over a month ago through a booking agent who is a friend of one of our employees."

The detective asked, "Could you give us that information?" He handed her a business card. Just call that phone number, and they'll forward your call to me."

Marjorie said, "I will get that to you on Monday morning first thing."

The detective said, "If we can connect some dots from booking agents and certain hotel chains to the housecleaning company and their employees, that would make our life a lot easier and your stay in our area more enjoyable—win-win for us and lose-lose for them."

I asked, "Does this happen all the time around here?"

The detective answered, "It's been on the rise for about a year. We found one link from people trying to save money, clicking on the wrong website, and having their credit cards completely cleaned out. Some are more sneaky; they just nibble away at your card, thinking you won't notice the twenty or twenty-five-dollar charge per month.

"I have to get going, but thank you for taking some of your time to talk. It's very nice meeting you both; have a great day."

Marjorie said to him, "You may have broken up a theft ring. Should I talk to Jennifer about what happened?"

"In general, but don't disclose that her husband's friend may be assisting an organization in stealing from their customers. She'll find out soon enough, and it could alert them to shut down or go into hiding. It could also cause friction between you two; we don't need that."

Marjorie and I took the kids downstairs for breakfast. Delores and Marie, came into the lobby, looking like they had no sleep.

Delores said, "Mm, coffee," and took my cup. She downed it and said, "Thank you, dear; where is more? Oh, good morning, Marjorie. What a night."

They joined our table once they had retrieved some Java with a breakfast roll from the buffet. They brought us each another cup of coffee and a breakfast roll.

Delores asked me, "Were you afraid that she might be armed?"

"You know, when you in that type of situation, you just react. You and the girls mean more to me than protecting myself."

Marie said, "My dad will alert the organization, to see if there is a contract out on you; if so, they'll let him know. He said you're making his life a little more difficult every day."

Marjorie said, "We need to alert all the ladies to wear their warning devices."

I told them, "These girls are the bottom of the food chain, easily replaced."

Delores said, "Let's take two pots of coffee and some rolls to the suite and one pot of hot chocolate. The girls should be awake by now."

We returned to our rooms, where everyone was sitting at the round table, happy to see us with goodies. John told me that their bathroom was free to use to shower and get ready for the day.

While they all were enjoying their goodies, I took a shower and got dressed for the day. The girls were already in their outfits from yesterday. They'd been told that the wardrobe crew had outfits for them for the Mardi Gras. They were still hugging and talking to their lambs.

The ladies needed to freshen up. While they were doing that, we had a knock at our door. The forensic team was returning to do more investigation and asked if we all could leave and use the other suite so they could finish.

We all gathered up our goodies and went into Marie and John's room through the door access to both rooms.

Marie took a shower first, then Delores, then Mama, and finally Papa. Soon everyone was ready for the day. Just in time, for the parade of limousines pulled in to retrieve all the guests for the Mardi Gras.

We went to our restaurant, where Leslie reminded them of the Albright scramble. The chef was ready to show her his version and gave her a sample. She took a bite and handed the plate to me. I had a taste and gave the plate to Marie and John. We all agreed that it was a great rendition of the original.

The group ordered twenty Albright scrambles with their own special beverages.

The meal was fantastic. The girls and the Wiloby children all received their favorite chocolate cupcakes with their names in white icing on top. All refilled and rehydrated, we were off to Jennifer's to see what Phillip's surprise is.

We had six limousines in a parade. That got the attention of the guardhouse, and they called Jennifer to make sure it was okay to allow them to pass through.

We all arrived, and the girls and the Wiloby children wanted to see her playhouse. Jennifer said, "I've been waiting for you to arrive since last night. I could hardly sleep."

Leslie asked, "Did you have a burglar in your house too?"

Jennifer said, "No burglar. Did you have a burglar?"

Leslie said, "Yes, Daddy caught her, and she's now in police custody."

Jennifer asked, "Is everyone all right?"

Leslie said, "We are all fine. Even our lambs were a little restless but settled down and slept real close to us all night long."

Jennifer had them all close their eyes while she opened up the front door. As they entered the house, they got very excited.

"It's beautiful. You have done a marvelous job decorating our house," said Sarah.

Leslie had to correct her, saying, "This is Jennifer's playhouse."

Jennifer said, "You know what, I'll share my house with you today, tomorrow, and forever. Please feel at home. You all inspired me to have one built. I would be lost without the playhouse.

"Follow me; I'll show you my surprise." They all went through the double French doors on her patio. "The entire top of the patio cover is a sundeck." Phillip had installed two corner tables with two bench seats on both sides with four-inch-thick all-weather cushions. They were painted to match the doors and gates to her backyard. The kids took turns sitting on the four benches, pretending to be at a resort.

Marie, Delores, Marjorie, Mama, and Papa joined them on the deck and saw the surprise. "Wow, nice surprise—they're beautiful."

Jennifer told them, "I cried when I saw them, I was so overjoyed. He even had a thank-you card attached. That will go in my guest book for everyone to see. My photo albums are ready for you to inspect; let me know how I did."

The kids all returned to the playhouse while the moms enjoyed the benches and tables.

Marie said, "We have a nice spot on our decks where these would work marvelously."

Delores said, "You decorated the house very nicely. Have you spent any time in the house?"

Jennifer said, "My husband has to drag me back into our home. Wait till you see the place lit up at dusk. I sat a plastic chair on the patio and enjoyed a cup of coffee looking at the lights from above. My neighbors and friends will be delighted to see the final outcome of the project.

"I had to keep it under lock and key since it was completed—turned off the light system after the first showing. I don't want a ho-hum from anyone. As a safety precaution, I didn't even let my husband see the place lit up."

42

The crews arrived to start setting up the backyard for the carnival, the cul-de-sac where her house was located was being blocked off by the traffic control company. All of the homeowners who would be attending the carnival had been notified that if they needed to go anywhere from now until the event started, they would be shuttled by either limousine or SUV.

The cul-de-sac would have the games for the adults and kids to play. On Jennifer's driveway would be the mechanical bull which Jason and his crew were starting to set up. There were at least a dozen trucks full of items for the carnival.

The cul-de-sac would be transformed into a fun zone with lights, music, and fried everything. They brought in a large truck full of sawdust to be spread on the street to give the event the true feeling of a carnival.

The crew setting up the backyard converted the place into Bourbon Street. The New Orleans chef arrived with his staff to start the food prep, and the temporary bar was being erected. Silvia was ready to have all guests put into a festive mood. They had an area in the garage set up for the ice machines and cases and cases of liquor, sodas, mixes, plastic glasses, bar napkins, olives, cherries, and all sorts of trimmings for every type of drink to be served.

Jennifer hired two assistants, Elizabeth, Rosalee, for Silvia; she tended bar at the country club where most of the guests were members. Jennifer had taken Silvia to the country club last night to introduce the two. Silvia was impressed and sized up Elizabeth as "a real professional, fast and efficient, good personality, and easy on the eyes."

The kids were having a great time on the patio deck. Jennifer gave them a box of beads to practice tossing them to one another. She showed them just how so the person below could catch them. "Don't want to break them."

The film crew was filming the transformation from upscale housing tract to the other side of the tracks carnival atmosphere. The booths were butted up against each other, so watching the film, you would never know the house behind the scene was a multimillion-dollar estate.

All the booths were being filled with sawdust on the flooring so that when filming the cameramen won't have to shoot at odd angles to avoid showing the floors. There were at least ten wheelbarrows spreading the sawdust; our landscape crews here were doing most of the spreading. They would return with their families once the sawdust was spread.

The carnival operators asked the girls, the Wiloby children, and the kids from Jennifer's family to give the booths a try. A ring toss, to land on a soda bottle, was the first booth set up, then throwing a dart at balloons hanging on a corkboard; with a slight breeze it wasn't easy to hit one. Then came toss the coin onto carnival dishes; putting the coin into the coffee cup was the impossible toss. There were at least twenty different booths once all were finished.

Jennifer's sisters were just like her, and their mom was exactly like the girls, just a little older.

I asked Delores and Marie to have them join the Ladies' Club and teach them how to do the grand entrance. They would blend right into the other forty-eight ladies.

Marie said, "You know, we would say okay, but we have to get a hold of Susanne and see if there are enough costumes for them."

Delores approached Jennifer's women relatives and said, "Ladies, I'm Delores. My husband, my best friend, and I were wondering if you would be interested in performing with our Ladies' Club this afternoon. We will teach you how to do a grand entrance and put you into outfits that fit the theme of the event. You will receive revenue from the magazine for performing."

Jennifer said, "You want them to perform with us? What a great idea! Mom, girls, you have to do this. It will be the highlight of the entire event."

Jennifer's mom said, "Oh, I don't know. I'm not much of a dancer, nor would I feel comfortable sashaying myself in front of strangers."

Delores told her, "With a little champagne and some quick lessons from Marie and I, between the applause from the crowd, the lights, and the music being played, you'll be in good hands."

Marie said, "We're all good. They brought plenty of outfits with them. Let's see what you girls have to show. First off, all three of you turn around slowly. Jennifer, show them how you do it."

Jennifer followed Marie's instruction.

Marie said, "See, ladies, follow what your sister just did."

They all three followed Jennifer's lead, and then Jennifer did it with them.

Marie asked her, "Do you have four champagne glasses?" And she asked Sarah to get her eight strands of beads, which she did.

Marie gave each lady a champagne glass, and Silvia filled each one.

Silvia said, "I have to watch this. Three new recruits, all gorgeous. You'll make my job just a little harder."

Glasses were filled. Marie, Delores, Silvia, Mama, and Jennifer had five additional glasses poised and ready.

"Silvia and Jennifer, go over by the doorway and come to me," said Marie.

Jennifer's brother put on the stereo with some very moving music, with a great beat, for the ladies to perform.

As they approached Marie, they both got very seductive in their moves.

Marie swatted Silvia. "Bad girl, but I liked it." She then asked Mama to show the ladies a more sophisticated entrance.

Marie said to Delores, "Your turn." Then she told the others, "This is a very talented lady. It will take you lots of practice to get close to her moves."

Delores wowed them with one basket full of swaying of her hips, one foot in front of the other, and a twirl, so poised, each move perfection.

Jennifer was helping her sisters practice moving, and Mama was helping Jennifer's mom do the same. "Loosen up, ladies," said Marie; "if you remain stiff, it will look odd." Silvia was helping the one sister.

The doorbell rang, and Jennifer answered it. There stood Denise, Eileen, Angel, Juanita, and Gloria.

Marie said, "Perfect timing. Show our newest ladies how you do the grand entrance."

The sound crew was putting together the music for the grand entrance as the girls all lined up and showed the ladies what to do.

Of course, they all wanted a glass of champagne or sparkling cider, and wow, just wow, they showed the ladies their best moves.

Jennifer introduced all the ladies to her family: "Everyone, they're all employees of Stockdale Landscape Construction."

Jennifer's brother said, "Is he hiring? I'm applying. How many more look like these ladies?"

Jennifer said, "All of them."

Jennifer's sisters and mom gave it a shot. They were pretty good but needed some more coaching.

Marie said, "Ladies, follow me." They went to the backyard and ascended the staircase of the playhouse. All the kids were on the patio, ready to watch the ladies perform. Janet was asked to join the ladies.

The chef's crew and the setup crews were busy putting up decorations when the grand entrance music started to play for Marie. "Okay, ladies. Silvia, Susanne, Jennifer, come to me." Marie and Delores were on the patio. As Silvia descended the staircase, the kids were hooting and hollering, and the ladies were applauding them with the setup crew and the chef's crew. Each lady showed off her best grand entrance, each one better than the last.

Denise told Eileen, "Let's make them drop something or walk into a post." They each put in one beautiful display of poise, glamour, seduction, and sensuality with each step until they reached the patio—and they both got what they were trying to achieve. One of the chef's crew walked into the barbeque, carrying a platter of meat, and another setup man missed a step on the ladder on his way down and almost ended up on the deck.

Delores and Marie showed the Cadillac of descents, and the applause was deafening, drowning out "Return to Me" for Marie and "Sway: for Delores." Both were stunning, just stunning.

Now that the ladies had performed in the living room and the staircase of the playhouse, Susanne informed them that the limousines were waiting to take them to the trailers for makeup, hairstyling, and an outfit for the Mardi Gras. She told the kids to head to the limousines so they could be outfitted first while the ladies were getting makeup and styling. She told Janet that she would go with the ladies and perform today.

Gloria put her arm around her and told her she would help her be the best she could be.

Jennifer's mom was Louise; Jennifer's older sister was Jessica, her younger sister was Merrilee, and her brother was Marcus. So all the ladies would be introduced to the guests by their first name.

Susanne had Jennifer, Louise, Jessica, Merrilee, and Candice get into the first limousine. Since this was their first fitting, it would take a little longer in case alterations were required.

Angel and Juanita would be dressed as a chauffeur and a chambermaid, respectively. Angel should be a crowd pleaser, and when Juanita performed at her last event as a chambermaid, the crowd went wild. She is finally down to a size where she and Angel can swap clothes. Juanita and Angel go the gym together and try to outdo each other in their workouts.

When the kids all returned in costume, the carnies kept prompting them to try and win a stuffed animal or a really nice Chinese toy. It didn't cost them anything, just bragging rights for any winner.

The boys enjoyed the arcade. Shooting BBs was fun; they only won a trinket or two, and Jerome was just three targets short of getting to the next level. He hit all the targets, but the target must fall over for it to count. Each target had a bull's-eye painted for the shooter to hit, but when you move up to the next level, the bull's-eye was designed not to allow the target to fall when it's hit. The carnie operator always said "Great shot" to the shooter.

The kids all tried playing each booth. They all received a soft vanilla ice cream cone dipped in a hard-shell chocolate coating. John and I went out front to help the girls win. We did worse than they did. John won a little toy car, and the operator said he'd scored the lowest score he had ever recorded. That really boosted John's ego. The boys and girls were winning some items; they would run upstairs and display them in the playhouse and then return to win some more.

The ladies were starting to return ready for the Mardi Gras. Silvia and the other bartender were in the first limousine returning so they could get the bar up and going. The aroma of the cooked meal was driving us all into hunger pains.

The girls, using their charm and talent to break the coldest heart, got some samples of the meat being cooked. The chef asked if they liked it. Leslie said,

"We're so hungry, the meat just disappeared in our tummies; our taste buds had to just release the meat so the tummy would stop crying."

The chef asked if they would like another sample. Leslie, now displaying her diplomatic side, stated, "If you could spare another sample, we would greatly appreciate the offer, but we would not want to take someone else's food."

The chef said, "If you can get me signed photographs of you and the others, I would consider that enough payment for the samples." Leslie took hold of her chin and looked down as if in serious thought. She asked the other girls if they thought that was a fair deal.

Marie walked up and asked the girls, "What are you up to, young ladies?" Leslie told her of the deal the chef offered them. Marie said, "You know, if you make it two signed sets of photographs, Delores, Mama, and I could also get a sample."

The chef said, "That would be fair. Is it okay with you, Leslie?"

Leslie asked, "How big are those samples? Our hunger pains are hurting something awful."

The chef showed her the sample size. "Would that help keep the hunger pains from hurting for about an hour?"

"Yes sir," said Leslie, "that size will soothe our hunger pain for an hour."

He had his staff fix up sixteen samples for our customers. He said, "You know, we have to feed the carnies running the booths."

The girls told the chef, "If you make up the plates of food, we will deliver them to the carnies running the booths."

The chef looked at Leslie. "Okay, young lady, how much would you charge me for your service?"

Now Leslie was very clever. Again she rubbed her chin and studied the ground. After a moment, Sarah, Kim, and Rebecca whispered in Leslie's ear, and she raised one eyebrow.

Marie told Delores, "I hope you're taking this all in. Watch her; here it comes."

Leslie asked, "Are you making dessert for the meal?"

The chef told her his staff was working on it "Why, may I ask?"

Leslie said, "Our favorite dessert is chocolate cupcakes with chocolate icing with a white squiggle or our names on top. We will serve the meals for that."

The chef said, "Leslie, that's a hard bargain but well worth the exchange. You have a deal."

The girls and the Wiloby boys carried the meals out to the carnies and Jason so they could eat before the Mardi Gras started.

Delores told Marie, "She will be dangerous to anyone she encounters at a negotiation table."

After all the meals were delivered, the carnies had the girls run their booths while they ate. Leslie became the barker, and as guests arrived she enticed them to play. "Everybody wins, nobody loses. Please try your luck, and treat that beautiful lady to a beautiful stuffed animal, or win some great gifts for your children or relatives. Come on, show us what you've got! Be the first one to have your beautiful wife or girlfriend carry around your trophy."

She had all the booths filled with people trying to win. She loved playing up to the males hitting the pad with the sledge hammer, trying to make the bell ring. She would feel their muscles and give them some encouragement; the wife would bet money that her hubby would ring the bell.

It was getting close to starting time for the Mardi Gras event. Susanne and Jason were standing at the entry gate of the carnival asking for everyone's attention. Susanne announced, "We have with us tonight from four different states our Ladies' Club, who are all poised and ready to do a grand entrance for your enjoyment. Maestro, music please."

Jason asked the crowd to form two lines in front of the booths. "Everyone in the backyard, do the same to make an alley for the ladies to walk between." They had four waitresses making sure the alleyway was ready for the ladies.

Leading off the grand entrance was Phyllis; then came the rest of the fifty-three ladies. They were all wearing very vibrant colors, with necklaces and arm and ankle bracelets of zirconium and diamonds, carrying glasses of champagne. They were all gorgeous.

Behind Phyllis was Jennifer's younger sister, Merrilee, followed by Susanne, then Sally, then Juanita, then Jessica, then Maggie, then Marjorie, then Silvia, then the twenty other ladies of the housing tract. Then came Nadine, Janice, and Louise, one after another, until the music paused. Susanne ran back through the alley of people to announce the last six ladies. Every lady thus far had drawn huge applause the entire length of the human alleyway.

Susanne said, "We did save a few of our ladies for last, who have mastered the grand entrance. Maestro, the special music for our final seven ladies. From Oregon, she is a Stockdale employee, landscape designer, field foreman, laborer extraordinaire, our little chauffeur, Angel." In a form-fitting black silk skirt, white silk blouse, and black bow tie, and spangled with as much glitter as the others wore, she entered the carnival area to deafening applause. She was giving it her all. Susanne pointed out, "She is the fourth lady of the Ladies' Club."

The song changed as Susanne continued, "She is from right here in Texas, also a Stockdale employee, our salesperson, Denise. As you gentlemen may have noticed, this young lady drives men literally to distraction: they walk into trash cans, miss doorways, and run into each other head on in airports. Two unlucky fliers accidentally stepped onto the moving walkway and fell on their rumps. There are numerous gentlemen with bruised ribs; one even had his fork knocked out of his hand from his wife's elbow in the ribs. She was not trying to draw his attention to her but trying to get him to stop gawking and drooling."

The song changed again, and Susanne introduced Eileen. "She is from Colorado and has worked on commercials, played bit parts on sitcoms, and is now starring in her own feature film due out in a couple of months. She and Denise have contests in airports to see what man they can give experience of a lifetime. Eileen too is a Stockdale employee—sort of; she worked there only one day before she was swooped away by the movie industry." Eileen was giving all of herself with every move, and the applause had to be hurting the guests' hands. She also had elbows flying from girlfriends and spouses.

When the song changed, Susanne introduced Gloria. "She is from Utah, also a Stockdale employee. Please look at the monitors; this is how she looked when she first met Fred Stockdale while working on her drawings. Something was not right, and Fred even told his wife there was something wrong. That night he had a vision, and the next morning he had to call Gloria and told her his vision. She thought he was insane, but he told her to go to her computer, watch the video, and change her hairstyle and color accordingly. Very reluctant, she told him, 'You're supposed to fix my landscape. How much more will this cost me?'

"Well, look what we have now: our precious Gloria, mother of four daughters who are either married or about to be married. Gentlemen, she is single." Gloria was showing off her stuff, so poised, glamorous, sophisticated, and sensual that her applause was as loud and appreciative as that for the much younger girls before her. Wow; just wow.

The song changed as Susanne introduced the next lady. "She now resides in Oregon. She is the mother of our leader, grandmother of all our girls and boys. She has taught the girls to make some of the best meals I have ever tasted, and she makes desserts with them. She is one fabulous lady. She is also the number three Ladies' Club member and has become my mentor. Ladies and gentlemen, Sophia!"

She entered the carnival area to applause and even wolf whistles from the gentlemen—glamorous, stylish, and sophisticated. The kids all joined her walking through the alley of people and giving her hugs. Mama was getting tearful; Rebecca ran to get some tissues from Susanne to help her dry her eyes. Papa met her coming into the backyard as the kids ran back to be with their moms.

The music changed to "Sway" as Susanne introduced the next lady. "She also resides now in Oregon. This is the number two lady of the Ladies' Club. She and number one lady are blood sisters. They were kidnapped together and later freed by Sophia's husband. This is one hot momma; she and lady number one are the mothers of the girls. She is also my mentor, she means so much to all of us: Delores!"

She came through the opening and gave an impressive grand entrance that was off the charts. The poise, glamour, seduction, and sensuality in every step were complete perfection. The girls and boys all were giving her hugs. Susanne handed Jonathan Wiloby, a box of tissues for the girls and Delores. When they reached the backyard entrance, I took Delores to the playhouse.

The song changed, and "Return to Me" started to play. Susanne introduced the last lady. "She also resides now in Oregon. This is the vision beyond all visions, the one who started the whole thing. Fred had this vision of her coming to the Grand Event, introduced by a master of ceremonies to a large crowd of guests and friends. There were four violins and one gorgeous lady singer." All eyes were on the staircase as she descended, gown sparkling in the sunlight, diamond necklace, bracelet, and ankle bracelet, satin high heels, picture postcard perfect makeup, hair styled to perfection. "She too was kidnapped and freed by her father; she also is an attorney: Marie!"

As Marie entered the carnival gate the entire entourage of ladies, the girls, boys, everyone swelled toward her, giving endless hugs; Marie was in tears. As all the ladies, girls, and boys at last entered the backyard, everyone was in tears. What a great moment to be seen by guests, family members, and viewers worldwide.

Susanne, her voice breaking, asked Marie, "Show us the grand entrance from the staircase that got this operation in full swing." Marie, in a form-fitted light blue satin dress, champagne refilled by Silvia with one huge hug, gave them a grand entrance they would talk about for years.

Marie was escorted by Delores to the playhouse porch, where Delores gave her a hug and then descended the staircase. Delores had on a form-fitting black dress so the band played the Hollies hit, 'Long Cool Woman in a Black Dress,' as Delores descended the staircase.

Marie was serenaded by "The Girl from Ipanema" and the crowd and the ladies were applauding to the beat of the song. Marie gave them a show they would never forget. I told Susanne, "There is my Mona Lisa; she does my vision beyond my expectations."

Susanne ran over to the band and had them play "Mona Lisa," so Marie was halfway down the staircase when the band blended the two songs together. She was a little startled but continued to the patio. At the final step she was again joined by all the ladies.

Marie asked Susanne, "Why did you change the song?"

Susanne said, "You are Fred's Mona Lisa; he said so."

Marie walked over to me through the ladies, put her arms around my neck, kissed me, and said, "I'm your Mona Lisa?"

"Well, I thought I had better tell you sooner or later, this event fits my feelings for you."

She was still embracing me when Delores said, "Break it up, or I'll get a bucket of water."

Delores and Marie then hugged each other, and the girls all got into the group hug.

I told Susanne, "If this doesn't sell over a million copies in a couple of days, nothing will."

Susanne said, "I'll bet we sell over a million copies before we sign off."

It was time to turn over the event to the carnival and the Mardi Gras. "Food and drinks are available," Susanne told everyone. "Please make yourselves at home. Get ready for the Buck Off and then the parade. Get some beads from the girls as they toss them to you from the balcony of the playhouse. Then at dusk you will see the landscape come alive."

The band started to play all genres of music. Most of the crowd went to the carnival side of the event, where the booths were mobbed by those wanting to take home a piece of memorabilia.

Soon the Buck Off was about to begin. Jason called for the scorekeepers, his judges, and the contestants to report to the bull ring. Once all the scorers and judges were set in place, he asked for the ten known riders who followed Jason from event to event.

The first to ride was One Buck Short. Once he was on the bull, Jason announced, "He is on level two and will be judged with other level two riders; all those who ride later will be judged as level ones." Jason started the bull on level two, and One Buck Short was thrown off in two seconds; the girls gave him a five, average. There were four other riders who qualified as level two riders, and they all did about the same as One Buck Short; one rider got a five-and-a-half-point average.

"All remaining riders are level one," Jason announced, "so all other riders with their names, please form a line and tell our lovely ladies keeping score your bull-riding name."

The first level one rider was Wrong Way. He mounted the bull facing the wrong direction, and the ladies said, "Turn around, Wrong Way." But as he had in Utah, he slipped off the bull, landed on his backside, stood up, and took a bow.

Kim had given him a point last time but no point this time. They told Jason, "He needs to get on the bull the right way so he can be bucked."

This time he had two lovely assistants help him onto the bull facing in the right direction. Jason told him to hold onto the handle with one hand, raise the other hand, and prepare to start the ride. He also gave the rider some pointers, telling him to keep his knees pressured against the bull during turns. "Are you ready?" he called.

Wrong Way made it through two turns of the bull before being thrown off. He got one point from Kim, for being brave.

The next rider was a local gentleman, Diddly Squat his wife had named him, saying, "It's what he does around the house." Jason gave him the same pointers as he gave Wrong Way. Diddly Squat did exactly that: fell off between the first and second buck. Jason didn't have time to even turn the bull. Kim gave him one point; she liked his name. The next rider was Rerun; "It's all he watches on television," said his wife. He did one half-turn. The bull went right, and Rerun went left.

The next rider's name was Alright Already; his wife said, "Yep, that quick." The bets from the ladies were getting hot and heavy. Alright Already was right in between the first two riders.

The next rider was Are You Done Yet. "Yep, every chore, and I mean *every* chore, I have to ask him the same question."

He was netting out lots of money that he might become the favorite; "It's only two seconds, for crying out loud."

"Well, a half second would have been a record for him."

The next rider was Confused. "Sorry, girls, after five years of marriage and lots of training, he is what he is, confused." He made it into fourth place.

The next rider was Do It To Me. "He needs directions or a manual; I've given up." He was tossed, now sitting sixth.

The next rider was What Do You Call That. "It's about his singing ability, not for human ears to hear." He ended up sitting fifth.

The next rider was One Timer. "I married looks," said his wife; "the rest came with the package." He may hold the record for the shortest time.

The next rider was Over and Over Again. "That's how many times I have to tell him to do anything, anything." He soon held the second shortest time.

The next rider was By Appointment Only. "He wants reservations. He wants me to text him a reservation; snow will have to fall on the equator before that ever happens."

The next rider was Strangers in the Night. His wife told the wife of By Appointment Only that that would be a blessing. "Do you want to trade?"

The other entries were Mama's Boy, Breaking Wind, Easy Does It, Feelings, Flasher, Itty Bitty, Oh Come On, Heartbreaker, On Again Off Again, No Job Too Small, The Ceiling Needs Painted, Stranger in the Night, No Socks, and The Good Shepherd. There were even more riders waiting in line; most of the remaining names were extremely funny. A couple were not appropriate, so they used each rider's first name to announce those.

After all the riders had finished their rides, the women were stuffing money in their purses, and everyone's sides were hurting from laughing so hard. "We have a tie," announced Susanne. "We had two riders who lasted four and a half seconds.

"Could we have The Good Shepherd and All Night Long return to the bull ring for our fourth ever Buck Off? The winner will get the dinner for two at Steaks Are Us; second place will get to drive the limousine. No, just kidding. He'll get to wash the limousine. No, no; ladies, what should the second place finisher receive?"

Several answers rang out: "An instruction book"; "Wash all the windows in our homes"; "A box of donuts"; "Lessons from Madame La Rue." Then came the crowd pleaser: "The same as number one." That was from The Good Shepherd's wife.

One of the guests was the owner of The Willows, a competitor to the Steaks Are Us restaurant.

Susanne said, "The winner will get dinner for two at Steaks Are Us. The runner-up will get dinner for two at The Willows. Riders, are you ready to rumble?" Then she winked at the crowd of guests and said, "I have longed to do that."

Jason said, "You both know you were riding at level one. To make this fair, we will move you to level two, a little more challenging. We'll have four level two riders go first so you can see how they manage to stay on Elroy."

The other four riders completed their rides, and one held on for five seconds. He would advance to level three at the next event.

All Night Long lost the coin toss, so he put on his glove, mounted the bull, stuck a hand in the air, and said "Let's rock." All Night Long nearly fell off under a second but regained his balance and went to three seconds before being thrown to the mat. The girls gave him high marks; he looked like a real bull rider.

The Good Shepherd was a local pastor from a neighboring church. He said a short prayer and stated that his dinner would be given to one of his needy families. He also presented the girls with a shepherd's staff when he heard they were raising lambs and gave them all a hug. All Night Long's wife accused him of bribing the judges.

The pastor mounted the bull and told Jason, "Could you please start the ride?" The Good Shepherd nearly fell off just like All Night Long but regained his balance and composure. The crowd was counting the seconds as they ticked upward, cheering on the pastor, but he lost his balance just before the clock clicked to three. The girls rushed into the bull ring to help the pastor to his feet. They gave him a hug and great marks for his score.

Both riders got a huge round of applause. Susanne announced that they were getting ready for the parade, so "Everyone, as we enter the backyard the girls and boys will be tossing out beads for you. Ladies, none of that to earn beads." The band was playing Cajun style Dixieland. Five of the ladies with the band would teach the crowd how to dance in the parade and then lead the guests.

The chef gave the kids plates of food for them to nibble on, and each received another cupcake, with more promised. Silvia and Elizabeth were extremely busy, mixing all sorts of drinks. They even taught each other how to make a couple of drinks that were new to them.

The parade started, and each guest had been given noise makers or other items to wave as they paraded into the backyard, the ladies in their outfits—wow, what a sight. The king of the parade was John, and the queen, by any other name, Marie. Delores and I were the prince and princess. We just had to wear the crowns and carry jeweled staffs.

Everyone was having a great time, dancing, singing, and cheering for the kids to toss them some beads. The girls and boys were very selective on who would get what string of beads.

43

Mardi Gras is the feast before the fasting of Lent. Those who celebrated every year were showing the other guests just what this theme was all about. First of all, eating—lots of eating. The chef was handing out plate after plate of food to all the guests; more and more beverages left the bar, mostly alcoholic, but a good number were just sodas with add-ons to make them look like mixed drinks.

Silvia was making pitcher after pitcher of non-alcoholic margaritas, a real crowd pleaser.

Susanne had a surprise for Marie and Delores. She waited till just before the lighting ceremony to tell the audience viewing as well as all the guests, "We have made dashboard dolls, similar to the hula girls people in the fifties put on their dashboards. Marie and Delores are in gowns, with a glass of champagne, diamond jewelry, and exquisite hair and makeup. They stand about four inches high. As you jiggle them, their hips sway side to side. They're very tastefully constructed, although a little pricey, the quality is first class."

Susanne said they would have all the Ladies' Club members available before the end of the year. "We're offering a Ladies' Club of the month, so you all can collect a new doll each month. We'll also offer the girls and the Wiloby kids for you youngsters." Marie and Delores put their dolls on a raised table, and Susanne tapped them to make them sashay for the crowd to see.

Susanne said, "We only have twenty of Marie and Delores available for sale today, but they're available online; contact the magazine to order via the internet." The twenty of each sold in about five minutes.

Jennifer said, "I want them for my desk at work, my office desk, and my SUV." Her sisters and mom, now official members of the Ladies' Club, would get measured and gowned in the next week. The Ladies' Club members get royalties for each doll purchased.

Marie asked Jennifer, "You won't take a bad day out on us, will you?"

Jennifer said, "You know I have never had a bad day since working for your company. I'll use them to show new customers some of your moves." As the three of them were jiggling them into action, the girls were giggling at seeing their moms as dolls.

Susanne told all of the guests, "And now, finally, the moment we have been waiting for. Kids, are you ready for the light show?"

They all yelled, "Yeah, please, please! We want to see the lights from up here."

"Okay," said Susanne, "we need all of your help to fire up the lights. Juanita and your crew, are you ready?"

Juanita said, "We're ready when you are!"

"Okay, everyone, loud and clear, on the count of three. Ready? One"—slight pause—"two"—another slight pause—"*three!*" Everyone was yelling, and the lights came on.

The kids were saying, "Everyone, come up and see the lights from our balcony. We'll come down, and you can come up—maybe twenty at the most."

Jennifer was getting hugs from everyone. "This is absolutely stunning," it seemed everyone was saying. The circular planter was in its full glory. The vertical light into the multitrunk olive tree was spectacular, with the wall washers and pathway lights gorgeous. Everyone was in awe of how it looked at dusk. The barbecue island had wall washers and the barbecue light shining down on the grill surface. The spa had it lights shining, including the ceiling fans with the multicolored lights controlled by the dimmer switch. The pathway lights illuminated the sidewalks, and the hanging light in the archway matched the front sconces, all with amber bulbs. The other ladies waiting for their landscapes to be started or completed gathered around Jennifer, hugging her and saying, "We can't wait for ours."

You could not ask for any greater reward than people coming up and asking me how we make such ambience in a landscape. Their homes are so humdrum compared to this; could we come out and visit them soon? I gave them business cards with Marjorie's name and phone number; we had brought brochures for a table display, but they were all gone.

Marjorie was going to have me tarred and feathered if their workload more than doubled. *She'll hire that hit man for sure. Oh, goody, she must be reading my mind, Here she comes; I can't dodge this bullet.*

Marjorie said, "Way to go, ace. Our brochures are gone, my business cards are gone, and Angel's business cards are gone. I'm speed-dialing my hit man as we discuss how you won't make it alive to the airport tomorrow. Did you have to make this place so beautiful?"

"Marjorie, my dearest love, you know me, you know I don't do things humdrum and boring; you know you get a good bang for your buck. You know I want the homeowner to enjoy the goodness of being outside and share the joy with their friends and relatives."

She said, "Nice sales pitch. Where are my thirty or more added employees we need to finish existing contracts like this one? You are aware that we have three more homes just about completed, with six playhouses already under construction on top of the three being completed? You also know that those clients are here seeing what you can provide. If we don't give at least equal to this, my phone will never stop ringing, and my finger- and toenails will be a complete mess."

"You're forgetting one major asset: job security."

"'Job security'? What about the therapy I will have to endure to keep my sanity? Let alone the double or triple amount of grocery bills to cover the additional alcohol I'll have to buy just to make it to tomorrow's mayhem?"

"Your bonus money will come in real handy."

She said, "I won't need my bonus money for the hit that'll be put on you."

"Wait until your Ladies' Club dashboard doll is available; you'll change your tune."

"I'll have them change mine into head-hunting attire equipped with a spear, blowgun, and poison darts, shipped directly to you."

I grinned. "You'll keep me posted?"

She said, "I'll take your photo off of the wall of fame, remove the glass, and use it as a dartboard in my office. Will that suffice to keep you posted?"

"Oh, if only the law would allow me to have two wives, I'd be in seventh heaven."

Gloria grabbed my arm and said, "You've been spending too much time with that woman. It's my turn."

Marjorie told her, "Have fun with him now, before I have him skinned alive."

Gloria asked me, "What got her so riled up?"

"You know, when I first went to Oregon, I gave her twenty new contracts. Then we met you in Utah the next week, and I gave her twenty more. She hasn't quite gotten over that, and today we ran out of brochures and business cards once the light show started, So many want this in their homes, that sort of put gasoline on the fire. I reminded her of job security, but that's not how she's looking at it."

Gloria said, "You know, dear, that I will help her if need be. She has nothing to worry about. I'll even send a couple of foremen; we all work together."

I looked her up and down. "Do you know you look fabulous?'

She said, "What are you up to now? I've been hit on all day by some older and others younger than me." She showed me a stack of business cards about a half inch thick. "These are just since the light show started."

"You know, I love the attention you have generated for me, but after a while it gets very old. I could write a book on just lines men use to try to entice me to respond. My daughters used to want to go to lunch but no longer after I was approached but not them."

I asked, "Do you need another vision?"

She said, "Do you want two women putting out hits on you?"

I asked her, "What gives me this pleasure of your attention to me?"

She said, "You owe me a dance, a slow dance. I gave a request to the band, and the next song is ours."

"I'll dance as long as it's not 'Nine to Five.'".

She said, "Hold on a minute. I want to change my request; great idea."

She returned just in time to dance to, 'Nights of White Satin,' she'd requested. The dance floor, any space not filled with decorations, was quickly filled with those who liked the song being played. It wasn't long till I was tapped by a young gentleman eager to cut in. Gloria was surprised and told me I still owed her.

I turned to walk to a safe area when Delores grabbed me and asked if I was finished playing with our office staff.

"I was just killing time waiting for the opportunity to dance with my bride."

She said, "Fat chance that ever entered your mind."

I told her, "Let's just dance and not be judgmental."

Delores was soon tapped by Sarah. "Can I dance with my daddy, please, Mom?"

Delores said, "We can all dance together. Join us."

Before the song ended, we had all four girls dancing in a circle. Then some of our Ladies' Club members asked the girls to dance with them. We must have danced to five or six slow romantic songs with all sorts of Ladies' Club members.

The king and queen joined us, which brought the guests into the mix. The patio was full of dancers; there were even some dancing on the upper patio.

Jennifer and her husband were one couple dancing above everyone, along with her sisters and their husbands. The band liked seeing the dancers enjoying their music, so they kept playing requests.

The Wiloby boys were now dancing with our daughters; there's a first time for everything.

Marjorie was dancing close to us, and I told her we could end up being fellow grandparents.

Marjorie gave Delores a look. "You get the even days, I'll take the odd days, and we'll share the holidays."

Some of the guests were being escorted by limousine to the church parking lot and their cars. The party was winding down; what a great event!

44

Insanity Determination

We all arrived at our hotel to be informed we had been given new suites. The forensic team had moved our belongings. They were still collecting evidence. The desk clerk told us, "Here is a note they left for you."

They did inform us that last night's desk clerk was being held as a coconspirator, facing numerous charges.

We received our new room keys and poured a pot of coffee and another of hot chocolate and collected two bags of rolls. The desk clerk said, "The bellhop will bring you two more pots of coffee and another pot of hot chocolate and ten more rolls. Give them about ten minutes; please enjoy your stay with us. We are so sorry for any inconvenience that we may have caused."

We headed up the elevator to our suites. On the elevator ride, Leslie told us they gave their winnings to the pastor who'd given them the shepherd's staff, to pass along to his needy families.

We all gave the girls hugs. Marie said, "That is so nice of you girls. What made you think about doing that?"

Leslie said, "We have so much, and they have so little. It seemed unfair for us to keep the items, even though we won them—it just didn't feel right."

We entered our suite and found a note from the forensic team: *We are sorry to have to move your belongings to another suite. We were still not done investigating the other three suites. Please make certain that we did not leave any of your possessions in the other suites. If you need further assistance, please contact me, Detective Morris.*

We all sat at the round table and sofas to enjoy our rolls and beverages. Bedtime was about a half hour away. The girls all wanted to sleep in the king-size bed with their sheep. They talked about seeing Scooter and Lulu and the sheep and calves. "We miss them."

Sarah said, "We really miss our fish at Whispering Pines Resort. Could we call them to make sure the fish and Mr. Frog are doing well?"

Marie said, "I will have them send me a photo of the aquarium so you will feel better."

She and Delores put their dashboard dolls on the table and got them to sashay from side to side. The girls just giggled. "Those are so cute."

Leslie said, "I wonder what ours will look like."

Marie said, "Susanne will send us a catalog when they are printed with all the figurines. I told them as fast as the club is growing, we may have to add another house just for the figurines. There are four classes starting up next week, and our class being run by Eileen and Janice is coming to graduation in two weeks—that's another fifteen women.

"Ours will start in two weeks. Silvia said she has ten confirmed with a possible ten more. Her lists keep getting longer, and she's running out of time to get the wedding planned."

We had a knock at our door; it was the bell hop with our needed refills. John gave him a tip for his efforts.

The girls found their favorite rolls, one apple, one raspberry, and two cherry. The ladies took their favorites, and Mama and Papa took theirs. John and I flipped a quarter for the crumbs.

We made the mistake of getting two stale rolls in our first two bags, so John and I used them as dunkers to make them chewable. John won the coin toss, so he got the crumbs from the second order. They barely covered the palm of his hand, so, being such a good friend, he ate one little crumb at a time.

He also expressed how good each crumb tasted. I told him, "Remember, I'm cooking tomorrow's dinner; I'll make yours very special."

The girls were finishing up their rolls and hot chocolate. I told them, "Time for jammies. Brush your teeth, and climb under the covers, and we'll come in for prayers, kisses, and tuck-in."

Delores found the night lights; thank goodness they were in her overnight case. It would not have been pretty if they were still in the other suite.

The girls said they were ready for all of us, so with John on one side and me on the other, we tucked them in. The girls said their prayers—for Scooter, Lulu, the lambs, the calves, the fish, their stuffed animals, and their newest lambs, making sure they were under the covers—"Don't want them to get sick. Please watch over everyone, and return them and us all home safely. Thank you for today. We all had a wonderful time. Help all the children who are needy or need a bed to sleep in and food for breakfast. Amen."

We all gave the girls kisses, told them how much we love them, and thanked them for giving away their winnings to the needy children. We turned out the light and made sure the night lights were illuminating the room.

We entered the living room and all went our separate ways to our beds. I reminded everyone to put the bar across their door so no one could enter; we forgot last night, and it was a disaster.

Delores and I shared one bed, knowing that I would get up before the girls woke up and move to the other bed so they could pounce on both beds.

We were both so tired that once our heads hit the pillows we were out. She did allow me to hold her for the couple of minutes before I was in la-la land. I let another golden opportunity slip through my hands.

I was so tired that I never did move to the other bed, and the four girls had only one bed to pounce on. So to make matters correct, I moved to the other bed and pretended to be asleep so they could pounce on me. They hurried up to snuggle under the covers and shivered and shook until they took all of my body heat from me.

Then I heard Leslie say, "Daddy, you know, our hunger pain is so severe, we are almost ready to cry from the pain." They all four went back to Delores and snuggled until the goodies and beverages arrived.

I picked up the phone and called the front desk. I asked if they could bring up two pots of coffee with cream and sugar and two bags of breakfast rolls as soon as possible. "My girls have very severe hunger pains."

The girl at the front desk said, "We have your order ready to deliver; we were expecting your call. He'll be there in about two minutes."

I got up and put on some clothes and retrieved a five-dollar bill out of my wallet for the tip. The girls grabbed two blankets off my bed and wrapped up inside them just as the knock on the door occurred.

The girls were all giggles, Delores poured them each a cup of hot chocolate and us a cup of coffee. Then came another knock, and the rest of the Albrights, Mama and Papa, entered. I called down for a second batch, and the desk clerk laughed. "The rest of the family just joined you, so he's on his way with more."

We were all refilled and beveraged up. "Let's get packing and ready for our strip search."

One more knock at our door, and Susanne was here. "All ready for another plane ride?"

I told her, "The pat-down is my highlight of our travels. Watching men fall into trash cans and walk into walls is my second favorite thing."

Susanne said, "My favorite thing is picking you and Silvia up at the airport with your kids and wives all made up as beggars." The flight returning from Utah sold out of videos in two days—over a million—and even today we sell over a hundred thousand per month worldwide. The eye-opener of that video is the response of the witnesses. That guy at the airport who threatened me and was taken in by security has many mixed reviews.

Susanne grabbed a roll and a cup of coffee and went with the girls to pack up their bags. They told Susanne that they gave the pastor the toys they won to give to his needy children.

Susanne said, "On tomorrow's show can you tell your audience what you did for the needy children? We'll show you girls being judges, and also we have you winning toys at the carnival." I'll call the pastor to have him talk to you. We will have him on via a computer.

Our family was ready, all packed, showered, dressed. Marie and John, with Mama and Papa, were all ready. A knock at the door turned out to be Jennifer and two chauffeurs ready to take our bags to the waiting vehicles. We thanked Jennifer for inviting us to her event. "We had such a great time," said Marie.

Jennifer said, "All of my friends and family want you to move into our tract. They adore your kids; they think you would liven up our community. There were still customers at my house until after midnight. They all were just talking about how beautiful my yard is compared to theirs.

"The light show got everyone's attention. I can't tell you how many texts I received of photos of the light show at different angles, all saying, 'Wow.' Three ladies and their husbands decided to get the playhouse with the deck on top; they loved the design. One was encouraged to become a mom; she can always work hard at the gym to restore her curves.

"I told her you decorated the playhouse extremely well; you added a special touch."

We were all in route to have breakfast and then get strip-searched.

The girls asked Jennifer if she would mind sending them their shepherd's staff by FedEx. "They'll probably take it away from us at the airport."

Jennifer said, "I'll be honored to ship it to you. How about next day delivery: would that work?

The girls gave her a hug. "That would be perfect."

We all ordered the Albright scramble with pancakes and got more beverages; the girls ordered orange juice. They were watching their weight. Leslie said, "We decided to cut down on sugar for a while."

Marie said, "No more cupcakes?"

Sarah said, "We are allowing some sugars to remain. That's one of them, but maybe only two per day."

"We will eat more fruit," said Leslie.

The girls thanked Jennifer for sharing her house with them. "That was so nice," said Leslie. "Your house is so pretty, we felt right at home."

Jennifer said, "You are all more than welcome to visit my house anytime you're in town. We'll have to shop at the Western Outfitter store when you come back. They called me yesterday, the best sales day they have had since the last event.

"Oh by the way, the five ranchers and their wives are coming to dinner at my house. They saw the program' they want to see the backyard and the landscape firsthand. They are bringing the meat, vegetable, dessert, side dishes, salads, and a chef with waitresses. I hired a couple of men to clean up the yard to make it look like new."

Susanne said, "It was the most controlled event we have ever thrown. Your guests were so respectful and kept everything neat and orderly. The caterer left the barbecue area spotless; what a wonderful man."

Jennifer said, "He told her he picked up all of my friends and neighbors' events and many more. His email box is full of requests for his catering service. He wants to rent one of our spaces for his Texas office."

Our breakfasts were being served, Susanne and the magazine crews would be flying to Oregon, on the same plane, and we planned a continuation of the party we attended last night. Silvia rode in the limousine with the magazine crew. She gave us all hugs; she and Susanne were sitting with the girls.

Murry had sent her a text of the animals having breakfast. The girls were excited; only a couple of hours and they would be at home with their friends. Leslie said, "We have so much to tell them. We were judges, we played games, we were in a parade, we did a grand entrance with our moms—we will talk with them for over an hour."

Breakfast in our bellies, we were on our way to the airport, singing and laughing all the way. We all gave Jennifer huge hugs: "Love you. Let's do this again next week in Oregon." We went to the front counter and checked in our bags; we don't want to mess around with overhead compartments. Quickly we were all checked in and off to get searched. We told the TSA agents that we were wearing security equipment and that they should not use any scanning devices.

The agent in charge called their supervisor for verification. It took another fifteen minutes for the supervisor to appear. He wanted to see our identification, which their agents had on the conveyor belt.

"We would love to show them to you, but you have our wallets and purses tied up at the conveyor belt scanner."

"You don't have identification?"

I explained it to him again, just a little slower: "Our identifications are in the tubs you provide to run them through the scanner."

The supervisor said, "I can't verify who you are without your identifications."

Marie said, "Grab on to something, sir. You're about to see our identification."

Marie pressed her security button, and five FBI agents with guns drawn came to her rescue.

Marie said, "Gentlemen, this is the supervisor who thinks we have no ID after being told three times our identifications are in the tubs being scanned by their personnel."

They took the supervisor aside, not very happy. "Our cover is blown," they explained, "and the people we're protecting are now vulnerable."

We were given back our wallets and purses, belts and shoes, and told to have a nice flight.

Marie said, "Have a great time being interrogated."

Delores said, "Maybe they can scan your brain."

We got to the terminal just in time to be called with all first class passengers to board. We all just kept walking right onto the plane.

When seated, Sarah asked, "Why are they always confused when we board the planes?"

"You know those security devices you wear? If they go through an x-ray machine, they will be ruined or they will go off. Then our agents will shoot first and ask questions later."

At last the plane was in the air. Goodbye, Texas; hello, Oregon. The girls were being treated like little queens. The flight attendants gave them lots of attention and asked them all sorts of questions. One gentleman was getting impatient, wanting something. One flight attendant turned to him, pulled a bag of peanuts out of her pocket, and handed it to him. "You need to wait your turn, sir."

When we landed, the girls got hugs from the flight attendants as they disembarked from the plane. The girls were wearing their new Western Outfitter apparel. They wanted to show the lambs and calves their new outfits. Of course they would also show Scooter and Lulu. They were so excited that they said, "Let's get our luggage and head straight home; no stopping at the restaurant."

When we all arrived at the luggage carousel, we met Murry, Stuart, and Doreen with three chauffeurs standing by. After lots of hugs and kisses, Silvia and Murry could have used a bucket of cold water thrown on them.

The girls asked Silvia, "Didn't all that kissing hurt your lips?"

In the limousines the girls said, "We'd like to see the animals before we go eat lunch. Would that be okay, Grandpa?"

Stuart said, "That is a splendid idea."

When they arrived at the house, the chauffeurs took the bags into the houses, and the ladies freshened up in a hurry. The girls went out to the corral. Scooter and Lulu were very excited to see them with lots of loving going on. The lambs were all right at the corral gate hopping around, full of lamb joy. Even the calves came to say, *Hello, glad to see you home.* The girls got flakes of alfalfa to feed the calves and sheep.

Everyone was ready for lunch, and the girls told Scooter and Lulu they would bring them back a snack.

Soon we were back in the limousines and on our way to the restaurant where our meals were being prepared. Stuart texted the head chef our estimated time of arrival. We were all seated in the banquet room when Marie got a text from Ms. Morgan. *They are prepared to do the assessment of Katy Wilkins at nine o'clock on Tuesday morning. Could you be ready in a studio by then?*

Marie asked Susanne, "Can the studio be ready by nine o'clock on Tuesday morning?"

Susanne texted the construction superintendent, apologizing for texting him on a Sunday, and asked if the studio could be used early Tuesday morning.

He texted her back, saying they would make it happen. *We may have to screen off one area where the crews are putting in the final touches.*

Marie texted Ms. Morgan saying that time would work.

Ms. Morgan texted back: *My husband, children, and I watched the entire Mardi Gras event. You all looked like you were having so much fun. My children want to meet your girls and the Wiloby children. Could we make that happen for them?*

Marie texted, *We have another event in Texas in three weeks. Would you and your family like to attend?*

Ms. Morgan replied, *Count on us. This will be a dream come true for my children. Thank you for being so kind.*

Marie texted Ms. Morgan, *I will have Susanne get you the itinerary and hotel info. You fill her in with the details of your family. I'll contact Jennifer and have you added to the list of guests.*

We had a fabulous meal, and the girls asked our waitress for a box. They wanted all the meat scraps collected to give to Scooter and Lulu. Our waitress told the chef what the girls requested. He said, "For their dogs? I make them a meal. Tell them I will make it special for their pooches."

The waitresses were bringing out the desserts: for the girls, cupcakes with their names on top, peach cobbler with vanilla ice cream with chocolate shavings and of course a cherry on top. They offered apple pie à la mode and lemon meringue pie, but I got custard pie à la mode. John got chocolate cream pie à la mode—not a good choice the ladies all got bites and left John the crumbs.

I told John, "Welcome to my world."

Marie said, "He didn't need all those calories," and she ordered him a bowl. of Jell-O.

I told him, "That's more than they would do for me."

The waitress brought John his Jell-O and a take-home box in a bag; "No peeking," she told him. They stapled the bag so the ladies could not peek either.

At last we all finished filling our bellies. Back in the limousine, we learned the girls wanted to spend time with Scooter and Lulu before dark.

Back at the homestead, everyone met at our house. The girls were told to change into their farming outfits; the ones they had on could get ruined.

45

Marie took Leslie and Kim to their house so they could change into their farming outfits. They took no time to change; then they were down the tunnel to Sarah and Rebecca's playhouse, where they said hello to Annie. Then they were down the staircase to the corral.

Papa had both Scooter and Lulu on the patio to greet the girls. He had the treats made by the chef for the girls to feed to Scooter and Lulu. Papa told Marie, "He cooked them two steaks and put in some cooked vegetables, almost the same meal we had."

Marie said, "But theirs were free."

Scooter and Lulu inhaled their meals, the girls admonishing them, "Slow down and chew your food at least twenty times before swallowing."

By the time Leslie had finished telling them how to eat properly, it was all gone. With her hand on her hip, she said, "Maybe later today after dinner, we can practice proper table manners."

Papa put his arm around Leslie. "Honey, that's how dogs eat: fill up their mouths and swallow. They loved the meal. Look at their tails wagging. That's how you know they enjoyed the food you gave them. Give them some love; they appreciate all the attention you can give them.

"Let's go look at all the new calves. You haven't seen the last load."

The girls were already at the corral gate, ready to enter the other pasture. They told Papa, "Three calves don't look like the rest of the calves." They had varied colors of beige and long eyelashes. They were so friendly, they came right to the girls, mooing as they approached.

The girls ran and peeled off four flakes of alfalfa for the new calves. That didn't last long when the entire thirty head encircled them. Papa, John, and I brought the girls more alfalfa; they could not get out of the circle of calves. The entire herd were mooing *Thank you* to the girls.

Marie, Delores, Susanne, Mama, Silvia, were all petting the calves and giving them alfalfa. The girls were instructing their moms how to give the calves the hay. Murry was standing by the corral gate listening to the girls giving directions and applauded them, saying, "That was perfect."

Silvia went over to the corral gate and put alfalfa into his mouth. "Here, dear, chew on this; give your vocal cords a rest."

Then the funniest thing happened. One of the calves had to go potty right on Marie's foot. She was not wearing her farming outfit.

Murry said, "When they raise their tails move out of the way."

"Great advice," said Marie. "Next time tell us before we get into the corral."

The girls were giving all the calves love, hugging them and petting them, talking to them, telling them how much they loved them. Then they decided to spend some time in their playhouse and told Scooter and Lulu, "Let's go play in our house." The dogs were learning their new phrases, and Lulu was up the stairs in a flash, Scooter only steps behind her.

Everyone else went into the house to the kitchen. The ladies all saw John's surprise sitting on the countertop. He was busy talking to us guys and watching the calves going about their business.

The ladies all agreed to take a peek and, if necessary, re-staple the bag. When they opened the box, they saw what they were expecting, a chocolate cream pie with a cherry on top. Delores checked the refrigerator and found enough peach cobbler from Thursday night's dinner. "We're good, ladies. Make some coffee, and dig in."

The pie was gone before we all turned around and headed to the house. The ladies had already put the cobbler in the box and re-stapled the bag. It was sitting about where John had placed the bag, ready to open it himself.

The coffee was nearly ready for pouring. John sat at the stove counter and asked Delores if she could get him a fork. Delores returned with the fork and a cup of coffee. He opened the box and was surprised. He said, "I thought she would have brought me another slice of chocolate cream pie. She gave me peach cobbler."

Marie told him, "They probably ran out of chocolate cream pie; it was very good."

John took a bite, looked at the bag, looked at the ladies, and asked, "Just how good was the second piece, ladies?"

Marie said, "John, there was no second piece."

John said, "First off, this peach cobbler is cold. Secondly, there are six pairs of staple holes in the bag; you all could have at least re-stapled it using the same holes."

I told John, "Check their lips for chocolate residue."

John looked at each of them very closely. On Marie's upper lip there was proof: one itty-bitty smidgen of chocolate. Busted.

John finished his peach cobbler and drank some coffee. It was time to start preparing for our dinner, the girls' hunger pains were fast approaching. I headed to the grill with oil and a paper towel and oiled the grill while the ladies were preparing the meat offering: steaks, pork chops, and hamburgers, with salt and pepper on each side, and hotdogs. *The girls have moved to the better quality of meat, hotdogs are for kids you know; they profess they are young ladies now and no longer kids.*

I'd received that sermon a few months back—quite serious, dedicated to assuring them that I was on board with their decision. Today the ladies added chicken breasts—*or are they crow, just to resemble chicken? These ladies can be pretty sneaky to say the least. One can never be too careful.*

They gave me a bottle of barbecue sauce to flavor the chicken, telling me the chicken was on sale and we needed to eat healthier—all good reasons to doubt that this was truly chicken. *I'll grill the birds on a lower heat, and during the early stages I'll apply the barbecue sauce so as not to caramelize the sugars.*

All meat was on the first side when John approached. He said, "How could they eat both pieces of pie and feel no shame?"

I told him, "Remember the story I told you about the game, their rules? They hold the ball until you want to play more than anything. You are determined to beat them; they hold the ball. You want to beat them even more; then they hand you the ball and walk away. 'Hey, you promised to play.' They look at you and say, 'We did play; you lost.' Then you say, 'What did we play?' They tell you, 'Ball, our rules, our game.' You say, 'We didn't do anything.' They say, 'Of course we played. I held the ball; you wanted the ball, my ball, you desired to hold the ball. Owning and desiring are totally different. I handed you the ball when the game was over.'

"You now are totally confused. She owned the ball; you wanted the ball. She gave it to you, but she does not desire to have the ball back. You got what you desired; she doesn't desire the ball.

"Your focus was the ball. As boys we wanted to win the game no matter what the sport; it was inbred in us from a very young age. We look at everything in life with that attitude: *Let's play; we have our game face on. What's the game?* When we go that route, we're doomed before the game begins.

"They just want to see how vulnerable we really are. Your pieces of pie were their ball. The tables were turned on that event; you both desired the same object. They won the coin toss and ran the pie into their stomachs without any interference from you.

"You left the bag on the countertop; they took it as a tease. 'How dare he tease us? He owns the ball, but he handed it to us'; three and out, so to speak. Their ball, and they ran the distance into the stomach score. John loses again."

John asked, "Why do we play any game with them?"

"Be serious, John. We have things, they have goodies. We want goodies; by nature, they don't desire things. We want to play, but it's their rules, their game. We will always be doomed."

The grilling was on schedule, and the girls were summoned to carry out the sides, salads, dinnerware, napkins, plastic cups, and the candle and candleholder for the loser table, Scooter and Lulu were following the girls, pausing to take a whiff of the meat cooking, knowing they would get treats.

John took time to pet both Scooter and Lulu while the girls were placing the items on the table. After a couple of minutes, the parade of diners filled the patio area, plates in hand. They chose the meat offering, of course, checking both sides to ensure it was cooked to their liking. Only one bird was taken, by Papa.

John said, "No chicken for the ladies?"

They all looked over their shoulders and smirked.

I told John, "It has to be crow if they chose not to indulge. Game over."

John and I joined the loser table with our wives. I commented how delicious the chicken came out and got no response from the ladies. They were indulging in rib eye steaks, baked potatoes, and baked beans; no time to converse.

When the girls came downstairs to finagle the remaining grilled items, as I opened the grill cover, they saw two pieces of chicken. Leslie said, "Only the beef and pork please, Daddy; no birds."

Marie quickly said, "Honey, that's chicken, remember?"

Leslie said, "Yes, Mom, but Scooter and Lulu prefer beef and pork. They leave the chicken in their bowls."

I gave them the remaining beef and pork, gave John another chicken breast, and put another one in the center of the table for the ladies to pick at it.

They wanted to know why I didn't eat the final piece.

I told them, "I was still trying to digest my lunch when dinner approached, so I was not very hungry to begin with, and I think my first piece still had the beak attached. It's pecking at my stomach wall."

The girls were ready for dessert, so the moms got up from the table to help serve the desserts. John said, "Did you give me a dessert earlier?"

Marie came over to him and put her arms around his neck. "No, dear, you ate the dessert the restaurant put in your bag. Don't you remember?"

John looked at me and said, "You are one hundred percent correct: their game, their rules."

The girls gave Scooter and Lulu the meat scraps. They were right: the dogs wanted nothing to do with the chicken. We decided that it would make a great lunch tomorrow for either John or me. The girls went out to say good night to the lambs, calves, Scooter, and Lulu, telling them prayers and singing them a lullaby—which was the first time we heard or saw them do that.

When they were finished, the light show was coming on, and they headed up to their house to say good night to Annie and her friends. Phillip's crew would be coming over tomorrow to move the smokehouse and put Annie's house where the smokehouse was standing, put a patio between the girls' house and Annie's, and connect all the playhouses with tunnels. They will put in the electrical, heating, and air conditioning as well.

The light show was nearly as impressive as Jennifer's, and we talked for over an hour about the event we'd attended. The girls said they couldn't wait to tell their audience about the event and hoped the Wiloby's would expand their show with their own version of the event.

Susanne said, "We will film the program tomorrow in your house, since the studio will not be ready until Wednesday. Once the studio is ready, Phillip's crew will assemble your playhouse in the studio, and then you'll be set to film forevermore."

The girls decided to wear their new outfits on Wednesday to help celebrate their new studio.

Marie asked Susanne, "Can we start teaching new students on Wednesday as well?"

Susanne said, "Let me check with Silvia to see when she told the class it was to start. We want to have a grand opening of the complex after Silvia and Murry's wedding and just before the next event in Texas or Utah."

Marie asked the girls where they planned to sleep tonight.

Leslie said, "In Sarah's room. We like pouncing on our bed; our bed is nice and warm, and Daddy gets up and makes us hot chocolate, and we get to cook."

Marie said, "So they're spoiling you?"

Leslie said, "Yes, they treat us very well. They even let us bring our stuffed friends with us, and Mommy puts blankets around us until our hot chocolate sets in."

She went on, "You and Daddy treat us very well too. We'll sleep in my bed tomorrow night, then Rebecca's bed, and then Kim's bed. We like moving around to each room."

Marie said, while getting hugs from all the girls, "You know what time it is?"

Leslie said, "Prayer time. We'll go get our pajamas and our lambs."

Marie and Delores said, "We'll all go with you. It's dark in your house. Get Scooter and Lulu to be our watchdogs."

The girls got Scooter and Lulu and then met their moms in the tunnel. Scooter was leading the way into the girls' playhouse. They had already turned on the lights from the tunnel entrance and followed Scooter into the tunnel leading to the house, making sure Mama and Papa's playhouse was illuminated too. They would be heading home after prayers; Scooter and Lulu would escort them home. I would call the dogs once we received the all-clear from Papa.

Once the second floor was clear, Delores stayed with the girls while Marie and the dogs went to the upper bedroom and kitchen, the house was clear of any intruders. The ladies, girls, and dogs returned to our home.

Presently the girls were getting ready for bed, and we were finishing up our coffee to meet them for prayers. The girls were trying to teach Scooter and Lulu to bow their heads for prayers; it seemed to me that in a short time they would catch on; they are that smart and well behaved. After prayers, kisses, and night lights turned on, the dogs even licked them good night.

Scooter and Lulu took Mama and Papa home, walking slower with them. They all got into the elevator to the patio, checking outside to make sure no one was hiding in the yard. Then they waited for Papa to unlock the patio doors, entered the house, and searched all the rooms. Papa called the dogs to ride into the elevator and let them into the playhouse. From there, the dogs headed back to our house so I could put them in the corral, where I gave them both treats. They really like the dog biscuits.

Delores had her cell phone in hand just in case someone was lurking in the bushes. Scooter and Lulu checked the livestock, making sure they were all okay, and then lay down in the beds the girls made for them.

Delores and I took the elevator to the second floor, checking on the girls; they were fast asleep. We knew we had six or seven hours of sleep time so no dilly-dallying around; we hit the hay to end the day.

Delores said, "If you hurry, we can get some loving in. I'll set the eight-second clock, cowboy."

When we looked at our clock on the night-stand, it was one o'clock in the morning. Eight seconds? This cowboy isn't timed in seconds but in hours.

*

It seemed we had just fallen asleep when our four little girls came pouncing on the bed. "Daddy, we're cold." Delores and I scooted apart onto the cold mattress so the girls could take every inch of the warm part. Delores and I shivered wanting hugs. I knew it was time for coffee and hot chocolate or maybe hot apple cider.

I was quickly up, dressed appropriately, in the elevator, and into the kitchen. The girls and Delores were still upstairs getting warm. They knew how long it took to have everything ready for them to consume. I also put three, two-packs of hunger pain medication on the table and started getting the pans ready for another mouthwatering, palate pleasing, tongue titillating breakfast.

The girls, Delores, and Susanne were all approaching the kitchen table. "Thank you, Daddy," said Sarah; "we needed our medication."

Delores gave me a hug and a kiss. Susanne said, "My turn," so she did the same as Delores. Then the girls all wanted the same. I told them all, "Thank you. Now I don't need to wash my face in the shower."

The girls all knew their duty stations and were ready to do their best. We had to make enough for everyone; in a matter of about five minutes our elevator had Marie, John, and Mama and Papa all entering the kitchen. The girls and I got more loving from Marie and Mama. They all said how nice it was to sleep in their own beds, and they slept like logs.

Marie said, "How about you guys?"

The girls said, "We fell asleep fast, didn't move a muscle all night."

Marie said, "Delores, did you move a muscle?"

Delores said, "How about a refill? Anyone ready for a refill?"

Marie said to me, "What did you do to my sister?"

Marie said, "Refill? We just got a cup of coffee and had hardly a sip. A refill?"

Delores gave her and Mama two pieces of toast. "Here, keep yourself occupied, while the rest of the breakfast is getting ready."

The Albright scramble was smelling really good. Leslie asked if she could sneak a bite. I put a spoonful on a saucer for her and the girls to nibble on while cooking.

Leslie gave me a hug and told me, "This is perfect. Great job."

It was nice. A simple little thing like that made me feel really good inside. I knew it made her heart feel warm as well.

Breakfast consumed and finished, the girls ran to the elevator and up to their rooms. They came back down the elevator in their farming outfits and got Scooter and Lulu from the corral. Lots of love was exchanged, and they brought them into the kitchen and fed them the scraps in their bowls along with a cup of dry dog food.

They also filled their bowls with fresh water, I observed.

We don't need a garbage disposal; the dogs really enjoy our cooking.

Leslie asked, "Susanne, should we give some hay to our calves and lambs now or wait for our filming?"

Susanne said, "Wait for the filming. It was so adorable to watch yesterday. Your audience will love seeing how you are treated by the animals. We'll have your moms stand outside the corral; no mishaps like yesterday, right, Marie?"

Marie said, "I look at the bright side: I get to buy another pair of shoes."

Silvia arrived, ready to chauffeur me to work. Today was new truck day for me. The schedule showed a meeting in the afternoon with an attorney to start proceedings of theft by MacDonald, the fired leadman. Stuart was also going to file suit against MacDonald. Should be a fun-filled afternoon.

Silvia said, "I need a pick-me-up before we head to the office; tough night."

I told her, "There are some breakfast rolls and a smidgen of leftover breakfast. If you would like some, help yourself."

There was only about three bites of Albright scramble and a piece of toast, but with the breakfast she was a happy camper.

Papa asked Silvia, "What time is Phillip's crew due to arrive?"

Silvia said, "Just before eight o'clock was the last time I heard them mention. Why do you ask?"

"We're thinking about moving the lambs and calves in with the other calves," said Papa, "because of the noise the crews will make moving the smoker and preparing the holes for the playhouse."

Silvia said, "Let me call Murry to see what he thinks."

She called Murry on his cell phone, and he told her that Scooter and Lulu would keep the livestock out of harm's way; otherwise it could be hard to separate the Texas calves from the calves that were already here. Murry told her, "Most of the digging is done by hand and wheelbarrows. The lambs and calves will be more curious or looking for attention than being frightened. Thank you for asking; see you later today. Love you; bye-bye, my love."

Silvia told Papa and the girls, "No need to move the animals. All the work is to be done is by hand."

I asked her, "Do you need a refill of coffee?"

Silvia said, "You know, that would be perfect; would you mind?"

I told her, I'd be delighted to fulfill your desires, and I'd be right back.

Marie and Delores finished off the pot. "Too late; we beat you to it. Make a new pot."

"Thank you, you're both so caring this morning. Love you."

With a fresh pot brewing, I returned to Silvia and told her, "It will be finished in a few minutes."

The girls and Papa were out feeding the lambs and calves with Scooter and Lulu getting their fair share of hugs and kisses. All of the livestock came to the girls without the help of Scooter or Lulu. It amazed Papa and me to watch the animals react to the girls.

I returned to the kitchen to see all the ladies drinking coffee and talking.

Marie informed me that she'd taken care of my customer. She also gave her some hunger pain medication; my meager breakfast offering would not satisfy a mouse, let alone a full-grown adult.

I apologized profusely, telling them, "I'm still learning how to be a servant to you ladies."

That statement got them laughing. "You'll never meet our standards," said Delores. "No man will ever meet our standards."

I asked her, "What about your buff gardener?"

Delores said, "He speaks no words; he knows his duties. He returns to his work once those duties are completed to my standards."

Silvia was ready to hit the highway. "We'll be late," she said. "Angel and Juanita will not be happy with us."

I gave hugs and kisses to my bride, my best female friend, her mother, and Susanne and told them, "Not to worry; I will return."

Silvia got into her vehicle and buckled up. She got us to our place of business a couple of minutes ahead of Angel and Juanita.

They were expecting fresh brewed coffee, so Silvia said it was her fault; she had to have some coffee and breakfast at my house.

In a few minutes all the ladies were sitting in my office with their cups full of coffee.

Silvia asked if the office staff could have Friday off to prepare for the wedding on Saturday.

I gave them my best boss look, pondering the alternatives, looking at all the photos on my office wall, pausing for as long as possible, knowing women can only endure so much delay. Finally I told them, "If you have all your work completed on Thursday. This is response and reward, basic psychology."

Silvia said, "So if we complete our responsibilities in a timely manner, we can have the day off, paid?"

"You know, there's no dealing with women. I don't know why men even attempt to negotiate with any of you.

"When are the rest of the Ladies' Club due to arrive?"

"They're all coming in on Wednesday and Thursday," said Silvia, "so we have planned a get-together on Thursday evening at the restaurant. You know that Maggi and Sally will be attending, your bunk buddies. I'm not sure if men will be allowed to attend."

Angel said, "Juanita and I need to complete a couple of plans. I have two more appointments scheduled in the afternoon, two presentations scheduled for tomorrow, and numerous calls requesting estimates. It was nice chatting with you two; off to work we go."

Silvia got up and brought the pot into the office to refill our cups. She took the pot back, returned, and sat down on her chair. "You served me earlier, and I served you now. We're even for today."

I asked her, "Are you getting nervous?"

She said, "About getting married or sitting across from my boss?"

"I'd love to know if I make you nervous, but I was asking about getting married."

She said, "The ceremony and reception are my biggest worries. I'm hoping nothing goes wrong and I don't make some huge mistake. I'm not used to being in the spotlight."

I told her, "Who would know if you made a mistake or not?"

She said, "The pastor is a medieval scholar. He wanted to get a PhD in medieval philosophy. He's the one that talked to us about having this type of wedding."

I told her, "I think it will be remembered by many people for a long time. You'll both be known all over the world."

She said, "Murry and I have been practicing speaking the language of yore."

She stood up and transformed into Maid Marian with a snap of her fingers. I became King Arthur, and it was "sire this" and "sire that." She took me back in time with her, mentally.

I told Maid Marian, "This could become dangerous for me. I may never return from this journey."

She said, "Maiden Delores would be forever grateful to me for taking you over the edge. The asylum would inherit a gem for research material."

After a few minutes, Silvia was back to her normal self. Angel and Juanita were applauding her from the doorway.

Angel said, "You are going to teach us all of this before Saturday, correct?"

Silvia said, "Boss, we need another day if I'm to teach fifty women how to act properly for thy lordship."

"Okay, Thursday and Friday off. I'll be setting up the new office at the new location upon final inspection tomorrow's scheduled appointment with the general contractor." I asked Silvia, "You can contact the rental company regarding the move?"

"Aye, aye, your lordship. I shall dispatch a scribe with your message. Anything else, your lordship?"

"Yes, be good enough to fetch my wench from the castle. I need another crow for my midday repast."

"Aye, your lordship. I shall send the buff gardener to deliver the message."

"You'll find an extra farthing in your stockings tonight."

"You're so generous, your lordship. I hope this does not leave you penniless?"

I returned to answering my messages, which I had neglected for five days. All of my office managers were not happy and had put me on restriction.

Charise said, "Stay at your computer until you finish, or we will divorce you as your office wives, do you hear me?"

As a dutiful office husband, I opened up my desk drawer, pulled a two-pack of hunger pain medication, pulled out another, opened them, and enjoyed four wonderful sugar-loaded cupcakes with my coffee, of course, I ran low on coffee and went to the coffeepot for a refill.

Silvia asked, "Mister Boss Man, why do you need more coffee? You know you get all jittery after two cups."

I told her, "I have a powerful thirst. I must not have drunk enough water yesterday."

"Uh-huh, thirsty—not buying that, my dear," said Silvia. "You were in your snack drawer. I'm telling all the office wives. You're in big trouble, mister. I read the note that Charise sent you, and she won't take your actions lightly. You'll be on restriction. Now you go back and clean up your messages; I want to see results."

I returned to my desk and finished the final cupcake. *So there, office wives; so much for restriction. I'll just highlight all these messages and hit the delete button. Let's see … oh no, I can't delete that one, or that one—or that one. Oh, come on, isn't there just one I can delete? This will take all day to complete. Why so many? I'd be happy with just a couple. I want the girls to feel they are needed as well.*

There's more than a hundred and fifty. I'll see if I can't set the machine up to say, "Message center is full; please try again later. Have a great day!" I'll set the limit at ten.

I was an hour into answering the messages when I received three more messages, from Charise, from Marjorie, and from Gloria.

Nice job; don't stop. We have oodles more to send you. We've been saving them up. NO MORE CUPCAKES until you finish your responsibilities, read Charise's note.

In my second hour of the arduous task I came across a message from a vendor: *If you won't have lunch with our salesman, we want to make you a cash account. Please inform your superintendents.* It was signed by a marketing director. I got the phone number of the owner of the company. *Okay, marketing director, your day is just about to begin.*

The phone rang, and was picked up. "Who may I ask is calling?"

"Tell Charles that Fred Stockdale, from Stockdale Landscape Construction, is on the line."

"Hold, please. I'll see if he is in his office." The lovely operator then transferred me to the marketing director instead of Charles.

She introduced herself and gave me her title, seemingly oblivious to who I might be. "Are you calling about having James come to your office for a sales presentation?"

"I'm telling you, no sales meetings, no lunches. I don't appreciate a middle management person telling me they are threatening me with a cash account unless I tell my superintendents. You are not the owner of the company. I want to talk with Charles, now."

"Charles is in a meeting; can you call back later? Hold on a minute—I have Charles's cell phone number. Sorry to bother you."

I kept the line open and called Charles's cell phone number. He answered, "Fred, my boy, haven't heard from you for some time. What's up?"

"Charles, your marketing director threatened to set me up as a cash-only customer unless I arrange to have a salesman give me a pitch. Was that your doing?"

Charles said, "Not my doing. If there's some new product that could help you with your line of work, I'll call you. Don't worry about what she threatened; you know more about what you're doing than our sales staff. I'll straighten this out. I hope this didn't affect our relationship?"

"No, Charles, I'm in four different states with at least twenty new employees to deal with. Your service is impeccable; I'm very pleased with our arrangement. But going cash-only would have me trusting superintendents with a company credit card, I'm dealing with an employee today who stole merchandise from the company and reordered the same product to complete the project."

Charles said, "Did any of the products stolen come from our company?"

"A couple of them were; I'll send you copies of the invoices."

Charles said, "I will check with our order desk with the invoices to find out what we told them."

I said, "Charles, you may need to have a nice chat with your marketing director about telling your customers something that you didn't direct her to say. It was very nice chatting with you this morning, and thank you for taking my call. Have a great day."

When I hung up, Silvia was standing in my doorway, hands on hips, with a look that said *I'm going to kill you.*

I told her, "You look awful cheerful; how may I be of assistance to you?"

Silvia entered my office and sat down across from me. "One of our vendors put us on a cash account. We aren't getting our order as scheduled until they receive full payment."

"Was the vendor Donaldson Materials?"

"Yes. That will mess up every project on our schedule."

"I just got off the phone with Charles at Donaldson Materials. His marketing director threatened that very thing in one of my messages. That won't happen. Call the store, and have them talk to Charles directly; his marketing director is getting spanked for going over his head. He was not aware of what she was doing to his accounts. Give me the phone number of the store, and get me the manager of the store. Your order will be there as scheduled."

I called Charles's phone again. He answered, "Is this a butt call?"

"No, Charles. Could you have your people call you office here in Oregon and tell them to ship our orders as scheduled? They want payment in full prior to shipping. I know this is going to have a ripple effect in all four states; please undo what she caused."

"I'll make certain that all of those accounts she threatened will be reversed right now. She was on the phone a couple of minutes ago. I'll go to her desk and call everyone into our conference room for a quick spanking."

Silvia came in and laid the store manager's name and number on my desk. "You know, this interrupted my nail polishing. This is not recommended on nail polishing day; we do have priorities."

I dialed the number of the store and got another receptionist who wanted details of my call to the manager. I told her politely, "If you were the manager, you would know the nature of my call, but since you are not the manager, I don't feel it is necessary for you to know. Give me the manager, or I'll just have to come down there to talk to your manager and your entire staff so you all will be informed. Oh, by the way, you are getting a call from your corporate office in a few minutes. I'm sure they will want you to screen their call."

After a moment another voice came on the line. "This is Richard Stone. How may I be of assistance?"

"Good morning, Richard Stone. I'm Fred Stockdale, the owner of Stockdale Landscape Construction. I was informed that my order will not be delivered until you receive full payment. Do you know Charles Donaldson?"

Richard said, "Yes, he's the owner of our company."

"I know Charles very well. He and I had a talk just a few minutes ago regarding the exact issue you raised with my office manager. You will receive a call in a few minutes that will return our account back to the way it was originally established nearly twenty years ago. If you don't get that call, please call my cell phone; they may have skipped your office."

Richard said, "You know we can't ship anything until that issue is resolved?"

I heard his receptionist tell him he had a call holding on line two. "It's Mr. Donaldson, the owner."

Richard told me to hold for a minute.

When he came back, he said, "Mr. Stockdale, we'll have your order to the jobsite within the hour. We're sorry about all of this, and we'll correct our files to restore your account status."

Silvia was still sitting at my desk, now with a huge smile. "Wow. How do you do that so nonchalantly? You spanked the receptionist verbally, and you told a store manager in no uncertain terms that he was wrong to hold up our order."

I told her, "If any of my office wives pulled that with any of our customers without telling me what they were proposing to do, it would not be pretty."

I asked her to send Charles our invoices on which MacDonald had procured duplicate products. "Make certain they go directly to him, not to the corporate email box." I gave her the name of the office manager. "Tell her it's important that only he sees what you are sending."

While she was gathering up the invoices for Charles, her phone rang. It was Delores; she needed to talk to me right now.

I answered, saying, "I'm sorry. I was hungry, and those cupcakes hit the spot."

Delores said, "What are you talking about?"

"I was caught this morning eating cupcakes without doing my messages. Isn't that why you're calling? My office wives are in a tizzy."

She said, "Nope, I don't even care if you eat an entire box of cupcakes. While we were in Texas, Murry put twenty hams in our smoker, and they are being smoked as we speak. Phillip's crew can't relocate the smoker until the hams are finished. Murry is here and told the crew that if they stopped the smoking process, the hams won't be ready for the feast on Saturday."

"Tell them I'll be there in a few minutes."

I went to Silvia's desk and told her, "Let's go to my house. We have another issue to address."

She said, "You know this is still nail polish day. You're making it too much like a normal workday. I was not prepared for all these interruptions."

"Drive Miss Daisy, and when we return, get my truck delivered to the office. Then you will be freed from driving me around."

"What's the issue we have to address?"

I said, "It appears your fiancé put hams in the smoker for your wedding feast. We can't move the smoker, or you won't have any hams for your guests."

"Oh, I forgot to tell Phillip. Rats, this won't make people very happy with me."

"I guess you'll have to face the music. Make yourself a note so you won't forget, or send me a message so in five days I'll respond."

When we arrived, Phillip's crew was getting ready to leave. I asked them to stick around for a few minutes to reestablish a game plan.

I looked over the situation, took out my trusty steel tape measure, and had Silvia hold the dummy end. The crew was more interested in what she was wearing than the situation at hand; she kept the crew's minds occupied.

I determined that they could dig the four postholes ten feet to the west. Once we could move the smoke house, they could dig two more postholes for an extended deck for the girls to have picnics on and watch their animals.

Murry said, "I should have thought of that. Sorry to make you come out here for something as simple as that."

I told him, "No, I needed to have a break from answering messages."

Silvia gave him a kiss goodbye, and we climbed back into her vehicle and headed back to our office.

I told her, "One quick stop before we complete our journey."

She said, "Happy Meal, correct? You want a happy meal."

I told her she was starting to look pale and frail, clearly she needed some nourishment.

Silvia said, "I'm getting pale from lack of sunlight. Incandescent lighting is horrible for tanning."

She texted Angel: *We are at McDonald's and want to bring you two something. What would you like?*

Angel texted, *Something filling for two hours, then we'll go to lunch. And diet soda; we are getting bored with coffee.*

At the order window, I said, "Four big breakfasts. That should fill them up temporarily." We returned to the office with the girls' filler-uppers.

Silvia texted my other office wives with her reward for holding the dummy end of the measuring tape.

The hit song years ago, "You Light Up My Life"? Well, Silvia torched mine. Oh, the repercussions I received from the joint email. My message board was lit up. *They will do things to me that would even make Boris Karloff cringe.*

Where is my truck? I could use a getaway right about now. I swear I will never understand women. Even Marie and Delores jumped on the bandwagon: *Just wait until you get home. You thought eating crow was below you dietary standards. Dream on, buddy,* stated Marie in her very loving text.

Marjorie, Gloria and Charise all tried to outdo one another's texts. They agreed that since there were so many trees in Oregon, they would find a nice sturdy one and use a nice sisal rope. *A proper hanging is too quick; upside down, feet to the sky, that would be more fun to witness.*

Then they thought I could be the human piñata, with fifty women holding broomsticks to swat me with. It could go viral, and they would all become millionaires overnight.

Silvia texted back, saying, *The breakfasts are so good. Nothing tastes better than free. Now it's not gourmet by any stretch of the word, but real butter, nice sweet syrup, scrambled Egg Beater egg, sausage patty made from artificial meat and flavoring to resemble the real thing, a nice greasy hash brown, with an overbaked biscuit and plastic dinnerware—he'll have to treat all of you upon arrival. I might even change our menu for the wedding. This is remarkable. Thank you, my lovely office husband.*

Jennifer texted, *Why wait until Wednesday? We could be there in less than two hours. You find the tree, and we'll change our reservations.*

46

A gentleman entered our office. "I'm here to deliver a truck."

I darted out of my office. "Really? I have my freedom back. Wow, can I have the keys? She'll sign the paperwork."

I was followed by Angel and Juanita, and we all got into the pickup truck. I warned them not to take too big a breath. "I want the new truck smell to last until I get home." I put the key into the ignition, turned it to Accessory, and heard a Mexican radio station.

Angel said, "That's the station my dad listens to. You have to change it. Here, let me change it." She said, "They play one old-timey song and then talk for ten minutes about nothing. Then there's five minutes of used car commercials, then three minutes from a local restaurant that no one I know has ever eaten at; the owners are Chinese."

Angel found an oldies station, and the girls were bebopping, "to songs that we carry inside," from the Vietnam era. Then they played a fifties love song, and the girls knew the lyrics and were singing along, I told them, "Enjoy, and please bring in the keys and place them on my desk."

Soon Angel brought in my keys, saying she'd gotten her ya-yas out. "Very nice sound system in your truck."

It was nearing showtime with the attorney to start prosecuting MacDonald for embezzlement.

Silvia said, "You have a Mr. Charles Donaldson on line one. Do you want to take the call?"

"Of course. You know, by next week you can surrender the telephone answering to the new receptionist. You have placed an ad in the newspaper, correct?"

Silvia said, "I'll get back to you in a few minutes."

I picked up the phone. "Charles, how are you doing this fine morning?"

"Mr. Stockdale, you have created a little problem for me," said Charles. "You know my marketing director you talked with earlier?"

"Yes, I remember talking with her. What happened?"

Charles said, "She is the sister-in-law of Mr. MacDonald."

I stated singing "It's a Small World after All."

Charles said, "Very clever Mr. Stockdale, but my little problem is not so little. We searched your invoices that you sent over to me. Well, it appears those were not the only invoices which your MacDonald and my little account manager were tangled in."

I asked him, "I'm due to meet with an attorney in about an hour. Would you like to join us in a conference call?"

"I have good reason to contact the authorities myself and have her arrested for embezzlement. Her signature is on thousands of dollars of duplicated invoices."

I asked Charles, "Could you wait for about an hour? Let me confer with our attorney and call you right away regarding arresting her either today or maybe tomorrow."

I referred him to the detective we used on the Albright case. "He's very thorough and very prompt."

I asked, "Are you sure she acted alone, and others aren't involved?"

Charles said, "This whole thing just sickens me. Looking at her makes my skin crawl. I trusted her so much, I gave her a promotion just a couple of months ago."

I said, "I'll send you MacDonald's résumé. You may want to check to see if this has been going on with other companies where he worked before."

Charles said, "You're just a bundle of great news. If this has been going on since the day we hired her, I'm such a fool."

I told him, "Call the detective, and tell him what you told me. He will do whatever is necessary to move everything forward."

Just as we were finishing our call, in walked Stuart, Papa, and the attorney. Murry and Silvia were only steps behind them.

I stood up. "Gentlemen, welcome to my humble office. Shall we take this to the conference room?" Our conference room was our warehouse. We'd had the crews clean up the floors, and the girls had set up two folding tables surrounded by eight plastic chairs. Two buckets of ice held bottled water and flavored iced teas, or there was our world-renowned fresh-perked coffee.

We all went in and sat at the table. The warehouse lights were breathtaking; they lit the ceiling but not so much the table. Angel was summoned to go to the nearest home improvement center and purchase two pole lamps to help the situation.

She asked, "Could I have the pleasure of driving your new truck?" I reminded her about taking only small breaths. "And don't roll down the windows."

She was off and running to get more light on our meeting. While she was gone, I told everyone what had happened this morning and the outcome of my conversation with Charles Donaldson.

Papa said, "You know, you are a one-man wrecking crew for the bad guys. I know after today they will have a few contracts out on you."

The attorney said, "You're telling me this may turn into multiple arrests?"

I gave the attorney the name and phone number for the detective we used during the Albright case.

The attorney asked Stuart if he was going to pursue prosecution of MacDonald.

Stuart asked Murry, "Do you think we have enough evidence to prosecute MacDonald?"

Murry said, "He worked for us for two years. We'll need some time to check how many projects he ran, go through invoicing to see if there were duplications, what liberties he took on each project. It could take some time."

Stuart told the attorney, "Yes, I'll hire an auditing service to trace his whole time with my firm." He looked at Murry. "We can't afford to wait too long or he'll flee the area."

The attorney called his office: "Call our detective, and have him arrest MacDonald and his brother today. Embezzlement against two companies."

Angel returned with three pole lamps; she even had the store assemble them. Sylvia asked, "How did you get them to assemble the lamps?"

Angel looked her over, starting at her face and shifting to her shoulders and then her hips. "My daddy said, 'Girl, you were given great gifts from God. Use them to your favor by being polite and cheerful and seeming confused or frail to get men to jump through hoops.'"

Angel said, "I had six men working to assemble the three lamps without taking their eyes off of me. Two even carried them to the truck and put bubble wrap around each one and cushioned them between the fender wells. I also got six lunch or dinner date offers."

I told her, "Can you imagine if you were in your chauffeur's outfit what more you could have gotten them to do for you?"

She said, "Your truck is only a half-ton. I would have had to make numerous trips and rented another storage unit."

With the additional illumination, we were able to set up a game plan. Silvia had Angel and Juanita bring in all the invoices we had uncovered during our search.

The attorney asked Stuart, "Do you have the invoices that show the discrepancies?"

Murry said he had one year nearly finished. "We are working diligently, scanning all of the vendors. We should have the majority of the projects completed before the end of next week."

Stuart said, "We will hire the auditing company starting tomorrow; we may have enough for you before then."

Papa asked, "Is he working at another contractor? Do you need some eyes on him?"

Stuart said, "Eyes would be wonderful. We have to keep him from fleeing."

Angel said, "Charles is on line two, to talk to you."

"Good afternoon, Charles. Do you have an update?"

"She is now in custody," said Charles. "It was not a pretty sight. She said things that should never pass a lady's lips. She obviously had no clue she was being watched. They also took my receptionist, who was monitoring her calls. She was hired when I promoted my account manager and just happens to be her niece. They also arrested my salesman.

"The detective had put a couple of pieces together. The salesman had worked with our account manager in the past. The detective wants to see just what the salesman and the account manager have in common; he thinks there is a nice marriage between them."

I said, "We should have MacDonald in custody before the days' end, along with his brother."

Charles said, "One little phone call from you upset their applecart so to speak."

I told him, "If you were planning on putting me on a cash account, I know you would have called me direct to discuss the matter. It was not like you would do that to me during an ongoing project."

He said, "We're bringing in an auditing company like your firm is in the process of doing to find out just when and how long this was going on. They told me my entire office staff and yard people will be questioned before this is all over."

"I'm sorry about causing everyone extra costs over this matter. I look at it as saving me money in the long run. Losing that kind of employee actually did my company wonders."

Charles said he had to go. "The detective wants to talk with me privately. Talk to you tomorrow, my dear friend."

Our attorney said, "This could turn out to be something huge, if it's a well-organized operation. I'll get my staff working to research each of the employees arrested. I will get with the district attorney's office to start issuing search warrants. Deliver the case to them so they can start the prosecution rolling."

We all returned to my office, where it was warmer and more comfortable, and talked for a few minutes. Then everyone went back to their real jobs.

Papa already had eyes on MacDonald and his family. He received a report that MacDonald was in custody. The gang must know that they were caught.

Silvia entered my office to say, "The other office managers told me you're still on restriction. No more unearned cupcakes until all your messages have been addressed. They put their foot down; they mean business.

"Marjorie said, 'Nice job, you're keeping law firms wealthy.'

"Jennifer wants to know if you're getting kickbacks. Charise said you will do anything to get out of doing your messages.

"But Gloria told the ladies, 'Don't pick on the man who changed my life. I owe him dearly. Be nice, and he'll change your life as well.'"

I returned to my messages; once again, I barely put a dent into the list. I quickly checked the list for sales calls and put them in a separate folder. I looked for the lunch brigadiers; they also went into a separate file. New customers who wanted to schedule an appointment were put into a separate folder. That left me with the "just what do they want?" file folder. *Now my message list doesn't look so horrible: open one folder at a time, and put new messages in it. Makes it a little easier to manage now.* Then I made a file folder for employees wanting me to chat with them. That took care of the entire list of messages. *Nothing accomplished but filing, but it sure looks nice.*

I pulled the employees wanting to talk to me folder first.

Upon opening the file, I dialed the first number. The oldest message always comes first. I called Jennifer, and she was excited that I returned her call. "It's been five days. We talked at the party but not regarding my questions."

I asked her, "Are your questions extensive? Could you email them so I can review them before answering?"

She agreed. "It will take me a couple of minutes."

I called everyone in the folder and asked them to do the same so I could continue knocking out the messages received to date.

Jennifer sent me her email. She had five questions, all relating to either the theme park or new customers; can we do this or that? One asked if I had ever done something for a customer like this before.

I spent a few minutes deciphering her questions. I emailed her back asking her to have Diego look at her questions. *I have done most of what you have asked; not certain if Diego has that kind of experience. I would not want to pursue job tasks unless the field has experience with that task. As to whether we would be interested in cleaning up a customer's garage: no, not interested. There are companies who do that type of work.*

I received an email from Charise regarding some field issues they were having with a couple of employees. I emailed her telling her to have Juan contact me; *If the employees are not following Juan's instructions, let them go. We don't need to have to babysit employees. Follow the instructions to the best of your ability; if you need further instructions, then ask the superintendent.*

Charise emailed me back: *It appears to me the two in question don't like one another.*

I replied, *Put the two on separate crews. Then if issues arise after doing that, then let the employee go. I'm not partial to attitudes; have our competition deal with them.*

This process went on until it was time to shut down the computer and drive my new truck home. I asked Silvia for a map from the office to our house. She said, "I'm going to your house for dinner; you can follow me."

The girls met us in the driveway; they'd seen us coming past the corral.

I asked them if they would like to go for a ride in Daddy's new truck.

Leslie asked, "Can Scooter and Lulu join us?"

I told her, "It would not be a family ride without Scooter and Lulu. The girls, Scooter, and Lulu all got into the truck. Sarah, Rebecca, and Kim were in the backseat of my extension cab. Leslie and Lulu were in the front seat, and Scooter stretched out on top of the console between the front seats.

We went to the store for hunger pain medication and some dog bones for our four-legged friends. We left the dogs in the truck while we shopped very quickly, spending maybe five minutes in the store. Then we headed back home listening to the oldies station, and the girls were singing along with a song they knew—truly fun. We pulled into the driveway, and were met by Marie, Delores, Silvia, and Mama.

"We wanted to see your new truck," said Marie.

I showed them the truck. The girls, the dogs, and I were standing on the driveway when the ladies all got in the truck and buckled up. Delores told me, "Get the grill going; we have company." Off they went, radio blasting, and they all looked like they were dancing as they turned toward where the studio is being built.

The girls asked if they could have some hunger pain medication—"And the doggies need a treat, Daddy."

"Of course. That's why we went to the store; I can't have my girls in pain. Not happening, never."

I also made them some hot chocolate to go along with their cupcakes. I broke the dog bones in half and gave the girls one half each. They had Scooter and Lulu sit and take the bones nicely, which they did. The girls naturally gave them loving along with the treats.

I went out and oiled up the grill while the girls ate their cupcakes and drank some hot chocolate.

Their mommas returned from their joyride in my new truck. They let me know they had sucked up all the new truck smell. Could I get an air freshener on my journeys tomorrow? They put in a preference for the French vanilla that I used in my other truck.

While the grill was heating up, Marie and Delores brought out a platter of meat offerings. They both were in that special, loving mood: their eyes had a twinkle, their expressions were inviting, and they both had on my favorite perfume. *Something is up; either I'm on this planet for my last day, or they need my approval on something.*

I lifted the hood and was placing the meat offerings on the grill when Delores asked, "Did you notice our new outfits?"

"I did, but I didn't want to ask if they were new, since if they weren't, you both would thank me for not paying attention to you. Turn around slowly; I need to fulfill my vision." Both the ladies turned around for me, looking over their shoulders while they turned, with their model smiles.

I told them, "You both look beautiful, great style, color, fits you like a high-priced glove, right skirt length, perfect."

Marie said, "We just wanted to let you know that your office wives along with us decided you needed to be taught a lesson for sneaking those cupcakes before you answered any messages. So we all bought a new outfit. Silvia could not escape the office so she will get one tomorrow."

She now had her arms around my neck, inches from my face, and said with a sultry voice, "Baby, we need new shoes to go with our new outfits. You want us to look our best, and we do represent your company, but after-five outfits with tennis shoes is not a very sexy look. Delores sidled closer and started running her nails up and down my back very seductively.

I told them, "You keep this up, and I'll burn our dinner. Let me flip the meat over, and then you can proceed for five minutes."

Marie put her hands on her hips, looked at me, and said, "Men are all alike. All they think about is how good the meat looks."

I told her, "And tastes. You would not be happy with me if it wasn't cooked to perfection."

Delores told Marie, "Let's finish him off; he was getting very close."

"How about after dinner and dessert? I'm serious; I don't want to burn the meat. We have guests, remember."

As they both headed for the kitchen, Delores turned and said, "Dream on, lover, dream on."

We four parents got the loser table. Mama, Papa, Susanne, Silvia, Scooter, and Lulu got to dine with the girls.

John said, "I like your new truck; the signage is very impressive."

"Your wife took all the ladies out for a spin after the girls and I returned from getting hunger pain medication and doggie treats from the grocery store. We took the dogs with us, and they guarded the truck while we shopped for them."

While we were all just sitting around the patio table, Marie said, "You have a knack for finding criminal activity that's been overlooked by those around you. As an attorney, I find this a rather interesting trait. You find things that keep the courts busy for a long time. So do you have a secret you can tell us as to just how these mishaps in society happen to come to your notice?"

"I'm a very inquisitive person. It's like putting together a puzzle: you look for a certain piece that fits the location you're trying to complete. If your piece doesn't fit, you keep looking for that piece. I just have a desire to find the missing piece.

"Yesterday, I answered some messages. I was told by a middle management person that the way I have done business with them for nearly twenty years was going to be modified since I wasn't willing to have a salesman visit my office. They were moving me from credit to cash. That meant all of my superintendents would have to carry a company credit card, and that's not going to happen.

"I called to talk to my dear friend, the owner, but the receptionist transferred my call to the account manager. She wanted me to set a date for the salesman to come visit. I told her I wanted to talk to the owner of the company. She hesitated to transfer my call, so I used my cell phone and called his cell phone, bypassing her. She is now in jail along with the receptionist and the salesman. She did not fit my puzzle."

Marie said, "So in your world, all pieces must fit together, or you keep looking for the right piece that does fit."

"Correct. You and Delores are the right pieces of my puzzle. You both thought you would fit but were reluctant to be put into the puzzle until John and I talked—and your two stories were identical. You two were the missing pieces to our family puzzle. I have to say my puzzle looks pretty good, suitable for framing."

It was nearing time to put the girls to bed. They came down from their house with the dogs and sat on our laps to get some well-deserved hugs and cheek kisses. They asked if there were any more meat scraps for Scooter and Lulu. I just happened to have a plate on the barbecue counter waiting for just this moment.

The girls went with Scooter and Lulu to their bowls in the kitchen to feed them the scraps. When I turned to head back to the patio table, I noticed a note hanging on the post of Annie's house frame.

I saw they had the posts and beams assembled, and the joists were also assembled. The note asked: *Where do you want the front door, toward the corral or the front of the house? Where do you want the staircase installed? There isn't enough room for the staircase as it was assembled at the other house.*

While I was pondering the note I was joined by Marie, Delores, and John. Mama and Papa, Silvia, and Susanne were in the kitchen making coffee. We all stood looking at the structure, and Delores asked, "What's the matter?"

I told them, "The staircase from Marie and John's house won't fit the area, so it can't be installed exactly as dismantled. I will have to do a quick design for them to follow tomorrow. I have an idea; I just need to put it on paper."

Marie said, "Okay, you got our attention. What is your simple fix?"

"I will flip the house so you enter from the patio after we move the smokehouse and build the second portion of the patio cover. Instead of a bridge between the girls' house and Annie's house, the entire patio structure we have will be attached to the new structure with a nice tunnel between the two."

Delores asked, "So the only staircase for the two houses will be the one by the other side of the yard?"

"The only other location where there would be enough room would be along the property line parallel to the structure. The front door would still have to be on the patio side; the French doors will face the barbecue area."

I measured from the post of the structure to the property line fence. "The staircase is three feet wide, so we have two inches to spare."

Delores said, "Can we do that so the girls are closer to the lambs and calves?"

"Anything is doable. Do you all agree with putting the staircase along the property line fence?"

John said, "No, I think that could lead to someone jumping the fence and going onto the second-floor deck and into our houses. How about the patio side of the structure?"

"I have the perfect solution. We'll put the staircase on the existing deck entering from the barbecue side."

Marie asked, "The girls will still have the ten-by-ten patio looking toward the corral?"

"Of course. We can get them some chaise lounge chairs for the ultimate tanning experience. I think we can even get six lounge chairs on that deck. Their own five-star resort. I can even put a misting system on the hand rails to give you a tropical misting rain, on those hot and humid days."

Marie asked Delores, "Do you think your buff gardener would mind turning on the mister valve during our sun bathing experience?"

Delores said, "He loves turning on the mister valve."

John said, "You're talking about a water valve, correct?"

Delores said with a smirk, "I just answered your wife's question. She didn't specify if it was a water valve."

John said, "Let's get a cup of coffee and tuck the girls into bed and say some prayers. Lord knows you ladies are in dire need of spiritual counseling."

The girls decided to spend the night in Sarah's room; Susanne got Rebecca's room. The girls put Scooter and Lulu into their beds and gave the lambs and calves lots of love, telling them, "Have a good night's sleep. We'll see you in the morning." That was all taken care of while we adults were discussing the location of the staircase.

Teeth brushed, jammies on, tucked in, prayers said, night lights on, and kissed on their foreheads, "Love you, see you all in the morning."

47

I didn't get what had been promised earlier in the day. I did get a rain check; I now had three shoeboxes full of rain checks. She would have to start making good on those pretty soon, or they would become useless, nonredeemable, with no satisfaction guaranteed.

We got pounced on before the rooster crowed; the girls were cold and needed warming up. Delores and I went to the cold edges of the mattress, allowing the girls to have our body heat. They all were shivering and badly in need of hugs. Delores and I accommodated their wishes. Then Leslie said, "Daddy, you know this all feels so good, and we are warming up quite fast, but it triggered our hunger pains."

"Say no more. I lost all of my body heat, but I'll put on a robe and make the hot chocolate and coffee and heat up some breakfast rolls, while getting ready to start breakfast. You ladies all get snuggled up and warm. See you all real soon, and bring down some blankets to wrap around yourselves."

Soon coffee was brewing, the hot chocolate was ready, the rolls were heated, and the pans were in place, oiled and heating up. Quickly sausage and bacon started to spit and sputter in the heated oil. I was cutting up the bell pepper, onion, and mushrooms to be placed in cooking sherry, when I thought, *Where are my little chefs?*

Just like that here they came, all wrapped up in blankets, even Delores and Susanne. I started to make the batter for the pancakes, laid out a loaf of bread, and started frying the hash browns. Delores poured the girls some hot chocolate, and Susanne poured coffee for all of us. The rolls were history in a matter of a couple minutes. Hunger pains take priority, and you can't waste time chatting; it's bite, chew, swallow, bite, chew, swallow, and lick your fingers for any residue.

The girls, now acclimated to the room temperature, started to take their positions, flipping hotcakes, turning sausages, flipping hash browns, making toast, and setting the table and countertop. The elevator opened, and in walked the rest of our breakfast guests. The girls got their morning hugs. Marie as always tried to get a taste, but "Not so fast, Mom," said Leslie. "The batter is raw; you could get sick eating raw batter."

All got seated at their favorite places, and Papa went and freed Scooter and Lulu from the corral. Soon they were both poised and ready, sitting by their bowls. Scooter would look back and forth from his empty bowl to us. Eventually Papa gave them a cup of dry dog food. It wasn't what they wanted; they could smell what was cooking and were simply waiting like good doggies.

They both stood by Leslie; she always gave them a taste of cooked pancakes. She just broke up one pancake and gave them bite-size pieces. Rebecca and Kim gave them some pieces of toast, and that seemed to ease their hunger pains until the scraps covered their dry dog food.

I had never heard either one bark to get attention. In a few more minutes the only sound was silverware clanking on the china plates heaped with Albright scramble topped by homemade salsa. We had spoiled the diners with more than a month of fine dining. As everyone was completing their meals, putting their spoils into the dog's bowls, rinsing off their plates, putting them in the dishwasher, the sun was now peeking in the kitchen windows.

The girls decided to get their farming outfits on to feed the lambs and calves. The ladies refilled their coffee cups and returned to their proper seats. John, Papa, and I all headed to our showers to get ready for today's activities.

I had to meet Phillip's crew to discuss the layout of the playhouse and staircase. Silvia got to drive to work by herself; I would use my navigation system to direct me to McDonald's and then to the office. One more day at the old office; then it would be just five minutes from door to door to our new office.

When I returned to the kitchen, gussied up for the office, ready for another thrilling day of responding to messages—what a waste of my talents—Susanne said she had contacted the rental company yesterday. "They will be at our office and remove all the unnecessary furniture and framed photos this morning and then finish up the move tomorrow morning. The interior decorator will meet them at the new location around ten o'clock."

I told her, "I'd better get to the office as quickly as possible to protect my stash of cupcakes."

I saw Phillip's crew arriving at the patio area. I excused myself, joined them, and talked with his foreman. I showed him my sketch of what we had discussed. He agreed that they could do what we wanted. They laid out the stretcher for the staircase to make sure it would fit the area. The staircase just fit with about two feet to spare. The front door panel would just be flipped from one end to the other end. The French door panel would remain the same as at the old location; pretty simple and easy to reassemble.

The smoker would then be relocated on Monday, and the rest of the patio cover could be built. We also discussed the deck to attach Annie's house to the girls' house. We planned to lay out the tunnel connecting the two houses once the deck was completed. We might have to use a forty-five-degree angle to align both doors.

I went back into the house and gave all the girls hugs and kisses. Gave the same hug and kiss to Delores, Marie, Mama, and then Susanne. She told me, "You know I'm a married woman," so I kissed her on the lips and gave her a real manly hug.

Susanne said, "What part of *married woman* did you not understand?"

Delores said, "Susanne, you have known him for over a year. He did that to be ornery and to get a response. You did very well with both."

I told the girls, "Have a great show today. Marie and Delores, give Mrs. Wilkins my regards. Prove beyond a reasonable doubt that she is not insane."

Marie said, "My first couple of questions to her will erase all doubt among the viewing panel."

I went to her chair and gave her another hug. "I know you can put her in her place. I hope the panel finds her sane."

Another smooch to my bride and of course pets to Scooter and Lulu—they were both really happy; they got a couple of bites of my Albright scramble, which put a smile on all who enjoyed breakfast—and I was out the door.

I stopped at McDonald's and got everyone a breakfast sandwich, all the same to cut down on any arguments, and a hash brown for each. I pulled into the office parking lot, distributed the three bags, entered my office to a fresh cup of coffee with my three beauties only a couple of steps behind me.

They all had their bags and a cup of coffee, sitting back in my comfy chairs, almost ready to thank me, until only one bag had ketchup. Smiles turned to frowns in less than two seconds.

I checked my bag and dumped out more smiles for the girls. Now we were all happy. Angel had a surprise for me. She and Juanita had finished up a plan for me to review. They would complete another plan today, leaving them only one minor item before they adjourned for a four-day weekend.

Boy, my breakfast sandwich was awful. I could use one of my cupcakes but didn't pull a two-pack out of its hiding place. Luckily for the girls I cut mine in half and told them they could have the other half; these had no comparison to the breakfast I had with my family this morning.

It was well received by all three ladies, my plastic knife came in handy. They even welcomed the hash brown, cut into three pieces.

Just as the girls had completed their breakfast sandwiches, in walked the rental company moving staff. They asked where they could start. Silvia showed them the office where the girls were working and put a sticky note on each photo, to indicate which office they would go to. She had Angel and Juanita get a pen and sticky note pad and do the same for all the photos on the walls; for the artwork, Silvia put the sticky note on the back side of each painting.

She also put a sticky note on each potted plant, real and artificial. Then she started labeling the unnecessary furniture. When the items were removed, you could hear an echo in the office. Soon their truck was nearly loaded with what was ready to be spotted in the other office. Silvia, freshened up, was ready to lead them to the new office. She told me that while she was at the new office, she would drop in on Marie and Delores, filming their portion of the Katy Wilkins trial. She would also check in on the girls to see how their first show at the new studio was working out.

I told her, "I'll see you tomorrow; it appears your day will be completed at the new office location."

Angel asked if she and Juanita could go with Silvia?

"If you go, you know the rules. You could forfeit havingThursday off; your choice."

With a little pout on her face she said, "You just like Silvia more than you like us."

I told her, "Come here." I gave each of them a fatherly hug. "You know, I'm only looking out for your best interest. I want you both to enjoy partying with the rest of the Ladies' Club. Finish up what you have to complete, and if you get done early, you can go pal around with Silvia, my girls, and my wives—I promise."

Angel said, "You know, you're the best office husband I could ever ask for. So we will get our work done by lunchtime and then go outside and play." They both hurried to their desks and worked diligently until their tasks in hand were completed. Just before the lunch bell rang, Angel brought in the finished work for me to review.

They had emailed Silvia to say they would be free to go to lunch with her. If she would wait, they would be there in ten minutes. Silvia emailed them stating that Marie and Delores would be joining them since the Mrs. Wilkins meeting was postponed until after the lunch hour.

Angel and Juanita gave me a hug, told me they loved me, and scurried out the door. I think they laid rubber out the driveway. Lunch date, young girls in a sporty car—stand back, boy, or they will run you over.

Wow, silence. Messages were being knocked off one at a time. After only two or maybe three more days of this, I could start to attack the ones I'd received yesterday and today. As I was knocking off a dozen more unessential messages, I received one from Charles. He said they had uncovered more invoices to various companies with different delivery addresses. His auditing company had invoices dating back to the week she was hired. *Little Levana Hugly may serve the rest of her life behind bars. My salesman, Oliver Wisecott, has been linked to Levana for years. And that cutie Jolie Witten is Levana's niece. What a nice trio I hired.*

Papa called me. "Are you sitting down?

"Just a minute, I'll check. Let's see, chair under my backside—yep, that appears to be my present position. What's up?"

"Silvia gave me the names of those arrested yesterday, and our staff has worked many hours tracing these wonderful folks. First off, Oliver Wisecott, not his real name, sort of confused us; he is a known hit man. How does that grab you?"

"If he's a known hit man, why would he want to be a salesman for a construction building materials company?"

"Great question, and here's your answer: he's worked with Levana Hugly for many years, cleaning up on stealing credit data to feed to their organizations. Now we searched his apartment—not legally, mind you, but we found a list of victims who needed to be taught a lesson. Your name was at the top of the list; your sales appointment that they were hoping you would take would have been your last day on this planet. He wrote in the notes, *Hit*."

"Oh, don't stop. You're giving me goose bumps. What else did you staff find?"

"Jolie Witten—not her real name either—she is Levana's niece. She is the one making the appointments, and with each one that has 'hit' next to the name, she receives a lovely bonus gift. She worked with Levana at another location, and both were caught by the company executives for embezzlement; three of their clients were hit. Before they left the planet unexpectedly their credit cards and bank accounts were wiped clean.

"Mr. Wisecott has an associate who was a master at the computer. While he was reviewing your account on the computer, he would take screen shots and tell you he needed a password to install their program for estimating and invoicing— their one-stop shop, so to speak. Your data was put to use while you waited for the final sales pitch. Once everything was in place you were disposed of."

After a pause, Papa went on, "Oh, one more thing: they all lawyered up and were waiting to be released on bail until we informed law enforcement and judicial departments that these fine, law-abiding citizens are tied to Mrs. Katy Wilkins. Twenty-eight counts of murder, no bail, book 'em, and throw away the key.

"I've called our FBI agent and informed him about the information we had on all three of them and forwarded the data over there. The agent asked, 'Just how did you find out this information, so fast?'

"I told him, 'Do you remember who you're dealing with?'"

I asked Papa, "So I did good?"

He said, "You have now saved my daughters' lives, your life—whatever list you're working on, whoever's on that list should pay you dearly for life. This is more than circumstantial; this is bordering on ironclad. Once Katy Wilkins's attorney receives this new evidence, she'll either bail or be embarrassed forevermore."

I asked, "Is there anything else?"

Papa said, "Your friend, Charlie Donaldson, is he married?"

"Yes, he's married to Evelyn Donaldson; why?"

Papa said, "Let met check on Mrs. Donaldson. Charlie has an MP beside his name."

"MP—what would that represent?"

"Missing Persons, we are guessing. There are five names on Mr. Wisecott's list with MP. They are more than likely the new donors of body parts.

"Call Charlie, and tell him a Jeffrey Gibson will be applying for his account manager position, he will be there to protect Charlie. I'll have Jeffrey Gibson, not his real name, at his office in about an hour."

I asked Papa, "Are you having fun?"

He said, "If this protects my family, yes. I'm having fun putting a lid on their operation. I'm not certain this will have much effect. These are still roaches, easily disposed of not much use to anyone but a few."

Papa had texted Marie to message Ms. Morgan regarding the arrests and what bearing they had on the Wilkins case.

Marie sent the text message to Ms. Morgan, who replied, *You know we can only use one rope to hang this lady, but the more ropes, the merrier. I'll inform her attorney. Thank you so much; see you in fifteen minutes.*

Papa told Marie to use both the alias names as well as their actual names to get a response from Mrs. Wilkins.

Papa was heading to the studio to watch the proceedings. He and Marie would have iPads. This was his dream come true; he loved this type of case.

I called Carlos to ask if he needed anything. "Silvia, Angel, and Juanita are out of the office for the rest of the day, and I have a meeting to attend. If you need anything, call my cell phone. Do you have the alarm code for the office?"

Carlos said, "I have everything I need for the jobs, and yes, I know the code."

"Great. I'll lock up and set the alarm. Have a great afternoon; see you tomorrow."

Doors locked and alarm set, I was off to the nearest drive-through and then to the studio to watch Katy in action.

I pulled into my second favorite greasy spoon, Dashboard Café and Nail Salon—*TOP NOTCH EATING HERE* is what the sign says.

I saw the menu board, and it all looked great. If this doesn't clean out your insides nothing will. You know it's quality food when they put your french fries in a plastic Ziplock bag to keep the grease on the fries from escaping. This would not be a meal to eat while driving; your hands could slip off the steering wheel, or you could be wearing grease spots on your clothes. I would just wait to arrive at the studio.

I pulled into the parking lot and found where everyone was located. Quiet as a church mouse, I sat at a table all by myself. But when I opened up a bag, everyone turned around and gave me a look like *Get out of here with whatever you just opened.*

I went outside and sat on the curb. Two birds stopped by for a handout, so I tossed them a couple of greasy fries. They walked away holding their beaks high. I asked them, "What, no seconds?" This had to be the greatest lunch on the planet; even birds turned up their beaks at a free meal. I'd never tossed a french fry to a bird who didn't get excited about food.

The two french fries lying on the asphalt were leaving a mark, so I picked them up and tossed them into the planter. I could not believe my eyes: two snails and four worms crawled out of the planter and made it across the parking lot to another planter. *This lunch is remarkable.*

My first and last bite of my double hamburger with cheese ended up in the trash receptacle. The french fries were leaving an oil slick in my designer paper bag, which was soaking up the oil like a sponge. I was leaving a trail of drips from the sidewalk to the trash receptacle. Even the soda they gave me tasted like they forgot to put in the cola flavoring,

That was the best diet meal I had ever eaten. You would not gain an ounce with one of their meals. Of course, you would still be hungry but a good deal slimmer.

I went back into the studio and watched the beginning of the panel making comments on what Katy Wilkins would see and not see. There was a lot of back-and-forth between counsel. Finally, it was agreed to show Katy the only two people who had escaped her web.

Ms. Morgan told Marie and Delores, "Please stand by while they bring in the defendant."

Katy Wilkins entered the room. She had a video screen on which to watch Marie and Delores. Ms. Morgan asked her if she was comfortable. She introduced Marie as an attorney and Delores as an ordinary housewife. "Marie has written some questions for you to answer; you need to answer them, Mrs. Wilkins. If you refuse to answer, then your request to plead not guilty on grounds of insanity will be removed from the records, and you will be back in the courtroom on Thursday. Do you understand before we proceed?"

Katy Wilkins said, "I don't know these women."

Ms. Morgan replied, "Mrs. Wilkins, you kidnapped these women, and they were freed from your captivity."

Katy Wilkins repeated, "I don't know these women. I told you, I don't know these women."

Ms. Morgan said, "Then you are not insane. I ask for this procedure to be cancelled and for us to return to the courtroom."

Judge Adamson stated, "Mrs. Wilkins, you may never have personally met these women. You hired people to kidnap them. You had your doctor send out information for their body parts to be sold. If you refuse to take questions from these women, then your insanity plea will be rejected. This is your last chance; you have one minute to decide, starting now."

There was a pause. Ms. Davidson asked if she could confer with her client.

Judge Adamson answered, "You have one minute for your client to agree to respond to questions, or we take this case back to the courtroom Thursday."

Ms. Davidson entered the room and conferred with her client, telling her, "If you refuse to answer, I can't help you."

Mrs. Wilkins asked, "If I refuse?"

"You have no defense, and you have already pleaded not guilty by reason of insanity. If you're not found insane, you could get the death penalty."

Katy said, "I don't know these women!"

Ms. Davidson said, "Your fingerprints are on their file folders, and you signed for most of their organs to be sold. You are dead to rights. Answer their questions, or back into the courtroom for the trial to continue."

Judge Adamson said, "Time's up. Will she answer, or do we all go home and meet Thursday?"

Katy said, "I'll answer their stupid questions. I don't know why, but if it makes you happy."

The panel was already making notes on her actions during this whole exchange.

Marie said, "How do you feel about seeing two of your potential victims freed, and you made no money?"

Katy said, "I don't know you. Have we ever met?"

Ms. Morgan interjected, "Ms. Wilkins, answer their question. You are not here to quiz them."

Marie repeated the question.

Katy said. "I'm not deaf. You were lucky; you had fools watching you."

Marie asked, "How many of your victims did you actually cut to pieces?"

Katy said, "I'm not answering that question."

Marie asked, "How many, Katy?"

Katy said, "You must be deaf. I'm not answering that question."

Marie asked, "One more time: how many, Katy? It's either answer, or you will get what you gave others."

Katy said, "Six people."

Marie asked, "How many years have you been mutilating bodies?"

Katy said, "How many of these awful questions are you going to ask me?"

Marie repeated, "How many years have you been mutilating bodies? Last time, or back into the courtroom."

Katy said, "You're really getting on my nerves, whoever you are."

Marie said, "Your Honor, we need to return to the courtroom. This lady is not cooperating."

Katy said, "Over twenty years. I need a drink of water."

Marie asked, "Who are you working for?"

Katy said emphatically, "I work for no one."

Marie asked, "Who is running your organization while you are in jail?"

Katy said, "Where is my water?"

Marie repeated, "Who is running your organization while you are in jail?"

Katy said, "I work for no one. Where is my water?"

Marie said, "Last chance, Katy. Answer the question, or it's back to the courtroom Thursday."

Katy said, "No answer without water."

Ms. Davidson brought her a bottle of water and a plastic cup, poured her a partial cupful, and left with the bottle.

Marie said, "I'm waiting. Answer the question."

Katy said, "No one."

Marie said, No one. Do you know Levana, Oliver, and Jolie? They got arrested today along with MacDonald."

Katy said, "I know the man in the moon. Are you going to arrest him as well?"

Marie said, "So you know these people. Do you also know the names on the hit man's list now in the hands of the FBI?"

Katy said, "You're nuts. You should be in here; I should be asking you questions."

Marie said, "There are nine names on his list with MP by their name; they are your next victims."

Katy said, "I don't know what MP stands for."

Marie said, "I didn't ask you for the definition. We know that stands for Missing Persons—who just happened to appear the day after all your friends got paid. Remember your parties at the clubhouse?

"I'm asking one more time: who is running your organization while you are in jail Answer, or else we'll see you in court Thursday morning."

Katy now glared at the video screen. "I should have axed you two the first night."

Judge Adamson stated, "I've seen enough. Ladies, can you provide me a report by tomorrow morning, or do you need more time?"

The three psychologists stated that tomorrow morning would be doable.

Judge Adamson said, "Guards, return Mrs. Wilkins to her cell. Marie and Delores, thank you for your time. I can't tell you how glad I am to see you both alive."

Ms. Morgan said, "I need to have information so our staff can contact those who have the arrest records. We might as well move them all to one location. We'll need another jail just for your case. It's amazing how many people are involved in this case. Can you get that information to my office?"

Marie said, "My father is right here. I'll let you two have a chat."

Papa got behind the monitor and talked with Ms. Morgan.

Marie and Delores both came over to me. "What were you going to eat? It smelled awful," said Delores.

"Well, on my way here I found the Dashboard Café and Nail Salon and hit the drive-through. I ordered a burger, fries, and a soda. It's now in the trash dumpster outside. It tasted as bad as it smelled; don't ever stop there."

Marie asked, "Was that your lunch?"

"That was my lunch—very dietetic, I might add."

Delores asked, "Just how much was that lunch?"

"I got the special, four dollars."

Marie asked, "Did they call it four-buck chuck?'

"No, it was the four-dollar deluxe burger deal."

Marie said, There's a Wendy's just out the gate; first street, turn right. It's on the right-hand side. The girls will go with you and get the chocolate Frosty. We'd like one as well, so get eight Frostys and eight french fries. Don't take all day; our hunger pains are just as bad as our daughters'."

I gathered up the girls. We all jumped into my new truck, and they showed me the way to Wendy's. We arrived and raced inside. The girls gave them their order: "Eight Frostys, eight french fries medium, and whatever he wants."

The girl behind the counter said, "Good afternoon, 'he'; how may I be of assistance?"

I ordered their burger combo with a Frosty and a Diet Coke. Very shortly we were back in the truck and had returned to the studio.

48

The Sentencing

Everyone enjoyed their Frosty, and hunger pains were next to none. The french fries were actually being dipped in the Frostys; I tried one and decided it was a girl thing. I actually gave my fries to anyone who hadn't quashed their hunger pain. They were consumed for a good cause; the girls wanted to head home to be with their lambs, calves, Scooter, and Lulu.

The ladies and Papa were about to leave in a few minutes; they would meet us at home.

The girls and I arrived home after singing at least two songs which were playing on the radio.

Leslie asked if they could get a radio for their houses. They liked the oldies station; it made them happy.

"Let's get moms and dads together to help fulfill your desires. I can also call the sound system company. They may have something we can put into your houses so they all have the same music with a device you can change if you get tired of listening to the same songs."

When we arrived, we all headed to the corral to free Scooter and Lulu and give the lambs and calves some needed nourishment and love.

The girls were a delight as I watched their interaction with the livestock and dogs. The animals received from the girls what we adults receive from them.

I walked over to the playhouse construction. They had the panels in place and had started framing the roof. The wrap around walkway, was framed and some of the decking in place. They had added six four-by-four posts to help support the walkway around the playhouse. I went under the playhouse; they had the subfloor in place, and I saw holes in the subfloor for the conduits. The cabinets were still in my garage, along with the hand-painted ceiling.

Those smoked hams were starting to make me hungry. I didn't know how the dogs could lie in their beds without craving the meat they smelled cooking.

Murry pulled into our driveway; he was here to check the hams. He added more wood to raise the temperature of the smoker.

When he opened the smoker door, the dogs' senses came alive. The both came over to get a better whiff of the hams. Murry told them, "In a couple more days you'll get a snack, I promise."

I asked Murry, "You will teach John and me how to smoke beef and hams?"

Murry said, "Of course. Once you move the smoker, it's ready to start smoking, and we'll stock the smoker with meats. We'll keep it running all the time. My dad wants to have some smoked beef for his restaurants."

The ladies and Papa joined us at the smoker.

Marie said, "Are they ready? They smell great!"

We all were looking at the playhouse and saw the front door facing the corral and the French doors facing the barbecue. The ladies were starting to get a feel of how the house would look upon completion; they liked the surrounding walkway.

Phillip's crew had installed the stringers for the staircase on the existing frame, and I saw a note attached to the stringer. *This may not work very well. Are you sure this is what you want?*

I told everyone that I had to draw another vision for our backyard to fit Annie's house to the girls' house; there might not be another staircase.

Sarah said, "That's okay, Daddy. Annie told us she doesn't need a staircase to her home. She just wants to be connected to our home, so we can visit one another. She loves our new home but needs her own home. She's really happy now seeing her home almost finished."

"Does Annie like your animals?"

Sarah said, "She loves our animals and Scooter and Lulu. They make her feel young again. Being back on a farm was her dream, and you made her dream come true."

"I'll talk with Phillip's crew in the morning about not using the staircase right now until I find a new home, or maybe they can use it on another playhouse.

"Are you girls getting hungry? Ready for some nearly burnt meat off the grill?"

Leslie said, "You have been doing much better than before. We love your pork chops and steaks. We are getting hungry; Scooter and Lulu are as well."

"Okay, I'm on my way to heat up the grill. Ladies, could you do me the honor of preparing the meat offerings so my dearest darlings don't have hunger pains?"

I got my oil and paper towel, cleaned up the grill and oiled it, fired it up, and waited for my beloved to deliver the meat platters.

It was only a few minutes until the girls brought out the meat platters, with a can of goose juice, with my special labels, one on each side, kissed by all four ladies. Each label had *Guess who* written on the label, was it Silvia, Susanne, Marie or Delores, I'll have to give them all a try and match each kiss to the label.

I told Marie and Delores that I needed to measure each lip print and have each lady pucker up to make that determination.

Delores said, "Honey, no, absolutely not. No kisses from anyone; I'm putting your lips on restriction. You know better than trying to persuade a woman; we weren't born yesterday."

I took her in my arms, had her pucker up, and kissed her. "Yep, that was the one I chose, yours. Only three more to go."

Marie told Delores, "He just does not listen. You told him no, no kisses from or to anyone. Time to put a hold on his after-hours adventures. Hummingbird, go back to your nest."

The girls invited Mama and Papa, Silvia, Murry, and Susanne for dinner at their home. We again got the loser candle in the holder; on the bright side, a meal by flickering candlelight makes it hard to spot any grilling flaws.

The dinner was fabulous, grilled to perfection, just enough goose juice to add that special flavor. Dessert was beyond perfect; the girls, Mama, and Susanna had made a dessert fit for royalty. Scooter and Lulu got the meat scraps and were all smiles.

Murry said, "Those dogs are in seventh heaven; they've never had it this good. The girls make them a new bed each week, washed, He gave Silvia a look and suggested, she might want to spend a couple days with the girls, to get trained."

If Murry kept that up, he'd be sitting at the losers' table permanently. At least Delores and I still had a slim chance, but a chance, to be the honored guests.

It's like waiting for an hour at a restaurant. They call your name, and you feel so elated you almost do a happy dance. "I got picked, and not the last one either, I'm so excited!" Then you see the table where you'll be dining, right in front of the restroom or the swinging kitchen doors. Your waitress or waiter is on their second ticket book; they're exactly like Mall Santa near quitting time: "What do you want, kid? Hurry up, my sleigh only carries so much. How about a jack ball? Next!"

"We told our waitress at least three times what we wanted to drink, but not one drink was right." Walking out after waiting for an hour was racing through our minds.

Delores said, "Honey, are you in there? Yoo-hoo, Earth to Mars, do you hear me? Dear lord, he's zoning again."

Marie got up, grabbed my shoulders, and shook me, hard. I asked, "Why did you shake me so hard?"

Delores said, "I have been talking to you for over five minutes, with no response. Where were you this time? Stock cars or Formula One?"

"I didn't qualify, so I went and had dinner with you guys. We waited for over an hour to get seated, but they put us by the bathroom door or kitchen door. We had a waitress who brought everyone the wrong beverage, and we waited over fifteen minutes to get our order taken."

John asked, "Was the waitress cute?"

I told John, "In all my dreams, the people are faceless, or I just don't pay attention to their appearance."

Delores said, "I can vouch for that. He and appearances are like oil and water. We were at my company party, and I introduced him to my coworkers, He chatted with them for about an hour. I asked him what he thought about my boss. He said, 'Which one was she?' 'His name is Randy. You talked to him the longest of all of my coworkers. Would you recognize him, if you saw him again?' 'Who?' That was the only company party we ever attended."

Marie said, "He is one of a kind."

Delores said, "Thank you, God; you joined me up with Mr. Unique. You owe me big, when we meet again."

It was nearing bedtime. The girls put Scooter and Lulu to bed, gave love to their lambs and calves, and gave the dogs two dog bones. They knew it was bedtime. The girls fluffed up their beds and added a little hay under the blankets; they will become great mothers someday.

The time was almost nine o'clock; the girls went to the restroom and got ready for bed, brushing their teeth, putting on their pajamas, and getting their lambs. They of course were telling them about their day and hoped their days had been as good. As always they said good night to the rest of their stuffed animals.

Leslie and Kim ran home to say good night to their stuffed animals. When they returned, out of breath, Leslie said, "They are all doing very well. I told them we will sleep with them tomorrow."

The girls were all in Sarah's bed; John and I tucked them in. Mama and Papa, Susanne, Silvia, Murry, Delores, and Marie all gathered and said prayers with the girls. Then we all gave them kisses on the forehead and cheeks, night lights on and working perfectly. "Love you; see you in the morning; sleep tight," and lights out.

We all departed to our homes and bedrooms. Susanne's house was only one day from completion. Her husband, Alex, was driving from Colorado, and the moving truck was due to arrive tomorrow or the next morning. We might see him tomorrow morning, maybe for breakfast. She was very excited for him to arrive.

Her husband had a new foreman riding with him. Juan was sending us another well trained foreman. He was a laborer on Marie and John's house and was looking forward to seeing them again. He planned to reside with Susanne and her husband until Murry could set him up with another employee.

Delores and I headed to our room, knowing we would have four girls pouncing on our bed before the rooster crowed.

49

It seemed we just fell asleep when our morning pouncing occurred. The girls were all shivering and needed to get warm. Delores and I split apart, and the girls quickly got under the covers to make certain they got all of our body heat. We of course got the colder parts of the mattress.

I knew the drill far too well to just lie there on the cold mattress. No, it was time to rise and shine and get the beverages brewing and pans on the stove, oiled and heated for our young chefs. *Now in the kitchen each step is being completed; we've established a great routine. Hot chocolate and coffee are both nearly ready, and just in time: here they come, Mrs. America and her court of princesses, all wrapped in the latest blanket attire.*

I have to have cardboard cutouts for crowns. The girls can glue on sequins to represent jewels; a great project on a rainy day for all the ladies to create. I'll ask Silvia where the nearest craft store is located.

Delores said, "No warmed-up rolls this morning? You're slipping, chef. You know what we desire; don't let such things slip from your memory."

"Say no more, your highness. They are in the microwave; allow me to serve you and your court." I delivered the rolls on a platter with a knife for them to carve the pieces they desired; I also gave them five small plates for personal service.

They all took a vote, and I won another day as head chef by unanimous decision. I was warned, though: "Be very careful; you're on thin ice," said Delores.

One at a time the girls took their positions at the grill and toaster; let the breakfast begin. We were soon joined by the remaining guests, all sitting at their designated chairs or bar stools, and the girls were serving them.

Leslie told us about watching a program where the waitress gave orders to the short-order chef: "Cluck with oink, cakes, burnt bread and greasy spud, a cup of mud, clean, and be quick about it, they're in a hurry. Make that twelve orders."

Marie said, "I'm not certain that sounds very appetizing, but I love it."

Our door bell rang. It was Silvia and Murry. Leslie said, "Hey, fry baby, that's fourteen orders. Please be seated; we'll serve you in a moment. Please take an issue of *Remodeling* magazine while you wait. We're celebrities, you know."

She returned to making pancakes. What a flipper she had become; her cakes were perfect.

Sarah asked for more sausages to fulfill the orders—and more greasy spuds. She asked if any of our guests had reservations.

Leslie said, "Nope, just walk-ins this morning. We heard there's a busload for tomorrow's breakfast."

Leslie said, "Daddy chef, can we get some outdoor heaters for tomorrow's breakfast? We don't want anyone waiting in our living room lobby."

Susanne said, "There will be three busloads, I'm afraid to tell you."

Murry said, "We have that handled; you all can take a breather. We are all geared up for the busloads."

Leslie ran over and gave him a hug. "My hands would get tired from flipping the pancakes. Thank you, love you."

Silvia said, "We want you to tell our chef your way of ordering meals. He'll get a kick out of how you order. We will give you a waitress apron, a waitress hat and a pencil you can have sticking out from under the band."

Susanne said, "Our wardrobe people will make that happen. It will of course be televised live."

Silvia said, "Leslie, we need you to write down what the terms mean so the chef can instruct his staff. Can you do that for me?"

Leslie said, "Of course. I'll work on that right after breakfast."

Silvia said, "This is going to be the start of one fabulous week."

Susanne said, "In about three hours your wedding adventure will be in full swing."

Murry said, "In about an hour, would you girls like to help us give the calves and lambs a bath?"

Leslie said, "You want us in our farming outfits?"

He said, "That would be perfect. My ranch hands will be here with the calf washer. We'll get it all set up, and another crew will clean up all the cow patties while the calves get a bath. You're going to love how we do the bath."

Papa went and retrieved Scooter and Lulu from the corral. They were all excited to be with everyone, knowing they would get some breakfast as well. They both went to the girls and rubbed up against them, their way of saying good morning, aware the girls couldn't pet them yet.

Murry said, "I'm totally amazed at how those two dogs have attached themselves to the girls. Scooter was really down when we went to Texas to herd up the calves, but when he saw the corral, his demeanor totally changed. He could hardly wait to get out of the truck and ran to the gate. I opened the gate, and he darted into the backyard to find the girls, running as fast as I have ever seen him run. He found the girls and was elated; I've never seen that kind of joy in a dog before."

Murry said, "I will have to take the girls on our next trip to Texas, in a couple of weeks, if that would be okay with everyone?"

Delores said, "You know, we'll go through the same feelings as Scooter. Three days without our girls will be very tough on all of us."

The girls were serving everyone with their breakfasts and even gave the dogs their own breakfasts, a little of everything.

Murry said, "I don't know if our restaurant can match this meal; wow, it's so good. You even have homemade salsa; unbelievable. Darling you need to take note; this meal is a man pleaser."

The ranch hands showed up with the fencing and the calf washer and parked next to the corral. Murry and the girls all went outside to meet them. Scooter and Lulu were the first to reach the corral gate, and they barked until they saw who it was. Then their tails were wagging.

Murry explained how he wanted the horseshoe shaped fencing to be installed. He showed the foreman the quick coupler valve for the water source and the electrical outlet to power the heat blower. All set, he told Scooter and Lulu to keep the calves from getting to the corral gate while the crew was bringing in the fence and washer.

Leslie asked Murry, "What is the game plan for washing the calves?"

Murry said, "The calves will come in through this entrance and walk along the fence line to the jets which will spray them with warm water. Then they'll move to where they will receive cattle shampoo, and then the second set of jets will rinse them off. You kids can towel-dry most of the rinse water off the calves, and then they'll walk through the dryers and back to the pasture for more grazing. While they're getting a bath, my other crew will pick up the cow patties and load them into a spreader that will spread them on another pasture."

"How long will it take?" asked Leslie.

Murry said, "We hope to be finished before lunch."

"How will you get the calves into the fence area?" she asked.

"Scooter and Lulu will get them into the chute."

Leslie said, "We have a better way, if you would let us."

Murry said, "Okay, I'll let you. This is how we've done it for years, but I would enjoy seeing how you girls can make it happen."

Leslie said, "Let us know when you're ready to start."

Leslie got the girls together, and they talked for a couple of minutes. Then they called Scooter over to them and explained to him what he and Lulu needed to do to help them. The Wiloby kids, just arrived, were standing at the fence.

The girls rushed over to them and had them come inside the corral. They told the newcomers what they had planned, explaining that they could help the ranch hands bathe the calves as they passed by. Would they like to help?

No one objected. The ladies were coming out of the kitchen to watch the calf washer in action. Joining them were Stuart and Doreen.

Murry told Leslie, "We're ready."

Leslie called for Clancy and Cameraria and handed Kim a handful of hay. She directed her to stand at the entrance of the chute, which she did.

To Murry's and Stuart's amazement all the calves were following Clancy and Cameraria behind Leslie. Sarah and Rebecca were standing about fifteen feet apart like stanchions, and the calves formed a line following the girls.

Leslie led them to Kim, who was walking backward showing the calves her handful of hay. She walked them right through the first jets which did their job, to the ranch hands showing the Wilobys how to apply the shampoo to the calves, and into the rinse jets. Then came the towel drying, which led to the heat blower and back into the pasture to get their treat of a handful of alfalfa. Scooter and Lulu kept the calves near the washer until the pasture was cleared of cow patties. Then they escorted the calves to the cleaned area while the ranch hands cleared the next area.

In about an hour all the calves were washed and back to pasture. The girls then led the lambs into the washer. All done in just over an hour.

Stuart asked Susanne, "You have all of that on video, correct?"

Susanne said, "We have the whole operation on video from setup to last calf getting a bath."

"I need as many copies as possible to show my customers at the restaurants. This is the most amazing thing I have ever witnessed. The calves just followed the girls and stayed in line from start to finish."

Marie told him, "The girls play that game with them nearly every day. They have the whole herd following them with Scooter and Lulu just keeping the calves in line. The girls sing for the calves while parading around the corral. At the end of the parade they give each calf a handful of alfalfa as a treat, along with a loving hug and pet while they eat their treat."

Stuart told Murry, "We've been doing this wrong for years. What a learning experience."

The ranch foreman said, "I've never seen anything like this in thirty years of handling cattle. No fuss, no yelling or screaming at one another—I'm in shock."

Mama brought out a pot of coffee, a platter of dessert for everyone, and beverages for the youngsters. "Come and get it," said Papa.

Everyone was standing around talking about what they'd just seen. Stuart gave all the girls and boys a huge grandpa hug. "What a great job you all just did. He even told the ranch hands, "Job well done."

One of the hands said, "We just set up the fencing; these girls did the rest. Wow."

Stuart asked, "Leslie, how did you know which calves were the leaders?"

Leslie said, "When we enter the corral, they're the first two to come to us for an alfalfa treat. They loved the attention we give them. We decided to call the boy Clancy and the girl Cameraria. We wanted to see if they knew their names after a week. When we stood at the gate, we called them, and they came, so we gave some alfalfa as a reward. We wondered if they would all follow us around the corral, so we started a parade. We would all sing a song, and the calves followed us. After we made a lap around the corral, we gave them all an alfalfa treat."

Murry asked, "Why didn't you want the dogs to herd them to the chute?"

Leslie said, "The dogs scare them some. They didn't do anything bad, but it would be like a punishment to them. It could take away the trust they have in us, and we didn't want to jeopardize that. They're our friends."

Stuart said, "I'm so proud of you girls for taking the time to make those calves trust in human contact. You just don't ignore them; you bond with them."

Marie asked him, "Could we talk in private for a second or two?"

They both got out of earshot of the girls. Marie said, "I don't want the girls to ever see the cattle they have taken time to raise be loaded onto a cattle truck to go to the slaughterhouse. Can you promise me that will never happen?"

Stuart said, "You know that's our way of making money and supplying our restaurants with beef?"

Marie said, "I know it, and you know it. They don't need to know it. It will break their hearts. These are very special girls, and they're very emotional at times. Don't ever break their hearts."

Stuart promised her, "I'll tell my foreman and Murry what we just discussed. We will make Clancy and Cameraria breeding stock; their demeanor is far above any stock we have in the fields."

He also said, "When they've calved, we'll have the girls raise their offspring once weaned."

Marie gave him a daughterly hug. "Thank you for all you've done for me and our families."

Stuart said, "I have to say the same to you and your families, thank *you*. We'd better get back, or you'll make me start tearing up; not good for an owner to show that type of emotion to his employees."

They returned to the patio table to see the platter was empty, but Mama was bringing out the second platter. "You thought you missed out? You don't know your mother very well. The girls and I made four platters full, knowing we were going to have lots of mouths to feed."

The girls and the Wiloby children all headed up to the playhouses, followed by Scooter and Lulu.

Janet with Brad asked, "Do you like being around all those calves and lambs?"

Leslie said, "They're our friends. We feed them, we love them, we treat them like family, and they return our love tenfold."

Jonathan asked, "Don't you get afraid being around them, that they may attack you?"

Sarah said, "No, they know who we are, and they love us. We're not afraid of them, and they're not afraid of us. We don't yell or scream at them; we give them hugs and pet them. If they do really well, we give them some alfalfa. We make sure they have fresh water."

Kim said, "Follow us, and we'll show you something."

They all headed downstairs to the corral. They opened the corral gate, and the lambs came running toward them. With all eight of them in the corral, each one held a lamb, gave them some alfalfa, and hugged them.

Janet said, "They're like puppies; they are so soft." She and Brad were sharing one lamb.

Rebecca said, "They've been this way since we first met them. They give us such a great feeling. We cry some nights when we have to leave them to go to bed; they used to cry for us until they fell asleep. They call for us right after we have eaten our breakfast, telling us 'It's time to play; where are you?'"

Janet asked Brad, "Can we get some lambs once we're married?"

Brad said, "Are you proposing to me?"

Janet said, "You asked me a few months ago if I would marry you when I came of age. Did you forget?"

Brad said, "I was only playing with you, my love. If we live in an area that allows such animals, and if our place if big enough, I can't see any reason why we could not have a lamb or a pigmy goat."

Janet said, "I want to live in the country, not in a big city. Where we live in Texas is about as close to a city as I would ever want to live."

Brad said, "We have a couple of years before we have to worry about all that. I just turned eighteen; I can't even sign a legal contract without my parents' permission and signature."

Leslie said, "You two do know that you could have a lamb in our corral, which you can visit anytime you wish. We'll raise it for you. You're stressing me out listening to this type of conversation. You have two years to decide if you want to get married. Take it easy, enjoy your time here. We enjoy having you visit our home."

Janet gave Leslie a hug. "I'm sorry. I really love your lambs. They are so loving; our little one just lay down on my lap and fell asleep."

Leslie said, "That's Rosalee. She is our most lovable. If she feels protected, she will do that. We all love her. We love all our lambs, but she returns our love.

"Know what? We need to see when lunch will be ready."

Sarah picked up Rosalee from Janet's lap and put her on the dog's blanket without waking her up. She said, "She must be really tired." As they exited the coral, Rosalee called out, as if saying, *Hey where did my warm body go?*

Janet returned to her, holding her and telling her she would be back after eating lunch. "I promise."

Leslie gave her some alfalfa as a treat along with a hug, and told her, "We all love you."

Even Scooter and Lulu gave her a doggie kiss.

*

I had to return to the office to clear my messages. Marjorie said, "You are not being a good boy. You'd better have them all caught up."

When I got to the office after stopping at Wendy's, my new favorite eatery, I opened up the new office to find a note taped to the door: *We need access to finish dropping off the rest of the furniture. Please call when you arrive.*

I dialed the phone number; the moving crew was dining at my Wendy's and would return in fifteen minutes or so with the rest of our furniture. The decorator and her staff were just arriving.

I told them, "The rental crew will be here in about fifteen minutes. They're less than a half mile from our front door."

I went to my office. There was only one chair, so I told the decorator, "Please make yourself at home. I don't mind standing."

Jessi with an *i* said, "I really like decorating offices instead of homes. Do you spend more time in the office or at home?"

I told her, "Waking hours in the office and sleeping hours at home. I try not to take a nap at the office. Lead by example, you know."

"How far do you live from here?"

I looked out the window and told her to come close. "See the three rooftops to your left?"

"Yes," said Jessi. "Is that where you live?"

"The house on the far left is our home, so my drive time is next to nothing. I don't even heat up the oil in my truck."

As soon as she was ready to sit back down, in came the rental company movers with the next load of furniture.

Jessi and the driver knew each other. She asked, "What's the office you have on the truck to offload first?"

He told her, "I believe it's this office. Could you make certain for us?"

I walked out with the two of them, and sure enough, my desk was right on the end of the truck bed. The offload took about a half hour, and they returned to our other office to finish loading the remainder of the furniture. They expected to be back in about an hour.

With my desk in place I plugged in my computer, hit the Start button, and bingo: the screen came on. Wow, a miracle almost. It said it did not recognize my location and would shut off in ten seconds, which it did.

Not being bothered by such trivial things, I dialed my office wife.

Marjorie answered, "The computer doesn't recognize your location."

"How did you know that?"

"I could tell by the ring of your cell phone," said Marjorie. "Silvia and I will be there in about five minutes to bail you out."

I looked at my wall clock. *Let's see how close to five minutes they'll really be.*

They pulled into the parking lot in three minutes. I told them to wait in the car for two more minutes.

Marjorie put her fist in my face. "You go sit in our car. We're on a mission: our margaritas are getting warm."

"Women," I said. "When it's food or booze, don't get in their way, or all Hades will break loose."

In less than three shakes of a lamb's tail, mission accomplished. They each had a two-pack in each hand. "Hunger pain medication you didn't need to keep in storage," said Silvia. "You're on restriction, remember?"

Marjorie said, "We know why you came to the office. You knew you had hunger pain medication you could tap into. The kids will thank you. Have a great day."

Delores called me. "They're showing the sentencing of Katy Wilkins on the cable channel. You should watch if you have time."

I went to Google and typed in Katy Wilkins trial, no such item found.

I tried a couple of our cable networks, but neither one was showing the sentencing. I called Delores back. "Where are they showing the sentencing?"

All I got was "Shhh" and a dial tone.

Jessi came into my office. I asked her if she'd heard about the sentencing of Katy Wilkins.

Jessi bent over my right shoulder, and after a couple of taps on my keyboard, there it was, just starting.

50

The bailiff was telling the court, "All rise for the Honorable Judge Adamson, presiding."

Judge Adamson said, "All be seated." He went on to tell the courtroom he had received three recommendations from the psychologists on the panel and stated their names. He read the first recommendation; she found no signs of insanity in Mrs. Wilkins. He read the second recommendation; she also found no signs of insanity in Mrs. Wilkins.

Then he read the third recommendation; hers was a bit more detailed, laying out the guidelines and indications for the insanity defense. The judge read aloud, "None of these criteria apply to Mrs. Wilkins. I can only conclude from what I witnessed that she may have a dissociative or 'multiple personality' disorder, which can trigger aggressive behavior. I don't believe this client is unfit for trial under one of the personalities, though I cannot make a settled judgment about any of the other personalities.

"I came to this conclusion during one the fits she threw, wanting some water. Her request fell on deaf ears, which irritated Mrs. Wilkins. She wasn't getting her way, and that triggered a sudden shift from a near-normal personality to a far different personality. Without clinical support for this evaluation, I cannot be certain."

Judge Adamson asked for a sidebar. "Counsels, please approach the bench."

Ms. Morgan stated, "Your Honor, none of the panel stated she was insane. Her original not-guilty plea must stand."

Ms. Davidson asked, "If she has a multiple personality disorder, doesn't that make her unable to continue with this trial?"

Judge Adamson told Ms. Davidson, "I'm ready to render a directed verdict based on evidence already presented. There will be no more questioning unless you want the defendant to appear on her own behalf. The prosecution may rest, and you can proceed to call her as your first and possibly your only witness."

Ms. Morgan stated, "Shackle her to the witness stand, put two armed sheriffs next to me, and I'll cross-examine her."

Ms. Davidson said, "That is not in judicial protocol."

Judge Adamson said, "Ladies, we have to make a decision. I agree with Ms. Morgan: she is a potential threat. If she is indeed suffering from multiple personality disorder, she could get violent, as the psychologist pointed out. I agree to shackle her to the witness chair and to have one officer in the courtroom armed with pepper spray—but not beside you, Ms. Morgan."

Both counselors agreed.

Judge Adamson told the bailiff, "Please call in two deputies, and have Mrs. Wilkins shackled to the witness chair."

He asked the sheriff in the courtroom, "Please escort Mrs. Wilkins to the witness stand."

Katy was more than apprehensive at this point. The other two officers entered the courtroom with shackles and proceeded to shackle Mrs. Wilkins to the witness chair.

Katy was moving about, struggling to keep from being shackled.

Judge Adamson told Ms. Davidson, "Please talk to your client and explain to her why she is shackled."

Ms. Davidson told Katy, "This is your last chance. Answer the questions by the prosecution. If you resist, the judge will dismiss the jury and proceed to sentencing. Remember, you're up for the death penalty. You're only making matters worse. Please settle down."

Katy was now glaring at Ms. Morgan and Ms. Davidson, hatred in her eyes. She told her attorney, "Free me, now! I'm warning you—free me now, take off these shackles."

Judge Adamson said, "Get a doctor into the courtroom, now."

The bailiff had a deputy call the courthouse doctor into the courtroom.

The judge said, "Everyone please stay put," and told the jury to leave the courtroom—"Now, do not hesitate. Then he said, "All visitors, clear the courtroom. Sheriff, escort these people out."

In a couple of minutes, a doctor and two medical assistants entered the courtroom.

Judge Adamson told the doctor, "Mrs. Wilkins needs a sedative. Be very careful; we're not sure which personality we're dealing with right now."

As the doctor approached Katy with a needle at the ready, Katy gave him a fearsome look and spat at him. "Don't come any closer, or I will do you bodily harm."

Ms. Morgan phoned the psychologist who had written the detailed recommendation. The psychologist, Stella Womby, was nearby and rushed into the courtroom. She saw Katy and said, "Please, everyone, give me some room with Katy."

The doctor told her he had a sedative ready if it was needed.

Stella Womby told Katy who she was and said she'd been called in to help her. "Who are you?"

Katy said, "Who wants to know? Set me free, or I'll do you bodily harm."

Ms. Womby said, "I'm here to help you, but I need to know who you are. Are you Katy?"

In a couple of seconds three of the chairs in the visitor section were upended.

"I will do you bodily harm if you don't free me now," said whoever was speaking from the witness stand.

During these moments, with everyone watching the program, a sudden coldness came across the room and just as quickly left. Rebecca said, "Annie must have been watching."

"She does that once in a while," said Leslie.

As Ms. Womby tried to get Katy to settle down, a stillness came upon the courtroom.

Katy started to struggle in her chair. "Free me, or you will all die!" said a satanic voice from Katy's mouth.

Suddenly Katy tried to stand up, looking at the doors of the courtroom, and said, "Get away from me. I'm warning you all, get away from me; go back to your graves. You're not free to roam. You have done enough damage. Be gone, all of you."

The doctor saw an opportunity and proceeded to inject Katy with the sedative. That caused her to get furious, and she got very close to grabbing the doctor, even in her shackles.

She was not settling down; rather, she was changing into another personality in front of everyone's eyes. Looking very bewildered, she whimpered, "What did I do wrong, Mommy? Why did you put these chains on me?"

Ms. Womby said, "You need to tell me what you did."

With a very strange frown, Katy said, "You're not my mommy. I don't need to tell you anything."

Ms. Womby said, "I'm your mommy's friend Stella. She asked me to come over for a visit."

"My mommy's dead. She doesn't know any Stella. Get away from me," said Katy.

Ms. Morgan was shuffling through her papers and found a name that she might recognize. She said, "Ms. Womby, come here," and handed her the name of Merriam Grossman.

Ms. Womby said, "I'm sorry, Stella had to go home. Do you remember me, Merriam Grossman?"

Katy said, "You! You used to beat me with a belt. You told my mommy that I must have fallen down. I hate you! Why are you here?"

Then she said, "Who is this man, He just pinched my arm very hard. I don't like him; tell him to leave."

Then in a changed voice, she said, "Merriam, why did you always beat me with a belt? You hurt me! You lied to my mom, and then she beat me after you left. You would not play with me; you just wanted to beat me with a belt. You're a very bad person. I'm going to tell my friend and he will cut you to pieces."

In a few minutes the psychiatric ward attendants showed up to restrain Katy and take her to the hospital for further evaluation. They approached her and had the deputies remove the shackles. They were telling her how pretty she was and asking, "Are you married? Do you have a boyfriend? How old are you?" while they freed her arms and legs.

They asked her if they could put a nice coat on her while they escorted her to the high school prom. They put a corsage on her wrist. She stared at the flowers and smiled. "You are such nice boys. How did you get into our house?"

They told her, "Your momma allowed us to come in and play with you."

They escorted her to the floor just a step of two in front of the defense attorney. Katy looked at the attorney and switched back to the bad Katy. She knocked both attendants to the floor, one with each arm to the left and the right. Then all of a sudden Katy herself was knocked to the floor, where she struggled, being held down, but by whom?

As she violently thrashed about, unable to get to her feet, what witnesses said appeared to be an inhuman figure suddenly left her body and then was gone in a flash. Katy lay on the floor motionless. The two attendants quickly lifted her onto a gurney, strapped her down, and wheeled her to a waiting ambulance.

Everyone in the courtroom was in a daze at what had just occurred. They all were very confused. Even the psychologist was beside herself, never having witnessed such a scene before in all her years in school and practicing.

Judge Adamson stated, "Court is in recess until tomorrow. I'll let you know the time." He stood up, visibly dazed, and left the courtroom.

Ms. Morgan told Ms. Davidson, "I don't know about you, but they don't pay me enough to deal with this type of behavior. I need something very strong to settle my nerves."

Ms. Davidson said, "I'm calling my therapist. I'll see you tomorrow, sometime."

Everyone exited the courtroom in total disbelief.

Back at the homestead, the girls hurried to their home to ask Annie, "What happened?"

Annie told them, "Merriam was her best friend, and she is still missing. My friends are with Katy to get her to talk. We know she knows where Merriam is. We have to find her; she is our last spookette. We have all the rest, thanks to your discoveries."

Leslie said, "Can we tell our Papa and daddies?"

"If they can help, go ahead. Tell them I need to find Merriam."

The girls were hurrying down their stairs as I arrived home from the office. I entered the house without thinking and said, "What, I mean what was that? I have never seen anything like that in my entire life."

Marie, Delores, Susanne, Silvia, Mama, and Papa were all in a daze. "We don't know what we just saw," said Delores.

The girls entered our living room. Leslie said, "Papa, Daddy, all of you—Annie wants you to find Merriam. She has been missing for a long time. She was one of Annie's best friends."

Marie's phone rang, it was Ms. Morgan. "Good afternoon, Ms. Morgan," said Marie.

Ms. Morgan said, "How much of that did you see?"

"We saw up to when the doctor entered the room. Then the program went back to what would normally be airing."

Ms. Morgan said, "That was totally unbelievable, I'm still shaking, and that's after three shots of bourbon. I'm going to have nightmares for years. We think she had a demon leave her body. She was held down on the floor, thrashing about, but couldn't get up—after she tossed two strong attendants to the floor with little effort. I need another shot; hold on …. That's a little better. I mean, she went ballistic in a snap of a finger."

Marie said, "You triggered something in her. Merriam Grossman was a friend of Annie, one of her first victims."

Ms. Morgan said, "What? Did I hear that right? Merriam Grossman was *whose* best friend?"

Marie said, "If you're not sitting, please do sit down, and record this if necessary. Are you ready?"

"I'm recording this only because I'm a nervous wreck," said Ms. Morgan.

Marie said, "This might take a few minutes to get you up to speed. Annie Closkey is the great grandmother who was dismembered at our first home. The developer is serving a life sentence for her murder, and he also was hired by Katy Wilkins to dispose of other bones in his concrete pours. Merriam Grossman was Annie's best friend, who has been missing for years. You see, Katy Wilkins went berserk when your psychologist brought up her name. Annie needs to know from Katy where her best friend is located."

"Wait," said Ms. Morgan. "Are you telling me you speak to spirits?"

Marie said, "Hold on to something solid. —Annie lives in our playhouse."

"Oh, that's it," said Ms. Morgan. "I'm checking into the state hospital tomorrow morning after my hangover dissipates. I knew this job would finally do me in."

She paused and then asked, "What was holding Mrs. Wilkins to the floor?"

Marie said, "The spookettes?"

"You are all nuts," said Mr. Morgan. "Can we have a sensible conversation tomorrow?"

Marie said, "Of course. Call my cell phone."

Delores said, "I take it she didn't handle that very well."

Marie said, "Four shots of bourbon might have played a role."

Delores said, "Do you think she'll call you tomorrow?"

Marie said, "I hope she calls and we can have a conversation without the influence of alcohol and our minds aren't hindered. I know she was traumatized by witnessing that event."

Leslie asked, "Can we tell Annie we'll do our best to find her friend?"

Marie said, "You tell Annie we will do better than our best to find her friend. We want all of this to end, not for our sake but for all those poor innocent people's names on the list they found—and all the other lists out there. Tell her we love her, and thank her; we know she sent the message to her other friends."

Leslie, her sisters, Scooter, and Lulu scurried out the door and headed back to their home to relay the message from their mom.

I told them I was totally amazed at what I was witnessing—how she changes from one personality to another in the blink of an eye. "She's not crazy; she's strange. Can you imagine being able to change channels in your brain, sitcom to horror film, faster than using a remote on a television set?"

51

"**I**'m ready for some dinner. I'll go fire up the grill; excuse me."

I got my oil, paper bowl, and paper towel out to the grill, lifted the hood, and spread on the oil. Fired up the grill, closed the hood, and waited for the platters of meat offering. I was just going through what I'd witnessed in the courtroom, still in a daze of unbelief.

Papa came out of the house and joined me at the grill. "I don't know about you, but watching that on television—feeling the cold air whisk by me and seeing the television switch to a preprogrammed event—I just had a vision of what my daughters would have faced."

The girls brought out the platters of meat and handed them to me, and Papa gave his two daughters a very fatherly hug. Tears were moistening all three faces.

"We owe our lives to Annie," said Marie.

Delores said, "Who would have imagined that the girls' imaginary mom would play such a vital role in our lives?"

They all three looked at me and came closer. Marie said, "You knew the playhouse meant something more than just an old shed, didn't you?"

I told them, "I knew it was an important part of the house. The structure was well built, and the tunnel leading under the house was well built. That meant the shed was used more than likely as a momma's get away. The windows could be opened. During the summer months there was lighting for the shed. When I heard that was where Annie was murdered, I knew we could not just throw the shed to the landfill."

Marie asked, "So putting the shed on top of the patio cover, explain that more clearly to us."

"When I sat in the folding chair where the shed had stood, I was puzzled as to just how to keep the shed near its original location, It came to me, *Put it on top of the patio cover*. I saw the girls running up and down the staircase and standing on their balcony to look down on where the shed used to be. Keeping the shed intact was a priority. I know why: that's Annie's house; that's where her soul resides. Once we complete the relocation of the shed in our yard, she can have her peace returned to her."

Papa said, "You know all this, and you don't tell anyone. Why?"

"People would just think I'm crazy or making it up to get attention, trace circles in the air around their ear, call me loony tunes, that sort of thing. If you had not seen what was being aired, you wouldn't have any interest in what I truly know. I'm very glad we salvaged the painting of the animals on the ceiling, knowing now that Annie painted them as a child.

"Annie watches over the girls. She is their keeper; she wouldn't stand for seeing them hurt when you two were kidnapped. She called together her friends and attacked your kidnappers, helping to free you, to protect your lives for her little friends.

"If I had destroyed her home and thrown it away as trash, you would not be with us right now. The girls would not have a secret mom, one who watches over them night and day."

Marie said, "You need to write all of this down. We all need to be reminded from time to time of what we are really blessed with and to show more appreciation to the unseen world. Somehow you have been blessed to see things we can't or won't admit to seeing."

"I'd better get this meat cooking, or else the girls will have severe hunger pains."

Marie gave me a hug, buried her head in my shoulder, and wept. Delores and Papa joined in on the hug.

We heard little voices asking, "How much longer before dinner? Our tummies are growling." All eight kids were coming down the staircase and stopped when the saw everyone crying. Busted. I gave them a warning look, and they turned on their deaf ears.

Leslie said, "That's okay. We can get some hunger pain medication from our snack drawer. Come on, guys. You too, Scooter and Lulu; let's get some snacks."

I started putting meat on the grill, which was sizzling hot now; searing the meat was easy.

The ladies returned to the kitchen to join Mama, Silvia, Susanne, Marjorie, Gloria, Nadine, and Marjorie. They all saw the puffy eyes and had seen all of us hugging. "Are you all right?" asked Gloria.

Marie explained to all of them what just occurred at the grill. Now all of them were tearing up, and Susanne grabbed a box of tissues from the bathroom and a roll of paper towels.

Susanne said, "We're in for a tough night. I can feel it coming."

Leslie asked, "Can we all help with the sides? We really are getting hungry. Huh, Mom?"

Marie put her arms around her daughter. "Let's go get those sides finished. We're sorry, we'll try to get it together."

Sarah said, "Even Papa is crying. We never see him cry. Is he okay, Mom?"

Delores said, "He's just a little sad."

Kim asked, "It's that trial thing you all were watching, huh, Mom?"

Delores told the kids, "Sit down at the table for a few minutes so you will understand what that trial thing is all about."

Marie said, "Delores, be careful. We don't need everyone in tears."

Delores said, "The lady on trial is the one who had Marie and me kidnapped. She is on trial for murdering at least twenty-eight people. Girls, Annie was one of those twenty-eight people. Annie helped free us from the kidnappers. We were all crying, thanking God for Annie and being alive today to spend more time with all of you. Seeing you all get the calves and lambs into the chute for their baths without yelling or screaming at them, how they all followed one another into the chute and got their baths and returned to the pasture—that would not have happened if your mom and I were not with you today."

Susanne gave them a box of tissues.

"You see, everyone, this trial is very important to our families, all of the Ladies' Clubs, and our very existence. That's why we're crying; we need to release all the tension building up inside of us."

Mama said, "The sides are finished. We need our servers to get the table set."

Off all the kids went, taking items to the table and talking to one another as they hurried with the task at hand.

"I told them, "In less than two minutes your dinner will be ready."

Leslie said, "Thank you, Daddy. Love you; see you real soon."

Papa was sitting at the table, still in tears. He said, "Thank you, son. Thank you for telling us what you had envisioned."

Here came the parade of beauties and handsome dudes from the kitchen. They were all choosing their meat offering and dishing up some wonderful sides. They grabbed a couple of dinner rolls and headed up the staircase to their house. The Wiloby kids were the invited guests. We adults got the flickering candlelight, which was perfect so our red eyes were less noticeable.

Lucky for all of us the plates were wax coated, so the tears would just leave a puddle on them. I had to cook the second platter of meat so all could have seconds; we knew the seconds will be required.

John said, "You sure know how to liven up a party. Is that inborn, or have you had lessons on making women cry?"

I told John, "Look at me, a face only a mother could love, and she died laughing.

"In school, every time I asked a girl out on a date, she cried, not for being overwhelmed. Nope, I was the only one who asked her out, and she was depressed."

John said, "It hasn't affected you any."

I asked John, "During physical education, as the team captains picked the players for their team, were you ever the last one picked?"

"In most sports, yep, always the last one," said John.

"I had two captains trade positions," I told them; "the one captain counted all the players and figured he would get me, so he allowed the other captain to pick ahead of him. Talk about an ego killer.

"When we played them in baseball, that captain played in left field, and every time I came to bat he moved in toward the infield. We had bases loaded with two outs, and my captain grabbed his glove off the players' bench getting ready to head to the locker room to take a shower. The pitcher threw me an inside pitch, and I sailed it over the left fielder's head and cleared the bases. We beat them as the coach blew his whistle. The team was jumping up and down. I was standing on second base and turned and headed into the locker room. We'd just beaten the number one team. No joy in Mudville, as the story goes. Nothing was more lonely than standing on second base while the rest of the players were celebrating our win.

"The other team captain walked up next to me and said it was a lucky hit. I smiled at him and said, 'You underestimated my abilities; it wasn't luck.'"

The second batch of beef and pork was nearing completion when my little ones approached the grill.

Leslie said, "Daddy, you know you're the best chef for grilling our meals. All of us are still craving just a smidgen more. Scooter and Lulu with the sad brown eyes are looking for more scraps, and we have no more scraps to give them. Would you happen to have just a few more pieces of grilled meat for us to fill our tummies and bring joy to our doggies?"

I told her, "Let's open the hood and take a peek."

Leslie's eyes lit up. She told the kids, "Bring your plates. The grill is full of steaks and pork chops."

Down came the herd of kids all asking for this piece and that piece. Then the ladies all lined up and chose their select cuts of perfectly grilled meat. That left me with two nicely burnt hot dogs—well, almost. John took one as a friendly reminder of his grilling days.

I took my lonely hot dog, cut it up into bite-size pieces, squirted a little ketchup on top, scooped up the last spoonful of baked beans, scraped the bowl for the last of the macaroni salad, and sat on the seat wall with the remains of my goose juice to enjoy the chef's dinner.

Delores came and sat beside me, eyeing my hot dog pieces, got her fork poised for some culinary delight, and plunged the fork into two pieces at one time. Down the hatch they went. She licked her lips and told Marie, "Hey, these are pretty good. You want some?"

In seconds my lovely little birds were pecking at my dinner. I handed them my plate so I wouldn't catch a fork in the hand and almost finished my goose juice until Marie cleared her throat and took the can from my hand/ "You were drinking that, were you?"

Lucky for me the manufacturers have rounded the edges of the aluminum top opening or I would have shed some skin. I answered, "Not at that very moment. I'm sure glad you ladies aren't bashful about sharing my dinner."

Delores asked Marie, "Did you hear something?"

Marie said, "Yes, something about sharing. He knows we get fifty percent of everything, correct?"

Delores said, "He should by now."

Gloria, my office wife, said, "What about my fifty percent?"

Delores said, "Too late unless you want his final baked bean?"

Gloria said, "Of course, that is better than nothing."

I told them, "Wait, I have dessert coming. You all can ransack that as well."

With all of their forks raised in the air, Marie said, "Talk is cheap. Bring on the dessert."

Mama and the kids had made three, three-tiered chocolate cakes with chocolate icing and white squiggles on top.

John asked if I was ready to lick the cake platter for my portion.

I told John, "They'll scrape the plates clean, knowing that otherwise we get the crumbs."

The desserts were being served by the girls and the Wiloby children. Everyone got a real piece of cake. I didn't hesitate to gobble it down, swallowing when necessary, chewing occasionally. *There, finished before they finished. I'll just go try my fork on their piece.*

All I received was Delores saying, "No way, José. Go away; you had your piece. We don't share this, nor do you get fifty percent. Mine is mine, and yours is mine. Do you understand women's rules?—our game, our rules. Right, ladies?"

Even my office wives all nodded in agreement.

I told Murry, "Are you sure you're ready for 'I do' as an agreement, not as a question?"

Delores said, "A very wise wife told him that not too long ago. Something like *bunk buddies* comes to mind."

John told me, "You would have had more luck walking through the calf pasture blindfolded and not stepping in it, like you just did with the ladies out here."

I told him, "But I wasn't blindfolded out here."

John said, "Even worse, my friend, even worse."

The light show started, and the ladies wandered upstairs to get a view from the playhouse decking. I loved hearing the oohs and aahs from the ladies; it brought, back memories of the good old days.

The kids were all talking about where they would sleep tonight—which house, which bed, and who would wake them up. It was fun listening to them make the arrangements. The boys wanted to sleep in the playhouse, since it's heated. They would have the lights in the house and tunnels.

Marjorie asked Marie and Delores if they would mind.

Marie said, "Hold on a minute. Leslie, Sarah, Kim, and Rebecca, can you all come here for a second?"

Then she said, "Marjorie, you have to asked the homeowners."

Marjorie said, "Girls, can the boys sleep in your houses tonight?"

The girls huddled up and acted as if they were in heavy discussion. Then Kim looked up and asked, "Do we have to cater to them?"

Marjorie said, "No, they are pretty self-sufficient. They may need a blanket and pillow."

The girls went back into their huddle, again acting like they were in a discussion. They looked at the boys, went back to the huddle, looked at the boys again, and finally turned to Scooter and Lulu to ask if they would mind.

Leslie said, "That would be fine with us. Scooter was a little nervous about having noise after dark, but he and Lulu decided if you make too much noise, they will tell you to be quieter."

Marjorie said to Marie, "Is it always this difficult?"

Marie said, "Even more, if you need a philosophical question answered."

Marjorie said, "I haven't had one of those in nearly a year now."

I told John, "That's a lady joke."

52

Everyone had a sleeping area for the evening, all bags in the proper room, and stuffed toys all collected. The boys had blankets and pillows, anxious to sleep in the playhouses. One major thing remained first: prayers with the girls.

Once all the bases were touched, everyone headed to their sleeping quarters. The girls all slept together in Sarah's bed, Susanne and her husband got Rebecca's bed, Gloria got Leslie's bed, Nadine got Kim's bed, and Marjorie got our guest room. *Tomorrow should be really interesting. Fifty women; only in the movies would that scenario even work out.*

Early the next morning, who needed a rooster when we had four beautiful daughters eager to slip under the covers to steal all our body heat, shivering to get loving hugs?

I got up and did my Daddy duty. Soon hot chocolate was warming, coffee was brewing in two machines, pots and frying pans were in place and oiled up, and toaster at the ready. Here came my lovely queen and her court, wrapped up in blankets. I'd learned my lesson from yesterday; the breakfast roll was heated and on a plate with a knife and small plates for the queen and her court.

Just as the sausages, hash browns, and bacon were hitting the heat, our elevator was dinging. The door opened, and in came our next-door neighbors and their guests, followed by our guests. Then came the boys, Papa and Mama, and Scooter and Lulu brought in by the boys.

The girls all got into position, flippers and turners in hand. The batter was on the counter, and the first pancake was browning, sausages were being turned, the oink was just about ready for some clucks, and there were fixings.

Our doorbell rang, and Delores, answered. Sally and Maggie were there with two pots of coffee, hot chocolate, and two bags of breakfast rolls.

Delores gave them huge hugs. "Come in, girls. Just in time to see how your buddy does as a chef." The girls all ran to Sally and Maggie and then scurried back to their posts.

Maggie offered to be the server. Leslie showed her the list of how she told the chef what to make.

Maggie started to laugh. "This is a great list. Can I make a copy so I can start telling our head chef to get with the program?"

Susanne said, "He will be enlightened in a very short while. Leslie will give him a lesson he'll never forget."

Maggie said, "Put some heat in your pants. Our customers don't have all day, you know. I can't live on one tip per shift, for crying out loud."

Sally looked at the list. "Can you make one up for me as a hotel desk clerk? This is so funny, I love it." She gave Leslie a huge hug.

Leslie had a plate ready stacked high with cakes. Maggie gave her another plate; she took the cakes to the table and told everyone to dig in. "We can live on one tip per shift, you know." She high-fived all the girls.

My Albright scramble was ready to take to the table while I started the second pan. Maggi went to the refrigerator and retrieved two more packs of sausages for Sarah. She took the toast to the table and told the girls, "Go eat; I'll keep burning the bread for you.

Sarah asked if she could get her some more greasy spuds, shredded. Maggi said, "Do you all know what she calls the food being served?"

We all told her what we were making by using Leslie's terminology. Oink and cluck in my pans, finger oinks and greasy spuds shredded here, burnt sliced bread there—"Mud in a cup lightened here," said Delores.

Maggi said, "We are going to have so much fun yelling that in the restaurant."

The girls were all starting to eat their breakfast. Delores put on some country music—classic Alabama, George Strait, The Judds, groups like that, and of course Reba and Dolly. The girls and boys were singing along.

Poor Scooter and Lulu were confused by all the extra people eating, I knew they thought, *Hey, what about us watchdogs? Did you forget about us?*

Leslie and Sarah both had a plate reserved for each of them cooling on the countertop. They both got up and served their most special guests.

Gloria came over to me and asked, "Is there anything you don't do?"

"Anything?"

"Oh," said Gloria. "Used the wrong term, didn't I? Not that, not now, silly boy."

Delores got up and gave her a hug. "Great job."

Gloria said, "I got to use that phrase at least four times now. In fact, I have a new one for you ladies to use: 'Take a picture; it lasts longer.'"

Everyone's tank filled, the kids headed to their house to make sure the boys hadn't left a mess. Then they all went down to give loving to the lambs and calves.

Leslie called for Clancy and Cameraria, who came to them with the rest of the twenty-eight head. Leslie handed flakes to each of the boys and to Brad to feed the twenty-eight. The girls fed their eight and eight and then helped the boys.

Leslie went to each watering trough and filled it with fresh water.

Phillip's crew arrived. They were going to put the roof on Annie's house this morning and start framing the deck to connect her to the girls' decks.

Marie received a call on her cell phone; It was Ms. Morgan.

Marie in a soft voice said, "Good morning, Ms. Morgan. How was your night?"

Ms. Morgan said, "Thank you for talking softly. I'm still a little hung over. Not a good idea, drinking four shots. It caught up to me, and I had an associate take me home and bring me to work this morning."

Marie asked, "Have you received any word on Mrs. Wilkins?"

Ms. Morgan said, "After the sedative wore off, she became quite a rowdy lady. She would probably not be invited back for another visit if they had the choice."

"Will the trial continue this morning?" asked Marie.

Ms. Morgan said, "I really don't think the judge is in any mood to see Mrs. Wilkins in his courtroom. I'll forward you the entire scene; you got cut off before the good stuff happened. Judge Adamson said it would be all right for you to see the entire event, since you both are key players. I will send you the video right now using your email address. Have a great day. I hope to hear from you soon; you can email me what you think of the video."

Marie told her, "You have a good day too. No more drinking for you today."

Within a few minutes they received the video from Ms. Morgan. The ladies, Papa, Murry, Susanne's husband, and I gathered around the computer and watched what was aired yesterday and then the remainder of the scene.

When we got to the portion that the cable company didn't air, we were all flabbergasted at what we were witnessing. We saw the ghostly figure depart from her. We witnessed her just lying on the courtroom floor motionless. We saw the sedative kick in and watched the attendants put her on the gurney and strap her down to keep her from attacking the lone attendant in the back of the ambulance.

Marie said, "Now you all know why we were crying last evening. This lady is not well."

Papa said, "If we had not freed you from your kidnappers, you might or might not have witnessed her true nature. And if you *had* found a way to get her in a compromising position to break free from her clutches and tried to tie her up, then you would have seen something that would have scared you beyond comprehension."

Delores said, "The evil part of her was very strong."

Marjorie said, "Either what we saw was real and there are true spirits of evil lurking about, or she just won the Academy Award. If they ever made that into a movie, it would have to be one ruthless woman to play her."

Marie said, "I don't know of any actress who could play that in this day and age."

Delores asked everyone, "What do you all think about the video we just saw?"

I said, "They won't sentence her until there is an evaluation of her sanity. I'll bet they call back all the professional psychologists and add a few more who deal in personality disorders to determine if she truly has multiple personalities or if she is just one convincing woman."

Papa said, "I saw a case like this years ago, not as severe. While in the asylum, the patient escaped and sought revenge. He was not quite as insane as the professionals determined. He killed two of the attendants, fled the building, and murdered three more people, just for the thrill of doing the killing.

"When they had him cornered, he cried like a baby, and they put him back in the asylum. A month later he did the same: killed two more attendants and fled the building. He stayed at large for quite a long time, and they found him dead in an apartment; natural causes."

Papa said, "They better be more than correct with this woman. She is a real danger; I watched her expressions and her eyes. She is a very serious person."

Marie asked, "Dad, do you think she enjoys watching people suffer?"

Papa said, "Ladies, I don't want to give you nightmares. She not only enjoys watching people suffer, but it's power over you that she enjoys. She is truly a dangerous person."

"Well, our limousines have arrived," said Murry. "We need to get the children ready for a ride to the restaurant."

Delores called all the kids. "Put the dogs in with lambs and calves, and wash your hands. Leslie, bring your list. The limousines have arrived."

Lightning Source UK Ltd.
Milton Keynes UK
UKHW012032091020
371334UK00003B/43/J